TWILIGHT

TWILIGHT

KRISTEN HEITZMANN

◊ BETHANYHOUSE
Minneapolis, Minnesota

Published by Bethany House Publishers
A Ministry of Bethany Fellowship International
11400 Hampshire Avenue South
Bloomington, Minnesota 55438
www.bethanyhouse.com

Printed in the United States of America by
Bethany Press International, Bloomington, Minnesota 55438

Library of Congress Cataloging-in-Publication Data

Heitzmann, Kristen.
    Twilight / by Kristen Heitzmann.
       p.   cm.
    ISBN 0-7642-2605-3 (pbk.)
    1. Single mothers—Fiction. I. Title.
    PS3558.E468 T88   2002
    813'.54—dc21   2002002466

Dedicated to those who serve

either heroically

or quietly

Rocky Mountain Legacy

Honor's Pledge

Honor's Price

Honor's Quest

Honor's Disguise

Honor's Reward

Diamond of the Rockies

The Rose Legacy

Sweet Boundless

The Tender Vine

Twilight

KRISTEN HEITZMANN is the acclaimed author of eight novels, including *Honor's Pledge* from her bestselling ROCKY MOUNTAIN LEGACY series. Raised on five acres of ponderosa pines at the base of the Colorado Rocky Mountains, Kristen has long held a passion for the state she and her husband call home. A teacher, a music minister, and a mother of four, Kristen delights in sharing her American heritage through the written word.

1

THE MAN WHO WALKS IN THE DARK

DOES NOT KNOW WHERE HE IS GOING.

John 12:35 NIV

THE THING ABOUT SERVING is that it isn't true service until there's nothing in it for you—no personal benefit, only pure sacrifice. Doing what you have to do when you can't give yourself a single reason, except someone needs it. And sometimes what you do looks just plain stupid. That explanation wasn't in the dictionary, but Cal had spent some hours defining it in his mind. He had redefined a lot of things these last months.

He stood now in the lounge of the fire station that served Montrose, population four thousand, and the surrounding county. By its nature the career he'd chosen meant training, dedication, service. He couldn't remember a time when he hadn't known he wanted to rescue people, combat destruction, take charge of any emergency. But some situations were beyond control.

Like the people lost in the terrorist attacks running into a building to save, rescue, aid, and the unimaginable destruction that followed. Pure service that cost them their lives. Cal's memories threatened to erupt, but he pushed them aside. Not now; not here.

He stepped up to the wall. The mirror threw his face back at him, each of his twenty-nine years leaving their mark in the lines around the eyes and the scar running white across his sunburned chin, shaved clean of the weekend's growth. He looked decent, manly, handsome enough if he wanted to go there. He wasn't vain—just assessing what he saw these days when he faced himself. It was about to change anyway.

White paint erased the chin scar as he shaped a smile outlined in red—a goofy, extravagant smile. He hid his blue eyes behind wrap-around sunglasses and pinched on a red plastic nose, then mashed his hair down like a mess of straw and pulled on the curly yellow wig. His uniform shirt took on a whole new look with the spotted, over-sized bow tie, but the emblem on the sleeve gave Spanner the Clown his purpose. Jokes, magic, laughter—all to grab and hold attention, promote memory. Climbing into baggy pants, he snapped the suspenders on his shoulders and stepped out into the garage.

The dented, red engine waited beside the smaller rescue vehicle. Cal stood for a moment, eyeing the old truck's length, the hoses accordion-folded in the back, the steps to the jump seat behind the cab where a man could crouch, the siren shrill in his ears, holding the side bars as the engine sped along, adrenaline transforming him into a machine primed for action. The new trucks were enclosed for safety, but not old Susie.

Stepping back, he made way for Rob and Perry to finish the checklist on the engineer's panel. Rob nodded, and Cal returned it, pretending he didn't notice the smirk on Perry's face, though it was how he'd have looked at one of them dressed like this. But he didn't judge anymore, not by appearances anyway. The real man was not on the surface—sometimes in the eyes or in the stoop of the shoulders, but never in the face he showed the world.

And that was the irony, Cal thought, frowning inside the white smile. Painting a clown's face was only a gross imitation of the mask-ing of humanity. Everyone just pretended no one knew. He took the boxed theater, props, and puppets from the shelves and went out into the glaring sunlight. Missouri didn't seem to know it was November. The air was warm and dry, and the daylilies along the road were put-ting out sprouts. Even nature could be fooled.

His scalp itched, and he stuck a finger under the edge of the wig to scratch as he climbed into his jeep. *Fremont Elementary, here I come.*

He could have dressed at the school and saved himself Perry's contempt, but kids were sharp. He didn't want them to see the man who would dress up as Spanner the Clown. He wanted Spanner to arrive. It helped the magic.

One year ago he would have never believed the tricks he'd taught himself in high school would become so important. That, and the drama classes taken for the heck of it. And his natural cut-up personality. It was crazy. He shook his head. Not crazy, just unexpected.

The drive was short, the walk inside routine. But the sea of children's faces made him tense. Eyes bright, cheeks flushed and plump beside their smiles, life and energy so thick he could feel it . . . and yet so precariously poised on the edge of tragedy. One wrong step, one minute too few . . .

He grabbed Rocky, the wooden-headed fireman puppet, and fixed the lever that worked its mouth firmly in his palm. But he kept the puppet still at his side as he stepped around the side of the theater. "Good morning, kids!"

"Good morning, Spanner!" They knew him from the last trip, maybe remembered his name came from the fireman's tool, the spanner wrench. If he could just know they would remember the message behind his tricks.

"Say hello to Rocky, kids." He held up the puppet.

"Hi, Rocky!"

"Hey, Rocky, tell us a joke." That from a husky boy near the back.

Cal thought fast. He'd already told every firefighter changing a light bulb joke he knew. He moved the puppet's mouth. "Did you hear about the monastery that sold flowers to pay for a new chapel?"

"No!" The childish voices struggled to outdo one another.

Cal made Rocky bob his head up and down. "Yep. But the flower seller in the village didn't like the competition. He told those monastery fellows to cut it out. Did they listen?"

"No!" The children collapsed in giggles. Cal loved that part.

"You're right!" Rocky shouted, clacking his wooden legs that dangled over Cal's arm. "They kept selling flowers. So that flower seller brought in the big gun, Hugh McHugh." Cal pulled the puppet back to face him and kept his mouth almost still as the puppet

11

pleaded, "I can't tell this part, Spanner. You tell it."

Cal made his own voice ominous. "All right, Rocky. If you insist." He looked over the young faces, waved his hand, fingers splayed. "Hugh McHugh stomped up to the monastery. Those little friars heard every step—boom, boom, boom. They trembled behind the door, then jumped back with each thump of his fist. The door flew open, and Hugh said, 'No more selling flowers!' Did the friars obey?"

The answers were mixed. Some defiant children shouted no, others called yes. Cal held his white-gloved hand in the air. "Yes, they stopped, and do you know why?"

Quiet now.

"Because Hugh and only Hugh can prevent florist friars."

The teachers around the gym rolled their eyes and laughed. Half the children laughed, and half leaned to a friend to get the explanation. Cal didn't wait. His reason for coming was fire safety, and he went right into his spiel.

After the school show he went back to the station, changed and washed up, then went home, more drained than he should be. It hadn't been that full a day: just paper work, code inspections, and one show. But seeing all those trusting faces, the innocence, little limbs, little minds . . . He dropped into his recliner. At the third ring of his phone, Cal picked up the receiver.

"Is this Cal?"

He grimaced. "Yeah, Ray. I'm the only one here, remember?" He tossed down the evening paper and popped the tab of his Coke. Its sweet effervescence took the bite from his mood.

"I got a job."

Of course. Ray only used the phone when he'd picked up an odd job from his newspaper ad. If Cal hung his head out the window, he'd see Ray standing in the garage apartment out back. Ray could have easily run up the outside stairs and told Cal in person, but he always informed him by phone.

"That's great."

It was great. At thirty-something, and balancing his lack on the smarts scale with his substantial strength, Ray took his work seriously and got top billing in the odd-job column. On the side, he helped his aunts, Mildred and Cissy, keep up the old country estate that Cal also called home. For that he got the garage apartment gratuitously. As the sole renter, Cal occupied the attic. Mildred and Cissy knocked around in the other two stories of the house in which they'd been born. Only the cellar was uninhabited, at least by humans.

"Yep," Ray said. "But I need your help."

That also was a given. Ray only called when he needed help. "Your employer will help in any way you need, Ray."

"She can't."

This was going downhill. "Why not?"

"She's not strong enough."

Cal hitched the recliner back until the footrest leapt out. "What's the job?"

"I gotta move a couch. It's a sofa sleeper."

"Move it where?"

"Downstairs. Around a corner."

He was getting the picture. "When?"

"Tonight. Now."

Cal pictured Ray's expression, the urgency in his normally bland face. Ray's jobs were the highpoint of his life, his way of saying he might not be much, but someone needed him. And that usually meant Ray needed Cal. What were friends for?

Cal massaged the kinks from his neck, swigged the Coke, and stood. "Okay." How exactly he'd become Ray's sidekick he couldn't say—probably no more than proximity and acquiescence. Cal couldn't turn him down, and that went a long way with Ray, who'd had enough rejection growing up.

The drive into town took longer than it would have if Ray had not insisted on reading the directions while he drove. Cal would have known the block and street by instinct, but Ray wouldn't let Cal near the strip of napkin he'd written the address on. This was his gig.

Ray's hammy shoulders hunched over the wheel with the paper trapped in the space between stem and circle. Every now and then he squinted his ruddy face at the hieroglyphics scribbled on the corner, and Cal couldn't tell from his angle if he could still see the road. Twice he sat on his hands to keep from grabbing the wheel as the edge of the pavement wobbled the tires.

Driving was Ray's most sensitive spot, maybe because it had taken him six tries to get his license. Cal guessed he'd run through all the driving testers and no one wanted to get in with him again, so they passed him. Now only Cal risked the passenger seat. But hey, if he hadn't wiped himself out yet, Ray wasn't likely to either.

After one final miscue, they pulled up in front of a blue-shingled house and climbed out of Ray's junker. Cal knew the street, but he hadn't been down this way in a while. The house was better kept than the ones flanking it. The paint looked fresh, and though the structure had the typical sagging of age and weather, there was an innate charm to the place. But then, he was a sop for old houses. More character than new. Just like people. What memories did those old walls hold?

Ray lumbered up the steps and rang the bell. Cal followed but stopped in his tracks when the door opened. She stood dressed in jeans and a T-shirt, her straight, brown hair hanging past her shoulders. She still had the melting brown eyes that reminded him of a spaniel pup. It was Laurie, pronounced "Lawrie."

She had been quick to correct him when they first met, but he'd made a point of mispronouncing it to keep her attention. He'd kept it, too, from the very start when she joined the Montrose High junior class his senior year. He hadn't needed to try so hard for her attention when she returned from college seven years ago, the summer her grandmother died. It was that summer that leapt to his mind acutely as they stood now without speaking.

What had been a boyhood crush had become, as his friend Reggie would put it, one of life's defining moments. He ached inside at the memory—and hoped it didn't show.

"Hello, Cal," Laurie murmured.

Rubbing his chin, Ray turned with a true "golly" grin.

Cal shoved his hands into the pockets of his jeans. What was it his mother used to say? Coincidence was God's way of remaining anonymous? It wouldn't be the first time he was the butt of some supernatural joke. "When Ray said he had a job, I hardly expected to find you." And in no way could he connect her to this old madam of a house. She hated anything old enough to have the price tags removed.

"Are you helping him move my couch?" She pushed open the door and stepped out.

"Did you think he'd move it alone?" Cal's knees felt weak.

"I guess not." She finger combed the hair back over her crown. "Come on in."

They followed her inside. The wooden floor of the entry and living room was the kind of tight tongue and groove that you wanted to slide on with stocking feet, though its finish was worn dull. Nothing broke its plane except a tired wing chair in the corner with a floor lamp beside it. Either she hadn't been there long or she was living a Spartan existence.

"I'll get you something cold." Laurie disappeared into the kitchen.

Cal tensed. If she brought him a beer . . . He hooked an eyebrow up at Ray. Would he say something like "Cal's not supposed to have that"? Swallowing a bitter taste, he gave the living room a quick scan.

The interior had not received the cosmetic boost of fresh paint the exterior had been given, and the absence of furniture accented the cracks in the walls. Ray could make quick work of that and slap on a coat of paint, but Cal didn't say so. That was Ray's call, though it suddenly felt personal. He'd have to be careful not to ruffle Ray's feathers. The last time he'd overstepped his assistant role, Mildred had cold-shouldered him for weeks.

At the foot of the stairs, Cal noticed a junior-sized baseball glove. He didn't want to think what that meant. But when Laurie emerged and handed him, luckily, a can of Coke, he noted the lack of a ring, though her fingers were as long and slender as he remembered. "Thanks." He took a swig and followed Ray as she headed upstairs, taking the glove with her.

At the first doorway, she tossed it onto a twin bed with a sports comforter. A pair of trophies perched on the windowsill, and in the corner a stuffed bear wearing a Padres hat. The next room sported only a pink bed and a dollhouse under the window. Two, Cal counted, and they weren't even down the hall yet.

Laurie stopped at the next door and waved her arm inside. Cal halted at the faint but familiar odor of clay. It must be her studio, and when he glanced inside, he confirmed it. Identifying the slip bucket and the wheel in the corner, he had a sudden attack of nostalgia, remembering a ganglier Laurie kicking the concrete wheel at the bottom, then attaching elbows to ribs for support as she cupped her hands over the mound of clay spinning between them. Little by little, working her hands upward, she'd dig in her thumbs until a gaping mouth appeared, then work the walls thinner with an imperceptible tightening of the fingers and thumbs.

Laurie led Ray to the blue couch along the wall, a Flexsteel sleeper. Well built. Probably lots of steel. She said it came with the house, and Cal guessed the previous owners hadn't wanted to move it down the stairs. Hanging his head out the door, he eyed the turn of the banister and knew why. He handed his Coke back to Laurie and told Ray, "I'll go first and be the brains."

Normally he'd have let Ray take the downward slope and the weight that went with it, but there was no telling what Ray would do with the turn, and if his driving was any indication, Cal was determined to be at the wheel. Ray grinned, hefting his end before Cal could find a fingerhold. Bending both knees, Cal lifted the other end and backed out the door. "We'll have to raise it over the railing at the .turn."

By Ray's grunt, Cal supposed he understood. As Laurie squeezed by to direct them, he smelled her. Giorgio, of course. The years flew in reverse as he started after her like a dog at heel, tugging the couch and Ray along. They made it to the turn with no trouble, and he braced his legs as he adjusted his hold. "Going up."

Ray hoisted his end so swiftly, Cal almost tumbled down the stairs, but he caught his hip on the corner post. It shifted dangerously, and he realized the whole banister could use shoring up, especially with kids in the house. He'd probably find a list of safety hazards if he inspected the place. He eased his hip around the post. Past the turn, they lowered the couch again and brought it to the place Laurie indicated in the front room, providing an ungainly companion to the chair. Slowly straightening with one hand on his back, Cal found her watching him with a crooked smile. She handed back their drinks, then pulled a twenty from her pocket, gave it to Ray, and thanked him.

Ray beamed, shoving it into his pocket with the closest thing to a gloat Cal ever saw on his face. "I didn't say I'd pay you." He waved a finger at him.

"No problem." That was another one of their little jokes. But it confirmed his earlier thoughts on service. Cal didn't add that this time seeing Laurie was payment enough. With one step toward her, he blurted, "How about dinner?" He saw the familiar pucker between her eyebrows and wondered what form her rejection would take, but she surprised him.

"I guess I owe you. I can scrounge something together."

That wasn't what he'd meant, but if she felt better cooking than going out, who was he to object?

Ray turned at the door. "Sounds great!"

Cal looked at him, slack-jawed. No, he hadn't a clue, and he didn't take a hint either.

Laurie laughed. "Come on, then." She led the way to the kitchen. "The children are with my mother for the night, so I haven't planned anything. I have some steaks to thaw if you want to start a fire."

She spoke over her shoulder, but Cal knew her comment was directed to him. "I put fires *out*, remember?" Seven years ago he had finished his initial training to become a fireman. Did she recall?

She handed him a box of matches and aimed him toward the back door. "Then you should be good at lighting them too." Now there was logic for you.

On the patio, he found an ancient grill, charcoal, and lighter fluid. Couldn't she just use gas like the rest of the world? He choked on the black dust that rose when he dumped out the charcoal, then saturated it and took up the matches. He could hear Laurie's voice and Ray's jovial answers through the screen. It wouldn't take her long to realize Ray's hive was minus a bee or two. But he was harmless overall.

When the briquettes had soaked long enough, Cal held a lit match to the pile. The flame leaped, and instantly his throat tightened and his hand shook as he tossed the match and stepped back. He swore. This was not the time to lose it. He scanned Laurie's yard, breathing, breathing. *Focus. Don't think.*

A swing set and sandbox looked as though they'd aged along with the ancient, fenced garden plot and the cracked and peeling bench that circled the massive oak in the center of the yard. Around the edge, shrubs and dry, clinging vines fleshed out the skeleton fence. The foundation was masked by flower beds of brown brittle mums and bachelor buttons, gone to seed. The beds smelled of mulch.

He had a hard time reconciling Laurie to this domestic scene. An uptown apartment with a steady stream of glittering, influential guests was more like it. But then, both of those were hard to find in Montrose. He went in and washed. Laurie was breaking lettuce into a bowl, and the microwave hummed.

"I think they're about defrosted." She tucked a strand of hair behind her ear and reached for the paring knife. Cal slid it to her, and she glanced up, meeting his eyes for a moment. She sliced a tomato onto the lettuce, flicked a gelatinous seed from her thumb, then set the salad aside. She removed the steaks from the microwave and handed them to him.

Forcing his jaw to relax, Cal carried them out to the fire. His friend Reggie would say this was therapy, and he should welcome the opportunity. He grasped the plate and what remained of his nerves.

The coals had white edges around small black centers. He must have doused them thoroughly to have them ready so quickly, or maybe they were those instant coals that didn't need fluid. He hadn't read the bag. With the long-handled fork, he stabbed the first steak and laid it on the grill. A shudder crawled up his spine as flame licked the meat, but he forked over the next, then the last, hearing the sizzle of the marinade as it met the coals. His hands began to sweat. "Oh, man," he whispered.

Laurie's hand on his arm made him jump, and he turned to find her standing with his Coke. "You always creep up like that?"

"I'm sorry."

He felt like pulling her into his arms as he had so many times, but he took the Coke and chugged it, looking away. "So where's Dad?"

"We're not together."

He'd expected it by her circumstances and the lack of a ring, but he couldn't tell by her tone whether it was good or bad. "Are you sorry about that?"

"Let's just say it's a long story." Now her voice had an edge.

"I heard you married some major league baseball player."

"Minor."

"Hmm?"

"Minor league. In everything but ego." Her tone was soft, but biting. "He played a season with San Diego, but it was mostly farm club stuff. Anyway, his father had better things for him to do."

"The senator."

"Ex-senator." A breath of wind flipped her hair across her cheek. Cal eyed the steaks. "So how'd you pick Ray for the job?"

"First ad in the column."

He nodded. "You didn't know he was my neighbor."

"No, Cal, I didn't know." With that hope-dasher, she went back inside.

The yard seemed gray and tired. After a few minutes, he turned the meat and congratulated himself on his steady hand. He could do this . . . as long as the flames stayed down.

Carrying the platter as a trophy, he joined Ray and Laurie in the kitchen. Ray had not moved, but Laurie had the table set around him. The swing of her hips as she carried over the salad and bread was unconsciously feminine. He used to follow her down the hall just to watch, but when he'd told her that, she'd gotten so self-conscious she had walked like a stick for weeks.

That memory surge didn't help, and he clattered the plate on the table, then sprang for Laurie's chair when she came over. His hand brushed her back as he eased the chair in, and the ends of her hair were like silk on his skin. His heart started pounding. Was she experiencing the same high-voltage sensations?

The steak was a little past the bloody stage, but not yet to a sophisticated warm, pink center. No one complained, so he didn't offer to throw them back on. The meat, the cold, crisp salad, and wheat bread satisfied the rumbling of his stomach, but only time alone with Laurie would fill the rest. Ray absorbed everything edible that came within reach, then stood to go as soon as he finished.

Good boy. Now keep on moving for the door.

Ray stopped, patted his pockets, and raised his eyes to Cal. Cal tossed him the keys. "You left them in the ignition."

"Thanks."

"I tell you what, Ray." Cal wiped his mouth and dropped the napkin on his plate. "You go ahead, and I'll find my own way home." His peripheral vision caught Laurie's surprise and the frown that followed, but she said nothing as she cleared the plates to the sink. He'd take that as assent. He stood and, with his hand on Ray's elbow, edged him toward the door.

Ray shrugged. "Okay. But I'm not coming back for you."

"No problem."

Cal watched Ray plod to the car, then returned to the kitchen. Laurie's back was to him as she rubbed the plates in the soapy water, rinsed them under the faucet, then stood them on the drainer. Her twenty-eight years didn't show. Her waist curved in smoothly beneath the T-shirt, and as she bent, the jeans tightened in only the right places.

As he watched her work, Cal drank in the sight of her, like some dream too good to be real. Now that it was just the two of them, the whole dynamic had intensified, shifting subtly from happenstance to purpose.

He couldn't be around her without purpose. But what it was this time, he wasn't sure. Just staying close maybe. Just believing she was there. But she wouldn't buy that, not with their history. She would read more into this than he intended.

Her body language grew tense, angry almost, and that was not surprising. The brush of her hair back and forth against her shoulders was like a pendulum ticking back the time. But not far enough.

She faced him. "Do you expect to stay?"

"Depends what you mean by stay." He had no illusions—even fewer when he saw the set of her jaw. And he hadn't even tried to provoke her.

She pushed back her hair with a damp hand. "Do you think you can just pick up where we left off?"

Cal's pulse throbbed in his throat. "Where we left off wasn't so great. How about where we started?"

Turning back to the sink, she grabbed a glass and, in her haste, smacked it against the counter. Glass flew over the sink and floor. She gripped the edge and stood there without moving.

He sucked in her tension like bad air. Whatever she was doing here, her plans obviously didn't include him. Big surprise. He stood. "I guess I misjudged things. I should go."

She didn't argue. Clearing the front steps two at a time, he started down the street. At this rate and distance, he'd make it home just when Mildred pegged him for a prowler.

———

Laurie drew a sharp breath as a glass shard pricked her finger. Gingerly, she extricated it and watched the blood bead. It clung to her fingertip in a perfect round sphere, then vanished in the cold stream from the faucet. Cal Morrison. As if she hadn't trouble enough. And yes, Cal was trouble with a big, bold, block letter T.

She fished another piece of glass from the drain. Her finger was bleeding again, and this time not beading, but running. She tossed the glass into the trash and angled the water around the sides of the sink. His hair was shorter, but just as blond, just as unruly. His voice, his stance, his eyes . . . the way his mouth tipped into that sensuous smile . . .

She was shaking. What had he expected? But that was Cal. Eternal optimist. There's always a way; just make it happen. She should have told him to go home with Ray, should have crushed any possibilities. She should have—

"Mommy?"

She spun as Maddie, in her coat and nightie, ran across the kitchen and plunged into her arms. In one motion, she caught and lifted her child. Maddie tightly wrapped her arms about her neck, lip trembling, her tiny chest still lurching with silent sobs. Laurie looked up.

She hadn't heard the front door or any sounds of entry, but her mother stood in the kitchen doorway now, lips pressed into their permanently pained expression. "No matter what I tried . . ."

"She's not used to it. This is all so new. The move, the change . . ."

"She doesn't know me. She might have, of course, if you had deigned to visit."

Laurie sensed Maddie begin to calm. "I came for Daddy's funeral. You saw them then."

Her mother's smile thinned her lips even more. It was so patronizing, her I'm-wounded-but-I-won't-argue smile.

Laurie accepted the guilt. "I'm sorry. It'll be better now. They'll get—"

"Maddie was scared." Luke came in, carrying their little overnight bag. He set it down and shook the brown shaggy hair from his eyes. He needed it cut, but she resisted. He'd grown too serious for his five years, and the shaggy hair offset his somber eyes.

"We'll try again. I'm sure in a few days . . ." She hated the entreating tone in her voice, more appeal than assurance.

Her mother pointed. "You're bleeding."

"I broke a glass. It's no big deal." She shifted Maddie to her hip and dabbed the finger with the dishcloth. "Thank you for bringing them back."

"I told you I would if there was a problem." Emphasis placed on problem, and a quick glance toward the source child.

Laurie deflected it. "I know you don't like to drive after dark." There she went, feeding her mother's martyr syndrome and heaping the guilt on herself. A reflex.

The sigh was expected. "Well, good night." Her mother's back in the brown boucle coat was straight and narrow as she let herself out.

Laurie took a long breath. The one stroke of luck was that Mother hadn't come while Cal Morrison was sitting in her kitchen. A shudder passed through her at the thought. She looked down at Luke. "Did you tell Grandma that Maddie was scared?"

He shook his head. "I didn't have to. She cried the whole time."

Laurie tightened her arms around Maddie's back and headed for the stairs. "Well, you're home now, punkin. We'll get you tucked in."

"With you, Mommy."

Laurie paused at the landing. She shouldn't. Probably she shouldn't. The women at the club had been appalled when she admitted her three-year-old still slept with her. Not every night, she'd been quick to add, but the damage was done.

"Okay. Until you fall asleep." She glanced down at Luke. "Did you like it at Grandma's?"

He nodded. "She made ice-cream sundaes. But she put pineapple on them." He scrunched up his nose.

Laurie smiled. "That's her favorite part."

"It's kind of yucky with chocolate syrup."

"I think so too. Jump into bed now, okay?"

Luke was easy. He burrowed between the sheets. " 'Night, honey." She flipped the light switch with her elbow on the way out.

Laurie deposited Maddie on the full-sized bed, removed her coat, and pulled the covers over her. She walked to the closet, undressed, and changed into her own pajamas, then climbed in beside her child. The bed creaked. What could she expect from an old one she'd found at a yard sale four days ago when she'd come back to Montrose?

She snuggled next to Maddie. Already the tears were dried, and sleepy eyes suggested a countdown of about four seconds to dreamland. Laurie smiled and kissed her daughter's forehead, then settled into the bed herself.

She supposed it was inevitable. In a small place like Montrose, she was bound to meet up with him sooner or later. She tried not to think of him walking home. Anyway, he liked walking. Guilt was not required.

Laurie laid a hand on Maddie's curls and snuggled in. After seeing Cal, she was glad not to climb into an empty bed with her thoughts, her memories.

2

AN ACT OF GOD WAS DEFINED AS

"SOMETHING WHICH NO REASONABLE

MAN COULD HAVE EXPECTED."

A. P. Herbert

THE NEXT DAY THE WEATHER CHANGED. Wet, gray skies capped the land, dulling Miller's Pond to putty as Cal looked through the long window of his apartment. Downstairs he heard Cissy on the vacuum in her twice-weekly ritual while Mildred drowned out the din with the hi-fi, which was worse by far. Cal prayed that one of these days it would shriek its last. He fantasized its insides giving out, a great metallic heart attack. Surely those things couldn't last forever?

As always on his free Wednesday or Saturday mornings, rain or shine, he made his escape to the woods. His wool plaid jacket was misted over by the time he reached the pond with pole and tackle box. Mildred had threatened him with death if one more crappie ended up in her freezer, but he could always throw them back. He was after the legendary large-mouth bass that haunted the lower end. It had been outwitting the fishermen since Cal was a kid, but one of these days he was sure he'd land it.

No wind stirred the pond as he approached, its surface rippled only by the occasional nip of a fish. The fading gold and red leaves of the trees were still. He was alone. Cal's rubber boots squelched in

25

the boggy ground as he searched out a place that might be less muddy than the rest. No matter. He'd be thoroughly wet before he was done, by the looks of it. A fiery male cardinal broke the silence, then flitted to a higher branch as Cal breathed the chill air. This cold snap would drop the leaves.

Cal cast and settled in, breathing the dampness as though he were half fish himself. He missed the nose of his old springer, Sadie, on his knee. He had almost put the gun to his own head instead of hers when he had to put her down last year. One of these days he'd get a new dog. But not yet.

Two bluegills later, he headed for the house, the fish over one shoulder and the pole on the other. He had already gutted the fish, one thing he would never again do on Mildred's back stoop.

His thoughts returned to Laurie. When had she come back . . . and why? She'd wanted out of the Midwest, out of Montrose, especially. Away from what she knew, away from him. A wet arm of redbud slapped him as he passed, and he wiped the moisture from his cheek. *Yeah, wake up.*

Her dreams had been bigger, wealthier, more urbane. His had always been small, like his expectations. He loved Montrose, liked knowing everyone, even when that meant they all knew him too. Kind of a two-edged sword, but he couldn't imagine living anywhere else. He'd like a place of his own someday with some land, but not far from town or the people he served in one capacity or another.

He reached the house and, waving to Mildred whose nose was pressed to the kitchen window checking him for fish entrails or anything worse, headed up the outside stairs.

The hole in his gut told him more surely than the clock that it was well past lunchtime. After tossing the fish into the refrigerator, he slapped together a ham on rye and sat in the recliner with a Coke. He eyed the can, picturing in its place the silver, red, and blue of a Budweiser. Immediately the crisp, malty taste filled his mind.

But he'd sworn off booze. It amazed him that his body had retained its strength after the punishment he had given it for a while. He patted his tight, lean stomach. Of course, as Mildred was quick to point out, he walked enough to wear holes in the ground.

She had once demanded to know what he thought he was

running from. Life, he'd said. Just life. Cocking her head like an over-grown peahen, she had informed him that he never would escape. Life would still be there waiting. And so it was.

The phone rang, and he jumped. In case it was Ray, he answered, "Cal Morrison."

"I think I owe you an apology."

He sat up taller. "Laurie?" Her voice warmed a place in him that had been untouched for too long.

"I overreacted."

"Nooo . . . not you."

"We can end this right now."

Cal almost heard the receiver homing in on her base. "No, wait. I'm sorry. No sarcasm."

"I see you made it home."

"Did you think I was still wandering?" He gritted his teeth at his lack of control.

She sighed. "Why do you make it so hard?"

"Can't help it, I guess. So how bad do you feel?"

"I beg your pardon?"

"Bad enough to have dinner with me? I'll cook." He waited through her pause.

"When?"

"How about seven? You can bring the kids." He wished she wouldn't, though.

"They're seeing a movie with Mother."

Better and better. It was probably the worst thing for him, but he needed to connect with her. He always had. "You remember where I am?"

The pause was predictable. "I remember."

Hanging up, Cal surveyed the damage: crusted cups and dishes on the floor and coffee table, several weeks' worth of newspapers, and discarded clothing. With four hours and a backhoe he could do it. With four hours and no backhoe, well . . .

Laurie hung up the phone and gripped her head between her hands. What was she doing? She paced across the kitchen and back with her head vised between her palms, then knocked her forehead on the wall. That hadn't been her intention. How did he turn her simple apology into a date? She knocked her head again.

"That's funny, Mommy." Luke wedged in between her and the wall. "What are you doing?"

Laurie smiled down at him. "I just asked myself that very thing." She straightened. Actually it was good. She would use this evening to establish the ground rules. That was necessary with Cal Morrison. Not that he followed them, but at least he'd know.

Luke reached up and hooked his fingers into hers, then wiggled his thumb back and forth. "One, two, three, four, I declare a thumb war."

Laughing, Laurie battled him, then let him trap her thumb. "You're too quick, Luke." She bent and gave him a squeeze. "Where's Maddie?"

"Playing dolls."

"Why don't you go be the daddy?"

"I don't want to." Luke shook his head with solemn eyes, then looked down.

Laurie realized her blunder. She stooped down to his level. "Where's my brave little guy?"

"Here." He looked off to the side, not meeting her eyes. And he didn't sound brave.

"Uh oh. Sounds like a job for Tickleman."

Luke bit his lip, trying not to smile. Laurie seized his ribs with her fingers, and he collapsed shrieking into her arms.

"I'm brave! I'm brave!"

She ruffled his hair. "I know you are. Now run and play with Maddie." She watched him walk away. She'd used simple terms to explain their situation, but it wasn't simple. She hadn't told him the half of it, and Luke knew it. And he hurt. Her own chest tightened inside. Had she done the right thing? A surge of anger jolted her. What other choice did she have?

———

Cal pulled the door wide. Laurie looked incredible. Her hair hung loose, and the short-sleeved pinkish sweater hugged her figure. She stepped in and circled the room. Catching sight of a sock in the bookshelf, he snatched it behind his back before she turned.

"I thought I'd broil some bluegill I caught this morning. That sound okay?" He dropped the sock behind the recliner.

"You're a better cook than I am."

They stood a moment. "Want something to drink?"

Laurie slipped the purse from her shoulder. "What I'd really like is a ramble through those woods out back."

"It's pretty wet."

She lifted her hiking boot beneath her jeans. "I'm ready."

"Okay. You don't have to ask twice to get me outside."

"I remember."

Cal grabbed a jacket from the hook. "Here."

Laurie opened her mouth to protest, but he hung the jacket over her shoulders anyway, not surprised she still had that stubborn resistance to the practical. But the branches would be dripping and she'd be soaked without it. He led the way down the zigzagging stairs and across the yard. Beyond the gate, he led Laurie into the bracken, then the woods. Walking silently abreast, they breathed the stormy air and the wet tang of the trees.

They broke into a mini-clearing fringed by yarrow, still nodding flat, faded, heavy heads. Laurie stopped. "Do you remember the night we staked out Breams Road to see if Mary Brite would come out on a broom?"

He noticed she skipped back to high school to connect, instead of their last time together. Understandable, considering the way they'd parted. "I remember."

"You had me convinced she was a witch. Did you believe it?"

"No. I just wanted to be in a car alone with you."

She twined her fingers together. "Is that still all you want?"

The question threw him. He didn't think about what he wanted these days. So he shrugged. "What do you think?"

She started walking again. The shadows slipped in, congregating in the trees as ragged storm clouds congealed overhead, blotting the last of the light.

Cal pushed aside a branch. "We shouldn't go far. The woods get thick out this way."

She slowed, then turned. "Can we be friends, Cal?"

Of course that meant "just" friends. "Why?"

"I could use one."

Jamming his hands into his pockets, Cal sensed the shadows scoffing. In *his* book she was his friend, his best friend, the one he wanted to curl up next to with mugs of hot chocolate. But she wasn't suggesting that. She was limiting.

"Okay."

"No pressure?"

He lifted a damp brown leaf from her hair, misted with droplets. "Why didn't you call when you came back?"

She ran her fingers over a birch twig, pooling the moisture into her palm. "I haven't been here long."

She had an amazing knack for answering what wasn't asked. Fresh raindrops struck the leaves overhead, finding the gaps. Cal grasped her hand, leading her back, then loped for the house as the storm gathered force. They clambered up the metal stairs together. Inside, he grabbed a towel from the bath, sniffed it, then tossed it to her.

She caught it at her face. "Nice shot."

"Want to see my three-pointer?" He whipped the towel back out of her hands, balled it up, spun discus fashion, then winged it up behind his back.

Laughing, she snagged it from the lampshade. "Better stick with lay-ups."

While she wiped her hair, he went into the cramped kitchen and laid out the fish. Brushing them with oil and lemon juice, he sprinkled on diced garlic and dill, then stuck them under the broiler. Laurie was taking her time in the other room. Probably seeing whether he'd graduated from comic books and sergeant thrillers to anything literary. She'd be disappointed.

He took out the potato salad he'd made earlier. The last thing was to cut the eggs on top, which he did as Laurie took a seat at the table.

"Want some help?"

"Nope. You want a Coke? Snapple? Got raspberry and peach." If she noticed he didn't offer beer, she didn't say so.

"Raspberry. Dinner smells good."

The fish were starting to crisp as the kitchen filled with the aroma. While the smell was great now, it wouldn't be so hot in the morning. He found two forks that matched and dug for napkins. No luck. He tucked folded paper towels beside the plates and held them down with forks and knives. At Laurie's amusement, he shrugged.

They sat at the small walnut table he'd built in shop his junior year. It was a good piece of work, but then, his dad had been a master with wood. Cal remembered watching for hours as his father shaped and sanded and stained. Maybe he'd absorbed more than he thought. When he put his own hand to it, he seemed to already know more than the instructor could tell him. Over the years he'd put together quite a few nice pieces and sold them.

But not lately. He palmed the top from a bottle of Snapple and tossed the lid into the trash in the corner. The timer buzzed, and he took out the fish. They could only have been better cooked lakeside as soon as they were caught.

Laurie complimented him twice. "I forgot what freshwater fish tasted like. I've been inundated with seafood and sushi."

"The scourge of the coast."

She smiled. "Something like that."

"Come back tomorrow, we'll do it again." He smiled. "I have more."

"I can't. I'm working."

"Where?"

She forked a fine, translucent bone to the side of her plate. "Maple's Grille."

He stared a long moment. "Why?"

"I have children to feed." She sounded defensive, tense.

He'd pushed a button, but as always, that didn't stop him. "What about child support?" Didn't her hotshot husband pay for his kids? What kind of jerk left her in the lurch working at a place like Maple's?

"Don't ask questions, Cal."

Something in her tone, warning him off. "I thought we were friends."

She set down her fork. "If we are, you'll respect that."

Keep out; don't touch. The message was clear. He leaned back. "Okay, then what about your pottery?"

She snorted. "Ever try to live on that? The adage 'starving artists' wasn't coined for nothing."

Cal reached over and took her hands, turning them palms up. He pictured them coated with the gray, gritty clay. He remembered the time she'd made a plaster mold of his face, first smoothing strip after strip of wet cloth over all but his nostrils. The feel of her fingers sliding over his features was the most sensuous thing he'd ever experienced. *Whatever happened to the mask?* he wondered.

He felt her smooth palms and searched the nails for telltale signs of her work, but found none. "Why the studio, then?"

She shrugged. "Tell me about you. Why haven't you married?"

"What makes you think I haven't?"

"If you had, you still would be."

He swung around and dropped his plate into the sink. "Haven't had much time to think about it."

"Too busy saving people?"

A quiver up his spine. "Not lately. These days I'm a clown."

She punched his shoulder. "Come on. Are you still a firefighter?"

He drank long on his tea, not coming up for air until he thought his voice would stay steady. "I'm not kidding you. I'm really a clown. That's what I do."

She waited. He stood and walked to the window. The rain made rivulets on the cracking sill and turned the tan siding muddy. One of these days he'd paint the place for Mildred and Cissy. "The official title is Fire Prevention and Safety Instructor. But the fact is, I put on my clown suit and entertain kids. Puppets, magic, the works."

"You're serious, aren't you?"

Cal watched Mildred's cat, Sienna, making her way through the underbrush, trying to reach the shelter of the porch. There was one open space she couldn't avoid, and she crouched low to the ground, then sprang through to safety.

Laurie's voice was soft. "I guess you're entitled to your secrets as well."

He turned and watched her drag her finger down the neck of the bottle. Her face looked tight, but when she glanced up, she smiled. He loved that smile. He'd gone to ridiculous lengths to coax it out when they were young, pulling antics he'd rather forget. Maybe he'd been a clown even then.

"You look good, Cal."

"You look better."

Her hair fell across her cheek. "Mother drilled me tonight about coming here."

"You told her?"

"Habit, I guess." Her quick smile was wan.

"You know, that's what I never could understand. Here I am, the nicest guy—"

Laurie laughed. "It's outrageous. I'm twenty-eight years old, and she's hissing at me through the screen to remember who I am."

"It always came down to that, didn't it." He jammed his fingers through his hair.

She sobered. "I'm sorry. I shouldn't have told you. The thing is . . ." She traced her finger around the base of the bottle. "I don't know who I am. I never have. Do you ever wonder who you'd be if . . . if one little thing had been different? Where you were born or when, or who your parents are or . . ."

"Who you married and who you didn't."

She sighed. "I wish you wouldn't do that."

"Okay." He leaned against the counter.

"Okay, what?"

"Okay, I won't."

She slid the bottle away. "I have to go."

"Because I tread on sacred ground?"

"Because it's late for the children. They're not used to Mother yet." She pushed back her chair and stood, hooked her purse over her shoulder, then paused. "Thank you for dinner and . . . for listening."

"What are friends for?" He beat her to the door and pulled it open. With the slightest indication, he would kiss her.

She slipped past. "Well, thanks again."

He watched through the window. Her head hardly bent as she passed through the wet halo of porch light to her car. Who would she be if one little thing had been different? Who would they all be?

Laurie snapped on the radio as she drove. Cal's place had brought a poignant stab to her ribcage. The last time she'd been there he had changed her life. She flushed with the memory. It wasn't so much the sight of it as the smell, the old house smell, wood and wool. It wasn't Cal's smell, yet it was, too, as though he fit the old place or it fit him.

He was so much the same—his smile easy, his eyes the blue of cobalt glaze. Out in the sun they lightened up, but inside . . . She turned up the volume. What was she doing? The last thing she needed was to revisit old ghosts. Before, it would have bothered her that Cal had things he wasn't telling. Now she was almost glad. It put them on equal ground.

She drew a long breath and released the tension in her shoulders. She had accomplished what she intended, established the relationship so he knew where she stood. Nothing, nothing could come of it. Not physical, not emotional. A slow ache tightened her throat. Her head knew the inescapable truth, but watching him move about the kitchen adding a sprig of this, a pinch of that, his careless sprawl in the old, creaking chair, the paper towel napkins . . .

Laurie smiled, then covered her mouth with her hand. She knew better. This could get dangerous too fast . . . as it once had. *"Who you married and who you didn't."* Even now, after seven years and six of them married, her time with Cal haunted her. Her friend Darla said they'd formed a heart bond. No one had talked about that in sex ed. No one had mentioned tearing out your soul, leaving part of yourself irreparably behind.

That was her own fault, spending all that time with him, knowing him better than she knew herself. How could she put him away and go on with her life? She had tried to, needed to.

When she confided to Darla five years after she'd married Brian that she still hurt over Cal, Darla claimed the karma of past lives had driven them together and torn them apart. There was also something about the alignment of stars and planets, things that were vogue in Darla's circle, but which Laurie didn't believe. What did she believe? Anything?

She slowed, then accelerated again as the light changed. The heart bond—that part seemed true. Not because of stars or reincarnated destinies. But because he loved her in a way she needed to be loved. No measuring up; no strings attached. It was still there in his face, that unconditional acceptance.

The way Grams had loved her. Grams, the one person in her family who had accepted her as she was, who had no plans for her but happiness, who had taken her on her knee and told her about Jesus. Grams had a different Jesus than Daddy's.

It was easy to believe in a loving God when she was with Grams. Somehow He came alive, and she felt cherished, just listening to stories about the God she couldn't see or touch. She believed He could see her, or at least she wanted to. But as soon as she went home her faith evaporated. God became the taskmaster she could never please. God looked like Daddy.

Laurie stopped in front of her mother's house and climbed out. Looking up to the window that had been hers, she shrank inside. She hated the house. She had hated it from the day they moved in three days before her sixteenth birthday. No, she hadn't had a party. She'd spent her birthday touring the high school with the other new kids.

She had picked up her schedule and met Cal, who was performing as student guide. Yes, performing. He was as amused by his selection as the others were shocked. Cal Morrison, class cut-up turned responsible citizen? Yet his antics were never malicious, and she suspected a bright, creative mind. He was always two steps ahead, quick with a comeback, clever and witty. From the start she wanted to climb inside his brain and learn how he did that.

Not that it would have done her any good. If she'd ever spoken back to Daddy with anything like Cal's remarks . . . She shuddered, rubbed away the mist that clung to her lashes, and stared up at the window of her bedroom, the ruffled curtains crisp to this day. Try as she would, she could not conjure the kind of happy family memories that ought to be connected with the tall, brick colonial, her staunchly Christian home. Firm and steadfast, stay the course, trample any seed of variance before it sprouts. Imagination? Bah! Creativity? Humbug. The law, the Word, and Daddy.

Maybe if she'd had siblings, a sister to lie on the floor with, share secrets, commiserate. But no, she wouldn't have wished on anyone the scrutiny, the never measuring up, the aching to be accepted. They lucked out, the ones buried in the Jefferson City cemetery.

What a morbid thought. Laurie walked up to the porch and went in, allowing herself the little rudeness of not ringing. Her mother returned the favor. Maybe they both needed to rebel a little. She stopped at the kitchen door and watched her mother cover Maddie's hand with hers and press the cutter into the cookie dough.

She was trying. Laurie had to hand it to her. With Maddie and Luke, Mother was trying. Maybe she had with her as well. Maybe when she was little, and she just didn't remember. Maybe even later, and she hadn't recognized it.

Her mother looked up. "Back so early?"

Laurie caught the tone and knew exactly what Mother was thinking. *No, Mother, we didn't stoop to your suspicions.* Nor would she. Hadn't she just established that, done the responsible thing? Wouldn't Mother ever give her credit for some sense?

"Looks like fun." She smiled at Maddie's floured cheeks.

Luke held up an oddly shaped cookie. "I made the bears."

"Yum."

"Want one?"

"If I can gobble its head first."

He held it out to her, and she bit the head off. "As good as it looks." Of course her mother had made the dough. That was a given. Marjorie Sutton never risked her ingredients on inexperienced hands.

Laurie's mood soured. "Maddie needs to get to bed, Mother."

"Yes, I know. But I had no idea how long you'd be with . . . Anyway, we're finishing the last batch now." She pressed the cutter herself over the remaining dough. "Wash her up at the sink, if you like."

Laurie worked the dough and sugar off Maddie's tiny fingers under the water. "Having fun, punkin?"

"We watched *Cats and Dogs.*" Maddie planted a sugary kiss on her cheek, then squeezed her neck with wet hands. How affectionate her children were. What did it take to drive that out of a child? Or had she, herself, been born deficient somehow? Had she ever squeezed her mother's neck like that, or God forbid, her father's?

She hooked Maddie on her hip and watched her mother slide the spotless cookie sheet into the spotless oven. Luke circled her legs in his arms. Her children were the only good things to come of the mess she had made of her life. What would she ever do without them?

3

THE BEST PART OF THE ART OF LIVING

IS TO KNOW HOW TO GROW OLD GRACEFULLY.

Eric Hoffer

HANDS JAMMED INTO THE POCKETS of his worn jeans, Cal stood outside the white brick walls of the Montrose Behavioral Health Center. In there you didn't wonder if you were cracking up; you knew it. And the best part was that everyone else was as cracked as you. He shook his head, thinking how belligerent he'd been. But he was past that now.

So why had he stopped there today? He drove by the center every day on his way to work, but this was the first time he'd stopped in the three months he had been out. Closure? Or had seeing Laurie made things harder to accept? Her expectations, her impressions were based on the man she had known, the man he'd been. What would she think now? He sighed.

A hand landed like a sledgehammer on his shoulder, and he turned to meet the smile, an awesome spread of lips, gums, and teeth as white as chalk. Cal couldn't miss the grin, blaring at eye level above the rock-like chin and giant Sequoia neck.

"Hey, man! How you been?"

Cal's own mouth spread. Pure Pavlov. When Reggie Douglas smiled, Cal smiled. At least he didn't salivate.

Dressed in his thin white coat, Reggie cocked his head and eyed Cal as he had each morning when he had come through the door of Cal's room. Cal half expected him to ask if he was regular and taking his vitamins.

"You're lookin' good. Whatcha been up to?" Reggie released his shoulder after a peremptory squeeze that made Cal glad this man was a friend.

"Oh, you know, clowning around."

"Yeah. My niece said you did her school."

Cal shrugged. "How're things?"

"Crazy. You know how it is. Good thing I got the Big Man upstairs in control." He hoisted his thick finger toward the sky.

"Yeah, good thing, Reg."

"Hey, Jack Smith got clean. Finally decided it was not worth the trouble to keep sneakin' stuff in."

Cal pictured Jack's haggard face. *"Come on, Cal. You got connections, don't you? Get me somethin' . . ."*

Cal swallowed. "I'm glad to hear it." He didn't have the sort of connections Jack had wanted—or that sort of addiction. Cal's had been strictly legal poison. Only stuff he had free access to as both a paramedic and consenting adult. Amazing what you could forget with booze and prescription drugs—until they grew horns and fangs and you were fighting for your life. He'd won the fight—so far.

Reggie squeezed his shoulder. "I gotta get inside. You coming?"

"Not this time." Cal jammed his hands into his pockets. "I think I'll stay sane for a while."

Reggie raised the shiny ridge of his sparse eyebrows. "Just get it close, man. Successive approximation. One little step in the right direction at a time."

Cal nodded. "Give Rita a hug for me." Rita James, M.D., Doctor of Psychiatry and part-time shoulder. She meant more to the department than any other resource, and personally far more to Cal than that. Like Reggie, she was a friend.

"You got it." Reggie zeroed in on the first set of doors. "I'll see you tonight."

Cal heard the slap of Reggie's pink palms on the door as his bulky shoulders, double roll of neck skin, and black, nubby head disappeared inside. He climbed back into his jeep and headed for the elderly care facility nearby.

Forty-two pairs of rheumy eyes fixed on him as Cal pointed to the charts, telling the residents of Oaklane Manor the best way to enter and exit a tub to prevent a fall. These occupants still managed on their own, unlike their counterparts in the nursing section of the facility, and fire safety wasn't the only concern he dealt with. When Billy rode his bike through a window, when Junior choked on a grape, when Grandma broke her hip, when a diner passed out, who got called?

Not that he minded. Helping folks was the heart and soul of what he did. That was the job. Or it had been. No, it still was. Prevention was as crucial as intervention. More so, because there was little you could do once a situation went bad.

Although the makeup and wig were back at the station, Cal threw in a joke. "There were three spinster sisters. The first decides to take a bath and goes up to the tub. With one leg over the side, she says, 'Now was I getting in or getting out?' When she doesn't come back, the second sister goes to check. She heads up the stairs and when she gets halfway, she stops. 'Was I going up or going down?' The third sister shakes her head exasperated, saying, 'Thank goodness, I'm not like them. Knock on wood.'" He rapped his knuckles on the podium. "'Now was that the front door or the back?'"

Chortles and snorts followed, and one purple draped woman removed her glasses and wiped tears from the corners of her eyes. Maud would be squeezing his hands when he finished, saying what a nice young man he was to come speak to them.

Flipping the chart, he started in on the fire prevention rules. "Make yourself a checklist. Turn off the burner, the iron, the . . ." His voice droned. Ed Mills in the white vinyl armchair snored long and low, then flubbered his lips with the expelled breath. His lips sank in between his gums, then flubbered out again. No one jostled him awake. Cal asked if they were all familiar with the emergency exits of the general facility as well as an escape route from their own private units. Heads bobbed.

No one looked confused, but he knew the disorientation they would face in a real emergency when smoke and panic concealed and distorted everything familiar. "Have an escape plan . . ." Could their aging limbs pull them along at ground level, where the air was cleaner? Could they move swiftly enough to escape the accumulating carbon monoxide, before even lungfuls of fresh air weren't enough to staunch the poison already in their systems? What of misplaced eyeglasses needed to locate the glow of exit signs, arthritic knees, and—

Ed snorted and shifted his position before resuming his snooze.

Cal moved his hands like a symphony conductor until Ed's snores settled into their regular pattern. His neighbors laughed, giving Cal good-natured smiles. Cal's chest tightened. Maybe a few of the sparky ones would see to their neighbors and friends. The rest was up to the men at the station and those called from their homes, even from their beds, to put their skills to the test. Cal tightened his grip on the pointer. Skills fail. Men fail. He closed the charts. "So remember now, think safety. We can't afford to lose the wisdom in this room."

Maud dabbed her eyes again, then honked her nose into a handkerchief. She was always touched that he cared enough to come. He never told her it was his job. And maybe it was more than that that brought him so regularly. He loved old people with their amused acceptance of their limitations, even the crotchety ones who complained about every ache. The more marginalized, the more he cared. Someone had to.

When he finished the presentation, Cal took the elevator up. It wasn't part of the job, but he always took a stroll on the confused floor. Sure enough, Martha was in the hall, stunning in an ankle-length beaded gown, her posture at eighty-four was elegant, her figure svelte. Her arms, covered to the elbow in gloves, swung just so with each step.

"I'm Martha, the Victorian." She engaged him with her eyes. "They said my baby died, but *I know* they stole it." Fallout from the days they didn't let women see their stillborn children. Sometimes Martha was clear as a bell, but when she was in her promenade mode, she didn't converse, she recited. She raised her chin again and walked on. "I'm Martha, the Victorian." Cal let her stroll and went into the third room on the right.

Here the woman was tied into a wheelchair to keep her from slipping out. She looked up. "Hello."

"Hi there, Olive."

She smiled, showing straight teeth. "Did I ever tell you my father was on the stage?"

"Is that so?"

"He was a comedian . . . and a tragedian."

They shared the laugh they always did.

"He had lovely white hair. Oliver DeForest. That was his stage name. He was a comedian . . . and a tragedian."

Cal squatted down and took her hand. "You doing all right, Olive? Anything you need?"

"My mother was a janitor."

"Nothing wrong with good honest work." Cal patted her hand and stood.

"Gladdy cut my eyelashes off. She was my half sister."

"Well, you have lovely eyelashes now, Olive." He framed her with his fingers. "Pretty as a picture."

She laughed. "Go on, you flirt."

Cal squeezed her hand. "You have a nice day, Olive."

"A comedian *and* a tragedian. Such lovely white hair."

Cal left her reminiscing and ducked into the other rooms briefly. He was on the clock, so he couldn't do much more than say hello. But that was enough. He walked out with a spring in his step.

After leaving the home, Cal headed for the library. Merv Peterson had earned himself an early inspection by twice calling in a smell of smoke between *true crime* and *mystery*. Both times the men had pulled the engine around to assess from three sides without seeing so much as a puff. Both times the interior proved sound. Merv took his position seriously and made sure everyone knew his importance to the library. But before Merv made this a habit, Cal intended to set his mind at rest and maybe slap him with enough infringements to discourage future overreactions.

Looking official in his uniform, with clipboard in hand, he sauntered into the stone-block building, pressed through the swinging half doors and made his way to the desk. Merv's hound-dog jowls dangled, and his lips parted when he saw Cal coming. Cal held out his hand, and Merv joined it with his sub-normal temperature palm.

"Did someone call?" Merv asked, darting his eyes to see who might have overstepped him.

"No. I'm here to inspect."

"Oh . . . well . . ." Merv spluttered.

"Don't worry. I'll whisper."

Cal found the two floors open to the public in relative good order, except for one blocked exit and an excess of flammables in a janitor's closet. These he wrote up, then descended to the cellar, flipped the switch that lit a row of bare bulbs along the ceiling, and eyed the ghostly shelves of out-of-date and out-of-mind literature.

"Whew." He blew a dusty cloud, then made tracks through the gray thickness that muffled his steps. It was like walking the catacombs; no man-sized spider webs, but a smell and silence of age and solemnity.

At the stone wall, Cal followed the wires up to the ceiling with a cloth from his back pocket, chasing the dust like fur before it. They were old, but sound. Must have been replaced since the place was built. He had hoped to make more of a point. Ah, an almost ceiling-high pile of periodicals in the back corner, beside the boiler room no less. Cal slipped the clipboard from under his arm. Now that should keep Merv busy for a while, especially as the man would never part with a one.

After a long discussion with Merv about the basics of fire prevention, Cal grabbed a bite at Benny's Burgers, went through the usual debate at the register, then let Benny comp his bill. Two years ago he'd breathed life back into Benny's son, who'd nearly drowned in a neighborhood pool. Benny swore Cal's cash would never be good in his store again. And after all this time, he still refused to take it. Cal almost stopped eating there, had been reluctant to return until word reached him that Benny was crushed by his absence. How many burgers was a boy's life worth? Cal made it in at least once a week. Best burgers in town.

Two more appointments and he called it a day. It was Friday. Poker night. Cal rubbed his hands. For some reason, he felt lucky. That feeling stayed with him until Ray caught him at his door.

"Cal!"

Cal turned on the perch at the top of his stairs. "Can't help tonight, Ray. Got plans."

"It's just a short job."

"Got poker tonight, Ray." He'd tried to include Ray once, but there was no bluff in the man at all. He'd felt so guilty over Ray's losses, he'd made them up from his own pocket, which wasn't deep to start with.

"But I need your jeep."

Cal leaned on the rail while Ray described the job. Ray's bomb wouldn't do it; that was clear. He'd planned on this time to make the place presentable, but . . .

"All right. Let's go." He headed back down the stairs. It wouldn't take too long to drag the trunk sections of a fallen tree into the woods behind Fred's house. And Ray was bobbing from one foot to the next like a kid going to the circus. Two jobs in three days was something.

Cal reached the ground. "Got chains?"

Ray nodded. "They're in my trunk."

That was one thing to be said for Ray's bomb. It had a trunk the size of Texas. "Move 'em over to the jeep."

Together they headed for Fred's, a mile away by road, shorter if you walked around the pond and through the woods. Cal pulled the jeep into Fred's backyard. Dogs came yapping from all sides, but there was no sign of Fred.

"He's not home." Ray climbed out of the jeep and greeted each dog as it slathered his hands.

Cal joined the melee. When they'd satisfied the dogs, he pulled the chains from the trunk, hooked the loops over his shoulder, and started for the nearest piece of the old elm that had rotted through and snapped in the last storm. Fred had sawed the trunk into six-foot sections, but they were half that much around.

Ray lifted while Cal looped the chain around, then attached the other end to the hook at the back of the jeep. It was rough ground between Fred's kennels and the woods, but the jeep could handle it. Ray's car would have lost its differential. They left the logs in a semi-circle at the edge of the woods like a boundary marker.

"Good enough?" Cal detached the chain from the hook after the last log had been placed.

Ray nodded. "I think so. He said he'd pay me tomorrow."

So they could have done the job tomorrow. But Ray wasn't like that. Everything was now for Ray. He wagged a finger. "I didn't say I'd pay you." The same old joke never got old for Ray. But with Benny's gratis burger in his belly, Cal just figured what went around, came around.

Cal clapped his shoulder. "Get in." They drove home, and Cal gave Ray a wave as they parted in the yard. That lucky feeling hadn't departed. If anything, it had grown.

———

Having slept like a rock following the poker game, Cal staggered to the kitchen. Thank goodness for Mr. Coffee. If everything could be that simple. A pain connected his temples, which was hardly fair since he'd refused Rob's Chivas and stayed clergyman sober. Boy, had Rita scowled when Rob walked in with the bottle. But it wasn't all about avoidance. Half the battle was resisting while in the presence.

It hadn't been difficult either. He hadn't drooled once, though Rita watched him as though she thought he might. She had difficulty leaving her professional role. Did she even have a life outside the loonies she rescued? Every man in the fire department had bent her ear at one time or another, debriefing whatever incident had caused stress, though most of them weren't court-ordered into her special treatment program. That was reserved for the truly deserving.

Shaking his head, Cal laughed. Well, he'd been lucky last night. It was always his lucky night when Rob brought liquor. He'd had him in his pocket last night by eighty bucks. Even Reggie owed him, although Rita had cleaned up. Not literally, unfortunately. He dug a Coke can from the sink drain and tossed it in the trash along with the unfiltered remains of Rob's Camels. Smoke still clung to the air.

There was something warped about a smoking fireman, but that was Rob. If he didn't get enough smoke in his lungs from the job, he provided it himself. Always on the edge, Rob. Together they'd pulled some pretty stupid pranks. Now they spent most of their time avoiding subjects Rob thought might kindle Cal's memories or his madness.

Cal contemplated the distance between them these days. On the surface, not much had changed. But there was stiffness, an unease that made it hard to believe they had known each other since they were three. Rob claimed no hard feelings for the fists Cal had thrown his way, and Cal believed him. No, it was the revelation of mortality Rob couldn't get past. Cal's meltdown proved they were human after all. That was the part Rob resented.

Rolling an unlit cigarette out from under the toaster oven, Cal remembered Laurie tucking one between her fingers and lighting up behind the gym. *"What do you think?"* she'd said, then frowned when he pulled it from her lips and crushed it under foot. *"I wasn't going to inhale."*

"I don't want to kiss a smoker mouth." He'd been a crusader then. He shook his head. He'd kiss it now, smoke or no. Splashing water on his face from the kitchen sink, he heard the coffee maker begin to sputter and steam, then release its brown stream into the pot. He traded the place of the pot with his cup, let it fill, then exchanged them again and drank. Ah, morning. What morning? The vacuum started downstairs. Saturday. The second bi-weekly torture began. He groaned when the hi-fi kicked in, warbling Wayne Newton through the floorboards. It was like living in time warp.

Gripping the phone, Cal called Laurie. "You doing anything today?"

"What's all that racket?"

"It's an old house."

"Oh. I have the children home today."

He switched the receiver to his other ear in hopes of overcoming the noise. "Don't you think it's time they met me?" It had been all of four and a half days since he'd learned she was back.

Silence.

"Laurie? Earth to Laurie . . ."

"I'm here."

"Have a nice trip?"

She laughed. "I guess you can come over."

"Something wrong? Are they mutants?"

"That's tacky." There was an edge to her voice.

So the kids were off limits for joking. "Sorry. Why don't we take them somewhere?"

"What doesn't cost anything?"

"It's on me." Cal took a long sip, letting the caffeine absorb into the tissues of his mouth, then swallowed it down.

Again Laurie was silent. A clue telling him what? Then, "I'd rather not."

Of course. Same old Laurie. One of these days she'd learn that it was also good to receive. And maybe she'd see he didn't expect much in return. "How about fishing? You and the kids can come here." The weather had warmed again, and the ground was sufficiently dry. It was reasonable, and it cost him no more than bait. She couldn't argue that.

"Luke would like that." Her voice sounded musey.

"That's your daughter, right?"

"Cute."

Oh yeah. "So I'll see you soon?"

"Okay."

He cleaned up last night's debris, and after a quick once-over, a shower, and shave, he was ready. Laurie's white Lexus pulled up in the drive, and they climbed out. Or rather Laurie climbed, a brown-haired boy, maybe five-ish, tumbled head first, and a smaller girl followed, reaching for Laurie's hand.

He started down, but they were intercepted by Mildred, and a minute later, Cissy homed in by way of child radar. By the time he reached the ground, both kids had a peppermint in their mouths, and Laurie was providing their vital statistics. Cissy and Mildred turned, Cissy's face dreamy, but Mildred's scowl firmly in place.

"Well, now that you've all met, we'll just be on our way." Cal scooped up the poles and tackle he'd left against the porch. Laurie pulled a food basket from the car and closed the door. The children waved to Cissy, who flapped her wrist like a chicken wing as they all set off through the grass toward the woods. The sooner he cleared Mildred's scope the better.

Laurie's son pumped his legs to match Cal's stride. "Did you ever catch a fish?"

"Sure, have you?"

Luke shook his head.

"Do you talk to 'em?"

46

"Fish don't talk." Luke gave him a gap-toothed grin.

"Well, not people talk. I mean fish talk."

Luke's sister drew up close, and Luke said, "That's Maddie. She's three."

Cal stopped and held out his hand, looking down into the dreamy face. Had Laurie looked like that at her age? Large, thick-lashed, brown eyes, blond hair curling around her shoulders, tied back in two bows. "Hello, Maddie. I'm Cal." Her hand was soft as a kitten's paw inside his calloused palm.

"Nice day to be outside," Laurie said.

"Yep." There was just enough chill in the air to raise goose bumps if they didn't wear their jackets. He noticed Laurie had clothed both children accordingly and was herself the picture of responsibility. *Guess that's motherhood.* Cal led the way until the pond came into sight, rimmed with copper-leafed trees. Then both children sprang forward and ran.

"It's kind of soggy there at the edge."

Laurie smiled. "Do you teach water safety too?"

"I've seen enough close calls." Too many. His concern raised a notch.

The air smelled of fall with a tang from the pond. Overhead a flock of ducks cut a lopsided wedge through the sky. He pointed. "You know why one line is longer than the other?"

Laurie's gaze followed his upwards. "More aerodynamic?"

"Nope." His smile quirked. "There's more ducks in it." He heard her sigh as he caught up to the kids, dropped the tackle, and set them looking for worms.

Laurie cringed. "Is that necessary?"

"No. But it's half the fun." He weighted the lines and added the hooks.

"Just so you know, I'm not sticking anything slimy, wiggly, or otherwise, on any hooks."

Cal grinned. "I didn't expect you were."

When the children wandered back empty-handed, he attached fluorescent pink marshmallow bait to the hooks. No sense losing his flies. Holding his hands over the boy's, Cal showed Luke how to cast, then helped Maddie do the same. He'd give her about thirty seconds before she got tired of holding it.

"We didn't talk to the fish." Luke tossed the hair from his eyes.

Cal looked at him. "You're right." He bent and rummaged through the box until he came up with a plastic straw. This he handed to Maddie and showed her how to sink the end into the pond. "Now blow, and whatever you do, don't suck."

"Cal . . ."

He nudged Laurie quiet. Why let adult concerns spoil the fun? Maddie blew, making bubbles, and giggled. The water lapped her pink canvas tennis shoe as she bent to blow again.

Luke tugged his sleeve. "What did she say?"

"She said, 'swim on down for the big bug party.'"

Maddie giggled again. Clicking her tongue, Laurie turned and shook out the blanket.

Cal reached out to help, took a corner, and tugged the blanket from Laurie's hands. "Oops."

"Grow up." Laurie caught up the edge with a glare, but he could see the smile behind it that wanted out if she'd just let it. He'd been after that smile as doggedly as he'd angled for that legendary bass. He tugged again, and this time she pulled back, bending her knees and digging in her heels.

Maddie dropped the fishing pole and ran for the blanket. Reaching her arms up around it, she staggered back and forth as Cal tugged and released.

"Stop it, Cal." Laurie half laughed, half scolded.

"Can't. If I let go, you'll both fall over."

"Just stop pulling."

Cal stood still, and Maddie dropped to the ground with the kind of laugh only a little girl could make.

Laurie raised her chin. "Now help me spread it."

How could he ignore that do-as-I-say mother tone? He spread his arms and billowed the blanket up, then maneuvered to bring it down on Maddie. Laurie shook her head as Maddie wiggled out from underneath.

Cal helped Laurie smooth the bumps, then hoisted Maddie on top and tugged her hair bow. "What's this?" He pulled a gold plastic ring with a shiny pink stone from her ear.

"A ring." Her fingers reached.

"How'd it get in your ear?" He slipped it over her thumb.

She giggled again. "It wasn't."

"Sure it was. Didn't you see me get it out?" He looked up and saw Luke's fishline bob. "Got someone playing with your line, son. Next time you feel a tug, yank up hard."

He stood and rescued Maddie's pole from the shallows, then took his place beside Luke. He showed him how to gently reel the line in and cast again. It took just over an hour, but with Cal's help, Luke finally landed a thrashing crappie, almost into Laurie's lap.

"I think we'll work a bit on reeling." Cal rubbed Luke's head. The look in the boy's eyes was as seeking as any he'd seen in Laurie's. Approval? Affection? Cal smiled. "Good work, Luke."

The boy rubbed the back of his hand over the splashes on his cheek, but Cal could see his praise had sunk in. He removed the hook and tossed the fish in the pail. "Wanna get another one?"

Luke watched it flopping. "Does it hurt them?"

"Nah. Fish don't have nerves like ours."

"Okay." Luke picked up his pole. "Let's get another one."

Cal patted his shoulder. "That's the spirit." The boy was sensitive, not wanting to hurt a crappie. He could spend time with a kid like that. Lots of time.

Cal caught the next one in less than ten minutes. Since it swallowed the hook, he had to cut the line. He set aside the poles, lifted the fish pail and took out his knife. Then he eyed Luke. "Now if we were Indians, you and I would go have a seat under that tree, and let your mom and sister take care of this."

"Not a chance." Laurie spoke with her back turned. "I'll make the fire."

Cal's hand tightened on the pail. "I thought we'd just broil them at the house."

"I promised the kids if they caught something we'd cook it lakeside. I even brought marshmallows."

"Oh." Marshmallows clinched it. "Come on, Luke." Cal took him far enough away to not horrify Maddie, then gutted the fish.

"Ick!" Luke looked a little pale as they worked, but Cal let him use his knife to hack off the heads.

Laurie had made a fire circle and started a small blaze. "I didn't think about a grate."

There was his excuse: Sorry, better take them to the house after all. But there was the marshmallow thing and two pairs of wishful eyes, so he said, "We can skewer them." He fashioned a tripod of sticks over the fire, tying it up with line from his tackle box. With his knife, he sharpened the end of two branches and skewered the fish at tail and top, then fixed them to the tripod with more fish line. These held the fish just close enough to roast.

"I'm impressed." Laurie smiled.

This was good. Cal grinned back. Impressed went a long way with Laurie.

Luke ran off to scavenge more wood for the fire. Glancing over, Cal watched Maddie dance in the long grasses. When a little breeze came up, she stopped spinning and reached her fingers up, closing her eyes. Cal could almost sense her little nerve endings feeling the brush of the breeze.

"She's kind of a hedonist," Laurie said. "Gets it from Brian."

"Ah. He has a name."

Laurie frowned, turning back to the fire. She poked the flesh of the nearest fish. "What do you think?"

"Not yet." Cal settled onto the blanket. "They're good-looking kids. High-class genes, I guess."

She didn't take the bait, just knelt at the edge of the blanket.

He shook his head. "It's funny to think of you with children. Not that I doubt you're a great mom."

She flicked an ant from a ridge of the blanket. "I know what you're thinking. Laurie couldn't be domesticated and selfless enough to have kids of her own."

"Children never factored into your plans. At least as I heard them."

She tucked her hair behind her ear. "No, they didn't. But you can't imagine how holding your newborn son for the first time can wipe away all the false notions of what matters most." She turned to him, the tenderness in her eyes almost painful. "There's nothing in the world I wouldn't do for them."

"I can see that."

"Can you?" She held her eyes full on him for the first time since she'd returned.

"Yeah. People change."

She smiled. "You don't."

"Why do you say that?"

She took a long breath and looked up at the clouds in the sky. "You're like the ground, or the trees, or the sky. Changeable, yes, but always essentially the same, no matter what blows your way."

"Depends how closely you look." Did he hide it so well? Could she really believe he was the same reckless optimist he'd been? He knew better now. His half full glass wasn't just half empty—it was smashed to pieces.

She pulled the lids from the coleslaw and cold vegetables. "I guess that's true for all of us."

Cal tossed a dry seedpod at her. "So what changed your mind?"

She stacked the lids together and tucked them into the basket. "Luke."

"Unexpected, huh?"

She nodded.

"Before or after you married Mr. Baseball?"

She glared. "After. Just. Brian was happy, though. He wanted the birth of his son announced while he was playing the World Series."

"Only he never played the World Series."

"No."

"Guess he didn't mind that while he was hearing his announcement, you'd be in a hospital alone somewhere having his kid."

Laurie settled onto her left haunch. "You'd better check the fish."

As she poured out cups of cider, Cal pulled the fish from the fire, avoiding the sight of the flames. He would have liked to kick dirt on it now, but for Laurie's mention of marshmallows. Setting the plate of fish on the blanket, he whistled through his teeth for Luke, who was stabbing a stick into the mud at the side of the pond.

Luke came running. "Can you show me how to do that?"

He tucked Luke's chin up and studied the gap in his bottom teeth. "You need all your teeth. Otherwise the air just goes through."

"When the new one grows in? Will you show me then?"

How long did it take a tooth to grow in? Would Laurie give him that much of her life? Cal mussed Luke's hair. "Sure."

Maddie screwed up her face at the fish, and Laurie produced a bologna sandwich. Luke ate his fish gamely. Proprietary pride, most likely. Crappie wasn't the greatest. As soon as they'd finished, both children dived for the marshmallow bag and stabbed them onto sticks.

Cal crouched beside Laurie, his muscles tight as he watched, elbows resting on his knees. Twice the children handed over their torched remains for his and Laurie's enjoyment, then returned to the fire with new ones. Every sinew in Cal's back and neck was on edge, like a slingshot, aimed and ready. His thighs burned with the position he held, but he couldn't sit.

It was torture watching them at the fire. How many marshmallows did they have to cook? A breeze blew Maddie's curls about her face. He tensed. A stick popped, a spark flew, and Maddie jumped. Cal lunged, crashing down into the grass with the child in his arms. Maddie screamed as they rolled, crying when he released her.

Curled on his knees on the ground, Cal covered his ears with his hands, teeth clenched. He didn't move or look up when Laurie lifted the child away from him. The flames were everywhere, the orange glow, the tiny form crouched under the chair, crying, crying—then the screams . . . His stomach churned, his muscles quaked. It was the screams he couldn't take. *Stop! Stop!* They faded.

Opening his eyes, he saw the pale green of the grass swaying in the autumn breeze. He glanced sideways. Maddie huddled in her mother's lap, tears sparkling in her eyes, and Luke knelt beside them, solemn. The screams had ceased; the air cleared, but not the thrumming in his head. Looking at Laurie and the children clasped together in stunned wonder, Cal understood their silence. What was there to say?

Laurie drew a breath, but before she could speak, he rasped, "I'm sorry," then staggered up and started for the house, blood pulsing in his ears. Inside, he splashed water on his face and buried it in a towel. His breathing slowed, and the tension drained from his muscles, replaced by lethargy and a slow throb in his right temple. If he could walk to the end of the earth, he'd drag himself right then. He was only half surprised when Laurie came inside.

"The kids are in the yard."

He nodded without turning.

She laid a hand on his arm. "Thank you."

"For?"

"Caring enough to be concerned."

Cal snorted. "I scared the wits out of her. She'll never roast another marshmallow as long as she lives."

"I told her you thought she was in danger."

Thought she was. Not knew, not saw. Just imagined in some warped place in his brain. Cal pulled away. "Would you mind going now?"

It was a long moment before the door closed behind her. He didn't watch her descend the stairs, gather up the kids, and drive away. But he heard them go. He spent the rest of the day in the woods. It was a bad habit, really, running away from life, but he'd just about mastered it.

A little before nine that night, he called Rita James. "Here's the scenario. We're having a picnic, roasting fish on a campfire. The kids are toasting marshmallows, and a spark flies up, maybe toward the kid, maybe not. I freak out, tackle her, and sit there panting like a rabid dog so I won't burst out crying."

"Sounds like a natural reaction to the situation, given your history."

"I'm a pyrophobic fireman."

"You're not pyrophobic. Fire triggers post-traumatic stress and causes panic symptoms. It's not fire you're afraid of, it's failure. Let go of the guilt, and you know the rest."

Cal leaned against the counter. "As easy as that, huh?"

"What do you want me to say?"

"How about telling me I'll be normal again."

Rita sighed. "What's normal? You had a death experience with extreme personal trauma. You already take on more than the usual responsibility for things beyond your control, and you have a marked inability to separate the possible from the impossible. Given all that, you have to play the hand you're dealt."

"Can I bluff?"

She laughed low. "Probably. Knowing you."

"Thanks, I guess."

"Cal, it hasn't been that long."

"Hasn't it? Feels like forever."

———

Laurie rocked back and forth, back and forth, Maddie's cheek hot against her chest, the little hand on her arm limp and soft. But even though the child had fallen asleep over an hour ago, Laurie hadn't moved to put her to bed.

She stared at the crack on the wall that meandered like an old waterway from the corner to the floor. What was wrong with Cal? What had caused his reaction, his lunge for Maddie, the tone in his voice when he told her to leave . . .

What had happened to him? She felt as though the earth had shifted. Somehow the sand had been sucked out from under her feet. *"People change."* Had he been telling her? Had he warned her he wasn't what he'd been? *"It depends how closely you look."* Was he saying underneath the same old Cal was a man she didn't know, wouldn't understand?

No one's perfect, he used to say. Accept yourself the way you are. Of everyone she'd known, he was the most sure of himself, the least concerned about what others thought. He always did things his way. She pictured him again, crouched, hands pressed to his ears like claws, blocking what? What did he hear?

Maddie slept. Laurie closed her eyes and rocked. She wanted to puzzle it out, to find the answers, but she couldn't. She'd been away too long. Cal had lived his life while she lived hers, and now there was a whole critical piece of it she knew nothing of. But it couldn't be helped.

She had Luke and Maddie to think of. Nothing mattered as much as they did. Nothing. She stroked Maddie's hair. Cal was right. She hadn't planned on children. She wasn't prepared for the joy when it happened, the miracle of holding Luke's tiny head cupped in her palm, and again with Maddie.

The love was so deep, so encompassing. She had never loved like that before, had not known she was capable of it. Something inside her had been starved for it, yet when it came it brought as many doubts and fears as joys. But she wouldn't trade one minute of it. Love that deep was worth the pain.

It should have knit her and Brian together. But it hadn't. The children were little trophies to him, something he kept on a shelf and looked at when he wanted to brag. He was too busy maintaining his image. She and Brian were swept up in the mirror maze of appearances, the express lane of power. With Brian's semi-fame, his father's senatorial influence, and corporate success Laurie had attained her dream. She belonged to the elite. And the elite had rules of their own, or none at all.

Laurie dropped her cheek to Maddie's head. It was late. She gathered the child up and carried her to bed. In her bathroom, she pressed a cold washcloth to her face. Fame, power, wealth. How fleeting it all was. She climbed into bed. How fleeting and ultimately worthless.

Closing her eyes, she pictured Cal, stiff and tense, his back turned to her, his voice a grating croak. *"Would you mind going now?"* Never once, in all the time she'd known him, had he ever asked her to leave.

———

The alarm jolted Laurie awake. For once her body clock hadn't wakened her ahead of it. Small wonder with the thrashing she'd done. She sat up and raked her fingers through her hair, then headed for the shower. She turned the white, cross-shaped enamel faucets that sent water up the metal tube to the head. The plumbing groaned.

She draped her gown over the rack, stepped into the claw-foot tub, and pulled the curtain around her. She tipped her head back to submerge her hair. The paint around the upper edge of the wall was stained a burnt orange and peeled. Closing her eyes, she tipped her head farther and let the water run over her face, feeling a heaviness inside she couldn't put words to. Listlessly she lathered her head with arms like weights.

Was she depressed? Three years ago she'd seen a therapist who warned against stress factors. If Laurie made a list today, she'd topple the scale. But she could not go there. She couldn't afford to. She had to be strong for Luke and Maddie.

As she rinsed, the pipe started a high-pitched whine that set her teeth on edge. She hated old houses: cracked tiles, noisy pipes, faulty wiring. So why had she come back and chosen one? Beggars couldn't be choosers, but it was more than that. She jammed the faucets into the off position. The cold one slipped back and started dripping, and she pushed it harder. This time it held. She climbed out.

Wrapped in a towel, she blew her hair dry, then pulled it into a French braid. She dressed in the skirt and blouse she wore to Maple's, plain enough to satisfy Maple, fitted enough to encourage tips. The thought alone depressed her. Even in college she hadn't waited tables. She had done work study in the library two semesters, and after that Daddy had taken up the slack since she'd proven she could handle academia.

Of course, what does one do with an art history degree in Montrose, Missouri? Or anywhere else for that matter. If she had gone for fine arts or commercial art . . . but Daddy wouldn't hear of it. *"They're all drop-out losers."*

Mother's focus had been finding her a suitable husband. And oh yes, Brian was suitable. Wealthy, known, good connections—better than Mother had dreamed. Not even her imagination could have conjured the son of a retired senator for her daughter. No, Laurie had done that for herself.

And wasn't Brian the epitome of all she'd wanted? No matter the indiscretions, infidelities, illegal substances. Laurie hadn't known about any of that at first. She'd been raw . . . bleeding really, though no doctor would have detected it. Grams' death had driven her to an intimacy with Cal that made her need him too much. So she had left him, returned to UCLA, and rebounded.

Unequally yoked. The phrase came to her mind now like a foreign language. Yes, she'd felt unequally yoked, never measuring up to the senator's son. Had he intentionally chosen beneath him to keep the upper hand? Had she intentionally chosen to perpetuate her unworthiness? But that wasn't how Grams had meant the phrase. She had talked about a spiritual yoke.

How Laurie had laughed, picturing the yolk of an egg. What did she know of oxen and the careful matching that must be done one ox to another to keep the yoke from wounding one or another of the beasts. But Grams had said, *"I'm praying for your husband, child. You're a daughter of the kingdom. You must marry a prince."* Well, she had, hadn't she? At least he had the trappings. But then, trappings could deceive.

Laurie looked at herself in the mirror. She tucked the hair behind her ear. In the white blouse and denim skirt she was a far cry from Mrs. Brian Prelane. Good. The farther the better. She went to wake the children. They'd have a muffin at Maple's before Mother picked them up for church. At least she hadn't tried to force the issue with Laurie. Luke and Maddie had enjoyed Sunday school last week, so she didn't make it an issue either. After the service they would stay at Mother's until Laurie got off work. Soon she would need to find a daycare. But there wasn't money for it yet.

Laurie crossed her arms, resting two fingers between her eyebrows. How many years had it been since she worried about money? She'd signed the checks at the club, charged her clothes at the boutique, dined and shopped and entertained herself without a thought for the cost. And the children had Gail: warm, efficient, ever present when Mommy had to slip out.

She hadn't left them often, not nearly as often as her friends left their offspring. They'd laughed at her midwestern roots that still idealized the traditional family. *"Honey, that's what we have nannies for. Just because we birth them doesn't mean the umbilicus hasn't been cut."*

Laurie bustled the children into the car, and looking into their cherubic faces, still sleepy eyed and puffy, she was glad she'd left those friends behind. At least when she left Luke and Maddie now, she had a worthy reason for it. Survival.

She drove to the run-down diner and parked in the back, then lifted the children out. "Now remember your manners and be quiet for Mommy, okay?"

Maple was in rare form. Laurie had gone right to work even before Mother came for the children, but now she stood while the wiry woman rummaged through the discarded fruit. Maple pulled three apples from the trash that Laurie had scraped from the bag rather than touch. "These are perfectly good. Cut off the soft spots and dice up the rest."

Laurie took them and eyed the oozing spots. Normally she didn't work in the kitchen. Lord knew she didn't belong there. But Barb had walked out, leaving Maple alone this morning. Looking at the apples, she was tempted to follow suit. But, God help her, she needed the job.

Maple snatched the fruit. "Go on out front. I'll do them myself."

Laurie pulled off the apron and escaped. The doors didn't open for ten minutes yet, so she made the coffee and wiped off the counters. Then she made sure each table was stocked with sugar, saccharine, and Equal, wiped down the salt and pepper shakers, and filled the napkin dispensers. Closing her eyes, she pressed a palm to her forehead. How long could she stand it?

4

SOME HAVE BEEN THOUGHT BRAVE

BECAUSE THEY WERE AFRAID TO RUN AWAY.

English proverb

REGGIE CLOSED CAL'S DOOR behind Rita and Rob as they left for the night, then turned back to Cal. "So what is it, bro?" Rita could not have missed Cal's mood, but it didn't take a psychiatrist to see the trouble in that man's face. She'd said nothing, but Reggie felt compelled. He'd been as much a part of Cal's "cure" as Dr. Rita James, and often as not, he'd been the one to initiate things.

"What's what?" Cal scooped up the poker chips and put them into the cabinet.

"What's got you holding fours against my straight, and not seeing Rita's bluff to your full house?"

Cal shrugged. "Not my night."

Reggie looked around Cal's place. It showed a distinct lack of effort. Not that he hadn't seen it worse, and he wasn't particular. Like Peter to Cornelius, he went where the Lord called him, and, like Paul, he did as the Romans. But so he didn't get a big head comparing himself to them, Suanne always shook her finger and said, "You just see you don't enjoy it too much."

And truth be told, he did enjoy these nights with Cal. The Lord had a mission with that man. But even unredeemed, Cal Morrison was a pleasure, the sort of man you could call a friend with no hesitation. No one Reggie'd had the grace to meet matched his sense of humor, a sense of the absurd and the ability to appreciate it, even when it involved him. Except tonight.

"If your face was any longer, you'd polish your boots with your chin." Reggie settled down at the small walnut table in Cal's kitchen.

Cal leaned against the counter. "Reg, do you ever wonder what's the use?"

Reggie's spirit quickened. "Don't have to wonder. I know what's the use. To all things under heaven there is a time and a purpose."

Cal rubbed a hand through his hair. He looked shaky.

Reggie's instincts kicked in. "You clean, bro?"

"Yeah, I'm clean. But I'm thinking hard about changing that."

"Rough week, huh?" Reggie eyed him. Something had brought him low since he'd seen him last Friday, but it wasn't fear, and it wasn't guilt. If he were to guess, he'd name the demon despair. "Don't let those thoughts in. You don't need that stuff."

"It's not a question of need." Cal closed his hand and cupped it into the other. Both were shaking. "I just want to bury it all in a long, deep stupor."

Reggie hunched over the table. "Bondage of the mind and spirit can be as debilitating as any physical addiction."

"Tell me about it."

"What's causing it?"

Cal turned a chair and straddled it. "I saw an old flame."

Reggie guessed he meant the female sort, though with Cal it could be literal. "It happens." He'd run into one or two himself.

Cal chewed his lower lip. "Yeah, it happens, but it doesn't always burn you."

"How'd it burn you, bro?"

Cal straightened, dropping his wrists over the chair back before him. "I had her and her kids over Saturday and gave a performance." He raised an eyebrow. "She looked at me as though I'd lost my mind." He clenched and released his hands. "Which of course I had . . . again."

Reggie had seen the performance Cal meant. PTSD, shell shock,

whatever you wanted to call it. People wouldn't necessarily understand, especially a woman who'd known him before. "God has a time
and a purpose for everything. I know that's not fair for me to say
when I have Suanne to snuggle with each night."

Cal's eyes took on a hollow intensity. "Do you think there's one
right person, one woman for every man?"

Reggie considered that. He believed God ordained marriage
between one man and one woman. He couldn't imagine any other
woman besides Suanne. But did that mean there was no other
woman he could have loved, built a marriage with? "I take it this one
was special."

Cal dropped his chin with an exhaled breath. "How does the
'love of my life' sound?"

"Overdramatic."

Cal laughed, but Reggie could tell it was forced.

"I'm not kidding, Reg. It's like she's the flame and I'm the moth.
But here"—he tapped his right temple—"I know what fire does to
me. And I don't want to crash and burn."

"Then you gotta hang tough. God created the laws of nature and
the heart. Just like gravity, things gotta work a certain way. You can't
mess with the order."

"Yeah? Wish I'd known that before we . . ." Cal closed his lips
and clasped his fingers together. "Before it went so far."

Reggie blew the breath between his lips. "There's not one of us
doesn't have things we regret. But God's bigger than that. He hung
our sin on a cross, and we just gotta believe He'll take it and make us
new."

He watched Cal struggling with that, knew the battle raged,
forces neither of them could see and only Reggie knew were real.
Cal wasn't a wicked man. In fact, he was a good man, better than
many. But it didn't matter, because in the end he couldn't do it himself. Cal's eyes came up to him, hollow and tense, and Reggie knew
before he spoke which side had won this time.

"I wish I could, Reg. But then I see a little girl with pigtails
going up in flames." His voice got raw, and he wore the haunted look
that Reggie had seen before. "I hear her screams." His throat worked.

Reggie sagged. Some things had no explanation. He could tell

Cal God's ways were above man's, His wisdom supreme. He could tell him somewhere in the scheme of things even horrors had their place. But there was a hand to his lips. Cal wasn't ready to hear it.

"Hang tough, bro. Don't give in."

Cal nodded slowly. "Can you sit for a while?"

"I can sit all night." And that's what he'd do if it kept Cal out of the bottle, or the pills, or whatever he might find to take away the memories.

Gradually the shaking stopped, and Cal looked bone weary. He put his head down on the table and closed his eyes. God may not have the victory yet, but between them they'd won this skirmish. Reggie stood, towering over Cal's hunched form. With the tenderness of a father, he helped Cal to his feet and got him into bed.

"You made it, Cal. One more time."

Cal shook his head, then sank into the pillows. "Thanks, Reg."

Reggie looked at him lying there. People didn't understand the courage it took for an addict to stay clean. Everyone had bad days. But a bad day to a drunk could be the start of the slide. Reggie looked up and closed his eyes. *No dreams, tonight, Lord. Guard his mind and his soul.*

As soundlessly as possible in that old house, Reggie let himself out. If Suanne was waiting up, he'd explain. But chances were, she'd gone to sleep hours ago. Funny, but Reggie hardly felt tired at all.

———

Two days later, Cal stood behind Ray as he lay on the red vinyl bench in the shed. With three hundred and ten pounds of weight, counting the bar, across his chest, eyes bulging and his face aflame, Ray puffed out his cheeks and pushed it up. Cal hoped Ray wouldn't drop it. The bar held one hundred and twenty pounds more than Cal's total body weight, and his biceps already pulsed from the curls. The bar dipped, and again Ray pushed it up before Cal grabbed and helped him sink it into the brackets.

"Whew, Ray. You're a better man than I."

"Your turn." Ray sat up, his perspiration pungent as an onion patch.

"I think I'll pass."

"Come on. I'll make it lighter."

"By fifty pounds."

"Forty."

"Okay, forty. But you be ready."

Ray grinned. There was something in Ray's grin that was less than convincing. Cal took his place, smelling Ray as he did. Ray adjusted the weights, and Cal gathered himself, then eased the bar down to rest on his pectorals and shifted his hands. "How many reps?"

"Ten."

"Five."

Ray paused, probably not sure how to divide the difference to keep arguing, and Cal pushed the bar up, expelling his breath as he did. It had not been that long since he'd worked out with the guys on the line. Though he never developed much bulk, he did possess a natural strength and musculature, inherited from his dad.

He managed a set of ten before he hooked the bar and rolled off the bench. His left shoulder joint popped, and he rotated it, releasing the strain. The blood vessels in his arms stood up like snakes. It was an ugly business.

Ray slipped a weight off the ends. "Now shoulder press."

"No thanks."

"You chicken?"

"No. Me tired." Cal shook his arms to loosen the muscles. "Listen, it's getting hard to breathe in here. You want to walk with me?"

Ray's face sagged. "It's dark."

"So?"

Ray stood sullenly. "I don't like the woods at night."

"Suit yourself." Cal loved the woods at night. Especially the time just between the day's glory and the splendor of the starlit night. That mysterious unformed twilight. When Sadie was around they had taken many twilight walks and romped long after dark under the stars through rain, snow, or what have you. Even when her hips had grown so stiff that he had to carry her up the stairs, she had never missed a walk in the woods.

The trees were mostly bare against the low November sky, their long, arthritic fingers clashing together in the chill wind. But the underbrush was still dense, some of it up to his shoulders. Cal turned up his collar and shoved his hands into his pockets. His pace was as brisk as the night, though he did not head anywhere in particular.

Once inside the shadow of the trees, he slowed because he could see only a little space ahead. The slice of moon faded in and out of the clouds. To his right an owl hooted its throaty call, then whooshed from its perch after some prey it had heard in the fallen leaves. Whatever it was would never hear it coming.

Cal circled back to the house but stopped mid-step, one boot grinding on the toothed edge of the metal stair as Mildred motioned through the window. He pushed open the lower-level side door obediently. He knew that expression.

"You know, Mildred, Ray's here to do whatever it is—."

"Ray does what Ray does. I need you to figure out the thump in my furnace." Her face said she wouldn't be talked out of it.

"I don't know the first thing about furnace thumps. I'll call you a repairman." He started for the phone.

"Hmmph."

He stopped. "What's that supposed to mean?"

"Nothing."

"No way. That was a meaningful hmmph."

Mildred shrugged. "You with all your training and lecturing."

"I don't lecture on furnace repair." A detail that obviously meant nothing.

"Keynote speaker at the city council banquet . . ."

Cal started for the furnace. "Show me what it's doing." He pulled open the panel and studied the guts of the heater. Everything looked in order as far as he could tell. The pilot was lit, the parts were relatively clean. "So what's the trouble?"

"It thumps."

"So you said, but I don't hear anything."

"It thumps when it blows." To prove her word, the furnace drew a long breath through the intake vents and the blower came on with a thump.

"Here it is. Whoever serviced your furnace missed the groove on the filter. Nothing serious." He refitted the filter. "But you'd think a repairman . . ." He glanced up at Mildred. "Uh, did Ray change these out for you?"

"Thanks for your time."

He stood. "Sure." They clumped up the stairs and found Cissy on the couch, smiling broadly. In contrast to her sister, she was gladly talked out of anything—except Wednesday and Saturday morning vacuuming.

"Well, you're set." Cal rubbed his hands.

Mildred grunted.

Cissy patted the pillow. "Why don't you join us? I have chocolate on the stove and corn in the popper."

"No thanks, Cissy. Another time."

"I haven't seen Laurie back." Mildred spoke before he could make his escape.

Cal turned. He'd expected as much. They'd lured him in, but he edged toward the door. "Nope."

"Did you scare her off?"

"Mildred . . ."

"Just as well. You're not in any condition for entanglement, and from the looks of her, she's not in any condition for you."

Cal stopped. "What does that mean?"

"It's written all over her. That woman's been hurt, and she's afraid."

Cal frowned. "She just doesn't open up right away."

Mildred huffed. "Show's what you know."

He knew better, but his fighting spirit flared anyway. "I know a lot."

"Maybe his vision's clouded."

They both spun on Cissy, and she blushed a queer shade of purple and sank into the couch.

"If his vision's clouded, that's all the more reason he shouldn't get involved."

"I'm not involved. Laurie's a friend from way back." And even that was pushing it now.

"That's deadly."

"What?"

"I said that's deadly. Was she your first love?"

Cal swallowed, then turned for the door, but not before he caught the knowing look Mildred and Cissy exchanged as he slipped from the room. After mounting the inside stairs, he crawled into his den to lick his wounds. He knew better than to take Mildred on. But he suspected she would have had her say whether he'd taken the bait or not.

He was still morose when the phone rang an hour later. "Yeah?"

"Cal?"

He leaned on the counter. "Hi, Laurie."

"I wasn't sure I should call."

He said nothing.

"Is it a bad time?"

"No."

"I kept waiting to hear from you."

Had she really expected it? "Laurie . . ."

"I understand why you haven't called, but, Cal, it doesn't matter."

He swallowed the dryness in his throat. "What doesn't?"

"Whatever caused you to react as you did. It hardly warrants an end to our friendship."

Cal rubbed a hand over his face. "Laurie, I'm not sure where to go with this. I think it would be simpler if we just let it ride." She was quiet a long time, but he didn't make jokes or try to get her attention.

"Does that mean you don't want to see me again?"

"It means we've gone eight days without speaking and survived it." Mostly.

"I see. I'm sorry I bothered you."

The line went dead in his hand, and he lowered the handpiece to its bed. Mildred would be proud.

Laurie hung up the phone. So that was that. She shoved away the hurt. It was better anyway. She didn't need him. It was time she stood on her own. But her legs betrayed her, and she stiffened the muscles. The mistakes, the decisions, the responsibilities—did she have it in her? Or was she just the failure Daddy thought her? Had her abilities been criticized, corrected, and denied right out of her?

Laurie pictured her father. Oh yes, she called him Daddy. But had she ever thought of him so? Wasn't Daddy someone you snuggled up with, ran to with your latest discovery, whose arms scooped you up when you scraped your knee . . .

She sighed. Was there even one time Daddy had praised her without adding "however"? However, if you had done it this way, if you had listened, if you weren't so emotional, stubborn, difficult . . . She had tried so hard to please him. Maybe it wasn't in her.

If Mother had once stood up and admitted he was a difficult man. If she had once let on that she herself despaired of pleasing him, once given Laurie permission to be herself . . . Grams had. *Oh, Grams!* And Cal had. He had taken her so much for who she was, it terrified her.

Seeing her affinity, he talked her into taking art, though Daddy said it was a waste. She fell in love with pottery, with creating things from raw material with her own hands. Mother refused to consider a potter's wheel in the house because of the mess, the smell. Besides, the pots she brought home from school were lopsided. Never mind that they were first attempts.

Laurie gave them to Cal. He still had them on his bookshelf, holding who knows what. She had seen them the other night. It was embarrassing. Over the college years she had improved greatly. But she guessed Cal didn't see the imperfections. He took things as they were, especially her.

Daddy despised him. The son of a cabinetmaker with only a high-school education, a disrespectful cutup destined for nowhere. The worst part, the part that made her ashamed to this day, was that she saw him that way too. As much as she had thrived on being with him, a little voice niggled inside that he was nothing, would be nothing, would go nowhere.

And he hadn't. He could have been anything. He could tally numbers in his head faster than she could press them on a calculator. He was bright, creative, good with his hands. He could succeed in any field he put his mind to, but here he was, a clown in Montrose, Missouri. Nowhere.

And she had told him as much when he asked her to forget her studies at UCLA and marry him. She hadn't known she belonged to him, that their lives were grafted together. He called her a snob; she called him a loser. He accused her of social climbing; she said he was stagnating in the cesspool of Middle America. She was sure that she had hurt him more than he hurt her—because he accepted her even though he knew her for what she was . . . and she rejected him.

Laurie closed her eyes. Her hand still gripped the phone in its cradle. She wanted to pick it up and tell him she accepted him, no matter what his trouble was, no matter what had caused his over-reaction, no matter what had happened in the years they'd been apart, she accepted him. But would he believe her? Did she believe herself?

She drew a long breath and released the phone. Anyway, it didn't matter. Cal was right. They'd gone eight days without speaking, and she, too, had survived. She would make it on her own. She had fled Brian's world. She had taken nothing but the children and what she could fit into the Lexus, and the Lexus was in her name.

––––––

When Cal got into work the following day, Frank O'Connor motioned him into the drab room that doubled as office and conference room. Reaching to the corner of the desk, Cal lifted the pink head on a black plastic base that read *Stress Head*. Cal squeezed. The vinyl features mashed together, then ballooned slowly back to their normal form.

"Great, isn't it?" Frank grinned, tonguing the gap between his front teeth.

Cal put the head down. "If you're into mashing faces."

"Good therapy, anyway." The red rushed to Frank's face as he sputtered away from his use of that word. "Sit down, Cal."

Cal sat.

"I guess you've noticed I got people dropping like flies."

"Flu?" The local news had carried the story last night. Much of Montrose was sniffling, hacking, and shaking with fever.

"So the doctors say. Some germ from hell." Frank ran a hand over the tuft of red hair that sprouted from the center of his rounded head like the mayor of Munchkin Land. "Now Rob's down with it, and you know him. He'll be out till spring. Fact is, I'm running awful short." He strained back the springs of his chair.

Cal fingered the head again, poking the nose in like a skull. It mutely reformed its blank features.

"I need you active."

"No."

"I know what you can do, and there's no one I'd rather have at my back." Frank peeled a stick of gum and folded it into his mouth. "This other stuff is fine, but it wasn't meant to be permanent or exclusive."

The entire head collapsed inside Cal's palm. "Things change."

"If you let 'em."

Cal stood. "You've got twenty-four volunteers."

"Half of 'em down sick."

Cal replaced the head on the desk. "Sorry, Frank. You don't want to see my act if it really gets hot." He passed through the doorway in two strides.

In the middle of the night Reggie Douglas woke. His eyes opened to the darkness and Suanne's soft breathing. He felt her warmth and soft curves against his side and almost reached an arm around and snuggled back in. But there it was again, the urging. *Okay, Lord. You got the reasons; I got the time.*

He pushed back the covers and slipped out of bed, dropping to his knees. It was nothing new, God putting someone on his heart so strongly it called him to action. Even the name was familiar. *Cal.* God had plans for that man. Cal just didn't know it.

Reggie's thick knees could hold up as long as it took, though. He'd seen harder cases than Cal fall like timber. Trouble was, Cal always landed on his feet. Even in the psychiatric center, when you'd think he'd been brought low, he didn't hit bottom. He still found something inside himself to fight back with.

Rita saw that strength and fed it. But that was psychiatry. He'd pray for her tonight, too. But right now, God's call was for Cal. He didn't know if Cal had a bottle in hand, if he'd suffered a recurrence of the post-traumatic stress, or if he was simply at a critical point as he'd been the other night. All Reggie knew was that God called him to wrestle for Cal's soul, and that he would do.

He bowed his head. *Ah, Lord* . . . Suddenly the night was fresh, and Reggie could go on forever. Cal Morrison had better watch out when that Holy Ghost power started to flow.

5

A DOG TEACHES A BOY FIDELITY,

PERSEVERANCE, AND TO TURN AROUND

THREE TIMES BEFORE LYING DOWN.

Robert Benchley

LIKE CLOCKWORK, the twenty-fourth of November brought snow Midwestern style. The local news was calling the event "Old Faithful," since that day had seen the first real snow for the last three years. Though deep, wet, and more than he wanted to tramp through on a cold afternoon after a frustrating day of inspections, Cal nonetheless did, because he had hit on the tracks that he thought might explain last night's whining.

At first he had thought by the yelps outside that Mildred's cat, Sienna, had attracted a hound. But when he went down, she was in her usual spot on the hearth, and neither Mildred nor Cissy had stirred from their sleep. The snow was coming too thickly for him to see far, and he'd shrugged it off and gone back to bed. He hadn't had time to search it out that morning, but when he got home from work there was clear evidence around the stairs and across the yard.

The tracks were three paw prints with a line running beside, which could mean the dog was dragging a hind leg. He followed the trail into the forest. Maybe one of Fred's hounds had strayed and been injured. He stopped. The snow was crushed down in a circular pit, and he bent to examine a tuft of reddish gold hair.

Straightening, he followed the track as it dipped into a dense thicket of redbud and chokecherry. The snow was falling again in wet clumps as he edged through the bracken. A whine encouraged him, and he pushed aside the branches to find the dog, a retriever mix by the look of her. She rolled to her side, exposing her lighter-colored belly.

"Hey, girl." Cal reached forward slowly, let her sniff his hand, then ran it over her head and throat. She had no collar. Carefully he felt down her side, and she yelped when he reached her hip. "What's happened to you?" He guessed she'd met a car, though the highway wasn't busy out this way.

She struggled to rise. He backed out, encouraged the dog to follow, and stiffly she did, holding the hind leg just at the top of the snow as he'd guessed. When they were in the clear, he examined her again. "What are you doing out here, huh?" She nuzzled his face as he stroked her and gave his chin a weak slurp with her tongue.

"Well, come on, then." He led her back to the house. She was just about played out by the time they reached it. He gathered the dog into his arms, carried her up the stairs, and laid her on the foot of the bed. Then he toweled her dry, gently avoiding the problem areas, and set a bowl of water beside her. She lapped it onto his spread. He first placed a call to Second Hope Animal Shelter, where a lost dog might be reported, then called Fred Higgins, who knew every dog in the area.

"Nope, can't say as I recognize the description," Fred said. "Davises got retrievers, but they ain't mixed, and none's got a white chest like you say."

"Would you mind taking a look at her?"

"Be over shortly."

Cal hung up and looked at the dog. "You have a home around here, girl?"

She wagged her tail but didn't move.

"Well, since you don't have tags, I'll have to call you something. How about Annie? You like that?"

She nuzzled his hand. Her ears raised as Fred clumped up the back stairs, and Cal let him in. Fred shuffled over. His overalls smelled of cigar smoke and grease. His nails were outlined in black, but his

TWILIGHT

hands were gentle as he ran them over her limbs. "Her leg ain't broke.
I don't think she's been hit. More like she jumped or got thrown
from a moving vehicle."

"Do you recognize her?"

"Can't say I do. She ain't from this end. No collar neither. I'd
guess she's been dumped."

Cal's excitement grew. "Who would dump a dog like her?"

"Who'd do anything? People got reasons."

"How bad is she, do you think? I couldn't feel anything broken,
but she's sore."

"She'll mend. You keeping her here?"

"Until I hear different." Cal knew she had come to him, just as
Sadie had, just as all the good things in life came when he wasn't
looking. He thought of Laurie and frowned, then stroked the velvety
ears and bony head of the dog. He'd handled that last phone call
poorly. A knee-jerk reaction. He watched the mournful roll of
Annie's eyes.

Fred pulled the orange hunting cap down over his ears and
headed for the door. "I'll keep my ears open."

"Thanks, Fred." Cal went down the inside stairs and found Mildred in the front room. "I have a dog."

"No, you don't."

"You know I'll take care of her. She won't bother you."

"She'll bother Sienna."

He pictured the old cat hissing her way around the yard. "They'll
get used to each other. When Annie's mended, she'll spend the days
outside. Keep an eye on the place."

"It almost killed you to put that other one down."

"That's my problem." Cal frowned.

Mildred grunted. "Where'd she come from?"

"I don't know. Looks like she's been dumped, but if someone
claims her . . ." He shrugged.

"Don't get attached."

"You sound like my grandmother Hazel."

"Smart woman."

Cal saluted and made his escape by the front door. Once the
night set in, the streets were going to freeze, but now they were

73

slushy and the jeep handled fine, tracing the path to Laurie's.

It had been three weeks since their chance encounter at Ray's couch moving. Three weeks after seven years, and all he could think of was seeing her again. Who was he fooling? Mildred? Himself? So he'd shown his dark side. She said it didn't matter. Maybe it didn't. She knew he was a clown; he'd only confirmed it.

He stopped for peace offerings at the Walgreen's on the corner of Lincoln and Wood. The place was a madhouse of people brought out by the storm. Storehouse mentality. Well, the power had gone down last year. Better for them to be prepared.

He chose a handheld video game for Luke, and for Maddie a stuffed puppy with a purple ribbon. Laurie was harder. *The next best thing to his hands*, the sign read over the electric foot massager. That would go over real well. Shaking his head, Cal took his place behind a gaggle of women at the cosmetics counter.

One pink-faced, dimpled woman spun his way. "Aren't you the fireman who works with the kids?"

"Probably."

"I teach at Fremont. You did the fire safety program . . . the clown and all."

"How'd you recognize me?"

She laughed. "I saw you packing up after you took off the nose and hair. I teach music, so I'm free the period after lunch."

Two people ahead were processed at the counter. He shifted, but she didn't move forward.

"I think you're just wonderful with the children. Do you have kids of your own?"

"No."

"It's unusual to have such a rapport. For a man, I mean. Not that some men aren't as nurturing as women, nothing like that."

Cal motioned her forward.

She turned back after a couple steps. "It's just that until they've experienced fatherhood, most men haven't tapped into their feminine side."

He smiled benignly.

She placed her gargantuan bottle of multi-colored bath beads on the counter and told the clerk, "I need White Shoulders." While the clerk unlocked the case, the woman added a Chapstick from the basket next to the register and rummaged through the discount earrings. Impulse marketing at its best.

"Is that all for you?" The young clerk scratched her cheek with a blue plastic fingernail.

"I guess so." The pink face lingered on a pair of orange loops large enough for aboriginal ritual use. She glanced back at Cal, and he shook his head. Sighing, she dropped them back. "Well, bye now." She at last made room for him at the counter.

Cal faced the clerk. "What's the nicest fragrance you have?"

"Eau de parfume?" She tapped a blue staccato on the counter.

"Do you have real perfume?"

"Eau de toilette and eau de parfume."

"Okay. What do you like?"

"I like Obsession." The blue stud through her tongue made her lisp it.

Obsession. Not exactly the message he wanted Laurie to get.

"Anything else?"

"Estée Lauder's Beautiful is the most popular." She reached into the case, sprayed a sample of it, and sniffed.

Cal sniffed too. Not bad, though it was only fifty-fifty that Laurie would accept it anyway. Still, Beautiful seemed a better fit. "I'll take that one."

The girl reached into the case. "Big or little?"

"Little. She might be more inclined to accept it." He smiled, paid, and headed out.

He arrived at Laurie's door with snow up to his ankles from the unshoveled walk. Tucking the bag under his arm, he rang. Maddie pulled open the door and, to her credit, did not scream and run.

"Your mom home?" he asked.

She did, however, close the door in his face.

Laurie sat at the potter's wheel with the spinning terra-cotta clay between her hands. She had a good center; it spun with almost no wobble at all. Surprising, given how long it had been since she'd thrown. Digging in her thumbs, she formed the mouth and drew up the sides, once and again.

She swiped the back of one wrist on the nubby towel hung over her shoulder to absorb the excess sludge as she worked. A rust-colored dampness ran onto her white T-shirt, but it didn't matter. It was a work shirt, and it felt good to be grubby.

She jumped at the rap on the open door, and the motion translated to a wobbly lip on the pot between her fingers. Dragging her foot on the spinning cement disk, she brought the listing pot to a stop.

Cal slouched against the jamb with his bad-boy stance and crooked smile. "Wanna go to the prom?"

Her heart lurched. How did he do that? She tugged the towel from her shoulder and rubbed each finger. "I already did. With the cutest guy in the senior class." And what was he doing there in her doorway after giving her the snub?

"Cute, huh?"

"You were, then." She rehung the towel on her shoulder.

"And now?"

She didn't want to think about now. But she scrutinized him anyway. Cute was definitely not the word anymore. "Kind of rugged."

"It's the scar."

It was more than that; the manly line of his jaw, the lean musculature apparent even through his jeans and sweat shirt, his ropy neck and tousled hair. "How'd you get it?" She chipped a dry edge of clay from the surface of her nail.

"Risking life and limb. I really am a good bet."

"I know that." More than he guessed. And more than she'd show.

He sauntered in, nodded at the wheel. "I thought you weren't throwing."

"I thought we weren't talking."

He shrugged. "I guess it won't hurt."

"That's big of you." Her tone was sharper than she intended, defensive. She had tried not to let his rejection hurt, but it had. She sliced the pot from the wheel and crumpled it back into the clay bucket, then plunged her hands into the tub of water beside the wheel.

"Sorry about the pot."

She shrugged. "There are more where that came from."

"It's good to see you working." Cal ran a finger through the reddish sludge on the metal disk of the wheel.

"You're the only one who ever thought so." Laurie dried her hands, catching a thin line of terra-cotta down the inside of one finger, glad she'd seen it before he did. Cal used to tease her about mechanic's hands. She wiped it clean. "How did you get in?"

"Maddie. Sort of. She did close the door in my face, but she used no bolts or barricades."

Both children stampeded the doorway at once. "Can we have our presents?"

"What presents?"

"From him." Luke thumbed Cal, and Laurie frowned.

"He has a name, Luke." But she glared at Cal. Here she was stinging from his rebuff, but making the best of it, and what did he do? Showed up with gifts and tokens, demonstrations of his affection. Or was it repentance this time? Or bribery, like throwing a steak to the guard dogs when you want to sneak in. Whatever the reason, he knew how she hated that.

"Can we?" Maddie piped.

Laurie fumed. He'd put her on the spot and he knew it.

He roughed up Luke's head. "It's okay by me."

That's right, make it worse. She looked at Luke's pleading eyes and sighed. The children took it as agreement and flew down the stairs. Laurie tossed down the towel and started after.

"Do they always try to occupy the same physical space?" Cal motioned her by, and she stalked through the door before he could get any closer. It was bad enough that he thought he could shmooze her with gifts.

The children were on their knees with the bag on the floor. She sat down on the sleeper couch. Cal dropped to the other end of it and hung his arm across the back. He looked annoyingly pleased with himself.

Maddie pulled the stuffed dog from the bag and squealed. She squeezed it to her cheek, then jumped up and squeezed Cal. With a raise of his eyebrows, he put an arm around her, and she wiggled into his lap.

"What are you going to call it?" Cal shifted her on his knee.

"Doggie."

"Seems to fit."

Maddie bounced the dog on his knee. "What would you call her?"

"Oh, I don't know." He tipped his head to examine the dog. "She's kind of fluffy."

"Fluffy. Her name is Fluffy." Maddie beamed and pressed the dog to Cal's cheek. He hugged them both.

Laurie bristled. What right did Cal have to worm his way into their hearts? To buy their affection? Especially after giving her the brush off? But why was she taking it personally? He was just a friend, making amends.

Her chest squeezed. He was so natural with Maddie. He wasn't trying to buy their affection. That was Brian's game. Brian had always tried to seem larger than life. He would have bought a pony or a ceiling-high giraffe instead of a child-sized puppy. He'd wanted awe from his children. From everyone.

"Tarzan!" Eyes wide and gleeful, Luke raised the handheld video game for her to see.

"Batteries are in the bag." Cal nudged it his way.

Of course, Cal would know just the thing to get for Luke. Her son had not stopped talking about him since the fishing outing. She could only imagine the barrage that would follow this visit. Laurie stood and pulled Luke to his feet. "And now it's bedtime."

"Aw . . ."

She held up a finger and he stopped. He could always read her moods.

"Can I play it in bed?"

"If you're ready in five minutes. Go on, Maddie." Laurie eased her out of Cal's lap and sent her running for the stairs. "Brush your teeth!" She ought to help Maddie. She ought to do anything to get away from there. She sensed Cal watching her and wanted to run up the stairs herself.

He glanced at his watch. "Isn't it early for bed?"

At least he had the sense not to question her before the children left.

"I have early mornings. At Maple's." Though she blessedly wasn't working tomorrow. "I keep their routine even when I'm off." Even so, it was early, though with the days so short the children might not realize. And she could limit the mileage Cal got from those gifts. He didn't attach expectations, but she did. Either way, she couldn't stop the turbulence within her. He was playing dirty. First he tells her to get lost, and she spends the week fending off the children's questions, then he shows up with bribes. "You know I hate—"

He tossed her a small box. "You didn't get yours."

She stared at the box. She wanted to throw it back at him, tell him she wasn't for sale, and even if she was, she was out of his range. She wanted to holler and stamp her foot and tell him to take his gift and—

"Go on, open it."

"You didn't have to do this." She didn't want him to. Brian, yes. She had expected gifts; they were her due. But not Cal. His giving was different somehow. It came from the heart. And she could not allow that.

"Don't get hung up on it."

He knew her too well. He'd known when he brought the gifts how she'd react, but he did it anyway. Why? Why did he consider it his duty to go against her grain? She sat down, faced him squarely.

He smiled. "Just open it." Cal tugged the flap of the box for her. "I know you like Giorgio, but it's a little hard to come by on short notice."

And she wouldn't accept it. She knew well enough the dollar amount on that. He was insufferable, but she reached in and slid out the bottle. Beautiful by Estée Lauder. It was eau de parfume, but she felt grateful for that. She'd been out of scent the last three days, and wouldn't dare squander what little money she made at Maple's. His gift was perfect.

"Oh, Cal." She pulled the lid off and spritzed the hollow of her throat. The aroma filled her lungs. A nice scent. Her skin burned beneath her collarbones as she leaned toward him. "What do you think?"

He shook his head. "I better not try. Besides, there's a new woman in my life."

It was like ice rushing from her head to her heart. Had he learned to be cruel? And anyway, what was she doing acting like this? She'd set the limits, and she knew why. Laurie closed the bottle. "Blonde or brunette?"

"Kind of a strawberry blonde, I guess. Brown eyes, long nose, shaggy."

Her fingers froze on the lid.

"I found her in the woods this evening. She'd hurt her hind leg." He grinned. "I named her Annie."

Laurie raised her chin. "She's a dog?"

"Retriever mix, as best I can tell."

Why was she surprised? He always tweaked her rope. "That's cruel, Cal."

"I thought it might take the pressure off."

She turned away, and he tugged a strand of her hair. "Hey."

"Hey what?"

"I didn't know you cared."

"I don't." She couldn't. She wouldn't let herself. Things were far too complicated as it was.

"Really?" He pulled her close and dropped his head to breathe her perfume.

She knew it was coming before he kissed her. When his mouth met hers a rush of warmth filled her. She'd expected it, wanted it. She'd probably even telegraphed it. Now she fought it and pulled away.

He searched her face, confused, hurt. He would be, after her ridiculous behavior, leading him on, flirting. What was she doing?

"You agreed to be friends." It sounded feeble.

"Why?"

Tell him the truth. "More reasons than I want to go into."

"It doesn't make sense."

She shook her head. "Nothing makes sense. It never has with us."

"Ah, come on. That's not true."

"I just can't, okay?" She needed him to leave, to move his body away from hers. She needed him to stop loving her. *Liar.* That's why she'd come, homing in like a wing-wearied pigeon to the one man who—*No!* The constriction in her chest pressed the air from her lungs in small, shallow waves. If he kissed her again would she stop him? Could she? *Tell him the truth.* Was that her conscience? Did she even have one? She'd done her best to ignore it for years now. But hadn't conscience driven her here? Conscience . . . and fear.

Cal leaned back. He studied her with eyes more understanding than she could bear, then held out his hand. "Okay. Friends."

Her heart sank. She looked down at his hand as though the gesture were lost on her. Then reaching out, she shook it, smiling faintly. When he left, she felt the void, the loneliness, the ache. She wrapped it around herself and cried.

6

WORRY IS INTEREST PAID ON TROUBLE

BEFORE IT FALLS DUE.

W. R. Inge

EARLY THE NEXT MORNING, Laurie struck a match and held it to the wick of the cranberry-scented candle on the metal shelf of the floor lamp. Luke's face glowed as he watched it ignite and puckered his lips to extinguish the match. After he blew, she handed it over, still smoking. "Run it under the faucet before you throw it away."

"Okay." He scampered to the kitchen, then returned to snuggle onto the sleeper sofa with her and Maddie.

A whole day. All to themselves. They'd had fried eggs and pancakes for breakfast, something Laurie rarely allowed herself, and now with a stack of library books beside them, she held both her children close and reveled.

It sobered her how much she cherished this time. Maybe she wasn't as evolved as her friends, as cosmopolitan as Brian would have liked. Maybe she was, after all, a product of Montrose, although it had always been expected she would exceed it. Maddie dug through the stack and pulled a book loose, flopping it into Laurie's lap.

Thanksgiving Mouse. It was only days before that holiday would be upon them. She shuddered, remembering the hours in the kitchen with Mother watching every move she made. The criticism had crippled her, and she'd been all too pleased to trade in the tradition of a family meal for the elegant spread at the club with Brian and his friends . . . but not Luke and Maddie.

Kids had stayed home with Gail and had stuffed Cornish hens, Gail's specialty.

Had Laurie ever cooked a Thanksgiving meal for her family? Ever had them all gathered together counting their blessings as Grams had insisted when they circled the table in Daddy's house?

"Read it, Mommy."

Laurie smiled down at Maddie's upturned face and opened the book. " 'There was once a mouse who lived all alone. His name was Sam.' " For some reason she thought of Cal. Would he have Thanksgiving with Mildred and Cissy?

" 'He was a very small mouse with tiny feet and tiny whiskers and a tail that was bent to one side.' " Cal was neither small nor malformed, but for some reason the analogy stuck. " 'The other mice looked down on him. "What good are you? What can you do?" they said. "We have no use for you." Sam turned circles and hopped on one foot. But the other mice scorned him. "Go away, we do not enjoy your tricks." ' "

Laurie looked at Luke, who was sounding out *tricks* with her. He looked up with a smile, and her heart flipped. Nothing must ever stifle his willingness to try, his pleasure in succeeding. Maddie turned the page.

" 'For weeks and weeks the mice gathered food for their Thanksgiving feast. Sam watched as they carried the large, tasty grains from the tall stalks in the field. He could not climb to the top, for his tail would not wrap the stalk and his feet were not strong. He had only one small grain that had fallen to the ground.' "

Maddie fumbled with the page, and at last got it turned. Laurie smoothed it and read on. " 'On Thanksgiving day each mouse carried the best of his grains to the feasting table at the top of the hill. Sam carried the poor small grain, which was all he had gathered. His head hung sadly when he saw the wonderful things the others had brought.' "

This time Luke beat Maddie to the page and turned it with deft fingers. Maddie pouted, but Laurie tapped her nose with a smile. "Look, Maddie, how sad poor Sam looks."

Maddie searched the page, her face filled with childish compassion.

" 'The mice were angry. "Is that all you have? Will you eat the good things we have brought? No, you will not. Go away, Sam. We have no use for you." ' " It hit too close to home. Sam didn't measure up, so he was not to be accepted. Just as she . . . just as Cal.

" 'Sam turned to go, taking his one small grain to have for his Thanksgiving day feast. Suddenly a gang of rats with long sharp teeth and angry eyes came to the top of the hill. "Go away mice. We want your food." ' "

Maddie's eyes grew large. Luke flipped the page.

" 'The mice were so afraid! They ran to hide. Poor Sam was left all alone. He was afraid, but his feet were not fast. His feet were not strong. He could not run away.' " Laurie turned to Luke. "What will he do, Luke?"

In answer, Luke turned the page.

" 'Sam turned circles and hopped on one foot. The rats stopped. The rats looked. The rats laughed. They laughed and laughed. They fell down and laughed. They held their tummies and rolled. Soon they were rolling down the hill. Faster and faster they rolled until they landed, splash, in the creek at the bottom of the hill.' "

"They liked Sam's tricks." Luke laughed.

"He's funny." Maddie patted the book.

Laurie smiled. " 'The mice came out. They looked at Sam. They smiled. They laughed. "Your tricks have saved us," they said. They carried him to the table and put his little grain on the top of the stack. "Hooray for Sam, our Thanksgiving mouse." ' "

Laurie stared at the cavorting mouse. More than ever it looked like Cal. She hadn't seen him as the fire-safety clown, but she could imagine the children's beaming faces as he taught them safety through skits or jokes or whatever he did.

"Now this one." Maddie landed another book in Laurie's lap.

With a happy sigh, Laurie settled into the couch. Nothing she'd acquired as Brian's wife compared to this—not the elegant home complete with pool and tennis court and gym, not the dazzling friends she met at the club for lunch, not the shops on Rodeo Drive, none of it. So help her, she was happier sitting in this old house between her children, reading stories.

Her father had failed, her mother had failed, and she had failed to make herself something grand, something elite, something wonderful. She was, after all, clay. She thought of the wrapped bundles of clay in the studio. It had been years since she'd thrown. But the first thing she had done when she came back was to retrieve her old wheel from Mother's garage.

Maybe today she'd use it again. She pictured Cal standing in the doorway. Maybe she'd make something for him. Maybe somewhere in the making she'd discover just what it was she wanted from him, and what she was willing to give in return.

The front door opened, and Mother stood there. If Laurie could have gracefully groaned she would have. "Mother? What's wrong?"

"I tried to call."

"I took my phone off the hook." So Maple couldn't call her in if someone else quit. She needed this day for herself and the children.

"My kitchen is flooding. I think a pipe's burst somewhere under the floor."

"Did you call a plumber?"

Her mother's lips tightened primly. "I never allow a strange man into the house when I'm alone."

Laurie nodded. So much for a full day with the children. She straightened Maddie, who seemed to have sensed the demise of their time together and was pressing into her side. "Would you like me to come over while the plumber works?"

"Bring the children, of course."

Luke groaned, but only loud enough for Laurie to hear. She turned to him. "Why don't we bag up the books and bring them along." She could always hope that her presence in the house would be enough, that she could still devote this scarce day off to Maddie and Luke. But she wouldn't stake her life on it. She gathered the children and the books and started for the door.

"Have you talked to Brian?"

Laurie stiffened and sent her mother a warning look. Her mother glanced at the children, then sighed, catching the unspoken message.

She wouldn't say anything yet, but at the first opportunity Laurie would have an earful. So much for a restful day. Laurie extinguished the candle and her hopes, then went out the door.

––––––––––

Cal awoke with a cramp in his leg from holding it bent. Looking down, he saw that Annie had worked her way to the center of the bed and lay in a square of sunlight that was too bright for early morning. They'd both slept late and awkwardly, hence the cramp. He nudged her with his foot. "Hey. This is my bed, and you're here by permission." She lifted her head, wagged her tail, dragged herself closer until her face met his, and licked his chin.

"All right, have it your way." So he was a pushover. He rolled out of bed, gratified to see her jump down and try her leg. She limped but didn't drag it as she had yesterday. He opened the door, hesitated, then carried her down the long stairs to the yard, hoping Mildred wouldn't see.

The dog didn't want to go far. She was quick about her business, then eager to return to the safety and warmth of his room. She tried the stairs herself, and Cal let her make it to the top, then patted his congratulations.

In the kitchen he started the coffee maker and brushed his teeth at the sink, a habit he'd acquired at the station on twenty-four-hour shifts, when he could only stagger one direction in the morning. That accomplished both necessities at one location. Annie stuck her nose into his palm, and he stroked her. What was he going to do with her while he was gone all day? After starting the coffee, he hit the bathroom.

It was there that he thought of Ray. He could hire him to dog-sit until Annie was recovered and knew the place well enough to be left on her own. When he finished his coffee, he dressed and headed for the garage.

If Ray hadn't been so groggy, he might have driven a harder bargain, but as it was, Cal got off easy: a six-pack of Bud and twenty bucks for the week. Not bad for the peace of mind. Annie was in good hands, he had no doubt. Ray was a softie for any animal, and her injury just about made a puddle of him.

He drove to the station, ready to be reprimanded for his tardiness. Instead, Frank O'Connor had a grin that divided his face when Cal entered. The gap between his front teeth yawned like a miniature mine shaft.

"What's wrong with you?" Cal hung his coat on the hook.

"Nothing at all." O'Conner grinned broader.

"I don't like that look."

"Oh, you're going to love it."

Cal hooked his thumbs into the top of his jeans. "Let me guess. I'm the keynote speaker for the women's auxiliary fund-raiser."

"Close, but even better. You get to be Santa Claus."

"I what?"

"You know, the gala. All that folderol?"

"What does Santa Claus have to do with anything?"

"It's traditional for him to show up at the end of dinner. Kind of usher in the shopping season right after Thanksgiving."

"It's not going to be me." Cal shook his head as Frank nodded.

"The women voted you in. Said you're such a natural with the kiddos. You got such a 'rapport.'"

Where had he heard that? Oh no. The pink lady in Walgreen's. Was she on the women's auxiliary? She *was* the women's auxiliary. "I don't do Santa. I'm not fat, I don't have a beard, and I don't ho, ho, ho."

"Aw, what's the difference? You do Spanner."

Cal's ears burned with indignation. "What's the difference, Frank? What's the difference?" His hands clenched. "The difference is Spanner saves lives, the same as you or anyone else in this department. I thought you understood that."

"Okay, okay." O'Conner came close and slapped him on the shoulder. "Look, Cal, don't get steamed. It's community service." He handed him the inspection schedule for the day. "I gave you a light load so you'd have time to swing by Lacey Matthews' place and get your costume. Ho, ho, ho." O'Conner broke into a belly laugh.

Cal eyed his boss right down to the still-rolling belly that hung over his belt. He and Frank had faced a lot together. It was Frank who had pulled him free of the debris at the foot of the stairs. Frank who held him back from tearing his way inside again when the flames devoured the guts of the old bed-and-breakfast.

Cal closed his eyes and forced his thoughts to the present battle. "I'll make you a deal. You do Santa, and I'll take the station Thanksgiving Day."

O'Conner stepped back. "Yeah?"

"Yeah."

"Active duty?"

"The whole deal." As long as he'd been with the department, they'd never fought the red devil on Thanksgiving.

O'Conner nodded. "Heck, if that's what it takes to get you back, you're on."

Cal held up a finger. "I'm only talking that one day."

"Whatever you say, Cal." O'Conner beamed.

Cal walked out feeling somehow swindled and definitely underappreciated. Spanner the same as Santa Claus? Maybe if he were Santa Claus he could have—

Cal expelled his breath in a hard rush. *Don't go there. Not even in your thoughts.* It should be no surprise that Frank held a low opinion of his work.

So the clown suit was demeaning. Did that change the message? If putting on a nose and wig and funny shoes would make the kids listen—he'd go in his underwear if it made the kids listen. He tossed the inspection clipboard into the jeep and got in. Inspecting was another area he took seriously, more seriously than he had before. Now he knew firsthand what happened when safety measures were ignored. If people cringed when they saw him coming, so be it. They'd shake his hand someday.

As Laurie had? He expelled his breath. So maybe the good old handshake was a little overdramatic. But wasn't that what she wanted? Four weeks, and he could measure the time by how often he thought of her. He was addicted to her.

The thought was grim. But that was his personality. Nothing lukewarm in his blood. No, sir. He just jumped in with two feet no matter what. When she was gone, married, lost, he had dated, worked, walked the woods like a maniac.

No, he hadn't spent the years pining. He'd hurt, and then he'd gone on, though if he were truthful, he'd made sure nothing too personal developed. But now . . . now he had another chance. Or was he fooling himself? Friends? Was it possible? He battled addiction every day. If he could kick the bottle, could he kick the Laurie habit?

He went through his day with more efficiency than usual, not even stopping for lunch. Frank had given him a light load, so he ran home for a quick change into jeans and sweater, then checked Annie. She was curled up with Ray while he watched TV, and Cal ordered her to stay.

He made a quick call, got a busy signal, and hung up. He didn't try again. The signal had told him what he needed to know. Grabbing his toolbox, he headed back to the place that had called his name all day: Laurie's house. He knocked. No answer. He rubbed his jaw and checked his watch.

The busy signal should have meant she was home. But maybe she'd gone in to Maple's for a dinner shift. His disappointment was palpable. As he turned from the door, Laurie's Lexus angled into the driveway. He leaned against the door and waited, catching surprise in her glance, but not irritation. That was good.

Luke was first out, running to him and stopping short with a skid. "I beat the first level."

Cal had to think, then grinned. "Tarzan?"

Luke held the game up. "I beat it at Grandma's."

Maddie ran up in white tights and wool jumper, Fluffy clutched to her breast. "Ruff, ruff." She held the dog up for his pat.

Cal felt a singular pleasure seeing them with the things he'd given. The joy of giving gifts was something else he'd learned from his dad. Jim Morrison had shown up at all times with little surprises for both Cal's mother and the kids. That same joy filled Cal now as he whiffed the cologne on Laurie as she joined them on the porch.

Just friends. He ordered his mind and body into obedience. "Hi."

"What are you doing here?" Laurie looked tense and weary.

"Got a busy signal on your phone. I thought you were home."

She inserted her key. "I forgot to hang it back up. We've been at Mother's."

"Can you play with us?" Maddie pushed the stuffed dog into his legs.

Cal looked down at her dreamy face. Something surged inside

him, an ache, a longing. "I came to fix your banister." He sent his gaze to Laurie. "That corner post gave badly when Ray and I moved your couch. It's a hazard."

She turned the knob and opened the door. The children ran inside, but she lingered. "I've told them not to lean on it."

"They're kids." Kids didn't think safety. Kids expected grown-ups to protect them, to make their world safe.

"Cal . . . " She sighed. "I've had a difficult day. Mother's pipes leaked, and I had to give up my time with the children to make sure she wasn't assaulted by the sixty-year-old plumber who came to fix them."

Cal's mouth quirked. "Well, you and the kids can do whatever you like while I fix your banister. I'll scoot out when I'm done, and you won't even know I was here."

She combed her hair back with her fingers.

"Unless you'd rather hire Ray." He leaned nonchalantly on the doorframe.

"I was doing SpaghettiO's for dinner."

"Enjoy." He tucked one hand into his pocket. "I'm not looking for a free meal, Laurie. I'd just like to shore up that banister before someone gets hurt."

She looked inside at the staircase. "I guess it's a good idea, but I'm honestly all out of polite conversation. I've even plumbed the stores of impolite."

Cal brushed her cheek with the back of his fingers. "I can imagine. Go feed the kids."

"You sure you don't . . ."

"While SpaghettiO's ranks right up there, I think I'll pass. Got work to do." He picked up the oversized tool chest and motioned her in ahead of him. "I'll try not to make too much noise."

"I feel bad."

"Don't go there, Laurie. I know you've spent the day with the guilt patrol, but you can give it a break now." He watched her battling that concept, then started up the stairs just as Luke darted back out of his room.

"Wanna see me fight the bad guy?" Luke scurried down to the landing with the video game still clutched in his hands.

Cal met him there. "Sure." He set down the tool chest and peered into the screen gripped in Luke's grubby fingers. He must have gotten some time outside at Laurie's mother's to accumulate that shade of gray.

"Luke," Laurie called. "Wash up for dinner. It'll only be a minute."

"I have to fight the guy first!" He resumed the game as he hollered.

Cal was torn between Laurie's orders and Luke's enthusiasm. "Beat him quick, son." He said the word *son* without thinking, but after it was out he felt another surge. He should not grow attached to Laurie's kids. No easy thing, though. They were great kids. And they were Laurie's.

"No!" Luke flounced against the railing, which visibly shifted. "I died."

Cal tensed, fighting both the connotation of Luke's words, and the peril the boy was in. He meant his game character died, but Cal felt the adrenaline start flowing. Not wanting a repeat overreaction, he caught Luke's arm and pulled him forward. "Stay off the rail, Luke."

"It's stronger than it looks." Luke hung the game by one hand and shook the rail with the other.

"Go wash up. Your mom wants you."

"I don't want SpaghettiO's." He dropped the game and shook the rail with both hands. "I want to help you."

Great. Luke was going to pit him against Laurie for sure. "You go eat, and if it's all right, you can help me later."

"Luke!" Laurie called with annoyance. "Wash up right now."

Cal winced when Luke argued, "I'm helping Cal."

"Run along, Luke." Cal nudged him.

But the child knelt down and unlatched his tool chest. Cal gripped him by the elbows and stood him up. "Mind your mom."

Luke shot him a glare. "Leave me alone, you . . . scaredy-cat." He jerked his elbows free and stomped down the stairs.

"Luke." Laurie caught his shoulder. "That was rude. Apologize."

"I'm not sorry." He pulled free and marched to the kitchen.

Laurie looked up and spread her hands. "Luke's usually not the one to act out. I don't know what's gotten into him."

"I've been called worse."

"That doesn't excuse it." She put her hands on her hips.

"Go have your dinner, Laurie." Cal squatted at the tool chest and took out the upper tray. He wasn't going to lose sleep over names called by a five-year-old. But it was an interesting choice. Had Luke equated the PTSD episode to being afraid? Incapacitated, over-amped, superadrenalized, sure. But afraid? It wasn't for himself he'd feared, nor hurt. But he stopped that thought before it bloomed into just the scene Luke remembered.

Laurie's and the children's voices came up to him in snippets while he worked. He didn't hear clear words unless one of the kids raised their voices, and even then Laurie's replies were barely audible. She hadn't been kidding about her drained state.

Cal had scarcely removed the newel post, shimmed the hole with wood fragments, and replaced the post when Luke made his way back down the hall below, dragging his fingers along the wall. He stopped at the bottom post and clung to it, swinging a slow arc right, then left by one elbow, before letting go and climbing. He toed each stair with a soft thump before mounting the next. Cal glanced at his progress but kept working.

At the landing, Luke dropped to all fours and slid on his knees to him like a beggar on a cart. "Are you mad?"

"Nope."

"Can I help?"

Cal seated the post tightly, pleased with the firm fit. "Hand me that wrench."

"What's a wrench?"

Cal glanced up. At Luke's age he could have named every tool in the chest and used most of them with help. But then, Luke's dad was not a cabinetmaker. "That metal one with the end like a claw."

Luke picked it up, felt its weight, then handed it over. "How do you do it?"

"Come here." He fit Luke between his knees and put the wrench into the boy's hand. Then he covered it with his own and tightened the bolt.

Luke tipped his head up with a grin, tickling Cal's neck with his too-long hair. Cal ruffled it and curled his arm around Luke's chest. "Now we'll check and tighten the balusters."

They worked together until Laurie came out of the kitchen with Maddie curled around her neck, sleeping. She carried her up the stairs and disappeared into the second room. Soft mews and one short cry reached them as Laurie no doubt readied the child for bed. A few minutes later Laurie joined them on the stairs. She pressed her hands to her lower back, elbows jutting behind.

Before she could order Luke away, Cal said, "Why don't you go have a soak? I'll shoot Luke off to bed as soon as we're done here."

Laurie debated, seemingly unsure whether to capitulate or hold her ground. She must have judged their interaction worthwhile because she nodded. "Maybe I will."

Cal refused to imagine her in the bathtub. *Just friends.* He and Luke started at the bottom and worked their way to the landing, then made the turn, checking and tightening the balusters to the top of the stairs. "I think we just about have it, buddy."

Luke raised and dropped his shoulders with a sigh.

"You've been great. Thanks for the help."

"Do I have to go to bed now?"

Cal took Luke's hands in his and crouched eye level. "What does your mom want?"

He looked aside, shrugging again. "Are you leaving now?"

"Yeah."

"You have to say good-bye."

Cal straightened and held out his hand. "Bye, Luke."

Luke shook his hand, then looked up with the most sorrowful eyes he'd shown yet. "We didn't say bye to Daddy."

Cal's stomach clutched up. "Why not?"

"Mommy said we couldn't wait."

Cal gave a slow nod. "I'm sure she knew best." But why not let a kid say good-bye to his dad? Even if there were hard feelings, as he guessed there must be for her to be living with no assistance or child support. He dropped one more time and gave Luke a hug. "Your mom's doing her best for you."

Luke hugged him tightly. "Will you come back tomorrow?"

"Not sure about tomorrow. But soon." He released the boy.

"Now show your mom how well you can get ready for bed."

Luke's obedience gave the truth to Laurie's earlier claim. Cal could see his eagerness to please. He wasn't sure what had set him off earlier, but they'd certainly made up. Not that it mattered. Nothing permanent could come of it. *Friends.* Well, okay. Luke could be his friend too. And Maddie for that matter.

Wasn't Spanner friends with every kid in town? He just didn't need the nose and wig this time. Cal gathered his tools and packed them up. Then he carried the tool chest down the stairs to the door. Glancing up once to where he hoped Laurie was getting some relief, he let himself out, then made for his jeep.

Laurie didn't hear him leave, but when Luke tapped the bathroom door and called his good-night, she assumed Cal had gone. "Good night, honey."

"I fixed the railing." His mouth must be pressed right to the wood.

"Good job, Luke. Thank you."

"Cal went home."

"Okay."

"He said bye."

Laurie drew a long breath. That had become quite an issue for Luke. Could she have handled it differently? "That's good, sweetie. Go to bed now."

She laid her head back and slid lower into the claw-foot tub. She should have given Cal something, even just her attention. But Mother had drained her, dropping comments all day about their wretched situation. What was she supposed to do? Fresh guilt assailed her as she pictured Luke under Cal's arm, his strong hand helping her son's small one to do something Luke could be proud of.

Already Cal had put out more effort to connect, to teach Luke, than Brian ever had. She wasn't sure what to think of that, and she was too dispirited to try. Avoiding Mother's questions, barbs, and urgings to call Brian had been battle enough.

7

I WILL SHOW YOU FEAR

IN A HANDFUL OF DUST.

T. S. Eliot

L AURIE COULD HARDLY REMEMBER feeling so tired, as though every muscle was sapped. She had worked a double shift at Maple's to cover for the second employee who quit during the three weeks of Laurie's employ. She had picked the children up from her mother's, taken them for fast food since they wouldn't eat the meatloaf with red stuff on top that Mother had made. Now she hustled them up to bed with as little ceremony as possible.

When they were settled, she went downstairs to turn out lights, then planned to go to bed herself. She didn't doubt her eyes would close the minute her head hit the pillow. Proverbial or not, she would prove the saying true. She locked the front door and pulled the living room drapes closed, then headed for the kitchen. She almost didn't care to take her bedtime vitamins, but she couldn't afford to get sick, and she was running herself ragged.

In the dim light of one hallway bulb, she went into the kitchen and headed for the counter where the vitamin bottles stood like bowling pins. She reached for the C first. There were enough germs circulating these days to warrant 1000 mg a day, 500 in the morning, and 500 at night. She took a glass from the cabinet and started toward the sink. Something crunched under her foot. Glass? She stopped, turned. A jagged hole in one lower windowpane swallowed the dim light from the hall. The door was closed and locked, but the window just above the knob gaped.

She swallowed her fear, eyeing the shards across the floor. How would the window break? Wind? A stone? A stick . . . wielded by someone? Who would break her window? And why? She had nothing worth stealing. The hair rose on the back of her neck. What if someone was in the house?

Her spine lurched. She lunged to the wall and flicked on the light, glancing all about her. A cold jolt of fear sliced up and down her back. The house was silent, but were they alone? *What do I do?* Go up to the children? Call 9-1-1? No. That was reactionary. It was probably nothing, an accident. She was overreacting.

Glass crunched under her feet as she crossed to the phone, dialing with trembling fingers. Not 9-1-1. Cal. She shouldn't even call him, she should deal with this on her own. But she was tired and afraid. Through the earpiece, the phone rang twice, and she almost disconnected.

Then, "Cal's Roto-Rooter. You fill, we drill. No job too rude, crude, or disgusting."

"Cal . . ."

"Laurie?"

"Can you come over?" She couldn't keep her voice steady.

"What's the matter?" He was serious now, all joking gone from his voice.

She searched for an answer, but words choked in her throat and came out a soft sob.

"I'm on my way." The line went dead.

She hung up. It was a mistake. She shouldn't have called. She was overreacting. Of course the house was empty. It was some punk's prank, some accident. A broken window for heaven's sake. Even if someone had broken in, they'd obviously not found anything to take. She didn't own a TV or electronics or any of the things thieves pawned.

She stood, fingers pressed to her cheeks, her thoughts locked and tangled. The clock ticked on the wall. She made herself walk into the hall toward the living room, so lightly furnished she could tell at a glance it was empty. The house was not large, two narrow stories, no basement. Steeling herself, she opened the coat closet. No one, of course. But she did take Luke's T-Ball bat from its place in the corner.

Armed, she went upstairs and checked the children's rooms. Neither closet was closed, and both were empty enough to provide poor cover for a lurker. The children slept through her search, warm, soft, and peaceful. How sweet they were. So free from cares. They had no idea, really, how their lives were changed. Even though Luke showed sadness, they were used to Brian's absence. It was nothing new.

They had stayed in L.A. while Brian was in Phoenix for the baseball seasons. He'd said he didn't want distractions. It was no different when he gave it up to do public relations in his father's corporation. Of course, that involved international travel, flights across borders that he made in his own Piper or his father's Leer.

Laurie shook her head. She had been so naïve. She checked her own room, still tense, but not as knotted as before. Her bathroom, behind the shower curtain, breath tight. But there was nothing there either. She went back downstairs. She'd tell Cal to forget it. She'd clean it up and—

The knock jolted her. He must have raced over. Drawing a long breath, she opened the door.

Cal pushed inside. "What's the matter? Where are the kids?" He was primed and loaded.

She squirmed. "They're upstairs in bed. Cal, I . . ."

He scanned the room. There was no way he'd let it go now. With a sigh, she led him into the kitchen and saw him tense as he took in the broken window in the door. He skirted the shards on the floor and inspected the hole. "Were you burglarized?"

Laurie fought tears—what foolishness was that? "What's there to steal?" She rubbed her face. "I came home and found it broken."

Cal looked from the window to her. His gaze probed, wondering, wanting to know more than she could tell him. She pressed her back to the cupboard. Why had she called him? Reflex. Now she wished she hadn't.

He took charge. "Don't touch anything. I'll call the police."

"No." She surprised herself, but a sudden thought had occurred. What if it was Brian? Had he followed her? Broken in and . . . what? "I've already checked the house. There's no one here."

He shot her a glance and reached for the phone. "He could have left prints."

She caught his arm. "I said no."

His eyes narrowed. "What's going on?"

"Nothing." *Everything.* If it was Brian—after what she'd done, of course he'd be angry, furious. She'd expected some reaction, expected it before this. She must have put him in a bad position. Maybe even dangerous. That was his own fault! But she couldn't risk—

"Are you in trouble?"

"No. Cal, really . . . it's an old house. Glass breaks. I called before I thought." She twisted her hands. "Besides, if someone did break in, they know now I have nothing to steal." She wished he would stop looking like that. How could she explain? How could she tell him what a failure she'd been, what a farce she'd been living? That it wasn't over, that she had been oblivious, ignorant, irresponsible.

Though his gaze didn't shift, he answered flatly, "I'll sweep up. Can you find some cardboard to seal the window?"

She dumped a box that held the children's shoes in the coat closet and brought it to him. He pulled it apart and taped it to the window frame. She was ashamed of the comfort she took watching him work. The way he moved, the way the muscles flexed in his shoulders . . . He handed back the tape. "Get someone out to replace that glass tomorrow."

She nodded.

"So did you torque someone off? Serve Maple's rotten fish or something?"

She smiled faintly.

"Seriously. Did you turn down a proposition?"

"Only yours." She tried to speak lightly.

"That wasn't a proposition."

"What was it?"

"A kiss. Just a kiss."

Laurie dropped her face into her hands. "I can't think." She didn't want to. Why would Brian break her window? Was it Brian? And why was she protecting him? Or was it herself, her pride?

Cal took hold of her arms. "What do you want me to do?"

She shook her head, still covering her face. *Hold me. Stay with me. Say the things you used to say that made everything all right. Take away the time and the hurt and the mistakes.* She said nothing.

He rubbed his hands gently up her arms and across her shoulders, soothing the stress from her muscles. "I can stay here tonight."

"No."

"I mean sleep on the couch. It's a sleeper, isn't it?"

She stepped back. "It's not necessary." She wanted it too much.

He tugged on her hair. "Forget necessary."

Her thumb tapped on her thigh. "Thanks for coming. I just needed a friend." She was surprised it was true. As she walked him to the door, she realized she had never considered him a friend. From the start he had engendered emotions too potent to be friendship. Now she saw through his jesting to something solid in his core. She wished she'd seen it sooner.

Cal's jeep fired grudgingly in the frigid air. He shouldn't be leaving. He should have called the police and ignored Laurie's protests. He had a bad feeling about this. Prank? Accident? Windows didn't break themselves. If he didn't have such bad history with Sergeant Danson, he'd go to the station now. He considered it, then shook his head. She'd asked him not to. And maybe she had her reasons.

But Laurie's tension had been thick as butter. Yeah, it was possible some kook had his eye on her. But from her reaction, her evasion, he guessed she'd brought this trouble with her. He also guessed—and this part wasn't hard—that the answers would not come easily.

Mildred was sharp, and she'd pegged something he missed. Laurie was afraid. Of what? Or who? Her ex? Maybe. It was the logical starting point. She'd been very hazy on the details of their split, reluctant to discuss him at all. She didn't look battered, but what did he know?

He popped the jeep in gear and jerked forward. Easing up to the light before his turn out of town, he saw a dark Firebird kill its lights at the end of the block. He noticed because, other than his own car,

101

it was about the only vehicle on the road. The light changed, and he cruised through the intersection and turned onto the two-lane highway that led out to the sticks and increased his speed.

Suddenly a car darted onto the highway from the old utility road, and Cal yanked the wheel to avoid it, veered, and spiraled off. His jeep banked off the side, then rammed into the far edge of the ditch with a shower of gravel and a sickening thud. His forehead smacked the frame, and lightning shot across his vision.

He blinked, stunned, as something ran into his eye, then turned to see a car tearing down the highway without lights. The Firebird? Jamming the jeep into reverse, he ground the tires until they bit and lurched the jeep back to the road.

His head swam, and when his vision cleared, there was no sign of the other vehicle. He swiped the blood from his eye with the back of his hand, and felt a sharp, slicing pain in his forehead. Dropping his head back against the headrest, he groaned.

Laurie tried to sleep, but it was like trying to breathe under water. Why hadn't she called the police? What if it was Brian? His audacity appalled her. Were there no limits? She may have strayed far from Grams' hopes for her, but she had not stooped to illegal, destructive— She heard a sound and froze.

A moment later the heat came on in the radiator. She released her breath. If Brian thought he was above the law, if he wanted to risk his own life, that was his business. She would neither participate, nor condone, nor look the other way. She had Luke and Maddie to consider. They might be irrelevant to Brian, but they were everything to her.

How could he even think . . . But she couldn't begin to get inside Brian's head. How did you understand someone who thought life was a game? Who'd been handed everything, including the physique and charisma to mislead the most scrutinizing eye?

Oh, how she'd fallen for his deception. But no more. Maybe she shouldn't have interfered, should simply have left. But there was the principle of it. She hadn't gone to the police then, though she should have, but she'd been married to the man six years, long enough to know his threats were real. And how could she ever explain to Luke and Maddie?

No, she'd done what she had to do. If Brian was angry, let him see her face-to-face. She'd tell him again just exactly what she thought of a father who—

Maddie let out a high whine and started to cry. Instantly Laurie was out of bed and rushing to her side. "Don't cry, honey. Mommy's here. What's the matter, baby?" She scooped her daughter up, covers and all, and dropped to a seat on the bed. "It's okay, Maddie." She looked frantically about the room for anything that might have startled the child. All was still.

Maddie opened dewy eyes. "A bad bird came in." She wrapped her arms around Laurie's neck. "It took Fluffy."

Laurie spotted the dog in the rumpled covers. "No, look, Maddie. Here's Fluffy, safe and sound." She pressed the stuffed animal into Maddie's arms. "It was only a dream."

"I want to sleep with you."

Laurie kissed Maddie's head. "All right." She carried her back to her own bed and climbed in with her. As Maddie nestled to her chest, Laurie found a drowsiness she hadn't before. She fell asleep dreaming of birds crashing into the kitchen window. Maybe it wasn't Brian at all.

———

Cal's head throbbed like a hammered two-by-four when he awoke, still dressed in yesterday's clothes. He touched the tender spot, new blood dampening the crust. He wasn't sure how he'd gotten home last night. Obviously he hadn't gone farther than the bed. Annie whined, thumping her tail and licking his ear. As he rose, pain shot through his forehead and up the back of his neck. Annie cocked her head, watching.

"Now I know how you felt a couple of days ago." He staggered to the door and let her out, then changed direction to the kitchen. It would take more than coffee this morning. Morphine would be good. He groped through the cabinet, popped eight hundred milligrams of ibuprofen, and drank from the glass he filled at the sink. He dropped his face into his hands, held his head until the vertigo passed, then saw the blood on his fingers. That it was still running meant the gash probably needed stitches.

He made his way to the bathroom mirror and confirmed his suspicion. After washing away the gore, he held a wad of cotton to his head while he dressed, then went to see Doctor Klein. He had seen the same doctor since he was twelve and wasn't surprised by the reception he got. He should have come last night; he was asking for infection; he ought to be in bed.

Four stitches and a whole lecture later, Cal left. It was a compromise. He wouldn't go to bed, but he'd take work easy today. No clowning around, Cal grinned to himself. And no driving, except to and from the station. That was okay. His neck and shoulders hurt like someone had worked him over with a crowbar, though everything was numbing nicely with the prescription pain-killer.

At the station, he slipped behind the cluttered desk and called Laurie. He caught her just going out. "Laurie, do you know anyone around here with a dark-colored Firebird?"

"I hardly know anyone here anymore. Why?"

She hadn't paused at all as he'd expected her to. "One ran me off the road last night."

Now she was quiet. "Are you all right?"

"I've been better."

"Oh, Cal . . ."

"Listen Laurie, can I take you somewhere tonight?" Now the silence was longer than he liked. If she refused he'd have to patrol her house. This wasn't about him anymore—about what he wanted for them. Laurie was in trouble. If at least she were with him . . . "Come on. What can it hurt to take in a show or something?"

"I can't ask Mom to keep the kids when I'm not working, and I don't trust a sitter with . . . this other business."

"How about Cissy? You could bring the kids there. She'd pay *you*." The pause stretched. Had he pushed too hard? Had he read more into her call last night than she intended? What if she didn't want his help?

"All right. Call me this evening." She hung up.

Yes! He'd gotten through. Eyes closed, he clenched his fist. If she were in trouble she might not want to tell him, but he'd get it out of her one way or another.

"Hallucinating, Morrison?" Rob walked in.

That was as close to a real jab as Rob had given him since his release. It felt good. Cal grinned. "Got a date."

"Been that long, huh?"

"Stuff it, Kilmer." Cal straightened in the chair. His sudden motion and the pain-killers made his head swim.

Rob leaned close. "What happened to you? You look a little peak-*ed*."

"Your concern is touching. I had a run-in last night with a black Firebird. Some nut who thought he owned the road."

"Huh. Hope you gave as good as you got." Rob tossed a sticky pad on the table. "Rita left a message."

Cal tore off the top sheet and stuffed it into his shirt pocket. When Rob left, Cal took out the note and dialed the behavioral health center. "Dr. Rita James, M.D., Psychiatry, hope to the hopeless and pillar of the fallen, please." He leaned back, crossed his ankles on the desk, and waited.

Rita came on. "Why does my receptionist always know it's you?"

"Why, Dr. James, need you ask?"

"Cal, are you on something?"

"Tylenol Codeine." He pulled the bottle from his pocket. "Courtesy of Dr. Klein."

"What for?"

"Head injury."

"Be serious."

"I am. I found a ditch with my jeep last night. The doctor laced my forehead and shelled out the drugs. Now, per our agreement, I'm letting you know."

"How many?"

Cal shook the bottle. "Two left. But I've had so many already I could be seeing double."

Rita clicked her tongue, and he laughed.

"Just kidding. I'm well in line, Doctor."

"The trouble with you, Cal, is you don't take mental health seriously."

"That's because I'm already on *the dark side*."

Rita huffed. "I'm not taking the bait, Cal. This is your official follow-up check-in call. Are you doing all right? No more incidents?"

"If you mean have I found myself under the table fighting imaginary fires, no, not lately." Not since he'd shown Laurie what he could do.

"Good."

"Wanna play poker Friday?"

She laughed. "Sure. I could use a few bucks."

"Pass the word to Reggie, will you?" He hung up.

It wasn't a bad idea using the day to catch up on paper work. That end of his job was not his long suit, and it was more of a mess than he thought. Enforced stability was the only thing that kept him at it. It hurt too much to stand up.

Six hours later he called it a day. He'd been dozing for half of it anyway. According to the prescription he was due another pill, but he wanted to be sharp tonight. He left the pain-killers in his pocket and headed down the stairs.

Rob was doing housekeeping in the lounge. It had been a slow day all around. "Who're you seeing tonight?"

"A flash from the past." Cal clapped Rob's shoulder and went out.

8

THE MAGIC OF FIRST LOVE IS OUR

IGNORANCE THAT IT CAN EVER END.

Benjamin Disraeli

A LITTLE AFTER EIGHT, Laurie went up the inside stairs to the door that opened from Mildred and Cissy's rooms to Cal's. She had left Luke and Maddie in the kitchen downstairs eating gum-drops and watching Cissy pop corn. She smiled. Under those conditions even Maddie was content to stay. She'd planted a kiss on her mommy's lips, then given her full attention to Cissy's candy jar.

Cal opened the door, and Laurie noted the stitched gash. He'd really taken a hit.

He covered it with his hand. "Sorry, I was changing the bandage."

She stepped in but glanced once more down the stairs. "Think they'll be okay down there?" She could hear Maddie giggling but knew how capricious her moods could be.

"You'll have to purge their systems, but they'll have a heck of a time." Cal ducked into the bathroom and came back with a new gauze pad taped to his forehead. "There. No more Frankenstein." But he'd have a new scar.

"Is it sore?"

"Not too." He reached around the refrigerator and pulled out a

107

plastic-wrapped bouquet of roses and baby's breath.

Laurie looked from the bundle to his face. It would do no good to scold. On that issue, he was deaf to her complaints. She took the bouquet, fingered a peachy bloom, and breathed its scent, then set them on the table. "They're nice, Cal. Thank you." She bent to stroke the dog. "So this is Annie. Why would anyone dump such a nice dog?"

"Don't know, but I sure do appreciate it. She keeps my bed warm."

"Lucky you."

He had the lights dimmed and Linda Ronstadt on the stereo, setting the mood. The sooner they were out of there the better. But looking around, she felt reluctant to leave. She couldn't put her finger on it, but though it was old and broken up by eaves and arches, his place seemed welcoming . . . and safe.

"Ready?"

Her chest tightened. "Cal . . . I'm not comfortable leaving the kids." That was true. She was tense, worried, though she didn't want to alarm him again.

"Oh?" He stepped close and took her hands. "You want to stay here?"

Yes! She wanted to be close to him, in his place. Nothing would happen between them, nothing they would regret. She just wanted the comfort of Cal. "We could watch a movie or something."

"Or something."

The gravel in his voice made her pulse race, but it would not go any further than that. She slipped her hands from his and took a step back, determined not to lead him on.

He shrugged. "Look on the shelf over the TV. See anything you want to watch?"

She crossed to the shelf and read the titles, frowning. All the *Terminator*s, several James Bond, the Indiana Jones series, *Gladiator*. Hadn't he finished with macho, fantasy heroes yet?

"My taste as bad as ever?" He met her there, took her hand, and pulled her close. "But you like my music." He clicked the CD remote to a new song, wrapped an arm around her waist, and moved to the rhythm and lull of Ronstadt's "Desperado."

It was a memory song for them. He used to call her Desperado, said she was searching for all the wrong things. How had he known? She swayed against him and dropped her head to his shoulder. She needed to be held, and, as always, he knew it.

He rubbed his chin in her hair. "We always were good together."

"All we did was fight."

"Not all."

No, not all. But that was past. Now it was different. It had to be. She'd blown her chance and changed everything. She had to live with that.

He circled her in his arms, held her close. "You fit better than anyone else. That's why I saved your place."

"You shouldn't have."

He threaded her fingers between his and said nothing.

She had to tell him. "Cal . . ."

He pressed their folded hands to her lips. "Don't say it. Just pretend that nothing else matters, but you . . ." He kissed her forehead. "And me."

She wished she could. She wished all the time and reasons that stood between them would vanish. But they wouldn't, and she knew that better than he. She tried to back away. "I'm not good at pretending."

"You, the great actress?"

"That was a long time ago. A phase. An attempt at finding myself. And you were the one with talent."

"You were good too. That time as Lady Macbeth—"

"That wasn't acting. I just put myself in my mother's place and imagined the possibilities."

He brushed his lips over her fingers and moved with her to the rhythm of the music. She couldn't stop him. As wrong as it was, she couldn't stop. Once again she was swept away by his presence, overpowered, even though he exerted no pressure. He just was. And it terrified her.

As the last strains of the song trailed into silence, he let their hands drop. "We need to talk."

That jolted her out of her romantic reverie. "You don't talk."

"That was before I knew how."

She remembered all her frustrated attempts at getting a straight answer from him. "You've learned?"

"I had a few months of intensive training."

"A relationship?" The thought irked irrationally.

"More like a crash course in life skills." He flicked a strand of hair back over her shoulder.

She raised her eyebrows, waiting.

"Group therapy. Debriefing an . . . incident." He looked away.

Cal in therapy? Incident? Was he offering her honesty for honesty? She could learn what happened to him, why he'd acted as he had with Maddie, all his dark secrets from the last seven years. He'd tell if she would? The thought crashed against her wall. She couldn't. Cal was the Lone Ranger. He'd take it and run. Instead, she reached a hand to his bandage. "How's your head?"

"A little woozy." He caught her hand and pulled her to the couch beside him, then hooked his arm over her shoulders.

She lifted it off and shifted over. Why did he have to be so physical? But she knew why. It was his nature to touch, and she'd given him no reason not to. She could now. She could tell him the part he needed to know.

He crossed his arms over his chest. "Tell me about Brian."

Her throat constricted. Had he read her mind? She half believed he could, but only because he knew her so well.

"And why you got married so soon after swearing you couldn't commit."

He'd certainly learned to force the issue. "I don't want to talk about that, Cal." Hadn't she made it clear? *Tell him.*

"You called me last night because you know you can trust me. So why won't you?"

"It's not about trust." Tension rose inside her like baking soda and vinegar. *Tell him everything.*

"What are you afraid of, Laurie? Or should I say who?"

She pushed up from the couch and paced to the window. "I hate it when you do this."

"Do what?"

"Question me and push me. Just like Daddy." She felt eight years old again.

And why did the paint water spill?

I bumped it.

And why were you painting in the first place? In the living room, on the carpet? Haven't you been told . . .

Cal stretched his arms across the back of the couch, waiting. She felt it in the knot of her stomach. Didn't he deserve to be told? Why? Why should he deserve anything?

Angry tears stung her eyes. "Do you have any idea what it was like with my father? Not even knowing myself because I was so lost in what he wanted me to be?"

"I was there, remember? I took my share of knocks."

That was true, even if it wasn't fair for him to disarm her. She dropped her hands to her sides. "I know you did. You were the only one who stood up to him."

"But that's not what we're talking about."

"Yes, it is."

"Okay, call me stupid, but how did we get from why you got married to how your father treated you?"

She paced to the recliner and picked up a throw pillow, then stroked the velvety blue surface and turned. "We're talking about why it didn't work for us. Isn't that what you really want to know?"

"Laurie, you have me so confused, I don't know what I want."

"It's about losing myself, Cal."

"What?"

She clutched the pillow to her chest. "I felt too much for you." She watched the emotion play across his face. In all their time together she had never admitted loving him. Even now she didn't say it. She couldn't. But he had to understand. "I'd lose myself in you. I'd be whatever you wanted me to be. Daddy's little girl all over again."

"You've got to be kidding."

She turned away. "I don't know why I'm wasting my time. You didn't understand before; you don't now."

"And Brian did? Or is that why you're divorced?"

She gripped the pillow, fighting the anger. Why was she here, submitting to this?

"If it's none of my business, say so. But something's going on here, and—"

"I never should have called you. I should have known you'd go overboard. You have a hero complex."

"Is that right?" Cal sagged on the couch. His face look harried. His voice was hoarse. "A hero complex. Well, I guess it could be worse. What did Brian have, Laurie, that you wanted enough to marry him?"

She flung the pillow hard, missing only because he deflected it. "What did he have that beat this penthouse suite in Nowhere, USA? Everything! He wasn't afraid to be someone, to use his talents. He didn't think poverty was a virtue. He wasn't content with mediocrity." What was she saying? Why was she defending Brian's twisted morality and holding it over Cal's head? It was herself she was describing. "Just stay out of my life, okay?" Fury burned through her veins as she stalked to the door and flung it open. What did Brian have that she wanted? Nothing. But she couldn't tell Cal that. He would see it all, the emptiness, the fear.

Cissy had the children on the floor cutting and gluing beans to construction-paper turkeys. Maddie's oozed like something out of *Alien*. Laurie drew a long breath and pasted on a smile. "I hate to interrupt this industry . . ." She heard Cal's door open upstairs but didn't look.

He wouldn't make a scene, not here in front of Mildred and Cissy. Mildred's knitting needles clicked furiously where she sat on the end of the couch. Laurie caught the glance Mildred sent Cal as he came down the stairs, but she didn't look his way. Why wouldn't he just leave it alone?

"Oh dear, I thought we'd have time for them to dry." Cissy clasped her hands.

Maddie held the sticky turkey up and the beans began to slide. "For you, Mommy."

"It's pretty, Maddie." Laurie set the picture down and tugged Maddie's mittens on. "Get your coat, Luke."

"If I move my turkey, it'll run."

"Lay it flat and put on your coat." She sensed Cal beside her. Gathering herself, she glanced up.

He held out the bouquet. A simple gesture, an offering, a kindness. Why did he do that? Make her feel beholden, forgiven, *cherished*?

She took the roses. "Come on, Luke." She herded the kids to the door. "Thanks, Cissy."

Cissy beamed. "We've had a lovely time. Bring them again, won't you?"

Cal reached the door ahead of her and pushed it open. "I'll walk you out."

"There's no need."

He followed anyway and waited while she buckled the children in. He stood by her door and pulled it open. "Be careful. It's wet."

She nodded.

"Laurie . . ."

"I know. I'm sorry, too."

He bent and kissed her cheek, his lips warm and dry. "Take care of yourself." It was there in his voice, something vulnerable, something she was sure she'd never heard before. He was saying good-bye, giving up on her at last.

Her heart ached. "You, too, Cal."

———

Laurie hustled the children up the stairs and brushed their teeth for them, even Luke's. Cissy and her candy jar. But the kids were bubbling. She could hardly hush them long enough to get jammied and in bed. Finally she gave in to Luke playing Tarzan for a few minutes and tucked Maddie once again into the big bed.

She didn't climb in next to her, though. She changed into her nightshirt and went back downstairs. Sleep wasn't likely to happen soon. She shivered. Drafty old house. Maybe a cup of tea . . . She snapped on the kitchen light and froze. The new window was shattered, the glass scattered on the floor, the cold air chilling the room. But that wasn't what froze her.

Light glimmered on the blade stuck into her table. Her knife, from her kitchen drawer that still stood open an inch. Someone had been in there, taken the knife, and jammed it through a sheet of paper into the table. She forced her feet to move to the table, to the note.

It was typed and printed, no handwriting she might recognize. With shallow breaths, she focused on the words.

I want the stuff.

Stuff? Oh no . . .

No cops or you lose the kids. Her heart chilled. The one fear that had kept her from acting the first time. He'd threatened it before, the time she told him she'd talk to the paparazzi if his infidelity didn't stop. And again when she learned he'd participated in a fraudulent deal. She could still hear the steel in his voice. *"I'll take the kids where you'll never find them. You know I can."* Could he? He had means she couldn't imagine. He didn't want the children, but he'd used that to control her.

She looked at the phone. No. She would not call Cal. He would push until he'd dragged every sordid detail from her. But what could she do? She pressed a hand to her mouth, staring at the note. Did Brian think she had taken it? She closed her eyes and pictured the white substance turning the hose water to milk as it ran down the pool drain. Bag after bagful, melting away.

Did he think she was stupid enough to take it with her? That she stole it from him? Hadn't he heard anything she said? A shiver slithered down her back. No, he had heard, and he'd let her go, shrugging off their relationship as he had so many other disappointments. But he didn't know she'd flushed the drugs before she left.

Would he come after her, threaten her? Had he sent someone in his place? Who? There were so many people who moved in his circles, people she knew nothing about. Some, she now suspected, whom she thought she had known. She pictured them cloaked in smiles, the beautiful people who did what they pleased, who made the rules but didn't follow them.

She looked at the hole where the windowpane should be. What if someone were outside even now, watching? Her legs jellied, and she gripped her throat. What should she do? Call the police? Tell all she knew? The system was slow. Brian would easily post bail, and she would never see her children again.

Grabbing a pen, she wrote on the same paper: *I have nothing you want. Leave us alone.* She jerked the knife out of the wood and slid the paper off. Then she balled it up, walked to the door and threw it out the opening. She backed away. She had no more cardboard to tape on, no hammer and nails. She hated to think of that hole and the chill air coming inside. She stuffed a towel into the hole, slid a kitchen chair over and wedged it beneath the doorknob, then did the same with the front door. Maybe it wouldn't keep them out, but she'd hear. Surely she'd hear.

Her breath rasped in her throat, and she clenched her teeth to keep them from chattering. She took the knife and slipped it into the deep pocket of her robe. Then she went upstairs and gathered up Luke, who had fallen asleep with his game still running in his hands. She laid him in her bed beside Maddie. Trembling, she locked the bedroom door, then wrapped herself in a blanket with her back against the wall and waited. She strained to hear, to discern any indication of entry below.

He was out of his mind to think she would walk away with a shipment of cocaine. Why would she take it? To use against him? Her purpose hadn't been vengeance, just escape. She wanted no part of his illegal games. How could Brian do something so reckless? Didn't he have money enough, power enough? But he wanted the risk, the thrill of getting away with it. Did his father know?

Laurie stared into the darkness. From what she knew of Stuart Prelane, Sr., he would look the other way as he did with Brian's other infractions. As he always had. If her youth had been stifling, Brian's was the opposite. He'd been allowed everything.

Now he had no compass at all, other than what he wanted and what he could get. She closed her eyes, picturing Brian's expression, cold and unflinching. If her accusations fazed him, he hadn't shown it. He'd grown too far from her to care what she thought.

And that's why he'd never guessed she would dispose of it. She had done it in secret, waited for her moment and dumped the drugs, then taken the children and fled. Not that it would take any great stretch for Brian to find her, to guess she'd gone home. She had known he'd be furious. But she'd never dreamed he would come after her for the cocaine.

The house was silent, no stair creaked, no door swung. She thought of the note she'd tossed outside. Did it lie in the yard? Or had he retrieved it? He had to believe her. She had no cocaine and nothing to show for it. The money he'd lost was his own fault. He should pay the consequences and leave her out of it.

But would he? Her eyes drooped and shot open, then drooped again. Every part of her felt weary, small, helpless. What could she do against him, against any of it? She was utterly alone.

Cal lay awake in spite of the full day he would put in at the station tomorrow. He was hollow inside. Had he thought he could make Laurie love him? Nothing had changed on that score. *"Penthouse suite in Nowhere, USA."* Had he called her because he feared for her, wanted to help her . . . or because she'd fit so well in his arms?

"It's about losing myself, Cal." Was he so selfish? No. His concern had been for her, still was. He needed to understand her situation if he wanted to help. But his hurt was too deep. The two emotions warred inside him and came out combative. He hadn't meant to go on the attack, but he'd done exactly what he'd sworn not to.

Friends. Where had his self-control gone, his determination to honor her wishes? Dissolved with each strain of Ronstadt's memory song. Laurie was still riding fences, and he hadn't convinced her to come in from the cold. He'd sent her out into it.

What if he had handled it differently? If he had not tried to force answers, but simply held her? He'd felt her surrender. But holding her while they danced had brought back Reggie's words. *"God created the laws of nature and the heart. Just like gravity, things gotta work a certain way. You can't mess with the order."* It had felt wrong in a way it never had before. Even so, if he hadn't let go when he did, they'd have been right back where they were seven years ago, and he knew they couldn't survive it again.

They needed distance. If she was in trouble, she could call the police. He was no good to her if she didn't trust him. And he was in back-up mode. She'd made it clear she didn't want his help. *"Stay out of my life"*—couldn't get clearer than that. Any connection would have to come from her. Cal wouldn't pursue her again. It wasn't healthy.

"Mommy? Why are you on the floor, Mommy?"

Laurie opened drowsy eyes to find Maddie's face directly in front of her own. An alarm was beeping, but not next to her head as usual. Confused and disoriented, she stared a moment into Maddie's brown eyes, then startled up with a rush of fear and scanned the room. Soft pre-dawn light poured into the window and spilled over the floor.

The door was still wedged shut, and Luke slumbered in the big bed. Maddie's blond curls hung in ringlets around her head, and the puzzled look hadn't passed. "Why are you sleeping on the floor, Mommy?"

Laurie cupped Maddie's cheek and forced a smile. "I wasn't comfortable in the bed, punkin." Laurie kissed her daughter's puckered lips and dragged herself stiffly up. She leaned over and stopped the alarm, smiling at Luke still sleeping right beside it. At least someone would be rested.

Laurie glanced in the mirror, not surprised at the grim visage that greeted her. At least she didn't have to work. Maple served so few on Thanksgiving, she'd allowed her the day off. Laurie was more grateful than she could say.

Not that the day would be any picnic. Mother had "requested" they spend it with her. Dread as palpable as last night's fear filled her. At least they'd be away from the house. Luke awoke and raised up to an elbow in the bed.

Laurie could see his confusion. "Good morning, sleepyhead. Happy turkey day."

He rubbed his eyes. "How did I get here?"

"I carried you."

His palms came down over his face. "How come?"

"Can't I want to have you with me sometimes?"

"Mommy slept on the floor." Maddie padded over to the bedside and pointed Luke's attention to the blanket lying in a heap.

Laurie scooped it up as Luke's eyes came to her, large and questioning, but some instinct kept him from asking. Maybe he didn't want to know. Laurie was thankful she'd concealed the knife before either child had seen it. That was two things she was grateful for today. She made a mental checklist. She would need it.

Luke slid out of the bed and trudged to the door. "When are we going to Grandma's?"

"As soon as we're ready." The sun wasn't fully up yet, but no doubt Mother already had the bird trussed and waiting. With a tight breath, Laurie opened the door and searched the hallway. The house was silent. Had Brian accepted the truth of her note? Was he gone? Would he leave them in peace?

She took Maddie by the hand and dressed her in an angelic rose chiffon dress, then tied her curls with two matching ribbons. Her own preparations were equally meticulous, though she dressed casually. As she bundled the children into the car, she made a mental note to have the window repaired again. She sighed. Glass. What a flimsy defense. But would it matter if she boarded and barred every window?

For a moment she considered calling Cal. He would help, she knew. He would jump in fireman style and play hero to her helplessness. Laurie frowned and turned the key in the ignition. She told herself no and made herself listen.

Mother lifted the small but painstakingly stuffed bird into the oven. Her lips made a hard line, though Laurie couldn't guess what troubled her this time. She'd done her best to cut and chop whatever was entrusted to her.

"Have you called Brian?" Mother's question was put so innocuously it took a moment to sink in.

"No." Laurie bit her lip. But she'd written all he needed to know on the note last night.

Her mother slipped the mitts from her hands and turned. "He is your husband, or have you forgotten that now that you've taken up with Cal Morrison again?"

Laurie glanced at Luke standing in the doorway. "What is it, honey?"

"The TV's snowy. I can't see the parade."

"Well, take Maddie and play outside for a while."

Luke shrugged and went to fetch his sister.

Laurie turned back to face her mother. "I haven't taken up with

Cal. He's an old friend, that's all." And probably not that anymore, not after her outburst.

Her mother sniffed. "Well, it's not my *affair*. Still, it seems a waste to trade in a Mercedes for an old Ford."

Laurie drew a long breath. Yes, a drug-smuggling demigod was no comparison to . . . what? A clown? Her heart ached at the thought. Why couldn't Cal have been . . . Laurie swallowed the bitterness. What if she told her mother everything, the empty nights, the wild parties, the lies, the drugs, and now the threats . . . Would it even matter?

"I haven't traded anything. Not anything worth keeping."

Her mother merely nodded, sufferance supreme.

9

C LICKING THE DOOR SHUT BEHIND HIM, Cal stepped out into the milky glow of sun in a veil of Midwestern sky. Still a little numb, he gazed out over the bristly tips of the alders and oaks as he walked to the jeep. The winter sun warmed his forehead, where he'd changed the bandage with remarkable dissociation.

Thanksgiving. With the chill in the air it was a proper "Over the River and Through the Woods" kind of day. He wondered what it looked like to his parents in Phoenix, where they had retired last year. Personally, he couldn't do without the seasons, the changing of the trees, the gray winter bursting into life. Warm all the time was like oatmeal every morning.

There was a dusting of frost on the ground with patches of snow in the woods, but the bare trees and the fog of his breath, the smell of the pine and the smoke rising from the farmhouse chimneys was perfect Currier and Ives.

Most of the guys would be spending the day with their families. Perry and Rob weren't married, but both had relatives in town. That's what it was all about—being thankful for what you had, for the people who mattered. Provided, of course, you had people who mattered.

Both his parents in Phoenix and his sister in Seattle had invited him to come visit, but he'd declined. Not that they didn't matter, of course they did; it was just that he hadn't wanted to face the concerned looks, the well-meant questions. *"What are you drinking, son?"* as his father popped the tab of a beer. *"Are you seeing anyone?"* in his mother's gentle voice. *"Maybe you should consider moving here."*

No, Montrose had his heart. These were his people, even if he was too damaged to serve them as he once had. Maybe that would pass. Maybe he'd snap out of it. Maybe he just had to find himself again like his brother Drew in Alaska, searching for identity in the wilderness experience. Cal might have considered going there, but he hadn't been asked.

Cissy came out on the porch toting a pail of birdseed. She wore a lavender flowered dress and a yellow-green apron with zigzag trim. She gave him the same smile she gave the finches darting on the rail around her. "Hello, my pets. Hello, Cal."

"Morning, Cissy."

"Are you having turkey with us?"

He shook his head. "I'm at the station today."

She clicked her tongue. "Oh, that's a shame." She scooped a teacupful of seed into one feeder.

The birds darted close, and Cal half expected one to perch on her head. *Feed the birds, tuppence a bag* . . . She seemed as happy among them as he'd ever seen her. No worry in her sweet doughy face, just pure contentment. He waved and left her to her feathered friends.

At the station Frank pulled on his coat the minute Cal walked in. "Margaret's so tickled about this she sent a homemade pumpkin pie to keep you company." He stood an ancient, olive green thermos on the table. "And hot spiced cider."

"You've been covering the holidays a lot of years. You deserve the break." Cal eyed the pie. "Thank her for me. That's really nice."

Frank didn't waste any time heading for the door. "We're going to Mary's to see the grandbaby. Margaret's helping Mary cook her first bird."

"That's great. Enjoy yourself."

"You know how to reach me."

"Yeah, I know." Cal waved him out, then settled in for a quiet day. With most everything closed, not many people were out and about. After browsing the current *Newsweek*, he went down to the garage and walked the length of the engine. It didn't shine as it once had, but every inch was clean and everything in place.

He pulled open the engineer's cabinet and fingered the controls. He knew this truck like his own body. At one time they had been almost one unit, man and machine interconnected. Lifting a spanner wrench, he balanced it in his hand. The tool of tools for a fireman. What you couldn't do with a spanner . . . He put it back and closed the doors.

A loud tone from the claxton device alerted him, and adrenaline surged as he picked up the hotline. "Lieutenant Morrison."

The dispatcher was not Frieda. A male voice monotoned, "Man down on Route D."

Cal listened to the specific location, then answered, "Engine two in service." The call would have gone out to the volunteers' pagers. Since it was a medical emergency, only the EMTs might respond, and that depended upon holiday availability. Taking the smaller search-and-rescue truck where he'd already stashed his jump kit, he hit the siren and sped out.

A car sat on the shoulder of Route D with hazard lights flashing, and the driver climbed out and waved him down. Cal parked and ran toward the bundle sprawled half on the road and half down the ditch. At the bottom lay a bottle of Wild Turkey. Guess the guy had drunk his Thanksgiving dinner first thing that morning.

After his own short romance with the bottle, Cal felt a singular sadness for the old guy and stood a moment, letting the emotion fade before he examined him. There was no hurry. He'd already noted the marked line of lividity—the top side of the face and neck white as wax, and the lower portion, where the blood had pooled, purple. By the angle of the head there was a C4 fracture, and "C4 breathe no more." A break that high to the neck would have blocked the ability to expand the lungs—a quick death. There were also abrasions and blunt head trauma. He'd been struck, probably by a car.

Cal shook his head. No amount of hurrying or life support could help this ragged piece of humanity. But he dropped anyway and checked for a carotid pulse. Maybe he just wanted to touch him, to give him the dignity he might have known in a kinder life.

He pulled his handy-talkie from his belt and radioed the police officer who was probably en route. "Yeah, I've got a DRT, looks like hit-and-run." DRT, dead right there. He was surprised at the sadness he felt saying it. He gave the mile marker on route D, then sat on his haunches and waited.

He looked up at the hum of an engine, tires on gravel and door closing. Patrol officer Simon Tate and Sergeant Danson, who more or less acted as detective. Danson's shadow loomed over him, and Cal shook his head. "Checked out a while ago. Internal bruising near the waist, head trauma, and abrasion." Again the sadness. Who was this old guy?

Danson stood like Matt Dillon, assessing the victim from his six-foot-four vantage, then turned to the driver of the other car, whom Cal had scarcely noticed. "Did you see it happen?"

The man was a stranger, dressed in an oversized wool tweed over-coat with a black muffler at his neck and a cell phone sticking out of his pocket. He pulled a pipe from between his teeth and said, "I didn't. I came over the hill and saw him lying there."

"Were you alone on the road?"

The man took a puff. "I'm not saying it's connected, but a way back, I was passed by a black sports car—"

"A Firebird?" Cal interrupted, and Danson frowned.

"Could have been. I didn't notice the model, but he was late for wherever he was going."

Danson asked, "Did you get a look at the driver?"

"Only that it was a man . . ." He eyed Cal. "About your age. I think there were others, at least one in the passenger seat. But like I said, I didn't see them having anything to do with this." He dropped his gaze to the corpse in the ditch. "What was he doing out here on a day like this?"

Cal shook his head as Danson searched the body for identification and came up empty. No name, no identity. Cal looked up and down the ditch for the parcel or pack vagrants usually carried. Except for the liquor bottle, the ditch was uncluttered. Not much to show for a life passing there.

Not much of a crime scene either, as far as he could tell. But that was Danson's job. Officer Tate finished taking down everything the motorist said, then radioed the coroner, Dr. McGill, who was also the mortician. Cal doubted McGill would find anything surprising in his autopsy. Alcohol in the blood, and death by blunt trauma.

"Will there be anything else?" The motorist emptied his pipe onto the powdery frost at the edge of the road.

Danson scowled at that fouling of the crime scene. "As long as we know how to reach you."

"The officer has my cell number." The man walked back to his car. With one more glance at the victim, he climbed in and drove away.

Cal stood with Danson. There was nothing more he could do. It was in the hands of criminologists now, such as Montrose had. Rarely did they deal with homicide, even vehicular. He turned to leave.

Danson stopped him. "What's this about a black Firebird?"

"One ran me off the road night before last." Cal touched the stitched gash.

"You might have reported it."

Cal shrugged. He wasn't sure why he hadn't. Maybe a macho desire to handle it himself, maybe more. But now they were talking vehicular homicide, with no witness. For all they knew this poor, drunk fool was weaving down the street or fell in front of the guy's wheels. That still made it hit-and-run, but it was a stretch to think anyone had hit the old guy on purpose. They had no I.D. on the vehicle. Not for sure. The old guy just got in the way of someone's errand, someone who didn't much care who got knocked down.

Cal hung the handy-talkie back on his belt and headed for the truck.

"Morrison?"

He turned.

"I want to know if anything else happens, you hear?"

"Yep."

The pie was exceptional. He ate it ravenously as he filled out the report. Nothing like a good dessert for covering a bad taste, and that hit-and-run had left a bad taste. He'd seen death, God knew. Even senseless death. But not deliberate. Not out here where folks still lived by the golden rule. He swigged the cider and it warmed him.

125

What was he thinking? They had no proof that guy's death was anything but an accident—freak accident of two objects following the same time-space continuum. For that matter, his run-in with the Firebird could be the same thing, so why was he even connecting the two?

The claxton device jarred him, jangling him worse than the first time. He answered the hotline and heard, "Uh, we got a cat poled at 1440 Walnut. Repeat—"

"Yeah, I got it the first time. That's Ida Blair's place, isn't it?"

"I'm sorry I don't . . ."

Some of the volunteer dispatchers were less adept than Frieda, who handled the higher volume times with ease.

"Engine two responding." Cal hung up. Where else in the country did the fire department still rescue poled cats? It was the chief's unnatural fondness for the fur balls that kept them at it. He pulled on his department-issue coat and once again took the rescue vehicle to the scene. As he drove, he tried not to think of the old guy in the ditch.

If he'd reported the Firebird incident before, would the man be dead now? Maybe. Probably. Chuck Danson could no more act on a sketchy, half-seen complaint like his than on a hit-and-run with no witness. Still, it hadn't been professional to keep it quiet. It had been personal.

He'd assumed that the Firebird was somehow linked to Laurie. Okay, maybe he was paranoid. Maybe he still looked for an excuse, a reason why she needed him. But that broken window could have been more than she let on. He'd mishandled that. He should have forced answers from the start. Even if it pushed her away, as he knew it would.

He swung the corner wide and headed down First Street. He slowed at Walnut and took in the scene. Ida Blair, wrapped in a quilt, stood under the electrical pole with a saucer in one hand and a stuffed mouse in the other. Her hair looked as though she'd already made contact with the wires. He pulled the truck to a stop across the street parallel to the pole and got out.

"Afternoon, Mrs. Blair."

"Oh, thank goodness you're here. Bootsey's got herself in a real fix. A real bad fix."

Cal looked up the pole at the gray-and-black tiger whose eyes gaped like an owl's. She was scared all right, but what did the stupid animal expect? "I'll fetch her down for you." He reached into the truck for his spiked boots and pulled them on.

Snapping the strap to the belt at his waist, he hooked it around the pole and attached the other end to the belt. Then grasping the ends of the strap, Cal dug the cleats of his boot into the pole and started up. With each dig, the cat's eyes grew wider and she tightened herself into a ball, nails impaling the wood. "Hey, there, Bootsey. Remember me?" He neared the top.

The cat growled low in her throat.

"Oh, you do remember."

The cat hissed.

"Come on, now . . ." He reached for the nape of her neck. Like a taut spring she launched herself over his head and sailed to the ground with a thud, then dashed to the back door Ida had left open.

"Oh! Oh, my baby, my poor Bootsey!" The milk from the saucer sloshed up her arm as Ida Blair followed her inside.

Cal slacked his weight against the strap and hung there. "You're welcome," he muttered, then let himself down. But he couldn't blame Ida. From the looks of it, she had no one but Bootsey to spend the holiday with.

He drove back to the station. It was empty and cold. When had it gotten so dingy? It needed paint. It needed light and bodies and laughter. He missed the camaraderie, the roughhousing. He missed talking through the trauma, knowing the others felt the same.

He shook his head. He'd changed all that . . . for himself, anyway. He'd pushed them away, kept it in. No one, not one man there had broken through the wall, not even Rob, especially when the booze made Cal wild enough to use his fists. He gripped the doorjamb and went inside.

His footsteps echoed up the stairs and, entering the office, he thumbed through the reports. Car alarm, poisoning, dog bite . . . gasoline fire, just a shed. No one injured, thankfully. Gasoline went bad fast, too fast. He stared at the wall, remembering his training, not just the fire fighting, but the chemistry of extinguishment, CPR trauma injury, EMT and paramedic certification, his red card that interfaced wild land fire and urban . . .

He was more highly trained than anyone besides Frank; he made and ran the training videos for the whole area. And what was he now? A clown. He dropped the reports to the table. "I can rescue cats. There's no better cat-nabber alive. So what if they hate me?" He rubbed the shoulder that was pulling a little from the climb. "And now I'm talking to myself. Not a good sign, Cal."

The silence hung like fog. Even the phone stayed quiet. The hours dragged. He spent them doing housekeeping, cleaning out cabinets, sorting, filing. He even washed down the walls. One call came in, a choking, but before he could respond, the victim expelled the obstruction, and he could hear everyone in the background cheering. He readied to go out anyway and check the choker's ABC's—airway, breathing, and circulation—but the victim got on the phone and spoke clearly and strongly. She was fine.

Daylight faded and evening drew on. He wished he could get the old drunk out of his mind. What a way to go. Alone and senseless, out on some road like an animal, road kill. There should be more to life, more than checking out with no one around to care. He felt morbid and depressed thinking about it.

Cal stretched, loosened his shoulders and back. Fifteen hours and he'd be home free—if nothing worse happened. The phone jarred him from his thoughts. His heart started to race, worse than before, worse than normal adrenaline alertness. Too many possibilities. Too many chances to screw up. He started to sweat and forced down the panic.

He lifted the receiver, braced for emergency. Laurie's voice brought a rush of relief, and he realized dispatch had not toned this call out. The claxton device had not sounded. He was getting careless. Details like that used to be automatic.

"Mildred told me you were there." Her tone was matter-of-fact, giving him nothing to go on. No fear, no contrition, only the sweet sound of her voice.

"I'm here till eight tomorrow morning. All by my lonesome." What was he trying to prove?

"Can I come by?"

His rush accelerated, the feelings he'd held at bay threatening again. "Sure." An unexpected overture. Especially after their tangling last night. He hung up and prayed the phone would stay silent. "Over the river and through the woods, to the firehouse she comes . . ." He strode to the mirror by the lockers and ran a comb through his hair. "She knows the way to make my day . . ." The phone rang, and he kicked the wall.

"Fire station."

"Cal? I forgot to ask if you'd eaten."

He let out his breath. Did one pumpkin pie count? "Not to speak of."

"Good. Be there in a minute."

He pressed the receiver home and held it there. If Mr. Dispatch ruined this . . .

Cal opened the door and stood outside to wait. The emergency tone would sound out there as loudly as within if he were needed. Laurie pulled up and climbed out of the car even as he reached for her door. She held a foil-covered plate balanced on a paper-wrapped package and looked as though her day hadn't been much better than his. "Mother's efforts. She let me cut and chop but didn't risk more than that." She followed him inside and set the plate, more like a platter, on the table in the lounge.

He just drank her in with his eyes, afraid one word might make her disappear. After all, he'd hallucinated before. And his mind was muddled enough after last night's fiasco. What was she doing there? Hadn't he let her go?

"Well, eat it while it's hot."

The aroma wafted into the room when she pulled the foil off. He tried not to drool as he snatched a fork from the drawer and sat down. She took the chair opposite, holding the package clutched to her chest.

He nodded toward it. "What's in there?"

"Something for you. Just something I had." She pushed it across the table to him.

She'd come bearing gifts?

"I'm sorry about last night." She looked sincere, biting her lower lip.

He didn't say anything to that. It was so un-Laurie to bring a reconciliation gift, he wasn't sure how to respond. He set down his fork and reached for it, pulled the paper off the book and read, "Selected Poems. Uh . . ."

"I know it's poetry, but there's some in there I think you'll like.

Robert Frost's. I always think of you when I read him."

"And you think it's time I got past *The Cremation of Sam McGee*?"

She smiled. "Like you, Frost loved the woods and . . . well, the road not taken."

What was she saying? The road not taken . . . their road? Better not go there. With Laurie it was never good to assume. Take things at face value. "Thank you."

"You're welcome."

She leaned back in her chair while he savored the turkey and stuffing and green-bean casserole, and suffered through the yams. "This is really good." Between bites, he relished her. Just having her across the table was so unexpected, a bonus he would never have anticipated.

"I'm glad you like it." She looked cute in the turtleneck and oversized flannel shirt. It reminded him of when she used to wear his.

It had amused her to knock around in his clothes. First his letter jacket, then his class ring, then his flannel shirts. Maybe he'd thought wrapping her in his trappings would somehow hold her. He'd been wrong, though.

She folded the foil into a compact square. "So . . . give me a tour?"

He wolfed down the last bites and wiped his mouth, then led her out of the lounge to the garage. He walked her around the ladder truck. "You saw this baby seven years ago. Remember we went for a spin?"

"I remember." She rubbed the fender.

To celebrate receiving one of the four paid positions with the department, he'd hijacked the engine and picked her up. She hadn't been overly impressed. *"Volunteering's fine, but why not learn a real profession?"* By that she'd meant something that paid better, required a suit maybe, diplomas on the wall. The things that mattered to her.

He turned. "That one's for search and rescue, medical emergencies. It takes the brunt of the load these days, except for fires. Still need the ladder for that." Something quivered inside. *Don't go there. Don't picture or imagine. Don't remember.* "Here's where we bunk." He dragged his thoughts back and swung his arm toward the adjoining sleeping quarters, a small eight-by-eight square with two bunks and a clothes rack. No good lingering there either. He headed up the stairs to the office and conference room.

"This is where we do business, training, that sort of thing. I'm in charge of the new recruits. I take them green and turn them out seasoned and ready for action." *Right. As though anyone is ever ready.*

"What else do you do?"

"Wanna see some magic?"

"Magic?"

He motioned to the stairs, and she preceded him back down.

"I won't do the costume if you don't mind. If a call comes in, I don't want to respond in clown makeup."

She laughed. "I'd guess not."

"Take your seat, ma'am. I'm about to dazzle you with feats of cunning and sleight of hand, wonders of such magnitude as never before seen within these walls." And that was true. He never did his act for the guys. He pulled down the box of puppets while she took the chair in the lounge. He positioned the wooden-headed fireman on his left arm and worked the lever to the mouth. "What's this, Cal? We get to play for this babe?"

"That's right, Rocky." He used his straight radio voice to respond.

"Wow!" The puppet rocked back. "Beats those runny-nosed kids any day."

"That's for sure."

"So . . . is there remuneration?" Cal lurched the puppet toward her and worked the eyebrows up and down.

She rested her chin on her fist, elbow to the table. It was obvious she wouldn't encourage him. But then, she never had.

He pulled the puppet back. "Nope. This is a free performance."

"I didn't mean money, bonehead."

"Who are you calling bonehead?" Cal rapped his knuckles on the wooden skull.

Laurie laughed.

"Hey, cut that out." The puppet ducked away.

"You sit here and behave yourself." Cal settled Rocky on the edge of the table and pulled out an aluminum pan full of wadded paper and an oversized lighter. He'd start with his best trick. "Now, then, would you be so kind?" He handed her the lighter.

She ignited the paper. It had taken him a while to work into this trick, but he didn't show it. He clamped on the lid. "Grease fire. Think quick; reach for the . . ."

"Baking soda." Laurie pointed to the box he held up.

"You hear that, Rocky? The lady's a sharp one."

Cal reached for the puppet with one hand and worked the mouth. "Pretty too. Brains and bod—what a combination."

She rolled her eyes. "I'm sure that line goes over well with the kids."

"Watch your mouth, Rocky. You can't insult an audience of one."

"It wasn't an insult." The eyebrows worked up and down. "Cal likes the brains. I prefer the—"

He yanked the puppet up by its neck. "One more word, and it's back to the box for you."

"You wouldn't."

"Try me." He clapped the wooden mouth shut with a snap.

Laurie shook her head, laughing. He fed on that laugh.

"Now, then. Pour the baking soda into the pan." He turned the vent in the lid, and she shook in the baking soda. "That's good." He spun it shut again. "Say the magic words."

Laurie said, "Abracadabra."

"No, no, no. We do fire magic here, lady. The magic words are stop, drop, and roll. Help me out, now. Stop . . ."

She spoke the words, and he flung open the lid to reveal the white mice scampering inside. She leaned forward. "How'd you do that?"

"Ah, ha, ha. *That* is the question. But I'm—"

The claxton toned.

"Grrr. Don't move." He ran for the garage extension, picked up the hotline, and listened to the dispatch. No getting around it. "Engine two in service." Cal hung up, snatched his coat, and met her in the doorway. "I gotta go."

"Go."

He leaped for the smaller truck, triggered the garage door and the emergency signal, and fired the engine. "Watch your ears!" He started the siren. Glancing in the rearview mirror as he pulled out, he saw her standing in the doorway, hands to her ears like a little girl. He wished he could just hug her.

Laurie watched until the lights and siren were gone. Turning back, she searched the big sterile room that held the trucks and gear.

Cal's place, his work. More than work, his identity. As long as she'd known him this was what he wanted to do. But she'd been surprised when Mildred said he was there today.

She must have misunderstood. Laurie thought back to the old conversation. Hadn't Cal intimated that he no longer worked in an active capacity? She walked through to the lounge and looked at the puppet lying on the table. She ran a finger over the wooden features and smiled.

How many men could pull that off with a straight face? He didn't sound stilted or stupid. And his magic had improved, though he was no slouch in high school. The kids must love his program. Luke and Maddie would. And the mice . . . It was all trickery, of course. But then, what wasn't?

She looked at the book on the table where he'd laid it. It was a silly sentimental gesture, more his own kind than hers. But she hoped it would show him . . . what? She took a pen from the jar on the table and opened the flap. Staring at the page for a moment, she thought, then wrote, *To Cal. A true friend is worth more than any lover.*

A step behind her made her jump. She turned to face Rob Kilmer with a breath of relief. But his expression was both concerned and annoyed.

"Laurie? What are you doing here?"

It was so direct she grew defensive. She waved toward the plate. "I brought Cal dinner."

"Why?" The word was thick with meaning she couldn't miss. Why her, why now, and what was she trying to do?

Uncomfortable under his gaze, she capped the pen and put it back into the jar. "It's Thanksgiving, Rob. I brought Cal a plate of turkey dinner. Is that so hard to understand?"

"Yeah." He rubbed the tip of his tongue along the edge of his teeth.

His manner irked her, and she turned it on him. "What are you doing here?"

"I came to make sure everything was under control." His tone said "I belong here, you don't." It was so clear he might have said it aloud.

"Cal's out on a call. Didn't you hear it?"

"I don't carry a pager when I'm off duty. It's against FSLA regulations to volunteer for the job I'm paid for."

"But you're here." She challenged him.

Rob stared, his animosity tangible. "I'm checking on a friend."

Laurie drew a quick breath. "Well, I was just leaving."

"Don't leave on my account." He walked over to the coffeepot and poured himself a mug, then turned. "When did you come back?"

"A few weeks ago."

"Didn't waste any time."

She looked away. How could she explain she wasn't there to hurt Cal or even to start anything again. She just needed a friend, and there was no one else in Montrose. No one anywhere, not like Cal.

"I just hope you know . . ." Rob cocked his jaw with a sharp breath, obviously unsure whether to say what was on his mind.

She waited, but he just shook his head and sipped the coffee.

"Why don't you say it, Rob?"

"All right, I will. He's been through hell this last year, something you wouldn't, couldn't understand."

Laurie pictured Cal curled up on his knees, hands pressed to his ears, gasping. No, she didn't understand. Cal wouldn't let her. Maybe Rob would explain.

But Rob's face hardened. "The last thing he needs . . ." He stopped and pointed the index finger of the hand holding the cup. "He got over you once. Why don't you leave it alone?"

She drew a slow breath and pulled the flannel shirt around herself. "Tell him I had to go, okay?"

"Leave him a note."

Laurie met his eyes, the hostility clear and unwavering. Well, she deserved it. In a way she was glad Cal had a friend like Rob. She scrawled a note onto a green Post-It pad, then gathered her dignity, along with the empty plate, and walked out.

10

A BLIND MAN WILL NOT THANK YOU

FOR A LOOKING-GLASS.

English Proverb

C AL REACHED MAPLE'S IN EXCELLENT TIME thanks to the lack of traffic. He grabbed his jump kit and rushed in. The handful of diners were all clumped around the overweight man on the floor—Harrel Draper, the mechanic at Lou's.

"Let me through." Cal pushed in and dropped to his knees.

Harrel belched and pounded his chest with a hammy fist. "Look, Dottie. They called in the cavalry."

He didn't look like a heart attack happening. By his smell, he'd slugged a few before hitting Maple's for dinner. A bad combination—enough booze to kill the natural defense against Maple's fare. If anything his color was redder than normal, so Cal decided against delivering oxygen until he'd taken Harrel's vitals. "Any pain in your left arm?" He wrapped the blood-pressure cuff.

"Nope."

"Shortness of breath?"

"Much as always."

Pulse was a little weak, pressure high, probably permanently so. "You on blood pressure medication?"

"Nope."

135

"I'd recommend you check with the doctor on that. Any other medication?"

"No. Some Rolaids sometimes."

Beth Summers arrived, Montrose's only female volunteer and a very competent EMT. She made her way through to them. Cal quickly gave her the SOAP—what he'd already learned subjectively, objectively, and his initial assessment, but he hadn't yet determined the plan. Clipboard ready, Beth took down the information and questioned Harrel further on medical history.

Cal took out the portable heart monitor. He suspected indigestion, but he would rule out anything worse. "Except for your pressure, everything's close enough to normal. But I'm going to use this machine to check your heart function. It'll show the rhythm."

Harrel shot a concerned look at the contraption as Cal opened his shirt and attached the sticky pads to his chest. The monitor showed a normal rhythm. All things pointed to chest pains from gastrointestinal distress, a common side effect of Maple's fare. Gas in the chest cavity could feel as sharp as a heart attack.

"I expect you have indigestion, but with your blood pressure up we'll order an ambulance." Though Cal doubted an immediate life threatening condition.

"No way. No ambulance." Harrel belched again.

"I need to recommend—"

"No ambulance, no hospital. Dottie overreacts."

Cal suspected that was the case, but departments had been sued over less. "Are you refusing follow-up care?"

"Dang right."

Beth drew a legal form from Cal's jump kit. "You'll need to sign this. It states that by your own will you've refused our recommendation for medical treatment." She handed the clipboard to Harrel. "Sign at the bottom."

With the nearest hospital being in Melbourne, and the ambulance coming from the same, it would save Montrose the expense. Cal took the clipboard back and slid it into the bag. "There are no signs of cardiac distress. When Dottie gets you home, take some sort of antacid." He glanced up at Maple, who stood glaring behind the counter. "Serving last year's turkey, Maple?"

"Very funny."

He helped Dottie haul Harrel to his feet and murmured, "Get him to see the doc. His blood pressure's high." He thanked Beth and sent her back to her Thanksgiving activities.

She smiled. "I didn't know you were back on the line."

"Just for today." Cal waved and climbed into the truck. He killed the emergency lights and drove back just over the speed limit.

Rob, not Laurie, was waiting in the lounge doorway when he pulled the truck in and closed the big emergency door. Cal climbed down. "Hey."

Rob nodded. "Everything okay?"

"False alarm. Unless you consider the inherent hazard of eating at Maple's." Cal looked behind him into the lounge.

"She had to leave." Rob cleared his throat. "She left you a note." He motioned toward the table.

Cal walked past Rob and read it. *I enjoyed the show. Had to run. Laurie.* Disappointment settling in his belly, he picked up the puppet and worked the mouth up and down. "Can't say we didn't try, buddy."

"You didn't tell me your flash was Laurie."

He turned to Rob, reading the concern in his face. "How'd she look?"

Rob leaned one outstretched arm on the wall. "She looked good." His tone was combative, but Cal didn't want to get into it.

"I had to run out on her. Wasn't sure we wouldn't find a class four substance infecting Maple's." He folded the puppet into the box.

"Cal . . ."

"You came to check on me?" Cal slid the puppet box to the shelf.

"I was done with dinner. Just thought I'd stop by." Rob eyed him hard. "Guess I wasn't the only one with that idea."

"Thanks, Rob, but I can handle it now." Cal unloaded the mice from the upper tray in the aluminum pan into their cage and dumped the ashes from the insert.

"You can, you know."

Cal glanced up. "Can what?"

Rob's gray eyes were intense. "Handle it."

Cal shrugged. "It's just this one shift."

"Doesn't have to be."

Cal put the mouse paraphernalia onto the shelf. "Yeah, but can you see Perry doing Spanner? I mean we all have our strengths, don't we?" He heard Rob's exasperated breath, but before he could argue further, Cal added, "Thanks for coming in."

"Yeah."

When Rob had gone, Cal took the book Laurie had brought and opened the cover to her inscription.

To Cal. A true friend is worth more than any lover.

He smiled grimly. "Yeah, yeah, I get the point." He flipped to the page marker she'd inserted into the section of poems by Robert Frost. "Acquainted with the Night." Well, it wouldn't hurt to read it, even if he didn't understand a word. He settled onto a cot and stretched out. *I have been one acquainted with the night. I have walked out in rain—and back in rain. I have outwalked the city light* . . . Cal braced his head on his arm, the poem resonating already. Where did Laurie get this stuff? Maybe she knew him after all.

He finished, unsure that he got the gist, but it painted a picture of ambivalence he knew too well. Once, if he heard a cry in the street, his feet wouldn't stop—they'd run to help, certain of success. But now? And then there were the lines, *One luminary clock against the sky proclaimed the time was neither wrong nor right.* Maybe that was it. He was trapped in twilight, caught between the surety of sunlight and the dark.

Cal frowned, glancing at the next offering. "Stopping by the Woods on a Snowy Evening." He pressed his cheek back to his palm. *Whose woods these are I think I know* . . . Cal felt himself there among the trees, the woods filling up with snow, the scent of pine and damp leaves, the chill and silence of a winter night. *The woods are lovely, dark and deep. But I have promises to keep, And miles to go before I sleep* . . .

There was something deeper there than the simple words implied, he suspected. But Laurie was right. He and Robert Frost did share an affinity for the woods. He glanced at the next, "The Road Not Taken." *Two roads diverged in a yellow wood* . . . He read the lines, then rolled over and lay back. That was dangerous stuff. You'd walk yourself right over the edge thinking of all the alternative choices. The what-ifs. He knew about those. He closed the book and rested his head on his arms.

This time Laurie had made the overture. That had to count for something. She could have left well enough alone. She wasn't looking to regain what they'd once had, that was clear. Then why had she come tonight? Why did Laurie do anything? She said one thing and meant another. She wanted things she didn't even realize. He closed his eyes. *A true friend . . .*

Cal sighed. No sense pondering what-ifs. They'd taken the road they took. His breath deepened, and he welcomed the fuzzing of his thoughts. With images of woods and roads filling his head, he surrendered to sleep.

He was jarred awake by the phone and sprang from the cot. Instantly alert, he noted the time. 3:05. The tone was not dispatch, but the business line again. "Fire department."

No answer.

"Hello?"

The line clicked, and he heard a child crying. His pulse started to race, more than it should. "Hey, are you there? Hello . . ." The crying stopped abruptly, and a low gravelly whisper rasped, "Child killer." The line went dead, and so did Cal's fingers on the receiver.

His spine chilled through to his chest. His breath constricted as the air around him flashed orange and the cries continued even though the phone in his hand began to intone, "If you wish to make a call . . ."

He couldn't breathe. His head spun. He dropped the receiver and clamped his hands to his ears, but the screams continued. Black smoke boiled two feet over the floor where he slithered spread eagle, one leg extended to the wall, the opposite arm lengthened by an ax handle. With his breath resonating inside his self-contained breathing apparatus, he focused on keeping his chest motion relaxed and shallow, stretching the air so he could search.

Had he imagined it, the cry so faint, it was hardly more than a whimper over the roar of destruction below? Somewhere in the back of his head intoned the fireman's prayer: Give me ears to hear the weakest cry. And he did. Somewhere ahead through the murk. A tiny cry, more of a whimper now. Inching forward, gripping the ax head and probing for the soft thud against a body, he fought the heat penetrating his gloves and Nomex hood.

Sweat stung his eyes straining through the gloom for any movement, anything to direct his course. There, in the corner, caged by chair legs, a huddled form. Small, too small. No one should be so fragile. He shouted, "I have one!" and crawled, leaving the wall, but holding to the lifeline, the hose that would lead them out.

He could just make out the contorted features, limp ponytails, knees drawn to her chin, two, maybe three years old, crying. Four more feet. He stretched out his glove. *Come to me, baby.* Two more feet and they could buddy-breathe his oxygen.

Cal tensed. The air glowed orange. Oh, God! Flashover. The force of ignition blew him backwards, down the stairs . . .

Sweating, Cal staggered to the bathroom and ran his head under the cold water of the shower. The noises stopped, and he flattened his back against the wall. His chest heaved.

He held out his hand, fascinated by the tremor. Raising his eyes to the shiny, gray ceiling, he blinked the water from his eyes and forced his diaphragm to slow. "Okay. What do you know? There was nothing more you could do. You followed procedure. The roof venting didn't work. That wasn't your job. You gave it your best shot. Two more minutes . . ." Stifling a sob, he ran a hand over his face. "Oh, God, two more minutes, and I'd have had her out!"

He smacked the wall with his palms and pushed away. He strode to the lounge and poured a cup of coffee even though the adrenaline already had his nerves on overdrive. He drank. The receiver dangling on the wall had stopped toning, and he walked over and hung it up.

He'd thought the crying was real, a child in danger. Could he have reacted? If the voice hadn't accused, could he have done the job? His throat ached. The click had shut off the cries like a switch. Why couldn't he shut them out of his own head?

Who would make such a call, and why? A thought landed like a rock in his gut. No. Ashley Trainor's family had not blamed him. That much he remembered: the grip of her father's hand in his bandaged one as he lay in the hospital, the child's mother sobbing but thanking him for trying to get their little girl out.

They had thanked, not condemned him. Yeah, he was drugged

at the time, but that memory was clear. Even though they participated in his nightmares when he imagined himself handing the child into their arms only to have it all blow up, he could distinguish that from the memory.

He pulled off his wet shirt and tossed it. Face it. It could be anyone. Everyone knew what happened. The paper had run the story. The town had responded in typical schizophrenic fashion—some hailing him as a hero, others condemning him as inept. It didn't matter. Nothing altered the fact that things happened as they did. And Ashley Trainor was dead.

He went upstairs to the office, dug the key out of Frank's pencil holder, and opened the lower right drawer. He slid his fingers over the half empty bottle of Southern Comfort, twisted open the cap, and brought it to his lips.

Closing his eyes, he drank, then capped the bottle and carried it back down with him.

Reggie's knees throbbed, but he didn't relieve them of his weight. Suanne leaned up on her elbow in the bed. "Reg?"

"Go back to sleep, sweet. I'm about my Father's business."

"It's four o'clock in the morning."

"I know. But I haven't been released yet."

She lay back down, and Reggie watched her side rise and fall in an even pattern. She didn't ask whom he prayed for. She never did. She figured that was between him and God. But Reggie guessed she knew and was adding her prayers just now in silence. She was a good woman. She held up his arms when they grew weary. Right now it was his knees troubling him.

Reggie allowed himself to shift just a little, then forced thoughts of discomfort from his mind. He armed himself and went to war for Cal.

Eight o'clock sharp the next morning, Cal put the empty bottle, his badge, and his keys on Frank's desk. Frank stood behind the chair, still in his coat and gloves, and looked from the items to Cal and back again. "What's this?"

"I quit."

Frank's cheeks were red from the crisp air, and he rubbed his running nose with his glove. "Have a seat, Cal."

"No thanks. I'll just be on my way."

"We've got too many years between us to not hash this out."

"There's nothing to hash. I'm through, that's all." Cal shoved his hands into his pockets.

"That ain't all. What happened?"

Cal jerked his chin toward the bottle. "That."

Frank looked at the empty bottle and shrugged. "Did you tear the place up, do anything felonious?"

Cal didn't answer. That wasn't the point.

"Rob said you did fine. I see the reports." Frank lifted the forms detailing yesterday's calls and responses. "You did your job."

Did his job? What if the cries had been real? What if he'd freaked out when a real child was in danger? *"Child killer."* Did someone believe that? Someone besides himself? If he had defied Frank sooner, heard better, seen better, let go the line to reach her . . .

Frank swept the bottle into the trash. "You can't let one slipup—"

"One slipup and people die." Cal's hands curled in his pockets.

"Let it go, Cal." Frank's face looked weary. "If you'd obeyed orders she would have died. You tried the impossible." He looked up, hazel eyes appealing. "I want you active."

Cal jerked his hand free and slapped the pink stress head across the desk. "Can't you get it into your thick head that I'm done? There's no law that says I have to be a firefighter for the rest of my life. I never signed in blood."

"No, but you sweated enough. How can you waste your training, your skill?"

"My skill is shot. And I'm sick of playing the clown." Cal's hands shook, and he stuffed them into his pockets. Frank had concocted that position for him. He'd given over the instruction, the training, the inspections, all of it to keep him connected until he was ready for action again. Cal knew Frank wanted him part of the department, but it couldn't be. The throbbing in his head intensified. "I quit."

"I don't accept it." Frank looked like a bull hunkered down.

Fine. Cal turned on his heel and went out. Frank would have to accept it. Sooner or later. He stalked to his jeep and climbed in. Maybe he could have driven worse, but probably not. When he saw Danson's lights behind him, he almost laughed. The perfect ending to the perfect nightmare. *Hip hip hooray. Take me to the clinker.* Cal pulled over. Danson approached the window, and Cal rolled it down but kept his gaze out the windshield.

"Watching your speed, Morrison?"

"Nope."

"Lane markers mean anything to you?"

"Sometimes."

"Got an attitude, don't you?" Danson leaned on the window frame. His breath smelled like hash browns and ketchup. "Frank told me you worked the holiday shift so he could spend Thanksgiving with his family."

Cal didn't answer.

"You take it slow home. I'll be on your tail all the way to Mildred's driveway."

Cal glanced over as Danson pushed back from the window. For a moment their eyes met, then Cal nodded. "Yes, sir." He rolled up the window and put the jeep in gear. Most of what Cal thought of the sergeant was true. He was a swaggering bully sort of man who liked to play the role of tough guy. But then, that was his job, and Cal wasn't by nature one of those who disrespected authority or even rules.

Though he was never averse to a prank, and, in general, thought most folks should lighten up, he liked order and respected those who, in any capacity, spent their lives protecting the public. He and Danson had never seen eye to eye on style, but they hadn't crossed swords until . . . Cal slammed his hands against the wheel as a shadow of last night's shakes started in his spine.

It translated to his hands again as he gripped the wheel and glanced in the mirror to see Danson on his tail as promised. Cal resisted gunning the gas pedal. No sense increasing the animosity. No sense to any of it. What had Reggie said? God had a time and purpose for everything?

Okay, God. What was the purpose of last night's phone call? What's the time line on post-traumatic stress? Or do I get to live with it forever? Cal scowled at the thought. He'd told himself he was in detox for substance abuse. Now he looked at the truth that Dr. Rita wanted him to see.

It wasn't booze and drugs he fought; it was a monster in his own mind. Failure. He closed his eyes against the throbbing of his head, then recalled Danson's cruiser just behind and returned his eyes to the road. His vision blurred, then cleared enough to make out the center of the road and keep to one side of it.

He wasn't still drunk, just suffering the consequences of it. He checked his speed and lightened up on the gas. He squeezed his palm across his eyes and focused. A time and purpose for everything? "So why is Ashley Trainor dead!" His sudden shout hurt his head, but it was the kind of hurt he wanted. "Didn't she have a purpose? You sure didn't give her time! You didn't give me time!"

He slammed the steering wheel again. "Two minutes! You couldn't give me two minutes!" The jeep swerved, and Danson climbed almost onto his bumper.

Breathing deeply, Cal controlled himself and brought the jeep into line. He just had to make it home, then he'd shed Danson and go to bed. He wanted sleep. He needed it. What did Danson say? Frank told him? Had Frank called the sergeant to see him home? A fresh fury started inside. Did Frank think he was cracking up again? Incapable of making it home unescorted? Did Frank think he'd do something stupid like . . . end it all?

Now that was a thought. Significant. One Dr. Rita kept digging for; one that Cal would never admit. *"I'm crazy, not suicidal."* And he'd given her his rascal grin. Cal swallowed. He wasn't suicidal. He'd seen enough ODs and slashed wrists to know that much.

He turned into the gravel driveway and waved the sergeant by with a single salute, then pulled the jeep to a stop. He held his head in his hands as he climbed out into the brightness of the morning. His legs were none too steady as he made his way to the stairs. Home free.

The knock on the window halted him. He didn't want to hear it, but somehow it penetrated his fog. He dragged his face up through his fingers and succumbed to the inevitable. Mildred pulled open the door. The excessive warmth and the smell of the fruitcake she held assaulted him. He fought the nausea.

"You smell."

He smelled? "I spent the night at the station."

"I don't mean that smell. I thought you didn't drink on duty."

"I'm no longer on duty." He squirmed under her gimlet gaze. "Did you need something?"

She shoved the fruitcake his way. "I made you this."

"Well . . ." He took it from her. "Thanks."

"You're welcome. And just so you know, it'll make your dog sick, so don't try it."

"I wouldn't think of it. Actually, I like fruitcake." Just not when he felt like this. He tried not to breathe the aroma as he went upstairs. He set it on the table and opened a window. Nothing wrong with the furnace today. He collapsed on the bed, pulled open the nightstand drawer, and shook four ibuprofen from the bottle. He swallowed them dry, then lay without moving.

The decision had been easy. He should have made it months ago. Seeing the disappointment in Frank's eyes had been hard, but he'd get over it. Cal's jaw tightened. The fact was, he was damaged, damage that went deeper than any training. And it wouldn't go away, not by spilling his guts to Rita, not by drowning it with booze and pills.

He shook his head. The Southern Comfort hadn't kept his thoughts at bay. Instead, it had churned up more memories—the dinner he'd had with Laurie's family, everyone sitting like mannequins at the table, their faces long and stern, and his adolescent attempts at joviality. They'd gone over like gum on your shoe. No wonder she'd broken free. He just wished she hadn't run so far.

But he knew now that he was no good to her. Maybe once— before the damage. Not anymore. The headache was subsiding, and he rolled over. Just before he drifted off, he jolted awake. The phone call, like the accident with the Firebird, had followed Laurie's visit. Was there a connection? Was it a threat? A warning?

He gripped his head, squeezing his eyes shut. Ignore it. Don't even go there. But his thoughts surged on. The voice had been indeterminate, hoarse and low. Male, most likely, but . . . Laurie's ex? The shell shock had set in so immediately, he couldn't be sure of anything.

By the time the trauma had passed, he'd drowned it with whiskey, a setback Rita would not hear about. Not from him anyway. He sat up, sleep no longer a possibility. He might not be what he once was, but did he have the luxury of giving up? Maybe Mildred was right. Maybe it was time to find a better way. Reggie had put it well. *"What's the point altering your senses? Live your life. It's the only one you got."*

That was wisdom. The trouble was figuring out how.

Laurie put on her best smile and brought menus to the couple at the counter, who took them without looking up. Funny how many people never looked her in the face. They talked with their eyes on the menu or stirring their coffee or looking at each other as though she were an intercom instead of a person. But she was getting used to that.

She glanced up as Cal sauntered in and took a seat in the corner booth. Her heart jumped, and she frowned. How could he still do that to her, just by walking in? Maybe, as Rob said, she shouldn't have gone last night, shouldn't have raised his hopes. It was just that she needed a friend, someone she could trust. And the truth was, she felt safer with Cal in her life than not.

She grabbed the coffeepot and went to him. Close up, he looked haggard. But then he'd worked through the night. He might not have been to sleep yet. "Breakfast or lunch?"

"I'm not that desperate. Think the coffee's safe?" He gave her a crooked smile.

"I made it myself."

His smile spread. "I was hoping you'd say that." He turned over his cup for her to pour. "I missed you last night."

"I couldn't stay." She almost told him Rob had all but run her off, but what good would that do? So she used the other excuse, which was also true. "Mother." She shrugged. Mother had contested her going in the first place. But there was also no point in going into that. "What are you doing here?"

"I'm celebrating."

"What?"

"My deliverance."

"Deliverance?" She hated it when he made her drag it out of him word by word.

"From work."

Boy could she relate. "I'm sure you're exhausted. Especially after a twenty-four-hour shift—"

"I mean permanently."

"Permanently." She rested her hip against the side of the booth.

"I quit the fire department." The blue of his eyes darkened.

Laurie stared at him. He couldn't mean it. As long as she could remember that's all he'd wanted to be. She'd teased him, saying most little boys grew out of their fireman stage. But not Cal. He'd stood at attention every time the fire engine passed, quivering with something vital, knowing that whatever it took he'd be one of them.

Seeing him there last night, having him take her around the station, pride had been there again in his voice, in his manner. And now he had quit? She should be elated. Now he could get serious, look outside Montrose for— What was she doing, imposing her own values on him? *Listen to what he's saying*. He was giving up his life. Why?

Why not? He was Cal Morrison. High on potential, low on motivation. She stopped the thought. It was unfair. Hadn't he thrown himself into the training over and beyond the requirements? This was not some disillusionment. He was leaving what he loved. "Why?"

"Tired of clowning around."

She didn't understand that. What was this clown part he played? Why was he entertaining kids with magic tricks when he knew so much more? The incident Rob mentioned? A fierce annoyance rose up. There were too many unknowns, and right now she had her own trouble. What did he expect from her?

"I'm having some friends for poker tonight. Want to come?"

"I know better."

He sipped his coffee, set the cup down. "It's not what you think."

"Sure."

"I swear. Everyone stays clothed."

Laurie glanced around as though Daddy could appear from the grave. Cal took her hand. She quickened at the warmth of his touch, but she did not want those feelings to start. She'd drawn the line, and she would keep to it. He flashed his smile again, but it seemed empty. Where was he? Why did he have to be falling apart now when she had nothing to give? She slumped. "All right, I'll come."

"Seven o'clock. I'll tell Cissy to expect the kids."

"I'll leave them with Mom. They're doing a lot better with her, and she . . . Well, she's alone so much."

"Suit yourself." He released her hand. "Good coffee."

Laurie recalled her other customers. If Maple saw her slacking . . . She hurried back to take the couple's order. When she looked up again, Cal was gone.

11

After all, it is hard to master

both life and work equally well.

So if you are bound to fake one of them,

it had better be life.

Joseph Brodsky

C AL SPENT THE DAY FIXING everything around the house that was chipped, scratched, or missing a screw. The hinge on the shed door, the half dozen dead branches, the peeling shingles . . . Mildred had no reluctance about accepting his help, though she had plenty of input on the how and when of each task. But the adrenaline from losing most of a night's sleep along with the sleeplessness that came with the post-traumatic stress disorder made him hyper. Manual labor was just the ticket. He poured himself into it with a vengeance.

Then he attacked his own rooms. Never dubbed a neatnik, he now scrubbed and scoured for more than two hours. Annie watched him, following from bedroom to living room to kitchen with a worried look on her face and a tiny whine now and then. Cal wondered if the folks who dumped her had moved, and she'd been subjected to a cleaning like this before losing them. "Don't worry, girl. I'm not parting with you. No chance."

Cal reached for the Robert Frost book of poetry and held it a moment. Why had Laurie visited last night? He'd intended to leave her in peace, as she obviously wanted. Then why had she opened it up again? Why bring him dinner, make his heart rush with just her presence? She knew the chemistry. She felt it.

Or did she? Did he imagine she cared the way he did? He opened the book flap. *A true friend is worth more than any lover.* He frowned. That's what she said, but all his instincts said otherwise. What was holding her back?

The broken window seemed to be a fluke, unless she'd kept any other incidents from him. That was possible. And there was the business of the black Firebird. And last night's phone call. The hairs stood up on his head. He shook the thoughts away. He had no proof any of it was connected. But what if someone was warning him off? Her ex? Was he some jealous maniac?

Cal wished she'd told him something more about Brian Prelane. Maybe tonight. Blowing his breath through his lips, he set the book on the shelf. It looked strange and a little lonely among Clancy and Grisham and Clive Cussler's Dirk Pitt mysteries. Turning, Cal surveyed the room. He almost didn't recognize it. But he'd worked himself into a tired enough state to try sleeping again. Sleeping without dreams, without the sound of that child crying. After all, he had to be at his fleecing best tonight.

After a decent four-hour nap, he pulled the door open to Reggie and Rita.

Reggie rubbed his hands together. "Hope you're feelin' lucky. I am hot today."

"You win the lottery or something?" Cal took Rita's blue suede coat.

"No, sir. I got Smilin' Sal to talk."

Cal stopped in his path to the closet. Smilin' Sal, who'd been in the center two years and had not said a word? He looked at Rita, who nodded back, then to Reggie. "How?"

"The power of the Holy Ghost. I am gifted with the mentally bewildered."

"Kind of a kinship, hmm?"

Reggie laughed. "You might say so."

"Congratulations." Cal held up a Coke.

Reggie shook his head. "No thanks. What you got in the fridge?"

"Nothing to put a dent in that appetite." Cal waved at Reggie's midsection.

Laughing, Reggie wrapped his enormous hands around Cal's neck and shook him like a rag doll. Cal fought free and looked at Annie wiggling her whole body with her tail. "Some protection you are. Sic, Annie!" She licked his hand, and Reggie guffawed.

"She thought you said *lick*, bro."

"If you men have finished with your machismo, I'd like a drink."

"Sorry, Rita." Cal tossed her a bottle of Snapple.

Reggie dug through the refrigerator chill drawer and pulled out a roll of liverwurst. "This all you got?"

"Pretzels and chips."

Reggie shook his head and took out the loaf of rye. "Mustard?"

"Bottom shelf in the door."

"So . . ." Rita accepted the glass he handed her and poured the tea. "What's this I hear about you leaving the department?"

Record time. What else had she heard through the hyperspeed grapevine? Cal shrugged. "That's what I love about you, Rita. You're so subtle, never pry, never . . ."

"Come on, Cal." She sipped. "Tell me what's on your mind."

He clicked his fingers. "I forgot my mind's on file with you."

She waited.

Well, she could wait. He wasn't going to tell her about the call, the little crying voice that had sent him over the edge. All things considered, it wasn't any of her business. He was no longer ordered into her care; she was a friend, nothing more. If she heard about the booze, he didn't care. He'd walked away, and it didn't matter.

She leaned on the counter. "Why did you quit?"

"Time to make a change."

"Oh? You have something lined up?" She tapped her fingernail on the glass.

"Maybe."

"What?" Brutally unrelenting.

"Maybe . . . furniture." The thought had sprung up in the nick of time. "Dad taught me cabinetry. It's always been a thought to try it someday."

"That's bosh, and you know it."

Cal frowned. He wished Rita didn't have X-ray vision. "It's not bosh at all. I'm good with wood."

"You made your table, didn't you, Cal?" Reggie spoke around the bite of sandwich.

"As a mere sprout. And other things over the years. Sold them too."

"And you're going to make your living that way?" Rita put a fist to her hip. "You know what I think? I think it's a cop-out."

"You know me." Cal spread his hands. "Cop-out Cal."

She shook her head, disgusted.

So what if she was disappointed. Add her to the list. "By the way, I'm having a friend join us. I'd like your impressions."

"Impressions?" Rita raised a suspicious eyebrow.

He knew that look. But he took the plunge. "Just check her out. You know . . ."

"Professional espionage? I'm surprised at you."

Cal sobered. "I think she's in trouble." He held Rita's eyes, willing her to understand, to take her mind off him and hear another need.

"What sort of trouble?" Rita gave no indication of submission.

"I don't know, really." It sounded evasive even to him.

"Who is it?" Reggie chomped off a hunk of sandwich.

"Someone I care about." Care about? The woman he'd loved most of his life, the one he'd walk burning coals to defend—if she'd let him. If he didn't lose it. If anything made sense anymore.

Rita tapped her fingernail against the glass, one of her tells. It betrayed tension and uncertainty. Cal always called the hand when Rita tapped her nails. Nine times out of ten he took it. Without releasing his gaze, she frowned. "Someone I know?"

"How long have you been here?"

"The four years I've worked with the department."

"Then no. She's from Montrose, sort of, but was gone awhile, and now she's back." Now there was clarity. He was muddying things, but he didn't want her to force more from him than he wanted to give.

"Why do you think she's in trouble?"

"A hunch." He had little else to go on.

Rita sipped again. "Stick to facts, Cal. Hunches aren't good for you."

"Thanks, Mom."

"Watch it." Rita tossed her dark, wedge-cut, gray-streaked hair. "Besides, when we socialize, it's strictly social. Separation of personal and professional. I'm here as a friend, not a doctor."

"Oh yeah. And that third degree a minute ago . . ."

"A concerned friend."

He knew better. Rita could no more separate out from her doctor mode than he could sleep without part of his mind being primed for emergency. But he let it go. He'd planted the seed, and he knew too well how it would worry her brain. No problem existed that she wouldn't try to solve. And if anyone trusted a hunch, it was Dr. Rita James.

A quick knock broke the tension, and Cal opened the door to Rob. "Brought a pal," Rob said, and Perry followed him in, complete with a twelve-pack of Budweiser.

Just the irritant he didn't need. Not the beer, the bearer. Was Rob making a statement, bringing along the one person he knew Cal wouldn't want? He hadn't told Rob personally that he'd quit. He hadn't needed to. Word would spread faster than any wildfire, and he saw in Rob's stance the hostility he'd expected.

Cal closed the door behind them. "We'll have a full table tonight." He crossed the room and pulled the card table from the closet, stood out the legs, and raised the flaps to make it round, then centered it in his living room. At Laurie's knock, he shouldered past Perry to the door.

With her hair pulled into a ponytail in a purple band that matched her gray-and-purple sweatshirt, she looked like a cheerleader, her melting eyes large and alluring. She *would* pick this night to look terrific. But then, when had she not?

Taking her hand, he pulled her in, breathing the Beautiful she wore. "Everybody, this is Laurie." Perry's immediate interest was no surprise, nor Rob's disapproval. "Laurie, you remember Rob."

She nodded. "Nice to see you, Rob."

"Here you are again." Rob's smile was less than convincing.

"Laurie, that's Perry, Reggie, and Mom." Cal pointed them out in turn.

Rita glared, then held out her hand. "It's Rita."

Laurie shook it.

While they all spoke platitudes, Cal took the coat from Laurie's shoulders. He leaned close to her ear. "I'm glad you came."

She smiled.

"Well, hail, hail the gang's all here." Rob pulled a new double deck from his pocket and tossed it on the table. "Or are there more women from your past coming?"

Cal's temple pulsed. Was Rob being intentionally obnoxious? "This is all of us." He motioned them to the table in the center of his living room and handed over the bowls of pretzels and chips. "Everyone grab a chair." He slid a kitchen chair to Rita, and another across to Laurie.

Rob pulled the plastic from the cards. "Don't let Cal and Laurie sit together. They communicate with their kneecaps."

Cal dropped down beside Laurie and hooked an arm around her shoulders. "Just try to break us up." He sent Rob a look. *Cut it out, buddy. It's not your business.*

Perry took the seat on the other side of her. Yeah, it was a tight fit, but not that tight. Cal eyed him. Maybe one day they'd click, but he wished Rob hadn't brought him tonight. Maybe this game hadn't been such a good idea.

He'd thought keeping the regular Friday night game would send the message of normalcy. Just because he was changing jobs didn't mean . . . But then, it did, didn't it? Everything would be different. He would be different. Cal frowned. He *was* different. He'd just stopped pretending.

Reggie sank into the recliner. "I can slip my aces into the pads." He bared teeth and gums, and Cal grinned back. One of these days he'd resist that smile—for his own self-respect.

Cal nodded to Laurie. "Don't try to cheat Rita. She keeps a magnum in her purse."

Rita shook her head. "It's mace. Highly effective and legally concealed."

"I thought women were going to that pepper spray to keep the men at bay." Perry looked at Laurie with bedroom eyes. Too pretty for a man, in Cal's opinion, but the women melted over them. Perry turned with a near sneer. "What keeps you off, Cal?"

"Don't know. No one tries." Except the one woman who mattered. He could feel the tension in Laurie's back.

She cleared her throat. "So. Who deals?"

Good girl. Cal turned to Rita, who seemed more intent on watching him than Laurie. "Lead us off, Rita?"

She gave no indication that she had any intention of honoring his first request, but if he knew Rita, she was processing Laurie's non-verbal signals. If he were crazy, she'd tell him. But would she tell him if she saw trouble?

Rob leaned around Perry. "Cal, did you hear what they got in Kansas City?"

"The smoke trailer?"

"Thirty-seven thousand bucks. Whew." Rob shook his head.

Cal tensed. "It's a good tool. I'd have liked to use one."

Rob grinned. "Like the kids go in and come out mice?"

Cal grinned back, but it was stiff. "Like the kids go in and come out alive." The silence thickened like paste. Cal swallowed, realizing he'd overreacted to Rob's jibe. "Think about it. Actual simulation of fire conditions and escape methods. The real experience, except heat and toxicity, of course. Now that's a tool."

"That's an expensive toy. The money could have gone to better use." Rob's grin was gone. "Ask any man risking his life on the line."

Cal bristled. What was Rob trying to do? Pick a fight? Couldn't he see anything past active duty? No. He hadn't ever understood Cal's "copping out," as he put it, and this latest severing was eating him. But they had been partners a long time, joined at the hip in more emergencies than Cal remembered. Anyway, it was past.

He broke the almost electric connection with Rob's gaze. "What'll it be, Rita?"

She named the game and dealt, but Cal could see she'd missed nothing. Rob was furious Cal had given up, but it didn't matter. Cal was through with the department, and it seemed his best friend as well. If Rob couldn't see past their mutual work to a core Cal had thought was there, then he'd let that go too. He glanced at Laurie.

She was the one thing he wouldn't let go easily. Cal frowned. Unless he had to.

Perry studied his cards, considered the bet, and shook his head. "This hand looks worse than today's road pizza." He tossed the cards down.

Laurie turned. "Road pizza?"

Perry stroked her with his eyes. "A cyclist bit the dust on the pavement."

"Did he die?"

"Nah." Perry shook his head. "But it was definite road pizza."

Cal frowned. He would not have used one of their cruder expressions with Laurie. But Perry lacked subtlety. Perry lacked a lot of things. He wished again Rob had not brought him.

The cards did not fall well. After three hours he'd bluffed his way into clinging by his teeth. If they were playing strip poker, he'd be sitting in his boxers. He drank from the Coke can and studied his hand. A pair of threes.

"That sigh isn't fooling me," Rita said. "I fold."

Reggie eyed him. Only he and Laurie still opposed him. "Too rich for this garbage." He laid the cards face down before him.

Laurie narrowed her eyes, challenging him.

"I call," Cal said and dropped the last of his chips on the pile.

Laurie laid down her cards. Eights and fours.

Cal tossed down his pair. "You win." He stood and with a grin, opened his cotton shirt one button at a time. Rob started a rhythmic clap and Perry whistled between his teeth.

Rita put a hand over his. "That'll do, boys. I saw enough at the hospital."

Cal froze. Was everyone out to get him tonight?

Laurie turned to her. "Are you a nurse?"

"I'm a doctor."

His stomach tensed.

"And you've treated Cal?"

Rita raised an eyebrow.

Laurie moistened her lips. "Then you know how he got the scar on his chin."

Rita turned to him. "How'd you get the scar, Cal?"

He wanted to wring her neck. "Fighting a fire." He pushed the words out and reached for his Coke, his eyes on Rita. If she betrayed him now . . .

"Twelve stitches," she said.

"So is the show over?" Perry shuffled the cards before him.

Reggie pushed back the recliner. "It is for me. I got an early morning." He nodded to Rita, "Dr. James," to Cal, "Beefsteak," then to the others, "*Adios* all."

Rita stood also, sliding her earnings into her purse. "It's always fun. Better luck next time, Cal. Nice meeting you, Laurie."

"I'll see you out, Doctor." Reggie waved back with a grin. "Call me tomorrow, Cal. I got something to run by you."

Cal eyed Rob and Perry. "Game's up when I'm busted, men."

"There're still three of us with money to burn." Tapping his finger next to his winnings, Perry smiled at Laurie. Cal imagined yanking him up by the collar, but Rob saved him the trouble, no doubt reading his intention.

Rob stood. "Time to hit the road, bud."

Perry downed his beer. His half smile to Laurie was all invitation. Rob clamped his shoulder and led him to the door. Timely. Very timely. At least Rob cleaned up his mess. Cal closed the door behind them and turned to find Laurie's eyes on him.

A slow smile spread across her face. "Would you have?"

He cocked his head and fingered the last button of his shirt. "What do you think?"

She brushed the hair back from her forehead, her fingers parting the hair into separate streams. "I'm not so sure."

"You're probably right. So did you have fun?"

"It was a little tense. With Rob." She erased a spot on the table with her finger.

"He's upset I quit."

She raised her brown eyes. "Is that it?"

"Sure." No need to recall Rob's other objections. "What about the rest of the gang?"

"You're still the life of the party."

He leaned on the doorjamb. "I don't know that Perry would agree."

She shrugged. "Perry thinks a lot of himself."

"He thought a lot of you too."

"He's not my type. I don't like moony eyes."

Cal smirked. "Good."

"You and Rita are close."

The tendons in his neck hardened. "Why do you say that?"

"I can tell. What did she treat you for?"

He slid the cards from the table into their boxes. "She heads the Critical Incident Stress Debriefing Team."

"Sounds serious."

"It is. Keeps us sane . . . most of the time."

Her gaze deepened. "Want to tell me about it?"

"Not really." He swiped the empty beer bottles from the table into the trash.

"Do you think it matters?"

"I don't know. Maybe." He dumped Rob's ashtray and stuck it on the bookshelf, then sat down on the chair beside her, his bare chest brushing her shoulder. "You smell nice."

"You sprang for it."

"Yeah." It was heady being next to her. All evening he'd wanted to touch her, hold her, communicate, as Rob said, with their knee-caps. He ran his thumb across her cheek.

"Don't." But even as she said it she leaned closer.

"What can it hurt?" His fingers slid into her hair.

"More than you know."

"I don't understand." He dug his fingers into its silky softness.

"I don't want you to." She closed her eyes.

He didn't need to. He kissed her lips.

Her voice was thick. "I have to go."

Annie whined, sticking her wet nose under the palm that lay on his leg. Cal sat back, rubbing the dog's ears. "When can I see you?"

"Cal . . ."

"When?"

"I don't know. Soon. It shouldn't be at all."

"Yes, it should." Her mouth was so close he could kiss it again. She said no, but she wanted it. Her signals were so mixed he'd need a multiple personality disorder to accommodate them all. But he took her at her word and resisted. "I'll call you."

"Okay," she breathed.

Laurie drove home, more shaken than before. It was getting out of hand, old feelings that had no place in her life today, old memories that made things worse. She tried to control her jitters when she went inside. Since the children were sleeping when she'd gone to her mother's for them, she had left them to stay overnight. Now she was alone, and the house was cold.

She walked through to the kitchen, hit the switch, and stared. The floor looked like something had been slaughtered there. It was smeared with blood, or something that looked and smelled like it. Across the wall was smudged, *last chance*. Her stomach turned over, and she put a hand to her mouth, gasping until she gagged.

Hands shaking, she grabbed a rag and held it to her mouth. "Oh, God. Oh, God." Why was he doing this? Was he punishing her for walking out? For destroying his goods? Why didn't he show himself? Ask her to her face? Why terrify her . . .

She looked again at the floor, and her head cleared. This wasn't Brian. It couldn't be. He was egotistical and reckless, but he wasn't sick. She looked at the black, gaping window and quailed. Who then?

Her legs almost wouldn't work, but she had to clean it up. What if she'd walked in with the children? Thank God they'd been asleep or they might have all trooped in for hot chocolate. This had to stop. But how? Last chance? Didn't he understand she didn't have it?

She crossed to the cupboard and took out the old corkboard, then nailed it to the door. Then she mopped the linoleum and wrung the mop in the sink as the water ran red. She wiped the wall clean, thankful now for the thick, almost plastic shiny paint, then sank to the chair and thought of calling Cal. She dropped her face to her hands.

No. She was already in over her head. His kiss had shown her that much. Her fists clenched with the sudden surge of emotion. She could not let things continue as they were. She hadn't meant it to reach this point. She had to tell him, but every time he was near, that same electric connection held her mute.

Maybe if they'd never—if she'd never—given in. She had known better. Even without Daddy's threats and Mother's tight lips, she'd known inside what was right. Her senior year in high school, after Cal had graduated, they'd spent most of their time together, but she'd resisted him. *Oh, Grams, where did I go wrong?*

It was for Grams' sake she'd held out against the pressure. Not just Cal's, but every date she had, it seemed. Grams made it sound a wonderful thing to be virtuous. But then Grams was gone, and Laurie so angry with God, with the Jesus who let Grams suffer . . .

She was striking back at Daddy, at God, maybe even at Cal himself. Striking back as much as reaching out for comfort, for love. If Daddy had known, he would have murdered Cal. For reasons Laurie still did not understand, Mother hadn't voiced her suspicions. Maybe she thought if she interfered Laurie would marry Cal. Maybe she would have. Laurie dropped her face into her hands. Why did she keep coming back to that night? Wasn't she past it yet? One night.

What would her marriage have been had she not known Cal first? Would it have made any difference? She might have been happy with Brian, might not have felt wrong every time they came together. Tears burned against her eyelids. She had to tell Cal. But how could she?

By the way, Cal, I'm still married. I know how you feel about that . . . She gave in to the tears. Did it matter that she and Brian had taken their vows on the beach instead of a church? That a vegetarian guru had officiated instead of a minister? That they had deleted "till death do you part" and said instead "as long as we both desire"? And she never had, really. Her marriage was a lie, a contract between two fools with no concept of unity or commitment. Did that change things in God's eyes?

She pounded the table. God was no concern of hers. His ways were too hard, too narrow, too controlling. Maybe Grams' Jesus was gentle and merciful, but He had died with Grams. And Cal had picked up the pieces. And he was there now. What they had once, they could have again. So why did it feel so bitter? Laurie pressed her palms into her eyes. *What have I done with my life? My children's lives?*

Luke. Maddie. Conceived of a lie, they were still the only point of light she had. If something happened to them . . . The shudder started at the base of her spine and shot up between her shoulder blades. Surprisingly it bolstered her. She would fight the demons of hell to keep her children safe.

Should she call the police? Risk Brian's threat? Could he take the children? It happened all the time, faces of missing children on posters at the grocery store. Did she think this podunk town's police department could find them? Besides, it was too late to call, now that she'd cleaned up all the evidence.

What then? She stroked her face with her palm, looked up at the corkboard. What a joke. Tomorrow she would install keyed dead bolts. And then another thought came to her. *Daddy's gun.*

12

You do not get a man's most effective

criticism until you provoke him.

Severe truth is expressed with some bitterness.

Henry David Thoreau

CAL PULLED OPEN HIS DOOR, only mildly surprised to see Rob back at his place. "Hey." It was mid-morning, and Rob was on his forty-eight hours off. After last night, he looked ready to speak his mind. Cal pulled a second mug from the cabinet and filled it with coffee. He handed it over, then leaned against the counter. "If you're here for answers, I'm clean out."

Rob sent him a look Cal couldn't decipher. Anger? Disappointment? "I thought you were finished with self-destruction."

Cal looked into his cup. "What's that supposed to mean?"

"You and Laurie."

Again, he was only half-surprised. That Rob chose to discuss Laurie instead of his quitting the department was an example of their noncommunication these days. "So?"

"So I thought you'd learned."

Cal swirled the coffee in the cup, then sipped again. "Can't help it."

Rob puffed the air out through his lips, kicked aside a chair, and sat down.

Cal took the opposite chair at the small table. "How'd she look to you?"

"Gorgeous, sweet . . . and deadly. For you, anyway."

"Why?"

"Come on, Cal. She's a fortune hunter."

"No, she's not."

Rob was unrelenting. "The kind who takes you for what you're worth and walks away."

"Well, I'm not worth much, so what have I got to lose?"

"I don't mean money."

Cal shoved the cup aside. "What then?"

"Your pride, your manhood. Your soul."

Cal sat back. "What soul? I thought you didn't believe in that stuff."

"Well, I think you'd sell yours for another shot at Laurie."

Rob still knew him after all. Cal frowned. "You're probably right."

"Forget it. Forget her."

Cal pressed his thumb over the dried dribble of coffee on the side of his cup and tried to rub it away. Yeah, sure. Forget the sound of her laugh, the beauty of her smile. Forget her silky hair between his fingers and the touch of her lips on his. Forget all their history, and the hole only Laurie could fill.

"Cal. You gave it your best shot—stood up to her old man, gave her a shoulder to cry on. She walked all over you and then walked out. Keep it that way."

"I don't think I can."

"Why?" Rob crowded the table, palms flat.

"She needs me."

Rob shook his head, disbelieving. "You have to believe that, don't you?"

Cal slid back the chair and stood. He dumped the rest of his coffee into the sink and rinsed the cup clean. Need and duty merged too closely to separate sometimes. Did he imagine Laurie's trouble because he needed to be heroic? Was Rob echoing Laurie's own accusations? Did he need someone to save to prove he still could?

"You've got it all wrong." Rob's voice took on an edge. "You hold on where you should let go, and punk out where you ought to stay."

So here it came, what Rob really meant to say. Cal rinsed the coffee from the sink.

Rob slapped his palm on the table and stood up. "You think I want to partner with Perry? You think I'd trust him with my life?"

Cal stared into the drain.

"Why can't you just get over it, Cal? It wasn't your fault!"

Cal turned. "Tell that to Ashley Trainor."

"Ashley Trainor is dead! We can't save them all."

Cocking his head, Cal saw the air starting to change, heard the buzzing in his ears. "Get out, Rob." He gripped the counter. "Get out."

Laurie took one last look around the kitchen in the morning light to make sure she hadn't missed any of last night's mess. Except for the corkboard nailed to the window, the room looked clean and innocuous. She went to get the children.

Her mother's face was puffy with a pinkish splotch on one cheek, her eyes hooded. Had she been crying? "The children are out back. Some of the neighbors came over."

Laurie passed through the hall to look out into the yard. Luke and Maddie were chasing about with three other children. With a smile creeping to her lips, she watched them play. It was good for them to have playmates. She turned and saw her mother watching her. The expression was hard to place; envy, regret?

Laurie knew all about regret. And that brought back last night's tension. How could she broach it without alarming Mother and revealing more than she wanted to? She folded her hands. "Mother, I'd like to borrow Daddy's gun."

Her mother's eyes widened. "What for? Is something wrong?"

Laurie waved a hand. "I'd feel safer about being alone with the children if I had it just in case."

And now the frown. "If you were home with Brian, you wouldn't need a gun."

The absurdity struck her. If not *for* Brian, she wouldn't need a gun. "I don't want to discuss that."

"No, of course not. What could I know about keeping a marriage together?"

Laurie swallowed a bitter lump. Oh, Mother had kept her marriage together, never interfering with the dictator's desires—and sacrificed every ounce of joy for all of them. Yes, Mother could tell her a lot. Pretend the drugs never happened, the infidelity, the shady deals. Your place is beneath your husband, under his heel. Laurie did not need to hear anything Mother might say.

Her mother turned, went to the built-in walnut desk beneath the kitchen phone, and pulled open the drawer. She took out the handgun. "It's not loaded."

Laurie joined her, took the gun, and felt its weight. She'd never touched it. Daddy had kept it locked in his bed stand. When had Mother moved it to the kitchen? Was she afraid as well, living alone? "Why don't you keep it loaded?"

"This is Montrose, not L.A."

Laurie didn't agree, but then, her threat was tangible. She could buy bullets at the hunting and fishing store on Breams Road. "Do you mind if I borrow it?"

"Take it." Mother started to close the drawer, then stopped and took out a thick manila folder.

"What's that?"

Her mother hesitated, then handed it over. "Some things of yours."

Laurie set the gun on the table, sat down, and opened the hasp of the folder. She shook out a stack of papers. They were drawings and writings she'd done as a child. Her mother had collected and saved them? She looked from sheet to sheet: the house they'd lived in before this one, the horse she'd always wanted in a field of flowers, herself with two little girls. Laurie stared at that picture. She had drawn herself in her favorite yellow sundress, but each of the other girls was in pink and they all had wings. "What's this?"

Her mother leaned. Her mouth tightened, and Laurie expected her to say "How would I know?" But she said, "You with your sisters."

"My sisters?" Laurie stared.

"There are a lot of those. Sometimes they're boys." Her mother's voice softened. "One of the babies was a boy."

Laurie flipped to the next picture. Sure enough, this time the three winged children were boys. But they were girls again in the next, four of them and they were all up in a tree. She looked at her mother. "I don't remember drawing these."

"They'd come in a rash. We'd bury a new one, and the drawings would start again, then dwindle."

Laurie almost thought her mother's lip quivered. She laid the pictures down and studied her mother's face. "Was it very hard? Losing them?" She was ashamed she'd never considered it before. She wasn't even sure how many babies her mother had lost.

The eyelids tinged with natural blue and brown hues came down over her mother's eyes. Her lashes were thick, but not as dark as Laurie's. Her cheekbones were well defined but not prominent. She was a lovely woman. "The hardest part was how your father took it."

Laurie turned away from her mother's face and squinted up at the corner, where a cobweb had escaped notice. It shocked her to see it. An imperfection in Marjorie Barton's kitchen? "I don't remember him grieving."

Mother shook her head with a sigh. "No. He was embarrassed. The thought that we could produce anything less than perfect . . ." She folded her hands tightly.

Laurie noted the pale brown spots flecking the blue-veined hands. She looked up into her mother's face. Why was she telling her this? They'd never spoken of the babies; at least Laurie couldn't remember doing so.

"You're lucky to have two perfect children."

Laurie stood up and walked to the window. Were Luke and Maddie perfect? Wonderful, yes. Bright and healthy, but perfect? "No one's perfect, Mother." Is that what Daddy had expected? She had to be the perfect one, just because she lived? She walked back around the table and sat down. "How did they die?"

Mother stretched out her fingers and pulled at the base of her middle fingernail. The nails were narrow ovals, except the one that came down into a hangnail point at the base. "The twins were stillborn. We don't know why. The next failed to develop a proper digestive system. He lived one day. The last was badly malformed. She lived the longest. Two weeks. Your father was terrified she might survive. After that we stopped trying." She looked up. "But we already had you."

"Was I first?"

Mother nodded. "I was nineteen when I had you."

"No complications?"

Mother shook her head. "Nothing to indicate every other birth would be . . ." She sighed.

"And they never figured out what the trouble was?"

Her mother pulled a poem from the stack of papers. "I was never told any reason." She held out the paper. "You wrote this in second grade."

Laurie took it. " 'Mother.' " *M—is for Marjorie. O—I love you. T—too bad the babies died. H—heaven is nice. E—everything will be all right. R—really truly, I promise.* Laurie looked at the precise, well-formed letters. Someone must have helped her spell. "Not much of a Mother's Day card."

"It was the best thing I got." Her mother's voice quavered. "Just knowing someone cared."

Laurie's throat tightened. Mother had been so unapproachable. How could anyone show they cared? But maybe she hadn't always been. Maybe she had grown that way with each passing grief. Laurie didn't know what to say.

Her mother stood up. "You can take all that with you."

"Don't you want them?"

"I'm cleaning things out."

Why did it hurt? The real surprise was that any of it ever meant enough for Mother to keep them in the first place. Laurie slipped all the papers into the envelope and tucked it under her arm. She stashed the gun into her purse. "I have to work at four. I'll bring the children back then."

Mother nodded. "They'll need baths. I can do it here."

Laurie nodded. "All right. I'll bring Maddie's bath toys."

"Don't bother. It clutters things up."

Laurie bit her lip against her argument and went out the back to get the children. She couldn't afford to antagonize her mother when she needed her help. Again, she realized how ill-prepared she was for this new stage in her life. Single-parenthood was no problem with unlimited funds and a nanny. It was a whole different picture now.

Especially with a madman trying to scare her witless. Laurie shoved the thought away. Sooner or later Brian, or whoever it was, would have to show himself. Then she'd explain she didn't have the drugs and that would be it. If not, Daddy's gun would dissuade them.

She caught Luke and Maddie by the hands as they ran over and chased each other around her legs. "Come on, you two. I'll race you to the car." She buckled Maddie into her car seat, made sure Luke was fastened, then headed for Roy's Shot and Tackle.

"Mommy?" Maddie kicked the heel of one pink canvas tennis shoe against the toe of the other. "Why is Grandma sad?"

Laurie glanced back. "Why do you think she's sad, honey?"

"Her mouth is like this." Maddie trapped her lips between her fingers and pulled the edges down.

It looked more like a duck, but Laurie got the picture. "Well, it's just . . ." What was it? A lifetime of nothing to make her smile? A permanent dissatisfaction? The joy sucked out of her by a chronically critical man? The pain of lost babies? Mother was a dry husk, stubble left behind in a harvested field. Laurie experienced something she hadn't felt before: compassion. Compassion for her mother.

"I don't know, honey. But maybe, between us . . ." She glanced into the rearview mirror at Luke in the backseat. "Between all of us, maybe we can help her learn to smile."

Luke nodded. "I told her a joke."

"What joke was that?"

"A joke Cal told me."

Laurie almost winced. Was it appropriate? Did Luke tell Mother where he'd gotten it? She shook her head, annoyed. She had to stop thinking that way, disparaging Cal for who he was. "What was the joke?"

"Knock knock."

"Who's there?"

"Duane."

"Duane who?" Maddie said simultaneously with Laurie.

"Duane the bathtub, I'm dwowning."

Laurie smiled. Leave it to Cal to resurrect something so old and make it new for Luke. She shouldn't have doubted him. "Did Grandma like it?"

Luke shrugged. "She said I did need a bath and made me wash my hands."

Laurie sighed, her newfound compassion waning. "Well, I liked it. Did he teach you any others?"

"Yeah. He told me a bunch when we were cleaning the fish the day he . . . jumped on Maddie. Mommy? Why did he jump on Maddie?"

"I've already told you, Luke. He thought she was in danger."

"But why did he hold his head and cry?"

"He wasn't crying. He was . . . I don't know exactly what it was. Do you remember the time you had the bad dream about the dragon? How you came into my room and you were shaking?"

Luke nodded.

"It's like that. Maddie reminded him of something, something scary that happened." Laurie parked in the small paved lot outside the store. She could get what she needed and maybe something little for the kids. The store was not large and the only thing she saw for children was a wire bin of brightly colored plastic balls. She distracted them with that. "Go look at those bouncy balls. Which one would you like?"

Quickly, she laid the handgun on the counter. "Could you please get me whatever kind of bullet this takes?"

The man looked at her quizzically.

"It's my daddy's gun and I'm not sure . . ." Why was he looking at her that way? "My father's dead, and my mother gave it to me for protection." Her voice shook.

Maddie's tennis shoes slapped the tile floor as she ran back. "I want the pink one."

Laurie turned as Maddie grabbed her legs. "I want the pink one, and Luke won't get it."

Maddie wasn't tall enough to see the gun lying on the counter, but Laurie shielded her anyway with a turn of her body. She sent a quick glance to the clerk. "Please just get me what I need."

Luke stood next to the wire bin that held the iridescent plastic balls. From the corner of her eye, Laurie saw the sporting goods clerk sorting through the boxes of bullets. She took Maddie's hand and walked her back to the ball bin.

"I don't want pink." Luke's face was firm, too much like Brian's.

"How about green?" Laurie lifted the ball out of the top of the bin and bounced it on the floor. Maddie swiped at it, missed, and chased it down the aisle. "Help her, Luke." Laurie returned to the counter.

The clerk pushed the gun toward her. "This is a Smith and Wesson .38 special, takes a .38 158 grain hollow point shell. Do you know how to load it?" He looked more than a little nervous. Did he think she planned to use it on him? What was so odd about a woman needing a gun for protection? But she felt nervous herself as she shook her head. She'd never touched a gun before.

He opened the box of shells. "Let me show you."

She watched first, then did it herself under his direction. Then he put the loads back into the box and handed her the empty gun. He moved to the register with the box of shells and rang it up. "That'll be twelve dollars and twenty cents unless you want that bouncy ball."

Twelve dollars! Laurie sighed. "Yes, I want the ball."

Luke ran up with it clutched between his arms. Laurie paid, then asked, "Where would I get dead bolts?"

Again that quizzical look. In a town like Montrose he must think her paranoid.

"There's a hardware store down the street."

Laurie drove until she found the store, then brought Luke and Maddie and the ball inside. She chose keyed dead bolts and the tools the package said were required. She paid and went out. Luke and Maddie bounced the ball between them. "Hold it in the parking lot, Luke. You need to watch."

She took Maddie's hand. Why had the man at Roy's Shot and Tackle made her feel so uncomfortable? Or was it her own tension that unnerved him? No matter. She had what she needed now, and she was not a freak, only a woman protecting herself and her children. As she pulled the car onto the twin lines of concrete that formed her driveway, Laurie looked at the house with a fresh ghost of fear. What would she find inside?

She reached for the bag with the bullets, and the one that held dead bolts, drill and hole-saw attachment, and screwdrivers. The man in hardware had assured her it wasn't difficult to install the locks. If only she could lock out everything harmful or tragic, every bad thing, every bad choice. But she couldn't. So then there was the gun.

She climbed out of the car. Maddie tossed the ball and chased it up the walk, but Luke held back.

"Mommy?" He turned his face up. "When are we going home?"

Home? Her heart sank. "You mean back to California?"

He nodded.

"Honey, we live here now."

"It's almost my birthday." His brown eyes held hers.

"I know. We'll have a party and—"

"Will Daddy come?"

A lump like a rock landed in her stomach. How could she make him understand? It wasn't possible to translate this mess into the thoughts of an innocent boy who loved his daddy in spite of everything. "It's chilly, Luke. Let's go in."

Luke planted his feet. "Will he?"

"Daddy's busy, Luke. You know that."

"He came last time. He brought me my car." His lip jutted. "I want my car." Now the lip trembled. "I want Daddy to come to my birthday."

Brian had made an appearance at exactly one of Luke's birthdays, the last one, where he'd impressed his son with the kid-sized motorized race car. Luke had driven it every day after Brian left again, even taking Maddie for rides. But Laurie was the one watching for traffic and making sure they didn't spill into the street.

"I know, honey."

"No, you don't!" His face reddened. It was so unusual for Luke to carry on that Laurie stood without speaking. "Why don't you like Daddy?"

Maddie's head perked up, and she headed back from the porch. Laurie's pulse raced with visions of broken glass, a shimmering knife blade, blood smeared all over the kitchen, horrible red words—last warning. What could she tell him? Your father does illegal things? And now he's crossed over to madness? How could she say, I need to protect you from the man you miss so much? "Luke, you don't understand. Some things are too big for little boys."

"I'm five."

She stooped down in front of him. "I'll call your daddy and see if he can come." That would tell her what she needed to know as well. Maybe they could talk it out, and Brian would call off the dogs he'd sent to frighten her. It seemed logical in the daylight.

"Call him now?"

Laurie shrugged. "Okay." She caught Luke's face between her palms and kissed his forehead. His pleasure seared her. How could he be so devoted to a man who hardly cared that he existed? They went inside, and Laurie shooed them to the bathroom to wash up while she checked the kitchen. It was dim with the corkboard over the window, but clean and empty. She expelled her breath and reached for the phone.

She hesitated only a minute before punching in the numbers. Gail answered. Laurie forced her voice to sound normal, the tone of a separated wife calling her estranged husband. "Hello, Gail. Is Brian home?" It was Saturday, after all.

"I'm sorry, Laurie, he's out of town."

She should have expected it. But the words sent that same plummeting thump inside her. "Do you know where?" Brian always left a forwarding number, though he was scarcely available on it.

"I'm sorry, I don't."

Laurie's mind clicked into excuse mode. He wouldn't need to leave it with Gail. She wasn't his family. "When do you expect him?"

"He didn't say."

Laurie sighed. By Gail's tone, Brian had painted her as the deserting wife and won full allegiance. But that didn't matter as much as Luke's disappointment. She could forget her hopeful sunlight solution to her own trouble. "Thank you." She hung up. It didn't prove Brian was in Montrose—he traveled all the time, gone more than home—but it proved he could be.

She opened her purse, took out the gun, and loaded it the way the clerk had shown her. Then she slipped it into the cabinet over the refrigerator, out of the children's reach, just as Luke bounced into the room.

"Did you ask him?"

She turned to her son. "Honey, Daddy's on a trip. I don't know when he'll be back."

Luke studied her face, his eyes darkening. Then he turned and ran out. His feet thumped up the stairs and his door slammed.

"Mommy!" Maddie ran into her arms, tears brimming.

"It's all right, baby. Luke's just sad."

Maddie started to cry, and Laurie sank to the floor, pulling her close and shedding tears of her own. She would have to go up to Luke, but how could she ease his terrible hurt? How could she help him understand what she couldn't fathom? Why had Brian done this to them? And was it somehow her fault?

Maddie was tired, crying just long enough to wear away the last of her resistance, before dozing off in Laurie's arms. Maybe she hadn't slept well at Mother's house. Big surprise. Laurie carried her up to her bed, looked at Luke's closed door, and decided to give him a little longer. He was one child who worked things through better on his own. Maybe that was a male characteristic.

She went back down and slid the contents of the envelope onto her kitchen table. One by one, she looked again at the drawings, mostly dated between her first- and fifth-grade years. They weren't all centered around her lost siblings, but none of them showed her with either parent. Some featured herself with any number of pets, none of which she'd ever had.

Her style was imaginative. She might have gone far with the right training. She read a cute story about a Christmas stocking, a fourth-grade effort. Nothing brilliant, but again the illustration was clever. Hadn't Mother realized she had talent? But artistic ability wasn't something they valued. Laurie laid the paper down.

Had she ever pleased them? Ever satisfied anyone? She closed her eyes, rubbed her temples with her fingertips. Luke had been given long enough. She stood up, looked down one more time at the scattering of pictures. Drawing a sharp breath, she jutted her chin. Wherever Luke and Maddie excelled—even if they didn't excel— whatever pleased them, made their little hearts sing, she would support it if it took every ounce of energy and every resource she had.

She went up to make peace with her son. Tapping at the door, she let herself in. He stood at the window, dropping the baseball into his glove, tipping it back into his hand, then dropping it again.

He turned to look over his shoulder. "It isn't you, Mommy."

"What do you mean, Luke?"

He looked down at the glove, then tipped it so that the ball rolled out onto the floor. It hit with a thud and rolled along the floorboard to the heating vent, where it wobbled to a stop. "Daddy doesn't want me."

She wanted to cry, knowing firsthand the pain of believing what he did. And a lie from her would change nothing. Children knew. They knew. She walked in and sat on the side of his bed. "Come here, Luke."

He came and stood between her knees.

She wrapped her hands around his waist, looked into his face. "Your daddy loves you more than anyone in the world." Except himself, and maybe that wasn't even his fault. He'd never been expected to consider anyone but himself, anything but his own needs and desires. "He just doesn't know how to do it very well. He would try harder if he could."

"I could help him."

Smiling, she stroked Luke's cheek. "If anyone can teach someone to love, it's you, sweetie. You taught me." She flicked the tip of his nose with her finger.

His eyes teared. "Why can't we try?"

She swallowed every one of the reasons that leapt to mind. "Maybe we can. Someday." For Luke's sake, if she believed it was best for the children, she would face even that. "But right now, Daddy's making some choices that mean we can't be with him."

"Like training camp?"

She shook her head. "No. Bad choices." She held a finger to his lips. "Please don't ask me to explain. Do you believe that I'm doing the best I can for us?"

He nodded.

"And you know I love you."

He reached around her neck and rested his head against her. "I love you too."

She closed her eyes against the tears that burned to the surface. She had wanted the perfect life for them. Perfect. Her mother's words chilled her, *"two perfect children."* No, she didn't want perfection. What then?

Cal reached into the jeep and slid the crate of clown paraphernalia off the seat. It was a sure bet no one in the department would take over that job. Well, that couldn't be helped. It wasn't his problem anymore. He wouldn't think about the sea of little faces that might not learn the message he'd tried so hard to get across. Someone else would have to teach them.

He started across the yard, saw Ray attacking Mildred's rugs with a broom. It was a toss-up whether the rugs hanging on the line or the broom was getting the worst of it as straw snapped and flew with each whap. Cal paused. "You might try that with a shovel, Ray. Packs a better wallop."

Ray stopped and looked at the broom bristles standing out like a bad hair day. Cissy would be hard-pressed to ferret out the dust bunnies with it after this beating. Ray turned it upside down. "I guess a shovel might work. What's all that?" He nodded toward the box Cal held.

"Clown gear. Puppets."

Ray grinned. "Is Rocky in there?"

Cal nodded. "Come see him sometime. He'll be rooming with me now."

"I will. Maybe I'll have him over for a cold one." Ray laughed.

"Better than he'll get at my place. He's already complaining."

Still laughing, Ray looked at the broom in his hand. "Guess I'll try the shovel."

"Better ditch that broom where Mildred won't see it."

Ray sobered. "You think?"

"Nah." Cal shook his head. "Just needs a little trim around the ears."

Ray looked up quizzically, then guffawed. "Yeah. Around the ears." He plucked off the worst of the broken straws.

Cal headed up to his room, stowed the crate on his kitchen table, and took a Coke from the refrigerator. Ray's mention of a cold one resonated inside. He popped open the soda with a *fiss* and a thin wisp of mist, hoping the caffeine would kill the craving. He chugged until he had to come up for air, but he still missed the bite and malt of a long-necked Budweiser.

A heavy step creaked up the stairs outside, Ray coming for Rocky already? But he opened to Reggie. Had the man divined his immediate struggle? Or did he intend to lay in as Rob had?

"Yo, Cal. I got a function I'd like to take you to."

"Function?" Cal pulled the wig from the crate. "Do I come in costume?"

Reggie grinned, and despite his best efforts, Cal couldn't help but return it.

"No. You just come as you are."

Cal's antennae went up. "Would this be a church function, Reggie?"

He nodded his big head. "Yup. And I got word you're supposed to be there."

"Let me guess. The big man, right?" Cal quirked an eyebrow.

"That's right. And when He speaks, His saints listen."

"Well, I'm no saint. Sorry to disappoint you." He reached into the crate and held out the jar of peanuts. "Help yourself."

Reggie pulled open the lid and a spring snake leapt out. Reggie flung it, both arms flailing, then scowled. "That one's so old, it's not funny."

"Wanna bet? Wish I had a Polaroid." Cal retrieved the snake.

"Ha, ha."

Cal stuffed the snake back into the jar. "What did you think of Laurie?"

"I thought she was lovely. 'Course, I prefer a little more fluff . . ."

"Did Rita say anything?" He glanced up, watched Reggie's face.

Reggie shook his head. "Mum's the word. You coming tonight?"

"If I do?"

This time Reggie swung his head with meaning. "Don't expect me to pump Dr. James. You want her to play, you gotta handle that yourself."

Cal expelled his breath. "All right, I'll come. But don't expect much."

"You don't know the Big Man if you can say that." Reggie

grinned, waved, and headed out the door. The stairs creaked and moaned as he descended.

Cal stared at the door. *No, Reg, I don't know the Big Man. And I can't say I want to.* He wiped his hands dry and shoved them into his pockets.

————

Four hours later, Reggie returned, and Cal met him at the base of the stairs. Banging his arms against the cold, Cal slid into the seat beside him. "You know, Reg, I'm only doing this because you're a friend. I slept through enough services as a kid."

"This isn't a service as such."

"What is it?"

"A prayer meeting."

"You didn't say anything about people laying hands and rolling in the aisle." He'd seen that on TV, rows of people laid out at the sweep of the evangelist's hand. No thanks.

Reggie laughed his deep, belly-rolling laugh. "Relax, bro. You're in the hands of the Master."

"That's what I'm afraid of." Cal dropped his head back against the seat. He should never have agreed to this.

Reggie pulled up to a small frame house with a couple of seedy willows at either side. Cal got out and trod the crumbly walkway reluctantly. Reggie hallooed at the door, then pulled it open and waved Cal in.

Cal stepped inside a room crammed with furniture—definite violation of fire codes. On one wall was posted the Ten Commandments. Across from that was the Twenty-third Psalm complete with pastoral scene. A bent and grizzled black man shuffled into the room from what Cal guessed was the kitchen.

"Brother Reginald," the man boomed with a voice larger than himself.

Oh boy. Here we go. Guess I'm Brother Calvert. Hallelujah.

"Brought a friend, Brother Lucas. This is Cal."

Cal shook the wrinkled hand. Did the bathroom have a window? Why hadn't he brought his ax? Four more people came to the door. All black, all large, three women and a young man.

"How you doin', bro?" Reggie spoke into his ear after introducing him.

"I feel a little pale."

Reggie laughed. "Don't worry. More whites are comin'."

A blond, pimply youth and an elderly woman made up the whites. Another half dozen African Americans made the ratio four to one. He felt conspicuous. He had expected to disappear into the back of a congregation, not sit like a specimen in a circle of the faithful. In spite of the cold outside, the room was getting plenty hot.

Brother Lucas stood and raised trembling hands. The others all got to their feet. Cal stood too. Beside him Reggie started to sing "Amazing Grace." His voice was deep and strong and perfectly on pitch. The rest of the group joined in. No instruments, no hymnals, just a circle of believers singing. As Cal looked around, it touched him somewhere deep.

They held nothing back, and when the song ended, many waved their arms and hollered in jubilation. That was a little much. One woman jumped up and down, and Cal watched with fascination the bobbing of her body parts. This was not church as he knew it. After a few more songs, Brother Lucas started to pray, or rather, he talked.

Cal watched his face smooth into a sublime expression. He spoke with a tenderness, an intimacy, an almost unworldly joy. And his words were simple. "Father God, I know you're here. You promised to be among us when we gather in your name. We thank you already, for what you mean to do tonight. There's not a one here who doesn't know you or won't come to. You called us by name."

Cal edged into the wall. He could guess their thoughts. Who among them didn't know the Lord? He felt naked and not too proud of his physique. Whereas in the natural realm his almost six-foot, lean, and muscled body was all right, it now felt like a new paper cover on a ratty textbook. He thought of things he'd said and done, things he hadn't thought of in years . . . and things he'd thought of all too recently.

He stole a glance around. All the eyes were closed, the mouths murmured "amen" and "thank you, Jesus." Beside him, Reggie's lips moved, but silently. Cal was an outsider, invited, but not included. That was okay with him. He'd know better next time.

Besides, what had he done that was so bad? Nothing worse than the other guys. Take Perry. He slept with a new woman every week. Rob had smoked a thing or two besides cigarettes. Frank . . . well, Frank did go to church every Sunday, but he could swear like a sailor when you riled him. They all had their faults. Why should he be any different?

He hadn't noticed everyone had taken their seats. He sat down in a listing armchair while Brother Lucas shared a text of scripture. Cal didn't hear much of it. He watched a small brown spider climb up the wall. He checked his watch.

Then he watched the drizzle bead on the windows and noticed the gaps where the aluminum window separated from the wall. A dampness, or at least the watermark of one, spread out from the corner over the wall. It looked like packing tape had been stuck there and shreds of it remained. Now others were talking.

"Aunt Mary's arthritis is better, praise Jesus. She wrote a whole letter this morning without pain."

"Thank you, Jesus."

"Amen."

"Hallelujah."

Cal startled when Reggie spoke up. "Smilin' Sal gets better and better. She's still not talking much, but every day has something to say."

"Oh, hallelujah. The Lord is faithful."

There was a pause, and Cal hoped and prayed—well not exactly—that they didn't expect him to say anything. He was relieved when they all stood up. They sang another song, then started hugging. The bobbing woman gave him an embrace he wouldn't soon forget. He sidled toward the door.

Reggie clapped his shoulder. "Ready?"

"Yeah." He waved halfheartedly to all the invitations to come on back again, then climbed into the truck with Reggie.

Reggie's grin was characteristically large. "Well?"

Cal shrugged. "It's not really my style, Reg. Nothing personal."

Reggie fired the engine. "That's practically the same thing I said the first time Brother Lucas asked me along."

"Yeah?"

"Took me two years to go back." He swung the truck into the street.

"Why did you?"

"Well, things got a little rough. I needed some serious power. Sunday religion wasn't enough to cover what was coming down."

Cal stared at him. "What was coming down?"

"When Suanne was three months pregnant, they found a malignancy. Uterine."

Cal winced.

"Yeah. Trouble was, they couldn't treat the cancer without losing the baby. She said no go. She wouldn't sacrifice the child."

"What happened?"

"I joined up with those people back there, and we begged God for a miracle."

"And?"

"The baby miscarried, and Suanne got treated. Full hysterectomy. She won't be having any more."

Cal shook his head. "And that made you keep going back?"

"It's not what happened to the situation." Reggie patted his chest. "It's what happened here."

Cal sensed what he meant. He'd felt it when Reggie started singing, he'd seen it on Brother Lucas's face. It made him want to run for the woods.

"Now, I could either gripe about us not ever having kids, or rejoice that Suanne was healed of the cancer. Things either make you better or make you worse."

No denying that.

"Having that group, and coming to know God personally, made me see the good side."

Cal nodded. Reggie had talked before about knowing God, talked like Jesus was his friend. Cal knew the jargon, had even sung the song in Bible school one year: *Jesus is your friend, He's the one next to you . . .*

"That group of people meets Wednesday and Saturday nights in prayer and thanksgiving, and I tell you what, they storm the gates of heaven. You might not have noticed tonight, but when your eyes are opened, then you'll see."

Cal glanced his way. Reggie wasn't shy in pointing out Cal's lacks.

"But you gotta know that prayer meeting's not the only place to find God. The Big Man doesn't limit himself to our smallness. If you got roots, start there."

Cal didn't answer. Roots. Did he have roots? Sure, but his roots connected him to the ground, to his home, to himself. His folks had been believers, but once he got old enough to resist, they hadn't made it an issue with him. They'd let him choose, and he'd done what any normal American youth would, given the freedom. Nothing.

Reggie pulled into the drive, and Annie came running, leaping for the car door.

She was as good an excuse as any to beat a hasty retreat, but Cal hesitated. "Look, Reggie, why did you ask me there tonight?"

"Like I said, I had a word. I don't ask why."

"Well, what reason would your experience tell you?"

Reggie rested his hands on the steering wheel and turned his head. His face was soft and serious. "That you're heading for tribulation, my man."

Cal shook his head. "Wish I hadn't asked." He pulled open the door and got out, more annoyed than he ought to be. Annie danced about. "Thanks, I guess." He waved, then headed for the stairs. Tribulation. As though he wasn't there already?

Inside he rubbed Annie down, then picked up the phone and called Rita James at home. "Well?"

"Well what?"

"What did you think of Laurie?"

"Don't set a woman up unless you're ready to be weighed in the same balance."

He could hear the stern exasperation in her voice. "Okay, so you held my tail to the fire. What did you learn?"

"If you want to know about Laurie, ask Laurie."

"She won't talk about it." He switched the receiver to his other ear.

"Do you?"

"Do I what?" He picked up a bread crust and tossed it to Annie.

"Talk about your problems."

Cal half laughed. "That's all I did for two months."

"I mean to Laurie." Rita's tone was indomitable.

"That's not what we're discussing." This was reminiscent of all the conversations he'd had with Laurie lately. How did they all get turned back on him?

"You have your defenses; she has hers."

Cal straddled a chair. "So she's hiding something?"

Rita laughed. "You're not going to catch me up, Cal. You're smart, but not that smart."

"Come on, Rita. If Laurie's in trouble—"

"Then she has the right to choose her own help, her own way of dealing with it."

Cal leaned against the wall, his exasperation growing. "Will you talk to her?"

"She hasn't asked me."

Cal slammed his palm on his thigh. "What about all those days I didn't want to talk?"

"That was different."

"How?" he snapped.

"You were a patient."

Cal swallowed the tightening in his throat. "I hate that word." He hung up.

Whistling for Annie, he stalked out to the woods. The night was deep and under the trees, deeper. And it was cold. Damp cold. The drizzle had stopped, but his breath came white and chilled his face as he walked. Pressing his way through the brush, he made out the lights of Fred's farmhouse, then turned south. There were parts of these woods even he didn't know. He struck out for new ground, wanting to put his mind on something else, someone else. The darkness took form around him.

Annie perked up her ears, looking to the right. He'd heard the snap, too, but she dropped her head and continued prancing at his side. Her leg troubled her only when they went too far, too fast, as they were in danger of doing tonight in his current mood. He was sweating inside his light jacket, not a good sign. If the shakes started, he'd begin to crave the bottle.

Then he thought of the old drunk lying in the street and shook his head. Maybe that sight would keep him from the slide. Frank's Southern Comfort had not made him want more, had not even satisfied. It wasn't a drink he wanted. It was . . . what? To stop feeling so hollow?

"It's what happened here—" and Reggie's hand on his heart. Was Cal missing something big, something crucial to his makeup? Did he need God to change his focus, put together the pieces he kept trying to fix? Rita didn't think so. She said he had it inside him to get over it all. Let go of the guilt. Reggie said let go and let God. Cal didn't know how to do either.

Changing direction again, he pressed through a stand of birch and dropped to the bottom of a gully. This he followed east until he heard Kriley Creek at an intersecting cut. Its song was clear yet subdued as it ran unconcerned toward Miller Pond. May as well follow the creek back home. Annie would be tiring. He reached a hand to her head and got a cold, wet nose in his palm.

After another tramp, he left the creek and passed through the last of the woods to Mildred's yard, the house, shed, and vehicles ghostly lumps in the darkness. Annie's ears perked, no doubt sensing home and hoping for a treat. She nudged his hand, then paused, staring into the yard. Cal kept on. If she smelled a varmint and wanted some fun, he only hoped she wouldn't wake Mildred.

He passed the shed and jerked his head at a motion beside him. A dark form separated from the shadow and knocked him sprawling with something hard between the shoulder blades. Annie bayed, dodging in and out, teeth bared, as the man-shaped silhouette raised a bat. Cal glimpsed the head covered in a ski mask, then rolled, catching the blow in his shoulder. He cried out as his arm went numb for a second, then screamed pain down to his fingers. He was too slow to avoid the next swing, which caught him just below the last one.

"Keep away from Laurie, jerk." The man raised the bat again, but Annie took his leg between her teeth. Bellowing, he kicked her free, then ran behind the shed and into the darkness.

Cal dragged himself to his knees, cradling the injured arm with his other. Annie whined, licked his face, and nudged him with her nose. "Thank you, girl." He felt her for injury, but apart from shaking, she seemed fine. "Guess you can tell when it's the real thing." He worked himself to his feet, wincing.

13

FOR WHAT IS YOUR LIFE? IT IS EVEN A

VAPOUR, THAT APPEARETH FOR A LITTLE TIME,

AND THEN VANISHETH AWAY.

James 4:14 KJV

C AL STEPPED GINGERLY TOWARD THE HOUSE, care-
ful not to stumble or trip. A sound caught him up short, and
he tensed. He was pretty worthless with his right arm out of com-
mission, but he wouldn't be taken by surprise again. He reached the
outside stairs just as a light blared on and Mildred pulled open the
door, shotgun primed.

"It's me, Mildred!"

"What's all the noise? You're staggering like a drunk."

Even sober. And Mildred didn't mince her words.

"I met with a bat."

"What kind?"

"The baseball kind."

She lowered the gun. "You can't stay away from trouble to save
your life."

"I didn't look for it. It found me."

He yelled when she grabbed his arm and pulled him inside.

"Where's the damage?"

"About where you're gripping."

Cissy shuffled up, gasping when Mildred pulled his shirt open to

185

reveal the purple welts and swelling joint. "Oh my." Her hands flew to her mouth. "Oh my."

Mildred scowled. "Get an ice pack, Cissy, and stop 'oh my-ing.' It's probably not as bad as it looks."

"It's as bad as it feels." He submitted to Mildred's inspection and probing.

Cissy rushed back with a blue plastic bag. He jumped when Mildred applied it.

"It's a gel pack. Doc Klein gave it to me for my knee when it swells." She shifted the pack on his shoulder.

"I'll take it from here, Mildred." He stood up, holding the pack in place.

"Did you get a look at him?" Mildred eased the shirt over the ice.

"He was masked."

"Figures." Mildred looked like that was his fault. "Likely took you for a prowler out tramping the woods in the dark."

Cal knew better. Only one person would warn him off of Laurie. "Thanks for the ice."

"You better have that looked at."

He nodded and Annie jumped up. "Come on, girl."

"Who would want to hurt him?" Cissy whispered as Cal climbed the inside stairs. He didn't hear Mildred's words, but he could imagine her reply.

He sank onto his bed, still holding the ice in place. It did little to alleviate the pain, but if it kept the swelling down, the healing would go better. What was going on? If he hadn't been so riled by his conversation with Rita, he might have paid better attention. Then again, he might not have. He wasn't used to looking over his shoulder. Was Laurie? If so, she hadn't admitted it. She'd been single-mindedly evasive. Was he a pawn in some game she played with her senator's-son ex-husband? Or was she in more trouble than he knew?

He considered the facts. One, the black Firebird running him off the road after seeing her broken window. Two, the phone call after Laurie's trip to the station. And now strike three. Was it her presence at the poker game last night? Had someone watched them? Out in the sticks he didn't worry too much about closing the curtains. And he *had* come on to Laurie, though it hadn't been his intention. Brian would have caught an eyeful in those moments after the others left. It wouldn't be the first time a man harassed his ex-wife when she tried to get close to someone new.

Cal gingerly moved his shoulder. Was his attacker Laurie's ex-husband? If so, did he have some history of aberrant behavior? Domestic violence? Was that what Laurie wouldn't talk about? That, too, was common enough, and Laurie was just the sort to fall into it. Well, there was only one place to learn the truth.

Throwing on his coat, he went down to the jeep and slid in. With his left hand, he put it in gear and spun the wheel. For some reason he saw Reggie's face in his mind. Tribulation. Maybe the Big Man knew what was going down, but Cal could only guess.

It took Laurie forever to come to the door. Cal noted the new dead bolt as he stood there, shoulder throbbing. It was both reassuring and troubling. She'd taken measures to protect herself, and that was good. But why had she needed to?

"Who is it?" Her voice sounded shaky.

"Cal."

The lock slid, and the door opened. Cal looked into Laurie's face. Fear and relief mingled there, and Cal's heart thumped when he glimpsed the butt of a handgun in her robe pocket. She was in trouble. He knew it with every fiber. And whether she liked it or not, he was going to get her out of it.

She crossed her arms against her chest. "Cal, what are you doing here? It's eleven-thirty."

He pushed past her and checked the doors at the back of the house. She'd added keyed dead bolts there, too. He caught her arm as he passed back and pulled her along with him. "We need to talk." He stopped at the faded sleeper couch and sat on the top edge, then peeled back his coat and shirt and bared his shoulder.

She gasped. "What happened?"

"My guess is Brian doesn't want me seeing you."

She stared. "That's crazy."

"Someone came at me with a baseball bat."

"That doesn't mean anything." She was evading. It was there in her eyes and the tone of her voice. "Ball players aren't the only ones who wield bats."

"He had a major-league swing."

She closed her eyes.

"He told me to keep away from you, Laurie."

She shook her head.

Cal grabbed her arms, wincing with the motion. "I want to help." Pulling her close with his one good arm, he kissed her mouth, kissed her hard and long. Not his intention again, but she melted against him, shaking. She had to let him in, trust him enough to tell the truth, to let him help. He kissed her again, slowly, then cupped her cheek in his hand. "I love you, Laurie. I always have."

He wasn't sure what answer he expected, but not what he got. "Well, don't." She pushed him away.

"Yeah, right." Not loving her was like never drawing oxygen again.

"I mean it, Cal. Go now, and don't come back." Her voice shook.

Why was she pushing him away? Did she think he couldn't handle it? That he'd freak out and fall apart? He'd never felt so strong and determined. Nothing would scare him off, no attacks in the night, no accusing phone calls. "Does Brian own a black Firebird?"

Shaking her head, Laurie stalked to the wall and back, the tension defining her features sharply. His airbrushed image of her wavered. There was something hard inside. He didn't care. He'd break through that too. "Who did you expect at the door tonight? Why do you have a gun?"

"Stop it, Cal."

Stop trying to protect the woman he loved? Stop trying to show her she wasn't alone, that together they'd make it right? "Laurie, I know you're in trouble."

She turned on him. "Just stay away from me, okay?" She pulled the coat back over his shoulder and pushed him toward the door.

"Is he abusive? Does he hit you? Is that why you left?"

"No." She reached for the knob.

With his left arm, he held the door shut. "Why won't you let me help?"

"Because you can't." She pressed back into the wall, looking trapped and frightened. As much an admission as he was likely to get. Was it pride? Did she think he'd judge her? Didn't she know that wasn't his way?

He cornered her with his arms. "That's why you came back here. To let me help."

"I was wrong." A vein stood out in her temple.

"If your ex—"

"He's not my ex."

Cal stood still. He met her eyes and saw there shame and fear and confusion. "What?"

"We're not divorced."

"But you said . . ."

She ducked under his arm and stepped away. "I never said it. You just assumed."

Cal's blood rushed. "You never said otherwise. You let me think—" He clenched his hands. She'd led him on, not in words, but she'd known how he would be, and she'd allowed it. Encouraged it. Why? To make her husband jealous? "No wonder he came for me with a bat! I'd have done the same in his place!"

Tears started in her eyes, but it didn't move him. He'd pursued, kissed, and held another man's wife? He'd held illusions of them together, working out their differences, caring and sharing love until death did them part. She had used him. Just as Rob said. She had come back and made a fool of him. After all, fool was only one step away from clown.

Well, he'd wanted the truth and gotten it. He swallowed the bitter taste in his mouth. What he'd said was true also. He loved her with the same mind-numbing grip he'd felt the first time he saw her. And it still didn't matter. He yanked open the door and left.

Driving home, he kept his eyes peeled for any motion, any vehicle, anything out of the ordinary. He was as pressurized as a discharge port ready to blow. But now he knew that if Brian came after him, he'd be justified. Laurie was still his wife.

Laurie pressed her back to the door, shaking. The terror she'd felt, wakening to the banging on her door, her rush to the kitchen for the gun. Then seeing Cal wounded . . . it was all she could do not to scream. But the children, her children were upstairs sleeping, safe, oblivious, and she had to keep them that way.

What other choice did she have? A man with a bat? A major-league swing? She pressed her hand to her eyes. Would Brian go after Cal? Why? To keep her unprotected? No cops, he'd said. Cal wasn't a cop. But she had looked to him for help, for safety.

Why wouldn't Brian just confront her face-to-face? What was this terror game? And now she had lost Cal. Of course he was furious. She'd known he would be. She had done that herself, keeping the truth from him at the start. Why hadn't she told him everything? Before old feelings had gotten in the way, before he was injured.

She pictured his bruised and swelling arm. Brian had struck him? Added violence now to his behaviors? She didn't want to believe it. They'd been married six years, and she thought—she *had* thought— she knew him. He'd been caustic and threatening, even malicious, but never physically violent.

Maybe it wasn't Brian, maybe . . . *Stop making excuses!* She had to face reality. Did she know the real Brian Prelane? She hadn't known he used cocaine, certainly hadn't known he flew it across international borders. He could be some drug lord for all she knew. He could be a killer.

Her knees trembled. His note had said no cops or she'd lose the kids. Could he take the children to some foreign country and leave them there? She would never know where. She gripped the gun in the pocket of her robe. What should she do? What *could* she do?

What if she'd told Cal it was Brian. Asked him to help her. She couldn't. If Brian could attack him with a bat . . . *"He told me to keep away from you."* That was Brian loud and clear. She didn't want Cal hurt by her mistakes. She brought one hand up and pressed it to her face. No, she hadn't wanted him hurt, but it seemed that was all she did to Cal Morrison.

She should never have gotten close again. Laurie knew he wouldn't accept friendship. And neither had she. It had taken everything in her to separate from Cal's embrace. And more than that, to tell him the truth. But now he knew. And he despised her. He who valued faithfulness, who embodied it. That's why she'd kept silent, let him believe . . . The guilt was hers. Just as it was before. Cal loved her. And she wasn't capable of love.

———————

Cal leaned on the doorjamb of Sergeant Danson's office. He'd slept poorly, when he slept at all, and the last thing he wanted was an audience with Chuck Danson, but the early morning phone call had demanded it. One didn't exactly tell Danson you had better things to do. And in truth he was sick of spinning his wheels, trying to make sense of things and failing. Laurie had lied to him. Maybe not in her words, but in her actions.

She had used him. Yes, she had said she wanted to be friends, and *he* was the one who pushed that limit. But he wouldn't have if she'd told him the truth. Her being married would have changed every-thing. It did change everything.

Cal frowned. "You wanted to see me?"

The sergeant took in the homemade sling. Cal had decided against professional treatment. It might cause too many questions since it was obviously a battering wound. He knew to keep it immo-bile, and unless there was a fracture, that would be sufficient.

"Another run-in with the Firebird?"

"No." Cal didn't explain further.

Danson held him in a steely glare, then looked down at the papers on his desk. "Took a while, but we got an I.D. on that hit-and-run."

"Driver or victim?"

"Victim. Flip Casey."

"Flip Casey."

"And that's his legal name. Or was." Danson stood and came around the desk. "Took some time for anyone to notice him missing. It was the bartender at the Blue Note who finally did."

Danson tapped his pen against the edge of the desk. "I sent the body to the morgue. Besides his name and address, there's not much more to know. He lived alone, mainly drank his meals either at the Blue Note or on the street, and talked sports. Hardly knew what day it was, but he had a mind like a trap for any sports trivia. Folks at the bar thought he'd make his million one day on one of those game shows."

Cal shook his head.

"Most valuable thing we found in his shack was an autographed Mickey Mantle trading card."

Cal considered that. "So what do you figure?"

Danson clicked the end of his pen against the wood. "Probably drank himself past the point of no return and never saw the car coming."

"What was he doing out there?"

"God only knows." *Click, click.* The pen point jumped out and vanished, jumped and vanished. "You got anything on that Firebird?"

"Why would I?"

"I thought maybe you had some personal connection . . ." Danson eyed him.

"If I do, it's one I don't know about." Not a lie—he knew nothing for sure, and anything he suspected would show him for the idiot he was.

Danson drew a long breath. "Well, I'll expect to hear—"

"Yeah, I know. But I'm not officially involved anymore."

"So I heard. I also heard Frank never accepted your resignation. As far as he's concerned, you're still on the books."

That was news. "We'll see how long I draw a paycheck. Not even Frank can pay me for nothing."

Danson shook his head. "What is it with you, Morrison?"

Cal stuffed his free hand into his pocket and slacked a knee, the bad-boy stance Danson took as rebellion. He didn't answer.

"I'll have my eye on you."

What else was new? Cal nodded without comment. "See you around." He walked from the office past dispatch, waved to Frieda, and kept going. What did he know anyway? A glimpse of a black car, a crank call, and a masked attack. The sergeant was a practical man with a healthy disdain for lunatics, and already Cal suspected Danson put him in that category. If he started crying wolf on Laurie's ex— Laurie's husband, in present tense—Danson would commit him again.

And he was sure not going to do Danson's legwork for him. He was through with the department, through with that hit-and-run, and through with Laurie. He went out to the street, sucking in the frozen air, then climbed into the jeep and drove home. Leaping from the jeep, he found Ray puttering in the garage. "Get your pole, Ray. Let's go fishin'."

Ray grinned, fetched his old-fashioned fishing pole, probably Mildred's grandfather's, from the look of it. Cal ran up for his own pole and tackle, then whistled to Annie, and they walked together to the pond, where Ray dragged a huge log over for them to sit on. It was good to have Herculean friends.

"Nice work," Cal told him and sat down. He baited his hook. "Mind casting for me?"

Ray took Cal's pole and sent the hook out into the water. "What'd you do to your arm?"

"Banged up the shoulder some." If Mildred and Cissy had kept mum, he saw no reason to worry Ray with prowlers in the yard. After all, the attack had been personal and posed no threat to anyone but him. Cal took the pole back and willed the tension away. He could think of nothing if he just tried hard enough.

Ray cracked sunflower seeds between his teeth and spit the hulls on the ground. The sky hung low, a milky mass that matched the gunmetal water. Nothing was biting. Nothing cared. Cal blew on his gloved fingers. "Got anything going these days?"

Ray turned. "Like what?"

"Like . . . work."

Ray shook his head. "Nah. I helped Fred with a tractor last week. He paid me good."

"You do good work." Cal shifted his seat on the log.

"Yeah?"

"Yeah."

Ray looked at him as though making sure he really meant it, then smiled. "Say, Cal, you know any women who might . . . like to go out sometime?"

Cal shook his head, laughing. "I'm as bad on my luck there as you, right now."

"You got Laurie." Ray's eyes could have been those of a ten-year-old.

His words sank in and bored a hole right through him. *No, Ray, I do not have Laurie.* Cal shook his head. No point telling him the crazy ins and outs of it all. He looked out over the pond, the water dull and unattractive. "You ever wonder what it looks like to the fish looking out? What do they do under there all year?"

Ray shrugged. "I don't know."

"Well, there's something for you to chew on."

"Yeah. I think a lot about things."

"Like what?"

He hunched his shoulders and played with his line. "Like why people are good at some things and not at others. And why some people are good at lots of things and some . . ." He shrugged.

"You know, Ray, you have a lot going for you."

"Yeah?"

"Yeah. I mean, Cissy and Mildred are just crazy about you. I bet you were always their favorite nephew."

Ray grinned, nodding.

"And you get to live in this great place, go fishing with me, work with Fred . . . You just need to see the good things."

"My mother used to say that."

"Isn't it amazing how smart mothers turn out to be after all?"

Ray laughed as though it was the greatest joke. Then he sobered. "You're a good friend, Cal. I don't have too many friends."

"It's not about numbers, Ray. Just being real with the ones you have." Cal made a note to include him more often. Standing, he pulled his line from the water. "That does it for me."

"You didn't catch anything."

"Nope. But that's not always what matters."

"It's not?"

"Nope." Cal gathered his things and started back for the house, hoping Ray wouldn't sit there until he froze. A thirty-one-degree day was not the time to lose oneself on the banks of Miller's Pond. Glancing back, he called, "Don't stay long, Ray. It's too cold."

Ray nodded and waved. Annie rode Cal's heels as he walked, and he reached to stroke her head. If someone came to claim her now, they'd have to fight him to the death. Snow flecked the air as he walked, not quite able to make up its mind to fall for real.

Digging for his keys, he got into the jeep and drove across town, as Danson had known he would, to a neighborhood he rarely visited.

He sauntered into the Blue Note and ordered an O'Douls. That alone should mark him, drinking a non-alcoholic beer in a blue-collar bar. Rita would be proud.

The place was rough even by his standards, but he could sense the camaraderie in the joined stares that turned his way. A handful of men circled the pitted, scuffed pool table, and a corner TV spit out the hockey game. The walls were the color of greenish sludge, but not much of them showed around the hodgepodge of neon signs and booze posters, some dating back to his dad's time—and not for nostalgia, but because they'd been added to and not replaced.

He sipped through the foam on his beer and waited while the bartender served rotgut to a man twice Cal's size with tree limbs for arms. The man glanced his way, then took the stool beside him. "Haven't seen you before."

"Nope."

The man downed his shot and chased it with half a beer. "Aren't from this end, are you?"

"No."

"There's a surprise." The man laughed, revealing the space for an incisor and eyetooth. Cal guessed the tooth fairy hadn't rewarded their loss.

"So what do you do, mister?"

"Magic."

"What?" He pressed his hammy palm to the bar.

"Magic." Cal pulled a deck of cards from his pocket and shuffled. "You have a name?"

"Brady. You?"

"Cal." He fanned the deck face up for Brady to see, then flipped it over and shuffled again. "Cut the deck, Brady."

Brady cut.

"Now take a look at that top card. Got it?"

"Yeah, I got it."

Cal put the deck together and fanned it toward Brady. "Okay, slip it in anywhere." He slid the deck closed and laid it on the bar, then swigged his drink. "You a gambling man, Brady?"

Brady snorted. "I might be."

"Ten bucks says I know your card without looking."

Brady sat a moment. "You're gonna tell me my card without looking in the deck?"

"That's right."

Brady reached into his pocket and unrolled a ten-dollar bill. "Let's see yours."

Cal pulled a ten from his wallet.

"Okay, what's my card?"

Cal clapped him on the shoulder. "You're a big guy, Brady. Got some meat on your bones."

"So?"

"So . . ." Cal reached into Brady's collar and brought out the card, laying it face up on the bar. "That it?"

Brady blew through his lips and swore, then slid his ten Cal's way with a grin. "But now I'll be watching you."

"You come here a lot?"

"Every day."

"Then you knew Flip Casey."

Brady sobered. "Everyone knew Flip." He nodded to the bartender who'd joined them. "This is Burt. He's the one told the sergeant something wasn't right. Flip hadn't missed a night in years."

Burt placed a second fake beer before him. "How do you know Flip?"

"I was the EMT on the scene."

Brady reevaluated him, then shook his head. "Heck of a way to go."

"It was quick." Cal gulped the drink. "Any idea why he was out there?"

Brady shook his head. "Never knew him to leave the neighborhood. You, Burt?"

"He didn't have a car. Didn't even own a bicycle."

Cal straightened. "Did you see him with anyone new? Someone you didn't recognize?"

Brady squinted. "You think he was killed on purpose?"

"No. As far as I can tell it was a hit-and-run. But I can't figure what he was doing out there."

Brady eyed Burt, who shrugged. "He was a crazy old coot, but we miss him around here. He could tell a tale."

Brady grinned. "Like the one on how he got his name. Mother asks what should we name him? His dad says, I don't know, flip a coin. Mother says, I ain't namin' him heads or tails, so his dad said, name him Flip."

Cal laughed, wishing he'd known the old man before he found him in the ditch.

Burt swished Brady's shot glass in the wash water just behind the bar. "He could pull your leg into tomorrow."

"Kinda like you." Brady slammed his palm into Cal's shoulder.

"Aah!" The pain screamed through him. He'd removed the sling before going in, and now seriously wished he hadn't.

Brady frowned at his reaction, no doubt taking him for a light-weight.

"Had a run-in with a baseball bat." He gritted his teeth, gripped the shoulder, and willed the pain into a small part of his brain.

"Something to do with Flip?"

"I don't know. Have you seen a black Firebird around?"

Brady narrowed his eyes and nodded. "A short time back. Parked across the street there." He waved out through the front window. "That's a car you don't see much around here."

The pain was diminishing, and Cal rotated his arm. He'd have to see the doctor. Probably should have already, but he didn't want to do any more explaining. "Flip mention any baseball players?"

Both men laughed. "One or two, maybe." Brady swallowed the rest of his beer and turned. "Flip ever talk about anything else, Burt?"

"Oh, football, hockey, basketball—"

Cal interrupted, "I mean recently. Did he mention meeting a ball player?"

Brady turned. "The man with the bat?"

"Maybe."

Burt shook his head. "I don't know. But I guarantee you, if a ball player came in sight, Flip'd know him."

"Minor leagues?"

"I don't know about that. Maybe."

"Did he follow the Padres?"

"He followed everyone, sat here from open to close and watched everything that came in on satellite. Mind like a trap for faces and stats."

Cal tossed both tens on the bar and stood. "Can you tell me where he lived?"

Burt leaned both hands on the bar. "I let him stay in my shed out back, end of the alley. It's not much of a place, but better than what he had, which was zilch."

Cal glanced toward the back door.

"You can look if you want. Won't find much. Police didn't."

"Thanks."

Cal pulled his collar up around his chilled neck as he made his way between the sooty brick buildings. At the end of the alley, he found the shed. He reached a knuckle to the door, then realized no one would answer his knock. He tried the knob, and the door all but fell open.

He went in. Against the back wall stood an army surplus cot with what looked like a packing blanket crumpled at one end. Some small comfort for a drunken man to sink into. Cal rubbed his chin and surveyed the rest of the room: a camp stove propped up on one leg and a brick looked as though it could burn down the whole place, a Formica-topped table yellowed with age, no latrine or sink. Flip must have used the Blue Note's or the alley.

Cal toed a pile of rubbish along the wall. He doubted a forensics team had been sent in. No one had any reason to suspect foul play. Flip was a worn-out drunk who got careless.

Cal kicked aside a bottle of Beam and a rotting newspaper. It wasn't the sports page, and he guessed it had served a different purpose than reading. Warmth, maybe. He slid his foot through the rest of the debris, then glanced around the room again. He didn't know what he had expected to find. Brian Prelane's calling card?

He strode back to the jeep and went home. The comfortable clutter of his own place surrounded him, but he was suddenly aware of the loneliness. He, like Ray, like Flip—each in his own little world. Islands of nothingness. He sank into the recliner.

At least if he or Ray were wiped out, there would be people who missed them. Then again, the men at the Blue Note missed Flip. Maybe everyone had someone, even if it wasn't anyone important.

He was tired. His shoulder ached. Brady's pounding hadn't done it any good. Leaning his head back into the chair, he probed the shoulder. It was sore all right, but not as bad as it might have been. He closed his eyes. The warm drowsiness was a welcome succor, and he sank into it.

Then he was crawling on his belly, the effort wearing him out. He could hardly drag himself across the floor, his movements slow and exaggerated as though he were weighed down with lead sleeves and pant legs. His breath was tight, strained, but no, he was keeping it shallow on purpose, stretching the air.

Where were they? He knew they were there. But he couldn't see through the smoke. He wished he had his ax handle to reach farther, but he'd lost it somewhere. Or left it behind. With his left hand he pulled out more empty hose. It caught, and he tugged against it, but no more came. He'd reached its limit. He could go no further.

But he had to. He saw them now, huddled together under the chairs, Laurie and Luke and Maddie. The smoke swirled around them in black gusts. Luke and Maddie were crying, but Laurie just sat there, looking away. If she was aware of him, she didn't show it.

He tried to call but had no voice. He yanked again on the hose, but it didn't give. All his training said don't let go. His hand felt frozen to the nozzle. He sensed the air in his SCBA thinning. He was running out of time. He called again, this time forcing the sound from his lips. Laurie didn't turn.

Wrenching his hand from the hose, his lifeline, his way out of the darkness, he stood, lunged forward toward them, calling, then dropped to his knees. Horror spread through his chest as the charcoal air took on the shades of hell, the ghastly orange glow in the moment before the room reached ignition temperature. Flashover. *No!* Their screams reached him piercingly clear. He only hoped this time he wouldn't be blown free.

Cal opened his eyes, sweat stinging them as he blinked at the room. His chest was heaving, his hands clenched and damp. He didn't move, other than to scan the space around him. The sun had come out from the clouds, and the rays slanted across the room. Not much time had passed, but he felt as sluggish as Rip Van Winkle.

His throat ached with emotion, but he still didn't move. His limbs were useless weights hanging from his body. His mind was dull, damaged. He was glad Laurie was lost to him. What good was he to her and her kids? What good was he to anyone?

14

WHAT A MAN IS ASHAMED OF IS

ALWAYS AT BOTTOM HIMSELF; AND HE IS ASHAMED

OF HIMSELF AT BOTTOM ALWAYS FOR BEING AFRAID.

R. G. Collingwood

CAL STOOD UNDER THE SHOWER in the late afternoon, letting the water wash away the residue of sweat and fear. This latest episode had left him stiff and shaky. And tired. Tired of it all. Rita had recommended the clown act. *"Do something positive to counteract the guilt."*

And together with Frank they'd brainstormed Spanner the Clown as a training tool for fire safety at the schools and community events. It was valid. Cal had to believe that. Making kids fire-smart had value. The inspections had value, and the training of the volunteers. But it didn't change things for him.

He rubbed his hand through his wet hair and turned off the water, angry and frustrated. He couldn't protect himself from every possible scenario, couldn't stop his own subconscious thoughts. There was only one way to kick this thing—and that was in the teeth.

He toweled his head and dressed without shaving. With a pat to Annie's neck, he grabbed his jacket and went out. The jeep fired sluggishly in the cold, but he was too worked up to let it warm for long. He put it in gear and drove to the station.

Frank was in his office and looked up, brows raised, when Cal walked in. The gum he was chewing to keep from wanting a cigarette filled his cheek like a small animal. He laced his fingers and leaned forward in the chair but didn't speak.

Cal came to a stop before him without the normal greeting, just, "Put me on the line." He saw his words hit home, though Frank neither whooped nor laughed.

"Active when?

"Just fit me in the rotation."

Frank leaned sideways to see the clipboard. "That'd be Thursday."

"Fine." Cal shoved his hands into his pockets and looked around the office. His uniform would be in the locker downstairs where he'd left it. But this time he wouldn't wear a clown suit over it. The only thing he'd add would be fire protection gear. He turned to go.

"Cal?"

He looked back over his shoulder.

"Welcome back." Frank showed the gap between his front teeth.

Cal smiled in return, but it was a little like smiling down a freight train with your ankles chained to the rails. He went out, sucking in the winter air with purpose. It was the right thing. It had to be. Hiding behind a clown face hadn't helped. Maybe suiting up in turnout gear would. At any rate, he didn't know what else to do.

He got into his jeep and drove. Though he'd carried the address in his wallet and had an open invitation since leaving the psychiatric center, Cal hadn't seen Reggie's house until he pulled up in front of it. Modest. That's what he'd call it in lieu of less tactful terms. It was near the place they'd met for the prayer meeting and pretty much on a par with it, though he imagined Reggie could do much better with what he earned at the center and Suanne's income as well.

He climbed out of the jeep and leaned against it. Did he want to do this? Before he could climb back in, Reggie caught sight of him from the window and waved. Cal pocketed the keys and headed up the walk, parallel planks over wood mulch. He halted at the stoop to make way for the aluminum screen door to swing open.

Reggie held it there with one muscled arm for Cal to enter. "Throw another chop on, Suanne. We got company."

Cal stopped just inside and looked at the Coca-Cola clock on the wall. "I didn't know it was suppertime. My body clock's messed up."

He knew Reggie would understand. Post-traumatic stress wreaked
havoc with the sleep cycles.

"No problem. There's always room for more."

"I don't want to interrupt. We can talk another time." Cal leaned
toward the door.

Reggie's hand came down on his shoulder, his sore shoulder.
"Bro, I've been expectin' you."

"You have?" Cal ignored the pain. "What, you got a memo from
the Big Man?"

Reggie laughed. "Not this time. I just surmised you'd be wantin'
to talk."

"You surmised . . ."

"Frank called Rita, Rita called me. Said you went back on active
duty."

Cal slacked his hip. "Already? I just left there."

Reggie grinned.

For the first time, Cal resisted. "Should I hire a billboard, let the
whole town know?"

"Nah." Reggie shrugged. "They already know."

Cal dropped his chin to his chest and forked his fingers through
his hair, leaving it standing like newly mown hay.

"Well, come on in and close the door." Suanne swung her hefty
arm at them. "You're letting out the heat."

Reggie closed the door obediently. "Suanne, honey, this is Cal
Morrison. Cal, my angel wife."

She was a plump, saucy sort of angel with red pouty lips and
knowing eyes. "Well, take off your coat, honey, and stay awhile. You
like pork chops?"

Cal nodded. "Yes, ma'am, I do."

"That's good, cuz you're gettin' one." She sashayed back into the
kitchen.

"Isn't she a dream?" Reggie's eyes were locked onto the space
she'd just vacated.

Cal studied him a moment, a pang starting inside. "How long
have you been married?"

"Fourteen years."

And their affection was tangible. "You're a lucky man, Reg."

"Not lucky; blessed. And I thank God every day for that woman."

Cal looked around the room, furnished with Herculon couch and recliner, not unlike his own. The bookshelf looked like the devotional end cap at the grocery store. The paneled wall had one oil print landscape in a cheap wood frame, and an old Magnavox TV with rabbit ears stood in the corner. But the place was clean and tidy.

"Come and sit, bro. Suanne'll call when it's time to set the table. That's my job. That and the dishes. You can help with both."

Cal took a place on the couch, and the recliner conformed to Reggie's bulk.

"So, now, what's on your mind?"

Cal sent him a wry smile. "I figured you'd tell me. The way news travels, you must know more than I do."

"What I know is you've gone back active."

"And what does Dr. James think of that?" Cal rubbed his palm along the Herculon arm.

"She didn't say. Only if I talked to you, to have you call. She wants to know you're doing things in the right order."

"My forte?"

Reggie smiled. "So why are you back?" He wasted neither time nor words.

"Running away didn't help. Maybe facing it will."

Reggie shook his head. "Only one way to change things. Put your trust in God."

Cal wasn't surprised. Maybe he'd come to hear that. At any rate he'd expected it. "I have to do it on my own, Reg."

"You remind me of someone."

"Who?"

Reggie grinned. "The Apostle Paul. Yessir. It took a major wallop to get his attention, bro."

"The Apostle Paul."

"You see he was on the road to Damascus . . ."

Cal listened, half polite, half interested. Actually more than half interested. Reggie was a natural raconteur, but it was more than that. Something in Cal wanted to hear, wanted to know what power Reggie had found that changed him. Right now, Cal would change into white mice if it would make a difference.

───────

Laurie was still smiling from the tickle time with Luke and Maddie as she walked downstairs. Nothing eased her heart so much as the unrestrained laughter of her children. She'd even allowed them to pummel her with the pillows before tucking them in and sharing enough kisses to get them all through the night.

It sapped her deepest reserves to keep up the front for her children, to not let them see the toll fear and grief were taking. She had called Mother six times through the day to make sure the children were all right. It would be so easy for Brian to go there, to take them and vanish, though she suspected his threat was more to control and torment her than any real desire to take his children.

Mother had grown suspicious. *"Is something wrong?"* What could be wrong in her mother's fantasy world of perfect husband, perfect life? *"I just miss them today."* Yes, she'd lied. She couldn't shatter Mother's dream. Her marrying Brian was the only thing Mother had wholeheartedly approved, the only time Laurie had felt truly accepted by both her parents. She had arrived. In spite of her faults, her deficiencies, she'd actually made them proud.

Her throat ached. It was all an illusion, but one she clung to even now. She'd lost Cal, driven him away. Maybe she should try to reach Brian, apologize for her stupidity, her pettiness. Maybe she shouldn't have cared that he chose a little excitement, illegal and immoral though it was. He was her husband. Isn't that how Cal saw it too? And God?

She had left God out of her decision to marry, run from Him as she had from Cal. Like a cat after a glittering bauble, she would topple the tree to get it. And when she landed with shattered glass ornaments and tangled wires, there was no one to blame but herself. If it were only herself, she might have stayed in the destruction. She deserved it.

But there was Luke and Maddie. What if they had found the cocaine? What if as they grew, Brian allowed them to experiment, as he'd obviously done. What if they were caught with it, if they overdosed? Let them think her the unkind, unforgiving one. She would not risk their lives.

Their little voices upstairs grew still, and as the silence deepened, her weight of fear and uncertainty returned. She looked around, searching every shadow. She hated this house. If she could pick up and leave, she would. But how could she? She'd hardly scraped enough together to keep them all fed and warm. And where would she go?

No, like it or not, this was the scene she had to play. She drew a breath and reached for the kitchen light. She'd left the dinner dishes until after Luke and Maddie were tucked in for the night. But she shuddered every time she entered the kitchen these days. She flicked the light on.

"Hello, Laurie."

She stifled the cry with her fist, certain it had carried up the stairs, praying the children hadn't heard. Why was she even surprised? She had sensed him there, this man she'd married but scarcely knew anymore. Looking into his handsome face, she saw a stranger, something she'd acquired along the way but didn't recall how. She drew a ragged breath. "What do you want?"

Brian motioned her into the kitchen. They would talk; she would explain; he would leave. If he made trouble, there was the gun in the high cabinet over the refrigerator. But how would she get to it? *Don't panic, just do what he says.* She'd reach the gun if she needed to. But as she entered, she saw two other men. One, a Latino with sharp dark eyes and hair pulled into a high, tight ponytail, was almost expressionless and stood in front of the refrigerator. The other man, with blond-tipped spikes and chain collar, was pure L.A.

"Hello, Mrs. Prelane." A spark of recognition ignited when he spoke. *Alex Dieter.* He had the kind of ruined voice you couldn't forget, the kind a crowbar to the larynx left marred. Or at least that was the story Brian had given her when she'd met the man at a party. She remembered him now, but she hadn't known Brian had any close association with him.

Dieter smiled, each tooth thin and spaced alone. The effect was ghoulish in the overhead light of the kitchen. A wave of fear passed through her. What was Brian doing with men like this? Why would he choose them for companions? Did he always have to be on the edge?

Dieter waved a hand decked with diamond cluster rings and a thick silver bracelet with a golden gecko. "You have something for me?"

She drew herself up, willing the fear from her voice. "I don't know what you're talking about. I told you that in my note." She looked to Brian hopefully.

He gave her nothing. Hollow-eyed with stress lines beside his mouth, he seemed agitated, angry. Of course he would be. If they could just talk alone. Why had he brought these henchmen? And how . . . She glanced at the door behind them. Her brow furrowed.

Dieter laughed, a terrible sound in his broken throat. "If you're going to add dead bolts, you ought to lock them."

Laurie thought back to the hours just past. Could she have left it unlocked? Yes, Luke had searched the backyard for his shoes. Then she'd rushed them out the door to Mother's and still arrived late for work. She hadn't checked the door when she came home, just brought them upstairs for their bath. Her breath escaped. She wasn't used to living in fear.

But she felt it now. Her eyes darted to the high cabinet.

Dieter's smile turned nasty. "Where is it?"

Her heart jumped, but she realized he didn't mean the gun. Why did Brian let this punk do his talking? She shook her head, looking confused, playing stupid. If she lunged for the cabinet, the Latino would stop her. Why hadn't she kept the gun on her? Because she didn't want the children to know.

"Just give it to him, Laurie." Brian's voice was tense. He didn't know what she'd done; he didn't understand.

"I don't have it."

"Who does?" Brian edged closer, muscles taut. "That boyfriend of yours?"

Cal? She pictured the swollen welt on Cal's shoulder. Now she knew it *was* Brian who attacked him, scaring him off, forcing away her only source of protection and comfort. She was lucky Brian hadn't cracked Cal's skull. "He knows nothing about this. I hosed it down the pool drain before I left." She saw the blood leave Brian's face, making a stark contrast between pale skin and jet black hair.

His throat worked, the larynx jumping up, then dropping. "Not even you could be that stupid."

His shock transferred to her. What was he saying? What . . . She now realized Brian was not in control here; he was afraid.

"You wouldn't be that stupid, would you?" Dieter flicked out a silver stiletto blade. "Not when you have such lovely children, Mrs. Prelane."

Laurie's eyes jumped from the knife to Dieter's face. Icy fear shot through her, silencing her. A quick glance at Brian affirmed his matching fear. It was real, tangible. What had he done? What had she done? *Luke. Maddie.*

Her mind suddenly calmed. It was as though she separated from the frightened shell that had surrounded her. She saw it now, the dangerous depth of her stupidity. It wasn't Brian she had to fear, it was what he had bought into—a world so dark and sinister she hadn't recognized it. Her act of retaliation was now a deadly mistake, one she could pay for with her life. Both she and Brian could pay. But not the children.

She glanced again at the cabinet. She couldn't reach the gun. She would have to use her wits alone. She must be convincing. If she could buy even the smallest window of time . . . "I don't have it here. I'll have to get it."

Brian's eyes closed, and she heard his breath escape. He, at least, believed her.

She turned to Dieter. "Give me some time." If he said no, she would lunge for the gun.

Dieter's expression was hard to read. He fingered the chain at his throat and glanced at his dark shadow. Laurie looked from the man to the cabinet. The Latino's eyes narrowed. He turned, looked upward. Laurie's throat tightened. He reached up, opened the cabinet, and took out Daddy's gun. Laurie's breaths came in heaves.

Dieter took the gun from his companion. His gaze shifted to her. "Did you think this could stop us?"

How had they known? Did she give herself away? She was no good at this! She looked at Brian. He should know that. She hadn't been able to play his games—wife swapping, thrill seeking. She

thought of Cal. *"You, the great actress?"* She drew on that, pulled herself up. "What do you expect? I had something to protect." She
meant the children, but let them think it was their cocaine.

The gun was loaded. Dieter could use it on her right now. But
that wouldn't get him his drugs. "Have it here tomorrow night."
Dieter turned with a jerk of his head.

The Latino followed. Laurie looked at Brian. For a moment she
thought he might speak. There was in his face something of apology,
something of regret. Then he, too, went out.

The kitchen wore the bleak look of an empty stage. Laurie
looked around, her breath shallow. For the first time in her life, she
considered a selfless act. For her children, she could die.

––––––––––

The phone jarred Cal out of the first decent sleep he'd had in too
long. Annie's head came up from his chest in startled concern as Cal
scrambled for the receiver.

"You awake?" Danson's voice was not one he'd care to wake up
to every morning.

He looked at the clock. 4:45. "Awake?"

"I need you to meet me on Route D."

Cal raised to one elbow. "Last I looked, I didn't work for you."

"Drag your tail out of bed and get down here. I've found your
black Firebird."

Cal listened to the dial tone a moment before hanging up. Found
the Firebird? Brian Prelane's Firebird? He pressed his palm to his eyes.
Was it any wonder he'd slept like a baby after Suanne's pork chops
and an evening of real companionship? He didn't want to pick up his
life where he'd left it. But what choice did he have with Danson
waiting?

Annie's nails clicked on the wood floor as she jumped down from
the bed, her eyebrows arched up in worry. He opened the door, hoping her pattering down the stairs wouldn't disturb Mildred. He never
let her out this early, but Danson had made it necessary. After mini-
mal preparation, he headed out into the darkness, coffee in hand.

Annie tried to join him in the jeep, but he ordered her to stay
and she curled up at the base of the stairs. Cal's head cleared as he

drove. What did Danson mean he'd found the Firebird? Had he stopped Brian for some infringement? Would he question him about Flip Casey? Cal shook his head. Then why order him to meet on the highway?

Cal knew as soon as he spotted the scene. The ambulance was there, lights flashing, Danson's cruiser and another behind it. An accident, but this time it looked like the Firebird got the worst of it.

Cal stepped from the jeep and walked to the roadside where the Firebird had lodged in the ditch. Lit by spotlights, the scene looked stark and eerie. The windshield was shattered and blood-smeared. The driver had been extricated and lay on the frozen ground, shrouded.

What on earth? Cal glanced at Danson. The steely gaze met his. With a swift dip, Cal reached for the blanket and pulled it back. He wished he hadn't. This was no blunt trauma death. The features were erased by the damage of an exiting bullet fired at close range. The black hair was crusted with blood. He dropped the blanket back.

"You know him?" Danson had come alongside.

Did Danson think he could I.D. that mess? But he had a guess, didn't he? His thoughts slammed into the front of his brain, just as his head had slammed into the jeep's frame when this same Firebird ran him off the road. "No." Cal's throat felt like detox.

"Car's rented to Brian Prelane. Name mean anything to you?"

Cal sucked the air. Was it Laurie's husband lying there? It didn't make sense. Then he saw again the gun in Laurie's pocket.

"You still own that rifle?"

Cal jerked his head. "I haven't used it in months." Not since . . . since shooting out the tire of Danson's cruiser on an angry, drunken binge.

"I'd like to see it for myself."

"Why?" And then it hit him. "You don't think . . ." He looked back at the telltale hole in the Firebird's window. "Oh, come on, Danson."

Danson took his Matt Dillon stance.

Cal's mouth went dry. "So come inspect it. See for yourself." It wasn't his rifle that had shot Brian Prelane. Was it Laurie's gun?

Danson's eyes narrowed. "What aren't you telling me? What do you know about this?" He waved his arm over the corpse.

"If you suspect me, why don't you take me in right now? Book me, Dano." What was he doing? Why was he protecting her? Again the thoughts slammed forward. Had Laurie killed her husband? He'd smelled her fear.

Danson came up chest to chest. "You have a smart mouth, Morrison. And you better believe I'll lock your tail up if I find one thing to indicate I should."

Cal kept silent. It would take all of an hour's work for Danson to learn more than enough to do just that. Cal had already admitted being run down by the car. Add to that his history, past and present, with the man's wife . . .

He ought to come clean, tell Danson what he knew. But something, maybe Laurie's fear or the pain he'd glimpsed in her eyes, held him mute. If Brian Prelane had battered Laurie, if she'd been driven to it . . . Cal felt a protective rage. He had to get to her, had to learn the truth before telling Danson anything.

Cal shoved his hands into his pockets. "You know where to find me." He turned away and reached the jeep without Danson stopping him. As he climbed in and started the engine he saw the sergeant's unwavering gaze.

The first order of business was to switch cars with Ray. If Danson suspected a connection, he would have him watched, in which case his jeep was well enough known to mark him around town. Ray's Chevy bomb would be a far cry from that.

He pulled the jeep into the gravel circle under the eaves and climbed out. Before he could head for the garage, Cissy opened the house door. "Oh, thank goodness you're back."

He stopped. "What's the matter?"

"What's the matter?" Mildred pushed past to the porch. "I told you there was trouble. But did you listen?"

Cal bristled. "I'm listening now." He needed answers, not scolding.

She held out an envelope.

He mounted the steps and took it. *Cal.* In Laurie's handwriting. He tore it open. *Please believe I wouldn't ask this if there were any other way. I don't know where else to turn. The children shouldn't pay for my mistakes. Please, please keep them safe. Take them somewhere they won't be found.*

Cal swallowed his fear and confusion. Looking up at Mildred, he searched for something, some clue to— And then Maddie slipped between the two sisters, pressing herself into Cissy's legs.

Cissy stroked the child's hair. "Laurie brought them not more than half an hour ago. You weren't home."

Laurie brought them? After shooting Brian off the road? Cold rose up inside. He didn't want to think . . . this was no time for conjecture. He stared a moment, then handed Mildred the note, turned, and called over his shoulder, "Keep them here. And don't open the door to anyone."

He ran for the jeep, all thoughts of Ray's Chevy washed away in the panic that now filled him. The sight of Brian's ruined face stayed in his mind. Someone, some thing had done that to him. Had Laurie killed Brian and run? Or was she herself the prey? He gunned the gas pedal and spun from the yard.

———

Laurie looked again into the rearview mirror. There was only the beginning of morning light to show her the car following. The best she could hope was to put enough miles behind her to give Cal time to escape with the children. She closed her eyes against the pain. Putting a hand to her mouth, she breathed in and out hard, fighting the overwhelming rush of terror.

She had to believe that he would keep them safe. He may despise her, but he would protect Luke and Maddie. Who better? Hadn't she seen it the day he lunged for Maddie beside the fire? It was pure instinct in him. He'd keep them safe from harm. And that's what mattered. Not Brian. Not her. Only Luke and Maddie.

Before she reached the edge of town, the Mustang with rental plates was behind her. She wasn't sure how she knew it was them. It wasn't the Firebird Cal had questioned her about. Maybe Brian was in that car somewhere up ahead, waiting to cut her off. She had hoped to get farther. Maybe she could still talk her way out. Buy time. Time for Cal and her babies to escape.

After Brian and his partners had left last night, she had waited in the dark, almost paralyzed, fearing the moment she stepped outside. But at last she'd had to risk it. And she'd slipped out, slipped out with her children in the small hours and made it to Cal's. Her courage had almost failed when he didn't answer his door. But then Mildred was there, taking charge, assuring her. Maybe it was better not to face him. The note saved her from that.

She had told Mildred only that it was an emergency. The note had explained nothing. But Cal would take them away, take them somewhere safe. It didn't matter where. She might never see them again, but they'd be safe. A stabbing pain, so real it stopped her breath, shot through her. What choice did she have?

If only Brian had . . . But then, she couldn't blame him. Even now she recalled his fear. He hadn't known, hadn't understood. In a way he was just a child himself, always looking for one more thrill, one more way to prove himself.

The Mustang drew up close behind her. She saw two men inside. Was it Alex Dieter at the wheel, or the Latino with no expression? Neither looked like Brian in the dim light. Where was he? She searched the road ahead, expecting him to dart out and run her off as he'd done to Cal. *Oh, God, what do I do?*

God? It was the first time she'd called on Him in too long. Once, for a while, she'd tried. She had even believed, given her life in the simple prayer Grams had led her through. But she'd turned her back when Grams died. Had God forgotten her then, too?

Cal pulled the jeep to a screeching halt and ran for the door of Laurie's house. He didn't have to break the lock. It was done for him, the wood of the old door splintered away from the new lock. He pushed open the door and went inside. Daylight streamed over the upturned sleeper couch, slashed and ripped apart.

It was like a scene from a movie, everything thrown about and smashed. The kitchen was the same, the cupboards stripped, their contents scattered. A search? Would Laurie have trashed her own place? He turned and rushed upstairs. The beds were slashed, the clothing tossed about, closets demolished. He knew already the house was empty, but the cry came from him regardless. "Laurie!"

Only a hint of echo. He dropped his face to his forearm against the doorjamb. Where was she? And why hadn't she let him help her? He went down to the kitchen where the back door banged in the wind. Probably the exit route, and by the amount of heat still present in the room, it hadn't been that long.

He heard the sound of sirens and from the window saw Danson and company heading around the corner. With scarcely a moment's thought, Cal ran out the door and around the side of the house. He laid rubber, just as Danson screeched to a halt and hollered for him to stop.

Cal drove like a madman, watching for them to follow. Either he'd lost them or they didn't care to give chase. After all, they knew where to find him, and their first concern would be searching Laurie's house. Of course, his presence and flight would gain importance once Danson ascertained the trashed house was empty.

Careening up to the Suttons' colonial brick house put Cal in time warp. How many times had he driven defiantly in his old Pontiac to pick Laurie up for the evening? Not as many as he'd have liked, but more than the Suttons could stomach. He took the masonry-tiled walk at a lope and banged on the door.

Marjorie Sutton opened it. She was a thinner, paler version of who she had been, but he recognized the expression. No matter how she aged, she would always wear the same tight, weary expression.

"Is Laurie here?"

She shook her head, surprise and concern betrayed in the eyes. Cal jammed his hands into his pockets. He hadn't expected her to be, but he'd hoped.

Laurie's mother stepped back. "Come in." A command, not an invitation. His presence on her doorstep, where the neighbors might see, must be a greater evil than admitting him into the sanctuary. But he didn't have time with Danson on his heels; he needed answers fast.

"Please." Her voice was tight as she waved him inside.

Cal stepped over the threshold just far enough for her to close the door behind him. "Mrs. Sutton, do you know what's going on?"

She stood stiff backed, hands folded at her waist. "I'm always the last to know. I hadn't heard she left Brian until she showed up here with the children." She headed into the living room, leaving Cal no choice but to follow. "As far as I knew they were perfectly happy."

Cal glanced at the picture she indicated with one hand out-stretched. He would have preferred not to see a radiant Laurie draped in lace and pearls. For a moment, he had eyes only for her, the smile emanating from her whole face, the excitement of the moment shining in her eyes as brightly as the sun on the ocean behind her. She had attained everything she wanted.

Then he looked at the man beside her, dark hair, white teeth gleaming. Wide shoulders, broad chest, an athletic stance. It was hard to see past their idyllic happiness to the brutality of what he'd viewed that morning. Had Laurie. . . ? Anything was possible. She was duplicitous and confused. But that didn't explain the condition of her house.

He rubbed his palm over his jaw and looked back at Marjorie Sutton. "Laurie's in trouble."

"Then it's your fault."

Cal swallowed that. He should have known she'd take that tack. It intensified his own suspicions that one misstep would land him in the slammer. And then what good would he be to Laurie? Once Danson made the connection . . .

"She's gone, and her place is all torn up."

Marjorie Sutton stood unbelieving. This was getting him nowhere. He pulled out a pad, wrote down Mildred's phone number, then tore off the page and held it out to her. "If you see or hear anything from her, call this number." He could see by the tightening of the lips she would refuse. "Mrs. Sutton, Brian Prelane is dead. And Laurie's missing."

He watched her pale and knew from his training he should have warned her first. He caught her elbow and eased her into a chair. There was no time for more. "Call if you hear anything."

She nodded numbly. Cal was concerned, but he guessed it would be only minutes before Sergeant Danson would be there to fill her in. Then she could make what she liked of it all. Somehow it would still come out his fault.

15

HOW MANY OF OUR DAYDREAMS

WOULD DARKEN INTO NIGHTMARES,

WERE THERE A DANGER OF THEIR COMING TRUE!

Logan Pearsall Smith

CAL DROVE HOME ON AUTOPILOT. Where was Laurie, and did she really expect him to take her children and hide out when she was in danger? Or was she making her escape? Dumping the kids and skipping town after shooting her husband?

Cal flashed on the shattered face. He felt no satisfaction. It was a wasted life. He puzzled his sympathy for the man who'd taken a bat to him and might have done worse damage if not for Annie on his ankle. It was what he'd seen in their wedding picture, a reflection in Brian's face of what Cal felt for Laurie—and in that he could pity Brian Prelane. Rob was right. Laurie took everything you had.

The children were in the kitchen with Cissy, but he searched out Mildred in the study. She fixed him with a sharp eye. "The police came looking for you."

"What did you tell them?"

"That you weren't here."

He let out his tight breath, thankful it had been the truth. Not only did he doubt Mildred would lie, but Danson would know it if she tried. "What about the kids?"

"He didn't ask."

Again Cal breathed his relief. No doubt Danson assumed Laurie had the children with her, imagined Cal would skip town and meet her somewhere after offing her husband. "I'll take them to the cabin."

Across the folding table lined with Christmas cards in neat rows, Mildred eyed him sharply.

He dropped to the wicker chair across from her. "You saw the note. Laurie wants me to hide them, and I can't argue since she's missing."

"Missing?"

"The house is all torn up. There's no sign of her." He didn't reveal the anguish that sight had brought him.

"I'll call the police."

"Danson's already been there."

Mildred's thin fingers laced together. "That's why he's looking for you."

"No. Laurie's husband is dead. Murdered." Cal jammed his hands into the sides of his hair. "That's why he's looking for me." He half expected her to take up the phone and turn him in.

Instead, she blew through her lips and said, "That tomfool hasn't the head for the job."

He looked at her from between his palms.

"Anyone with half a brain would know you don't have it in you."

Cal wasn't sure that was a compliment.

Mildred capped the pen. "My guess is a third party. She was afraid the first time I saw her. I think she brought this trouble with her."

Cal leaned forward. "I thought it was her husband."

Mildred snorted. "That was wishful thinking. It's always easier to believe the other man a monster."

Cal let that go. After all, it was half true. "I have to get out of here. Did Laurie send things with the children?"

"They have a suitcase by the door. But you won't get out in your jeep. They'll be watching the highways."

"They can't watch them all. Route double E will be low on their list."

"You have to take D to get there."

Cal frowned. Route D was where they'd found both Flip Casey

and Brian Prelane. Again he rubbed his jaw.

Mildred stood. "You'll take the Buick." She walked to the oak wardrobe beside the bookcase. Reaching up with more agility than Cal would have credited her, she pulled down a hatbox and set it on the table. His suspicion intensified as she lifted the lid to reveal a broad-brimmed bonnet sort of hat with ribbon tie. Mildred's garden hat.

"They won't know you in this."

"I won't know me in that."

Again the gimlet stare. "It's no worse than a wig and nose."

He opened his mouth to argue, but she went on. "To the country boys staking out the road you'll be a woman with children in a Buick, not a dangerous lunatic in a jeep."

He frowned at the word "lunatic," the first time she'd directly referred to his troubles in pejorative terms.

"Now." She laid the hat out on the table. "You'll need food and blankets. That place is a death trap. Your grandfather should have burned it before he died."

"I've caulked it some."

She snorted. "Not a word to Cissy. She'll be sick with worry. It'll send her to bed."

"She doesn't know already?"

Mildred shook her head. "I handled the police. She was in the kitchen with the children."

Cal bobbed his head once. "I think she'll notice they're gone."

Mildred glared. "She can know you're at the cabin, but nothing more."

"Mildred, I can't just stay at the cabin." He almost blurted out his intention to search for Laurie. "I'm supposed to be on active duty."

Mildred turned and fixed him with a stare that said about bloody time, but she didn't voice her thoughts. "You think you can just go in to work with the Lone Ranger on your trail? The minute you're spotted he'll haul you in, active duty or not. He was redder than a turkey jowl."

Cal slumped. It was true. But *someone* had trashed Laurie's place. Brian? Had he gone on a rampage and threatened Laurie? Had she killed him in self-defense? Or was there someone else? Someone

219

Laurie feared enough to give him her children to protect. "Listen, Mildred. Something's happened to Laurie." He knew it. Inside he knew she needed him.

You have to believe that, don't you? All right, so he had a hero complex. He needed to believe he could help her. Maybe he was the only one who could.

Mildred sighed. "Right now your responsibility is to the children. Give the sergeant time to come to his senses. Maybe he'll find Laurie for you. Now you better get packed. You'll wait until eleven-thirty, then go. It's women's auxiliary luncheon today. If there's anyone watching the yard they'll—"

"Think I'm you."

"Exactly."

Cal could say nothing that expressed how he felt about that. He released a slow breath. It was actually good to be ordered about. Especially as his brain was turning to mud. And Mildred was right. Before anything else, he had to see the children safely away. He started for the door.

"Calvert."

Wincing, Cal turned to find her holding out the hat. With a sigh, he carried it upstairs to wait out the time, knowing every minute would pass like hours. But there was no sense rushing off half-cocked. That's what Danson would expect, and he'd be watching for it. For a moment he wished he'd just told Danson everything he knew from the start. But where would that leave Laurie?

He paused at the stairs, heard Maddie's laugh waft up to him from the kitchen. He'd leave her and Luke with Cissy until the last possible moment. After that they'd be stuck with him.

———

There was nothing Laurie could do but yield to the Mustang and pull off to the side. The Firebird had not turned up, but she clearly saw Dieter and the other man in the Mustang as they edged her closer to the shoulder. Grimly Laurie brought her Lexus to a stop. She glared at Dieter as she held the button that lowered her window.

He didn't smile this time. "Where do you think you're going?"

"I told you I had to get it. Where's Brian?" She searched the

Mustang for his face, but it was only Dieter and the Latino.

Dieter's eyes were ice, glacial blue. The skin pulled tightly over his cheekbones as his lips parted for his ruined voice. "Dead."

The word hung on the cold air, a non-word, a senseless sound, something she couldn't comprehend. And then the letters reformed, came together with meaning, terrible meaning. Brian was dead? They'd killed him?

"Get out of the car."

Fear coursed through her. Fear and a terrible sense of failure.

All the while he drove, Cal fretted. Aside from feeling a complete fool in the hat, his thoughts and emotions were too jumbled to make sense of. Had Laurie killed Brian and skipped town? Was it Brian who broke her window and demolished her home? Was she defending herself by killing him? Then the deed would have happened at the house. Unless he took her, forced her into the car, didn't know she had a gun . . .

He kept seeing the wedding picture and their smiling faces. He did believe Brian had run him off the road and had a whack at him with the bat. But Brian was dead, and someone had pulled the trigger. The ruined face was imbedded in his thoughts as well. Could Laurie have done that? Could she?

His feelings were a mess. Rage and yearning and resentment. But then he thought of the fear he'd seen in her the night he learned she wasn't divorced. If he hadn't been so hurt and angry, he might have gotten some answers. If he hadn't cared more about his pride and loss, he might have learned why she'd run from her husband. *Left* him, as Marjorie had said.

Maybe he could have stopped this. *"Laurie brought this trouble with her."* Mildred had seen it. Laurie was in trouble, and if it wasn't Brian, she was still in danger. That was the thought he kept avoiding. It was easier, much easier to imagine her guilty, even of murder, than helpless and in danger.

"Where are we going?" The little voice broke through his confusion.

He tipped the mirror to see Maddie's worried face. "My grandpa's cabin."

"Why?"

What could he tell her? That he was eluding the law? Hiding them at their mother's request, yet leaving her to face . . . Again the fear surged through him. He had to do this. Whatever Laurie had gotten into, he had to keep the kids out of it.

"I want Mommy."

"I know Maddie." *I want her too.* He tried to still it, to ignore it. But there it was, the persistent, not to be ignored, wanting. And it wasn't just physical; it was a longing of the soul, a need to know she was safe, a need to care, to love her. He was a fool.

Cal looked into the mirror again, and his eyes shifted from Maddie's clouding face to Luke, who was fingering the leather rifle that hung behind his seat. "Leave it alone, Luke. It's loaded."

Luke dropped his hand without speaking. Cal yanked the ridiculous bonnet from his head and tossed it to the seat. They were past the point of discovery. Twenty minutes more on this highway, then a quick jaunt along the dirt road that would bring them to the cabin.

"Say, Luke. What do you call . . ." He told a series of jokes just silly enough to catch their interest. Even Maddie laughed. Of course, they had no idea what was happening. He doubted Laurie had said anything more than she had to.

Rounding the bend, the cabin came into sight. Cal took a good, unbiased look at it. Mildred had a point. The porch sagged, the front window was boarded, and the flap on the chimney pipe coughed rust in the wind. He smiled. "Here we are."

Neither child spoke. He pulled to a stop and climbed out, then lifted Maddie down while Luke got out with Annie behind. Maddie curled her fingers into his and pressed close to his leg. Luke planted his feet and stared.

Cal thought fast. "Just like Davy Crockett's house."

Luke looked up. "Who's Davy Crockett?"

Cal put his hands on his hips and sang, "Davy, Davy Crockett, king of the wild frontier." Luke grinned, and Cal rubbed his head. "I'll tell you all about him, but first let's check out the cabin for coons."

Maddie's fingers tightened as they mounted the stairs. He pushed open the door. Like his grandfather before him, Cal didn't lock up the place. He figured if someone in the area needed shelter, they might as well make use of it. It didn't smell as though anyone had, not for a long time anyway. "You two have a look around, while I get us unloaded."

Luke and Maddie circled the room. There wasn't much to see. The single space held a bed, a dry sink, a stretch of countertop, and a wood-burning stove. A wooden table and chairs Cal's grandfather had built from the woods out back were the only furnishings. The floorboards were warped and uneven, but solid, and Cal had, as he told Mildred, plugged the largest gaps in the log walls.

He went to haul in their gear, thankful Cissy had fed the children lunch before they left. It took nearly two hours to get everything wiped down and fit for habitation. The bed on the wall would work for the kids, feet to feet, and he made up a bedroll on the floor for himself. The stove was in good condition, and he'd brought enough water for several days. Now if the roof didn't leak and . . .

"I have to tinkle."

He looked down at Maddie, then out the back window to the outhouse. "Okay. That's the bathroom out there."

"You take me?"

"Uh . . . sure." He took her by the hand and walked out, Luke tagging along beside them. For all his bravado, Cal could tell Luke was none too sure about any of this. Cal pulled open the door and ushered Maddie in, then closed the door behind her.

"It's dawk."

He noted her exaggerated baby talk. It had started in the car. A sign of distress? Rita would know.

He slid open the panel on the door. "That better?"

"It's still dawk."

He glanced down at Luke, then pulled open the door a hand's width, painting a stripe of light across one tiny knee and shoulder. "How's that?

"Okay."

"Next time we'll bring a flashlight." He gazed around at the edge of the woods while she took care of business. It had warmed enough that Luke stood comfortably in only a sweat shirt.

He nudged the boy's shoulder. "If you're American when you go into the bathroom, and American when you come out, what are you inside?"

Luke started to grin and shrugged again. "American?"

"Nope. European."

Luke stared a minute, then finished his grin and laughed. "European."

"Don't tell that one to your mother." Cal felt a pang. Would Luke have the chance? Would any of them have the chance to tell her anything again? Adrenaline surged. What was he doing in the woods? How could he do anything for her if he was stuck in the middle of nowhere with her children?

With her children. *"You can't imagine how holding your newborn son for the first time can wipe away all the false notions of what matters most."* Wasn't he doing exactly what she wanted? She'd entrusted her most precious gifts to him.

Maddie pushed open the door. "How do you fwush?"

"You don't."

"Yucky."

"Yeah." He took her hand again. What if he were buying Laurie time? Time to what? Run away? Would she leave Luke and Maddie for good? She'd left Brian, but that was different. *"There's nothing I wouldn't do for them."* She'd meant that.

He tightened his grip on Maddie's soft fingers and called, "Luke! Let's take a walk, scout out the lie of the land." Maybe they shouldn't leave the cabin, but if he didn't walk he'd explode.

Luke jumped off the rock he'd climbed, laughing when Annie frisked around them and then bounded ahead. "Will she get lost?"

"Nope. She'll keep us in sight." Cal straddled the narrow stream bed and lifted Maddie across, then handed Luke over. His shoulder hurt enough to remind him he should have had it looked at. He scanned the woods, wary. The sunshine was deceptively bright, glancing off the brown grasses and shiny branches of the bracken. Across the rise a blue jay called and flitted to a higher branch. Annie rushed back, licked his hand, and ran ahead again. He relaxed.

Luke ran after the dog. "I'm the scout!"

"Not so fast. I want you to stay close." Cal might have been talking to the dog for all the response he got. Luke's pumping legs carried him into the trees. Well, Annie would keep him tracked.

They hadn't gone too far when Maddie stopped, put up her arms, and said, "Carry me?"

Cal hoisted her to his shoulders, wincing, and she planted her palms against his forehead. "Watch your head." He ducked down under the branches, and her hands slipped over his eyes. "I can't see, Maddie."

She slid them back to his forehead, and holding her small calves, he pressed on. He could just make out Luke's brown hair through the trunks ahead. Annie traversed the path, and Luke cavorted behind her. Cal smiled. Luke reminded him of himself, the same carefree abandon, the sense of adventure any woods gave him. He could almost imagine they were there for a holiday. The only thing missing was Laurie.

His diaphragm convulsed. What was he going to do? He pondered her note again. *The children shouldn't pay for my mistakes.* Mistakes. The murder of her husband? *Keep the children safe. Take them somewhere they won't be found.* Found by whom? Not Brian. The authorities? Or someone else? Someone who trashed her place and threatened her now? A finger of fear found his spine.

Maddie squirmed on the back of his neck. "Put me down. I want to chase the doggie."

Cal stooped to lower her to the ground, and she bounced away with tiny springy steps. He rubbed his shoulder, willing the pain and the fear to subside. Mildred was right. The children were his first concern. At the moment, it was the only way he could help Laurie.

They spent as much time in the woods as circumstances would allow. Some of the time they walked. Some of the time they sat and Cal told them about the woods, about Davy Crockett and Daniel Boone, about his job and fires he'd fought, about anything he thought might keep the kid's minds—and his own—from Laurie. But then the meager heat fled behind wintry storm clouds. He brought the kids back to the cabin, stoked the fire in the stove, and cooked some hot dogs. Maddie wrinkled her nose as he doused his with mustard.

He pressed the bun shut with a frown. "You eat yours your way, and I'll eat mine my way. Ketchup on a hot dog is sacrilegious."

"What's that mean?" Luke's eyes were wide and curious.

"It means the real way to eat a hot dog is with mustard." He slid the mustard bottle toward Luke, who still shook his head. Cal grinned. "Suit yourself. You don't know what you're missing."

Though it was just past sundown, Maddie was already yawning when they finished eating. The walk had worn them all out. He shouldn't have gone so far, but he had needed it. Staking out his territory, maybe. Feeling out the land. Some primal need to secure his space. No one would take him by surprise out here.

He put the paper plates into the trash bag he'd hung from the edge of the table, and nodded to the children. "Pull that curtain across the corner and get into your pajamas."

They walked like automatons, first to the suitcase that held their clothes, then to the curtained corner. A few minutes later Maddie reappeared in a flannel nightgown with the tag sticking up under her chin. As far as Cal could tell it didn't matter, so he left it alone.

She patted his arm. "I have to brush my teeth."

"Here at the sink."

"There's no water."

"No running water, but there's a drain. We'll use the bottled water to rinse and wash it down."

Maddie ran the foaming brush over her teeth, then he helped her pour the water over the bristles and into the sink basin. Luke followed on his own. His fresh silence bothered Cal, but he wasn't sure how to broach it. "You all right, buddy?" He rubbed the boy's shoulder.

Luke nodded, laid his toothbrush on the sink, and looked up. "Is Mommy coming here?"

Cal considered carefully. "I don't think so, not tonight." In the morning he'd figure out what to do next. He couldn't leave the children alone. He'd been charged with their safety, something he'd made his credo this last year: Keep children safe and they won't need to be rescued. Laurie trusted him to do that. But they could hardly stay holed up forever. Even if Danson didn't want him for murder, he wasn't the sort to change identities and whisk the kids' faces onto a milk carton.

He got them tucked into the bed, and turned off the Coleman lantern. In the darkness, he climbed out of his jeans and slipped into his thermal long johns. The stove glowed, putting out enough heat for the small room. There wasn't much chance he'd sleep deeply enough to let it go out, but, just in case, he tossed another blanket over the children and slid into the covers on the floor. He was just about gone when he felt Maddie's palm on his cheek. Not the outhouse again . . .

"I'm scared."

"Of what?" His gruffness was pure exhaustion.

"Mommy lets me in when I'm scared."

He studied her standing like a waif in the darkness. "You'll be more comfortable in the bed."

She shook her head, and, sighing, he raised the cover. She burrowed in next to him, her back, soft and pliant against his chest. Gently, he curled an arm around, and she rested her cheek on his opposite bicep. He couldn't remember ever feeling anything quite like it.

"What is it you're afraid of?" he asked softly.

"The noises."

He listened. "That's just the wind in the cracks."

"It's scary."

"Nah. It's only air moving around. Did you ever have a birthday cake with candles?" Her head nodded against his shoulder. "And you blew them out?"

She nodded again.

"That was wind. The air you blew. That's all it is, only bigger."

She tucked a hand between his arm and her cheek and wiggled closer. It gave him a warmth deeper than her body heat.

"Still scared?" he whispered into her hair.

"No."

"Good." As her breathing slowed and deepened, he closed his eyes against the softness of her hair and sank into sleep.

Her skin was hot, and his breath was tight. Smoke filled the room. It began to glow. Chair legs separated him from the child. He reached, his breath echoing in his ears. The glow turned orange, burnt orange. Her screams split the silence. "No!" Cal jolted awake.

His chest had drenched Maddie's back where she lay, undisturbed by his jolt. Dropping his face into his hand, he sucked air into his lungs and smelled smoke. Looking up, he saw the stove was out. Had that and the child's body heat conjured the dream from hell? It didn't take much these days.

In the dimness of the coming dawn, he looked at Maddie's sleeping face. She might have been his little girl. The thought felt strange and unfamiliar. Why not? If Laurie had given him a chance . . . He stroked a finger over Maddie's hair, then looked across at Luke. He was burrowed down into the covers, but his breath misted in the chilled air.

Slipping out, Cal crept to the stove, balled up some newspaper, crossed a handful of sticks over it, then laid a log on the top. His hand shook as he struck the match on the box. Flame licked up, golden white, warming his fingertips. He held it to the paper, and it took hold, growing and engulfing. He watched it spread like a live thing to the edge of kindling and curl the skin of bark from a stick. Sitting back, he closed his eyes and absorbed the heat.

Luke stirred behind him, and he turned. The child muttered, then settled in and continued to sleep. Cal closed the stove doors and filled the coffeepot with water from the jug. He scooped coffee grounds into the percolator attachment and stood it inside, then put the pot on the burner to heat. He filled his cupped palm with cold water from the bottle and rubbed it over his face.

No hint of screams lingered in the room. No tint of orange. Only the faint wood smoke, and it didn't haunt him. This was progress. This was definitely progress. Rita would be proud. But what would she think of the rest?

Hey, he could always plead insanity. So he ran off with someone's kids. Fallout. Failure to debrief. But imagining they were his, now there's the plum Rita would pick. What is it, Cal? A latent desire to put yourself in Brian's place? Oh, not latent, Dr. James. See I was there first. He's the one who didn't belong.

Cal shook his head. He hated it when his brain did this. Hyperdrive. Why was he even thinking of life with Laurie? She was so messed up she made him look good. She used people, sucked them dry, and left them. She had misled him, let him make a fool of himself all over again. Then told him to get lost.

So why was he here with her children, eluding the law and playing Davy Crockett? He thought of the old Disney film. *"When I know what's right I just go straight ahead."* Or something like that. The trouble was, Cal didn't know what was right. That was Reggie's department. Was this the lightning bolt Reggie expected he'd need? Cal thought about praying, then shook his head. It would take a bigger bolt than this.

The coffee was bubbling up in the pot. He lifted it from the burner with a soiled towel and poured a Styrofoam cupful.

16

LAURIE WORRIED THE ROPE that held her arms behind her back. If they'd been so quick to kill Brian, why hadn't they shot her by now? She was the one who'd interfered. She glared at the Latino, Luís. She had caught his name when Dieter had ordered him to watch her. As though she could do anything tied up.

Where had Dieter gone? To find the children? *Please no.* She could bear anything but that. *Please let Cal have them somewhere safe,* her thoughts begged. Begged whom? She looked around the splintering barn walls. Who would look for her here?

Who would look for her anywhere? Cal? She hoped and prayed not. Prayed. Did she pray? These begging thoughts, these fervent wishes . . . were they, as Grams said, pleas to the Almighty? Was there a God, a Jesus who loved her?

She had believed it once, put her faith into simple words, and made Him her Lord. But she was so small, maybe eight, maybe nine, a child pleasing Grams, whom she loved more than anyone. It had never become more than that, never steered her path. Who was she to expect anything from God now?

But there it was, a small feeling, a tiny comfort. *You're not alone.*

You're never alone. She thought the words. It was her own thoughts, her own wishful thoughts. How she wished she could think away the fear.

Destroying the cocaine had been a knee-jerk reaction, a way to pay Brian back for ignoring her objections. She'd never considered the cost. She didn't even know how much the cocaine was worth. All she knew was that Dieter would not accept any more excuses.

Luís was looking at her with narrowed eyes. She felt naked and vulnerable. What would they do to her? How much could she bear? Torture? Rape? Maybe they would just kill her.

Cal took the children to the outhouse early, prepared with flashlight in the dim morning daylight. Maddie had a little skip to every other step and wiggled her fingers in the air. Luke all but plodded. This whole situation might be going over Maddie's head, but Luke was uneasy. What had Laurie told them? How much did he guess?

After they'd all made use of the latrine, Cal got them washed, as well as he could with cold bottled water, and had just poured out bowls of cornflakes when Mildred arrived in Ray's bomb. For a moment Cal thought she would come right through the porch. But she stomped the brakes and lurched to a stop.

He left the kids at the table and stepped outside. "Good morning, Mildred."

"No, it's not." She climbed out, pulling with her a full paper bag, and shut the car door with her hip.

"What's up?" Cal hoped it was her normal grumpiness, but her manner was just agitated enough to indicate more.

As she approached, Cal caught a glimpse of a yellow-and-green Crayola box and coloring books. "How's Cissy?"

"Home worried sick."

"I thought we weren't telling her."

Mildred mounted the stairs. "Sergeant Danson made it necessary."

Cal dropped a hip against the wall. "How?"

"He's issued a warrant for your arrest."

"What's the charge?"

Mildred refastened her grip on the bag. "For starters, homicide. But he also suspects Laurie's abduction and the kidnapping of her children."

Cal's chin dropped to his chest. "You told him I didn't have it in me?"

"I told him he was off his nut."

Cal raised his eyes.

Mildred shrugged. "In the meantime, you'd better have a listen to your answering machine."

Cal's head jerked up. "Is it Laurie?"

"Here." Mildred pulled a folded paper from her coat pocket. "It came in after Danson searched your place or he would have heard it too. I wrote exactly what he said. But the voice . . . *that* you have to hear for yourself."

Cal opened the paper to Mildred's exact handwriting. *Fireclown, are you listening? If you want to see her alive, bring the snow. Gray barn, Route DD. No cops.*

He read it again. Bring the snow . . . Snow. It hit him hard.

"You sniffin' snow, bro?"

"I already told Rita no. There's enough comfort in legal poison."

His heart pounded his chest. They thought he had cocaine? Was Laurie mixed up in that? It made no sense. Or did it? He pictured her torn-up house, furniture slashed.

Pieces came together that he didn't want to fit. *"The children shouldn't pay for my mistakes."* Could a drug-crazed Laurie have shot her husband and run? But he'd seen no addiction in her. He would have; he knew how it looked. Or had he intentionally missed it, imagined her trouble came from outside when in fact . . .

He ran a hand over his face, noticed Mildred's keen stare. She'd brought him the message, but did she have any idea its import? He swallowed his tension. He couldn't let on, not with something so dangerous. It was a minor miracle she'd taken his side over Danson so far.

"When did this come?"

"Right before I left." Mildred shifted the bag. "I went up to see what kind of mess Danson and Baker had made."

Cal flashed on Laurie's place. Whatever Danson had done wouldn't compare to that. "And?"

"It wasn't bad. Not much worse than you keep it at the best of times."

Cal cocked his jaw.

"While I was up there the call came."

If you want to see her alive . . . A shudder crawled Cal's spine. What sort of scum had Laurie? Had *they* killed Brian? His gorge rose, and for some reason he thought also of the vagrant, Flip Casey. Had they run him down too? Why?

He sure knew his names and faces and stats. Had Flip recognized Brian? And they'd taken the old man out, made it look like an accident. But they hadn't made Brian's death an accident. They'd made it murder, and him the prime suspect.

Were they framing him? For Brian's murder . . . and Laurie's? No! He couldn't allow himself to think of her dead. He had to picture her whole and unharmed. A trickle of sweat started down his temple. He had to find her.

He straightened. "What do I do with the kids?"

"What do I look like?" Mildred fixed him with her peahen stare. "I am neither so old nor so feeble that I can't manage two youngsters. I trust there's wood cut?"

"Plenty."

"And you've left me water."

"Enough."

"Then be on your way." She jutted her chin at him.

Cal hesitated. What would Luke and Maddie think if he deserted them? They knew Cissy, and she was a natural surrogate grandma. Would Maddie snuggle up with Mildred in the dark? The thought was difficult. But then, if there was trouble, Cissy would wring her hands, whereas Mildred . . . He could be back by nightfall. With their mother. He nodded. "Thanks, Mildred."

"By the way. I've an old suitcase in the same closet I found your hat. You could use that."

He gave her a quizzical glance.

"Cornstarch and Baggies."

"What are you . . ." With a rush he caught on. Mildred did

know! Sharp old bird, but . . . Her remark sank in. Cornstarch and Baggies? "You can't be serious. I'd have thirty seconds before some thug stuck in a finger and tasted gravy mix."

Mildred gave him the look. "You have a better plan to get near Laurie?"

"Any plan would be better than some hokey. . ." Cal's brain caught up to his mouth. He looked around in the morning light. What she suggested was crazy. But what were his options? If Laurie had cocaine, he didn't know where. So how could he bring it? But whoever had Laurie thought he could. Walking in empty-handed would buy him a bullet off the top. At least with a suitcase filled with cornstarch he'd get close.

Ridiculous as it seemed, it was the best chance they had as far as he could tell. It was either that or walk into Danson's office and explain, which would land him in a cell—and probably a straight jacket. He'd been there once. He wasn't about to do it again. He looked back at Mildred still waiting in the doorway. She was right. And she knew it.

"Have Cissy fetch what you need from the store." She started toward the door.

"Mildred, you're incredible." He leaned and planted a kiss on her crepe-paper cheek.

"Good heavens. Get off with you. Time's wasting."

But he saw the flush under her sallow skin, and her mouth worked at the corners. He took the stairs in one leap and pulled open the massive door to Ray's car. The keys were in the ignition. "By the way, what does Ray know?"

"That you're in some sort of trouble. Danson doesn't think him worth questioning."

"Good. Of the two, I'd choose Ray for smarts." As he slipped into the car, he thought he saw Mildred smile, not something he could swear to, but enough of a smile it warmed him.

The warmth faded into a chill of concern for Laurie as he drove. *"If you want to see her alive . . ."* She was alive. She had to be. He entered the highway and sped toward town. Driving Ray's Chevy into Mildred's driveway, he kept his eyes peeled for vehicles.

Danson didn't seem to have the place guarded. After all, he had limited resources and probably doubted Cal would return after making his getaway. Cal pulled around the back. Ray was lingering by the outside stairs. Cal waved as he climbed out of the Chevy and hurried toward him.

Ray followed him up the stairs. "You in trouble, Cal?"

"Nothing I won't get out of." May as well stay positive. Cal unlocked the door to his place and went in.

"Did you do it?" Ray stepped inside just behind him.

Cal turned. "Do what?"

"Shoot Laurie's husband?"

Well, Ray knew more than Mildred thought. "What do you think, Ray?"

Ray tucked his hands into the sides of his overalls. "I don't think you did. I don't think you'd do that."

Cal smiled. "No, I didn't. But convincing Danson of that is another thing." He walked over and pressed the button to hear his messages. The first was Rita asking for a call, a little too casually. Danson must have gotten to her as well. The second message started, and Cal's breath arrested.

Tension pulled the tendons in his neck as he heard again the cries over the phone and the voice . . . *"child killer."* Thanksgiving night at the fire station. It was the same hoarse, broken voice, like someone with a tracheotomy put back together badly. "Fireclown, are you listening? If you want to see her alive, bring the snow." Then the location. "No cops."

Fireclown. Cal gripped the table, aware of Ray's puzzled attention. He waited, anticipating the shakes, but the shock didn't come. No orange, no smoke, no screams.

"You okay, Cal?"

Cal nodded. He had to be. Route DD. He couldn't picture anything out that far. It was pure rural. That explained the gray barn. Just the sort of place to hole up. He started for the bedroom, but Ray was in the way. "I've gotta get through, Ray."

Ray moved over. "I want to go with you."

"No, you don't." Cal walked into the bedroom and to the closet. He pulled open the door and searched the shelf, then remembered he'd taken the rifle to the cabin. He sagged against the jamb, dropped his chin, and swore.

Well, maybe it was better. He had no doubts whatever that Mildred would use it if necessary. He'd seen her wave her shotgun his way often enough. Shotgun.

Cal turned. "Ray, you know where Mildred keeps her shotgun?"

"Under her bed."

Of course. Cal started down the inside stairs. He had never set foot, nor hoped to, in Mildred's bedchamber. But there was nothing to do but suck it up and go in. It was exactly as he imagined. Prim, immaculate, and smelling faintly of old roses. He looked at the militant bed covered with a white nubby spread. The pattern was perfectly centered.

Cal tried not to muss it as he lifted the edge to peer under the bed. A few dust moats huddled against the wall where even Cissy couldn't ferret them out with the vacuum. The shotgun lay front and center, right where an old woman could get at it. Cal dragged it free and straightened the spread, then stood.

Ray was right beside him, face earnest. "I want to go with you."

"You don't know what's involved, Ray. Besides I can't implicate you. That's aiding and abetting." He didn't expect Ray to understand.

"What about Aunt Millie?" Ray stood in his path. "She's aiding and a—betting."

"Aunt Millie's why you're not coming. If anything happened to you, she'd have my head more surely than Danson ever dreamed of."

Ray crossed his hammy arms. "You can't go alone."

"Yes, I can."

"What did you learn in fireman school? Never go in alone. Always take a buddy."

Cal could hear himself saying those same words to Ray. He hadn't known how much stuck. He sighed. "Ray, I would . . . I really would, but it's too dangerous. You don't know what we're dealing with."

"Do you?"

Cal checked the load on the shotgun. "Not exactly. But enough to know—"

"You be the brains; I'll be the brawn. Partners." Ray held out his hand.

Cal looked up at him. "Ray, you could get killed."

Ray nodded, still keeping his hand aloft.

"I can't be responsible for that."

"I'm responsible for myself." Ray hooked his thumbs into the overall straps, looking like an overgrown Huck Finn wanting adventure.

Cal grinned. He made a very poor Tom Sawyer himself, but if Ray was set on it . . . "You sure?"

"Sure." The nod was definite.

Cal expelled his breath. He could always have Ray hold back if it came to it. "Okay, but I drive."

Ray's grin was as broad as his face. He shoved his hand out again, and this time Cal shook it. They went together to the kitchen.

Cissy's face was flushed and flustered. She wrung her hands and looked at the shotgun in Cal's grip. "What could you need all that cornstarch for? Just a little bit will do for any recipe."

Mildred must have posed the request already. "This isn't for gravy, Cissy. It's just for show, and I hope to heaven they don't taste it."

She shook her head. "I might have to go to three different stores for that much."

Cal pulled out his wallet and handed her two twenties. "Go wherever you need to." He helped the coat over her shoulders and eased her toward the door. "It's all right, Cissy, really."

While she was gone, he and Ray rummaged the closet for Mildred's suitcase. Cal clasped it by the handle and pulled it out. It looked like a small bomb shelter, and weighed about as much. He set it on the table where Mildred's cards still waited to be written, and opened it up. It would do. It would have to. It was ludicrous to think he could pull this off, but it was the best chance he had to get near Laurie.

———————

Laurie watched Dieter standing like a specter in the dim light, her handgun in his belt during his turn to watch. She wished now she'd left the gun in Mother's drawer. As thugs went, they weren't highly armed. Not that it mattered. Either weapon was deadly, though she hoped for a bullet over the slow damage of a knife.

Her hands and feet had lost most of their feeling; her eyes were grainy with lack of sleep, her throat, tight and dry. Which man would do the killing? Dieter's glares were more chilling, but less threatening than Luís's. Dieter's pale eyes turned to her now. "You better hope your boyfriend, your fireclown, gets the message."

She didn't answer. She hoped anything but. Cal couldn't get the message, not if he'd left with the children. Not "if." She was no longer questioning, only believing that Maddie and Luke were safely away.

She dropped her head back against the wall and closed her eyes. Sheer exhaustion would make her sleep soon. What did it matter anyway? Brian was dead. She would be soon. Her own stupidity the cause of it all. That and Brian's. A flicker of sadness. Had it finally been dangerous enough for him? What had he proved? Poor Brian. Always trying. Like her.

She heard a car engine and tires on the dirt outside. The barn wall shook as the door pushed open, flooding the recesses with daylight. Laurie looked up as Luís walked in, dark and silent. Dieter raised his brows, but Luís shook his head. "Only the fat one and the retard."

It was the first time she'd heard him speak. His voice was soft and accented. But his words brought hope. He must mean Ray and Cissy were home. But no Cal. She silently sighed her relief.

Luís turned to her. "Where is he? Your loco fireman."

She cleared the night from her throat. "I don't know."

"Has he gone to sell it?"

"He doesn't know anything about it."

Luís came toward her, reached into his pocket, and drew out Dieter's knife. He flicked the blade up with a touch of his thumb. "Do you know what happens to people who lie?" He leaned and touched the blade to her chin. "They go to hell."

Hell. Was that her destination? The tip pricked, slicing in just enough to draw blood. She closed her eyes against the pain and fear. How could it still be there? She kept coming to the point of oblivion where she thought she could feel no more, and then they found a new source and plumbed it. Would he slice her face? She had to make them understand.

She opened her eyes. "I told you I flushed it down the pool drain. That's the truth. Now, why don't you just finish this?" They'd ended it for Brian; why prolong her terror?

Luís's eyes were like plates, no human emotion at all. The blade reflected her face as he held it pressed into her chin. She no longer felt it, but she would if he sliced. She tried not to think of her face in ribbons, tried to keep the fear from her eyes. Luke and Maddie were safe. She fastened on that thought and held it.

"Luís." Dieter's voice broke through her concentration.

The blade came away from her chin as Luís turned. Another tiny jerk of Dieter's head and Luís stood up and backed away. Dieter took out his cell phone, and for the moment she was free of either gaze. But they weren't through with her yet. Not until they had the cocaine. How long would they wait before they realized Cal was gone and she had told them the truth?

"Always tell the truth, Laurie. Jesus hates lying lips." She'd looked into Gram's eyes and known she could not tell Daddy she'd lost his watch. She had taken the gold pocket watch to show her friend the little tune it played when the lid opened. Daddy kept it in a box and never looked at it, but it was one of her favorite things to sneak out and play with. Now it was gone from her pocket, and Grams wanted her to tell Daddy what she'd done. Jesus wanted her to tell the truth. She'd started by lying to Grams. *"I'll tell him, Grams." "Good girl."*

Of course she hadn't. The watch wasn't missed for years. When it was, Daddy couldn't remember exactly where he'd kept it, though he'd thought it was the box on his dresser. *"Do you know what happens to people who lie?"* Her whole life was a lie. *"They go to hell."* Laurie started to shake. What if this life was only the start? What if what waited for her on the other side of the bullet was worse?

How could she turn to Jesus now, when she'd had so many chances and refused? She had wanted her independence, left her parents behind, married a man she didn't love because he had what she wanted—the wealth and power to let her be whatever she chose. Would she surrender it now to a God who wanted complete control, just like Daddy?

Tears stung her eyes and she forced them back. She would not show these men her fear, her weakness. She would not show God her weakness. Something inside her shrank. Was she doing it again? Making the wrong choice? She couldn't help it. She would never be perfect. Soon she would not even be alive.

———————

Cal had run upstairs for his coat and one last chance to think before he headed out on this escapade. He looked around the room, pictured Laurie in the chair, hair loose and soft, her half smile. Beautiful scent. He could almost smell it.

He jumped when the phone rang, all his nerves tensing. Reaching out he snatched the phone and croaked his name.

"You okay, man?"

The rush of relief was immediate. His system couldn't take much more of this. "Yeah."

Reggie's voice was none too certain. "You sure?"

Cal laughed dryly. "What have you heard?"

"What should I have?"

Cal sobered. "Nothing."

"You in trouble?"

Cal hesitated, then, "Yeah."

"Can I help?"

Cal pictured Reggie. Between him and Ray . . . "No."

"Then you remember one thing."

"What's that?"

"You got the Big Man in charge."

Cal slumped against the wall. "I know, Reg. But last time I said a word to Him, things didn't work out so well."

"That's His business. All you gotta do is ask."

"Yeah. Well, if you have an inside line, put in a call for me, okay?"

Reggie's voice softened. "I'll do that."

Cal placed the phone in its cradle. Wiping his forehead with his palm, he blew the breath between his lips. Now there was nothing but . . . His hand jumped from the receiver as the phone rang again. What if it was Danson? What if it was Laurie?

He picked it up. "Cal Morrison."

"If you think this is a game, you're mistaken." The voice sent a shiver down his spine.

"No game."

"Where is it?"

Did the man think he was a fool? Cal swallowed. "I'm bringing it now."

Silence for a full two seconds' count. "No cops." A click and then nothing.

Again Cal hung up and released his breath. Why hadn't he asked if Laurie was all right, demanded to speak to her? Why hadn't he done anything but act the sheep? Because he was a sheep. A stupid damaged sheep.

"Cal?" Ray's voice came up the stairs.

"Yeah, I'm coming." He held the delete button until zeros flashed on his machine, then took up his coat and threw it over his shoulder and headed down.

He lifted the suitcase, now increased in weight by several army stews' worth of cornstarch, and left Cissy fretting in the kitchen. "You stay here for a minute, Ray. Let Cissy cool down while I get this into the jeep. No sense her knowing you're coming."

He nodded. "I'll go out the front and walk around."

"Okay."

Cal headed for the side door. He reached the jeep, set down the case, and dug into his pocket for the key.

"That's far enough, Morrison."

Cal's head jerked as Chuck Danson stood up and came around the far side of the jeep. "Look, Chuck . . ."

Danson came on, chest at full sail, taking in the suitcase with his eyes. He must think Cal had packed to leave town. "You're under arrest for the murder of Brian Prelane. Anything you say can and will be held against you . . ."

Cal spread his hands. "Why would I kill Brian Prelane?"

"The oldest reason in the book after Cain and Abel."

"What?"

Danson reached for the cuffs in his back pocket. "Never mind. I'm bringin' you in. You can do your talking at the station."

Guests

TWILIGHT

Panic rising up, Cal held out his arms. Danson reached for Cal's wrist, but not quickly enough to catch it. The first blow to the jaw was lucky; it stunned Danson and gave Cal the chance for a second, which caught Danson in the left temple. His head jerked back and hit the side of the jeep, and the big man went down. He wouldn't stay out for long, though, and Cal worked fast to slap the cuffs onto Danson's wrists behind his back.

As he yanked the bandanna from Danson's pocket and used it for a gag, he heard Ray lumbering along the side of the house. Rounding the corner, Ray stopped and stared.

"Well, don't just stand there. Give me a hand." Cal tucked his arms under Danson's shoulders.

Ray hurried over. Together they dragged Danson to the shed. Cal pulled the packing blanket off the old tractor and wrapped Danson with it for good measure. No sense letting him freeze waiting for someone to find him out there.

Cal closed the shed door behind them. He wished he had a dead bolt, but the rusty rod would have to do. He shoved it through the latch and tested its hold, then headed for the jeep. Hands shoved into his overalls, Ray kept step. Cal glanced his way. "Welcome to the world of crime, Sundance."

Ray gulped back whatever he meant to say. They climbed into the jeep from opposite sides, and Cal fired the engine. Ray rested his hands on the dashboard as Cal backed and turned, then dropped them to his lap as the jeep pulled out shooting gravel behind.

Ray turned his head. "You mean Butch Cassidy and the Sundance Kid?"

Cal gave him a quick glance. "You ever see the movie?"

Ray nodded and looked straight ahead. Cal guessed they were both picturing the ending scene. It wasn't reassuring.

17

HE HAS NOT LEARNED THE LESSON OF

LIFE WHO DOES NOT EVERY DAY

SURMOUNT A FEAR.

Ralph Waldo Emerson

REGGIE HELD THE STEERING WHEEL and watched the road, but even on his way to work, he was praying, praying hard. Whatever Cal was doing, it wasn't good. Reggie could only hope it was right. At any rate, it was the first time Cal had asked him to pray.

That was a bigger step than it seemed for a man like Cal. Just his acknowledging the need was enough to pump Reggie's spirit. Maybe some of what he'd said the other night had taken root. He pulled into the lot and parked.

With his hands pressed to his face he drew a long slow breath and released it. "Father, into your hands I commit my friend." He climbed out and headed into the psychiatric center.

Rita was at her desk. She looked up with a sharp face. "Have you heard from him?"

"From whom?"

"Cal." Her eyebrow rose in a peak.

"I just spoke with him."

She pushed back from her desk. "When? How?"

"I called his place." He wasn't sure why; he'd just had an urging. And obviously it had been right.

245

"He's home?" Rita looked more agitated than he'd ever seen her. She reached for the phone, then set the receiver down and stared at it.

Reggie cocked his head. "What's going on?"

Rita stood up and paced to the window. "I should have seen it. I would never have released him if I'd thought . . . There was no sign of this kind of psychosis."

What was she saying, psychosis? Cal was not psychotic, and they should both know that. "Dr. James?" Reggie took a step her way.

She turned and tears brightened her eyes. "Could I have failed so completely?"

Reggie sucked his cheeks. "We all fail completely. It's our nature."

Rita half laughed, rested her palm on the desk. "Did you see it, Reg?"

"Maybe you should tell me what you're worried about."

She shook her head. "He said Laurie was in trouble. I should have known he meant himself. Was it a cry for help?"

"Rita, what kind of trouble is Cal in?"

Rita raised a hand and let it fall. "The murder of Laurie's husband."

Reggie's heart thumped. "Cal killed Laurie's husband?"

"Sergeant Danson thinks so." She stood up and stalked to the window. "You saw him, Reggie. Like a man drowning every time he looked at her."

Reggie sensed the darkness, a presence seeping into the room, tugging at his faith, hammering his foundations. He'd seen how Cal felt about her, heard him admit it. There hadn't been any talk about a husband, though. Only an old love that hadn't worked. Was it possible?

He had just spoken with Cal. Surely his spirit would have recoiled, sensed something more than concern for a friend. He sensed doubt now. Was it an attack on his mind? Rita had no defense against it, nothing but her own human judgment. He had to stand in the gap for her. "I don't believe it."

She turned, the dark wedge of her hair spinning and settling back. Her face was pinched. "Don't you?"

"I don't believe Cal killed anyone."

Her voice took on a higher pitch. "Do you think I want to? You know I care about him. But . . ."

He spread his hands. "What's the proof?"

She crossed the room to the file cabinet, pulled open the drawer and from that the folder. "This." She held it out. "Post-traumatic Stress Disorder. An inability to discern the real from the unreal. Lack of debriefing. Self-destructive behavior. Violence under the influence. He beat up his best friend, shot out the tire of Danson's cruiser."

All true. Reggie knew what the file held. But God knew there was more than that to the story. Cal was haunted, not vicious. And he was clean. Reggie could swear he was clean.

She dropped the folder onto the desk and returned to the window, arms crossed against her chest. "Add to that his obsession with the woman. Any third-rate shrink should have seen it."

Reggie folded his hands and dropped his head. *Lord, show me.* He still did not believe Cal had killed anyone. That wasn't the man he knew. But Rita had the facts, and they didn't look good.

She expelled a sharp breath. "I never should have made it personal. If I hadn't been taken in by his smile and his jokes. If I hadn't been more interested in his friendship than his . . . sickness. . . ."

Reggie saw her not as the confident physician but as a lonely, fragile woman. What would it be like as the only doctor inside these walls, trying to do her job without faith to show her the way?

"I compromised my professional abilities." She turned, her face no longer pained, but barren.

"Rita." Reggie stood up. "You are not God."

Her lips came together silently, and she looked at him.

At the inner urging, Reggie went on. "These people in here . . . they're not yours to save. They're not mine. They're God's."

Her brow furrowed, but still she said nothing.

"And whatever the truth of this is, Cal's in God's hands." Reggie held out his own. "And so are you. The question is whether either one of you will realize it."

———

Laurie trembled. She had heard Dieter on the phone, but it couldn't be real. Was he messing with her mind, trying to trip her up, make her change her story? Cal was coming? Bringing cocaine? What about the children? "No, no, no," she moaned. Luke and Maddie. They were the ones who mattered.

She'd believed them safely away. But how could they be if Cal was home answering his phone? He hadn't taken them. Hadn't hidden them. And when Dieter learned there was no cocaine . . . *"You have lovely children, Mrs. Prelane."* Her breath came in tight gasps.

The door banged open, and Luís came inside with two large gasoline cans. He set them down, turned to Dieter, and said something in Spanish.

Dieter grunted. "Put her in the hole."

Laurie cringed as Luís approached. He tied a smelly rag into her mouth, and then he grabbed her into his arms and carried her to the center of the floor. He laid her down and yanked open a rotting trapdoor. Then he pushed. It wasn't a long fall, but with her arms tied, the impact jarred the breath from her, and she lay gasping until it returned. Sobs caught in her chest as she rolled to her side and lay there. Overhead, she heard a sound of splashing, and the smell of gasoline stung her nose. She stared frantically into the darkness under the floor. Would they burn her?

A scream rose up in her chest and caught there, though the gag would make it futile. Only Dieter and Luís would hear. And God. She struggled to her knees, the rope between her wrists and ankles pulling painfully tight as it tangled. *Oh God.*

How could she pray? She remembered sitting on Gram's knee. *"Jesus, tender shepherd, look down upon this child . . ."* She started to cry, tears choking and burning their way out. What was the use? What was the use?

Cal approached slowly with Ray beside him, the jeep's low rumble sounding loud against the silence of the deserted farm. Only the barn and the blocks on which the house had rested were left standing. Had the house been lifted and removed? There was something unnatural about a home being carried away, but just now Cal was glad. It meant there was only one structure to search.

He braked the jeep far enough away to scope the situation. He would have liked to assess from three sides according to his training. But that would mean getting out of the jeep and circling on foot. He wasn't sure yet that was the best plan. He glanced at Ray. "Looks quiet."

Ray nodded.

Cal regretted having brought him. It was one thing to risk his own neck . . .

"There's someone in the barn." Ray pointed.

Cal riveted his focus. "How do you know?"

"I saw someone move. In that crack there next to the door."

Cal squinted. "You have good eyes. Well, guess this is the place. I'll go on alone."

Ray shook his head. "You take the suitcase. I'll carry the gun."

"No way."

"The way Aunt Millie does. Just holding it like I mean business."

Looking at Ray's face, Cal's nerves tensed. Ray didn't look concerned at all. That wasn't a good thing. "If we walk up with a shotgun, we'll start more trouble than we can finish."

"I won't start shooting unless I have to."

"No, Ray. Listen. You stay in the jeep. Give me cover, but don't be seen. Don't touch the gun unless you have to. I'll make the switch, then hope they leave town without sampling the wares. Cornstarch could wreak havoc with the sinuses."

Ray didn't get it, but that was all right.

"Get down behind the seats." That was no easy task for Ray, but he obeyed. Cal pulled the jeep in closer, certain they'd heard him by now. "Stay in the jeep, Ray." Cal climbed out and pulled the suitcase behind him, then walked to the center of the dirt yard. He made no move to go inside. Neither did he holler. He waited.

After a moment, the door opened. A blond-spiked punk stepped out. The sort of drug dealer you'd see in a bad comedy and know his role immediately. But there was nothing comic in this scene. It was deadly serious. Cal wished he hadn't risked Ray, but there was some comfort knowing someone guarded his back. Cal only hoped Ray wouldn't shoot while he was still in front.

The punk held a gun, a handgun like the one Laurie had wielded. Why hadn't she used hers to protect herself? Or had she thought killing Brian was enough? The gun barrel was leveled at his chest. And here he was armed with cornstarch. Cal leaned the suitcase against his leg. "Where's Laurie?"

The man gave a slow jerk behind him. Cal glanced at the barn. Something quivered his nostrils. Gasoline. It didn't fit. The old barn stood black and gray, patches of dirty paint and rusty tin on rotting wood. It was too long deserted to carry smells unless . . .

"The case." The punk lowered the gun and held out his other arm.

"Not until I see that Laurie's safe."

The man sneered. "Once you turn over the goods, you can go get her."

Cal shook his head. "I don't think so."

The punk raised his gun to face level. Cal looked from the barrel to the icy blue eyes behind. If Laurie was dead it didn't much matter what he did now. But if she lived, if she was just inside . . .

"Okay." He set the case down and stepped aside.

"Open it."

Cal stooped and worked the heavy latch. For a moment he thought it had locked, and he fumbled with it, tension wrapping his stomach tighter than the bands inside a golf ball. Then it sprang open catching his thumb knuckle. Leave it to Mildred. He pulled the lid open to display Cissy's neat packaging.

The punk looked down briefly enough to keep Cal from lunging for the gun. "Put it in the car." He indicated a Mustang with rental plates, Cal noticed, tucked within a ragged fringe of apple trees gone wild.

Cal guessed as soon as his back was turned he'd feel the bullets. But he bent and closed the suitcase, just as the punk swung his foot. Cal caught it in the chest and sprawled. A bang and scattering of shot enveloped him. Ray. He tried to holler, but the punk opened fire on the jeep, and Cal rolled wielding the suitcase like a shield. One bullet from the punk could end it, but Ray had his full attention. Cal got to his knees, swung the suitcase into the back of the man's knees, but with too little force.

The man whipped the butt of the gun into Cal's head and landed a kick to his chest. Cal fell backward expecting the shot. The punk must have spent his ammunition. He wrenched the suitcase from his grasp, turned, and ran for the car. The engine roared. Another man ran from the barn, and just behind him Cal heard the sudden whoosh of flame. The car raced out of the trees and took off in a cloud of dust.

Cal scrambled to his feet as the barn began to blaze. Ray lumbered in holding his bleeding bicep with thick fingers. Cal registered his presence and condition even as he stared at the flames climbing the barn wall. Sweat started down his back. He gripped Ray. "Can you drive?"

Ray nodded.

Cal shoved the jeep keys into Ray's bloody hand. "Get Danson out of the shed!" It was no use calling fire support. The barn would be gone before any vehicle reached it. Trusting Ray would go, Cal ran, his chest heaving as the flames reached up one wall and around the side, devouring the rotten wood. He stopped at the door, his feet one with the frozen ground, impotent stumps. His fists clenched at his hips. The air around him flashed orange; the screams echoed in his mind as the shakes took over.

"No!" Grabbing his ears, he lowered his head and threw himself at the door. The wood shattered around him, and he staggered through, assessing the situation. The back end of the barn was engulfed; the loft, an inferno; the smoke, a demon host dancing to the flames.

"Laurie!" He gripped a post and crouched to see. "Laurie!" He choked.

Dropping to his knees, he searched low, crawling and groping. His elbow banged into something. Liquid sloshed over his sleeve as the gasoline can tumbled over and gushed. Fresh flames burst around him. Cal rolled, yanked his coat off, and heaved it as it, too, burst into flame.

He gagged on the gasoline fumes, pulled off his flannel shirt, and tied it around his mouth and nose. This was insane! They'd intended to burn it all along. Laurie was dead. They'd find her charred body and maybe his too. It was a perfect setup. A murder and a double suicide. Or a double murder and a suicide. Either way, the crazy clown is to blame.

Squeezing under the sagging stall, he searched with hands and eyes, then swung over the side and searched the next. A burning section of roof crashed into the loft and cascades of sparks lit the floor.

He stared at the growing destruction. If he didn't win his way to the back now, there would be nothing left there to search. He fought thoughts of failure and futility. If he gave in, if he doubted . . . He hoped Reggie was on his knees because it would take nothing short of a miracle to pull this one off. In fact if ever there was a time to pray . . .

He got to his feet. *Help me, God!* And ran. With a thud, his leg sank through the floor. He fought to free it, but more boards gave way and Cal started to fall. Clinging with his elbows, he caught a knee on the edge just as the loft broke free and plunged down. Flames exploded around him. Cal lost his hold and dropped.

Just like before, with Ashley Trainor. He utters a prayer, even thinks a prayer—and boom, failure. *Thanks again, Big Man.*

The drop wasn't deep. Just under his own height—a hog shelter? For a moment, he crouched in the darkness beneath the roar of flames above, his senses straining, adrenaline pumping.

There was probably an outside exit down there where the animals were let in and out. But just now his business was not escape. He had to find Laurie, and every second made that less and less possible. He reached up and gripped the flooring.

Then he heard it. The muffled cry. He spun and yanked the shirt free from his mouth. "Laurie!"

It hadn't sounded far off. Over to the right, under the floor like himself. Was his mind playing tricks? Did he imagine what he wanted to hear, what he wanted so much, he conjured it now as he'd conjured other things, dreams, wishes? His chest heaved with choppy breaths as he hurried in the direction the sound had come.

The floor was uneven, shrinking the space to four feet high or less as it rose, probably a natural bowl they'd built over to save digging. After the brilliance of the flames, the darkness beneath was dense. He dropped down and crawled, feeling about in a semi-circle with each move forward.

His hands found her before his eyes did. She was warm, and she moved when he touched her. She turned her face, emitting a muffled whimper. She was alive. *God, she's alive.* God had heard . . . and answered.

Feeling for the nylon cord that bound her wrists behind her back, he cut it free with his pocketknife. In his head the seconds ticked. They were at base level. The best air was down low, and the thrust of the fire upward. But would the floor hold when the roof went? He cut her ankles free.

Laurie yanked at the gag in her mouth with a sob and lunged for him, trembling so hard he had to work to keep his balance on his knees. "It's all right." He held her tight, only half convinced himself.

Her frantic fingers dug into his skin. "The children!"

"They're safe." He eased her away. "But we're not. The fire's above us. It's venting through that patchy roof. But the whole thing could collapse any time." He shook out the gag and, though she balked, tied it again over her mouth and nose. "Come on."

They needed to reach the outer wall where they'd have some protection and possibly find a way out. He guessed that they were roughly centered, though he wasn't sure now which way they were heading. The only light came from the hole he'd broken through, some sort of a trapdoor, he guessed. The rest of the space was dark. He didn't want to think of the smoke also sullying their vision.

Smoke rises, but it crept, too. Any opening, like the crack under a door, the hole in the barn floor would admit it. And it was as deadly and swiftly debilitating as the flames. More so. Flames you could avoid. The smoke was insidious.

Okay, God. One more time. I need your help. Keeping Laurie against him, he rose to a crouch and pushed on. The sudden roar of the fire above told him another part of the structure had collapsed. So far the floor above them held, but his panic grew. They had minutes, maybe seconds, before— He shook the thought away with a physical effort. He had to trust in God.

Reaching out, he groped forward until he touched stone, rough crumbling stone. His breath expelled in a loud rush. The wall. Now if only there was an opening . . . But which way? He tried to get his bearings. The outlet would be at either side or the back. Three choices. He kicked himself for not assessing the structure before he ran in. Mistake number one.

He pulled Laurie close as a crash shook the floor and flames licked the hole in the center. The sweat ran down his back as he yanked her by the arm, crawling three-legged now as the ground rose, shrinking the space. His head grazed the floorboards.

Behind him, Laurie cried out and gripped her leg, her face screwed up in pain. Fire glow glinted off the jagged edge of sheet metal protruding from the ground. Cal hadn't seen it, had crawled past it with no warning for her. Now he looked from her to the flames gaining hold of the floor.

He pulled the flannel shirt from his face and tied it around her knee. "Wait here."

"But—"

"I'll be back." No sense in both of them groping for the way out when he was less and less certain there even was one. Maybe this farmer had a crawl space, not a hog shelter. Maybe there was no way out, no way except through the flames above. A shudder crawled his spine.

Help me, God. Don't give up now. I can't do it without you. He crept forward, his back brushing the floorboards. The heat of it scorched him. It was ready to flash. What he wouldn't give for turnout gear instead of the T-shirt he was down to. He shook his head. Not that even that would be any good in flashover. Only God could save you then.

As He had once? He didn't consider last time God's work. More like the devil himself. God didn't save a man like him and leave a helpless child. God didn't—Cal expelled his breath. What would he know? God could do whatever He chose.

Cal groped around a scattering of broken rocks. Reggie'd said God had a purpose. The night he spoke of Paul on the road to Damascus, he'd told Cal God had a time and purpose for everything. Even if Cal couldn't come close to understanding, he just had to accept. In Reggie's words, God didn't owe him an explanation.

Okay, God. Do whatever you need to. Change me. Take me. Whatever you want. Just let me get Laurie out safe.

The thought of her sent a surge of adrenaline. He fought the panic, straining to see as he groped, and felt a sudden rush of relief. Cracks of daylight showed through the warped storm door slanting above the small chute just wide enough to admit two hogs side by side. He hurried into the chute. With his shoulder, he pressed against the door. It held fast.

He groped back along the wall until he found the loose rocks, grabbed one up and crawled back. Feeling along the seam between the door flaps, he found the metal latch, gripped the rock, and swung. It cut into his palm as he smashed it again and again against the rusted metal. He dropped the rock and thrust his shoulder once more into the door. The latch snapped, and the door swung free.

He'd known the risk. It was the same as opening a window. It formed a chimney, a channel, but it was their one chance. Behind him, Laurie screamed as the center of the floor dropped like a flaming curtain to the ground, trapping them both between the sag and the wall.

Cal plunged back as gasoline fumes flew like glowing specters. Sweat stung his eyes and soaked his chest and back. His skin blistered as he dropped lower beneath the flaming edge of flooring and sol-dier-crawled even as Laurie dragged herself toward him.

They met, gripped arms. Overhead, Cal heard a wrenching and jerked his head up. Through the gaps of fallen flooring, he saw the main beam from the roof break free. He shoved Laurie into the wall and ducked as the beam splintered the sagging floor above him, crashing through and driving him into the dirt.

Laurie's screams sounded small, childlike. She was trapped in the chairs, caged by their legs. Her ponytails hung limp. *Come on, baby. Two more feet. We can buddy-breathe my air. Only two more feet . . .* Then she was gone and there was darkness.

Cal felt so alone it hurt. This was death, hell even. The awful void swallowed him in silence. *God. God!* But he was alone, the need in him his only awareness. A need so acute it overtook fear and want and any other human emotion. A void so empty he lost all sense of himself. He'd never known loneliness before, never seen darkness. A cry burst from him, but there were no sound waves to carry it. His thoughts dissolved.

Then a hand reached out from nowhere, a hand punctured at the wrist, an arm roped with muscle, and a calloused palm. It pulled him from the darkness in spite of the wound. Pain sliced up his side as consciousness rushed in. He opened his eyes and spit dirt. His nostrils sucked the acrid air, his skin burned. He welcomed the pain, gasping with relief.

Laurie bent low, her tears wetting his cheek as he lay muddled. "Cal?" She shook him.

Groaning, he raised his face from the ground. Fresh pain, sharp and insistent, shot through his side as he rose to his elbows and saw the end of the beam less than a foot from his body, new flames licking it. It could have crushed him, but it hadn't. A lightning bolt? Thank God he wasn't blinded. He wasn't making sense. This was no time to ponder theology. They had to get out.

Swallowing the pain, he rolled out from under the debris that had struck him. But not the beam. The beam had missed. How? Why? He couldn't ponder it. They had to move. He had to make them move, or next time he might not be so lucky. Lucky? Was it luck, or God? Whose wounded hand had he gripped? He dragged his knees up underneath him and pushed Laurie. "Go."

Laurie dragged herself under the last edge of flooring and into the small chute that led to the storm door. Cal crawled behind. Eight feet, six feet, two . . . He saw the tiny hand reach out to him. No! He shook away the thought. They were going to make it. This time they were going to make it.

Laurie gripped the frame and pulled herself out. He staggered up behind her, grabbed her hand, and together they stumbled toward the apple grove and collapsed. He lay, sucking air into his lungs in sharp gasps. His head throbbed, his ribs were knives in his side, and the cold air stung the burns on his back and legs, but they were out of it.

Laurie's cheekbone was bruised, and she had abrasions on her face, hands, and arms. The ends of her hair were singed, and she was red-faced and sooty, but he didn't see any serious burns. The worst was her knee, which bled right through the shirt as she rolled and fixed her eyes on the fury of flames, shuddering when the barn skeleton collapsed.

He laid a hand to her cheek, and she turned. Tear streaks ran through the soot and filth on her face, and her lips were cracked and bleeding. He couldn't tell if she was in shock or just scared and exhausted. But it was clear she didn't have much left to run on.

He assessed their predicament. The fire posed little danger to them. Once it consumed the combustible gasoline-treated wood, it should peter out on the frozen gravel surrounding the barn. But they had no shelter, inadequate clothing, no first aid without the jeep, and they were dependent on Ray finding his way back. Cal looked up. The clouds were low, and in these temperatures they wouldn't get far on foot, injured and depleted as they were.

His thoughts were already getting fuzzy. Too many blows to the head, and he could guess at other damage. If he had Annie . . . Where was she? She would find them, but no, she was with Mildred and the children, at the cabin miles and miles away. He shivered, his T-shirt little better than nothing.

"You're freezing." Laurie's voice broke into his thoughts.

He wiped the grime from his eyes. "I'm okay." But he wasn't. The pain and fuzziness were growing. And one thing he knew, Ray was terrible with direction.

18

LAURIE STARED AT CAL. It was sinking in that he was there, that this was real. And as that understanding dawned, she realized with acute sensation how close to death they'd been. She shook uncontrollably. "I thought you were killed. When that beam fell . . ." The thought brought a sudden ache to her chest. He could have been. One foot to the left and he would have been.

His voice rasped, "I thought they'd killed you already." He winced and lay back against a narrow trunk.

He'd thought she was dead? "But you came in after me."

"I have a hero complex." He pressed a hand to his side.

Hero complex. Her own words. She'd meant it as an insult, but what if he didn't? What if he hadn't been driven to save her at all costs? "You are a hero, Cal." She covered the hand that held his side with her own. "Is it bad?"

"Bad enough." He faced her squarely. "Laurie . . ."

"Don't talk. It's hurting you." Her own knee was throbbing, shooting pain down her shin. His injuries were much worse, gashes and swelling on the side of his head, burns and abrasions, and something worse with his side. She fought panic. What if he was . . .

"Listen."

"No." She put a hand to his lips. "Later." She moved close to warm him.

He drew a shallow breath. "I don't know what'll happen later. There's something I want to tell you." He slowly raised one knee and shifted his hip with a groan, then settled. "Eight months ago there was a fire. An old B-and-B on Wilton Street."

"Cal." Why was he forcing it? Was he in shock, delirious?

"They were doing a remodel. Had everything blocked up. Scaffolding . . . debris. They were careless."

His chest tightened under her hand as he spoke, more she guessed from tension than pain. But he kept on. "They were replacing the electrical, but something went haywire, literally. Once it started, the place took off like"—his voice grated—"nothing I'd seen before. We thought we had everyone out . . ."

Laurie's diaphragm seized as she guessed what was coming. Did she want to hear, to know what had changed Cal, damaged him? Why was he telling her now, when he'd just done what no one else could have, would have, done?

He closed his eyes. "A little girl . . . Ashley Trainor, two years old."

Laurie remembered the way he'd lunged for Maddie.

Cal held his hand to his side, and his breath caught. "Each parent thought the other had her. Too much confusion. Exits blocked. The building was a loss. We were pulling out to contain. Then we learned Ashley was in there."

The pain was deep in his voice. Pain deeper than any physical injury. Pain that had changed him, broken him. Laurie trembled. Cal had always loved deeper, cared more, risked more.

"Frank said no." He rubbed his palm along his thigh in distracted agitation. "But I disobeyed. I thought—"

"Cal, don't." Laurie touched his cheek. She didn't want his sacrifice laid bare, didn't want to know, to feel his failure.

He turned, teeth clenched, jaw tense. "She was alive." His eyes burned. "I saw her there, scared, unable to help herself."

Oh, God, that little girl! Laurie felt his torture, saw it in his face, thought of her own children and the horror of losing them. Little Maddie, trapped and terrified.

"I was so close." Tears welled in his eyes, red rimmed and haggard. "She was too little, Laurie. Too helpless."

Laurie's voice was a ghost. "She died."

"The place flashed. Ignition blew me out." He cocked his chin and looked up at the sky, one tear making a track down his burned cheek.

They sat in silence a long moment. Laurie could think of nothing to change what he saw in his mind, what she now knew had caused his erratic behavior. Like what soldiers experienced long after a war. "That's what Rita treated you for?"

He swallowed. "I went a little crazy. Hit the sauce and behaved badly. They slapped me with a medical suspension to clean up my act. Court ordered me into treatment."

"And?"

"And I came back the fireclown." He grimaced. "A position tailor-made for pyrophobic firemen."

Laurie's eyes stung with tears. "It must have been awful."

"It was hell. Still is sometimes." He formed a crooked smile. "You saw that for yourself."

"But you came in for me. You faced the fire, you . . ."

"I'm no hero, Laurie. Just a fool." He slid a hand around the back of her neck, pulled her forward, and kissed her lips. It brought more pain than pleasure, and not because her lips were cracked and scorched. It was because she didn't know what to feel. He drew back, and she was glad.

He pressed himself up. "Think you can walk?"

Her knee still throbbed and bled, but she nodded. "Can you?"

"Don't have much choice. Unless we get to the highway, no one's going to find us." He sat up, wincing. "Ray would have been here by now."

"Cal . . ." She laid a hand on his shoulder. He shouldn't move. He might have serious injuries from the falling debris.

"It's okay." He pulled himself to his feet.

Laurie was almost too tired to do the same, but she made herself follow. He held out an arm, and she hooked hers in. Slowly they started for the road. They hadn't gone far when the snow began—small, listless flakes meandering down, stinging her cheeks like tiny pinpricks. She raised her fingertips to touch the skin.

Her face was burned like sunburn from the scorching heat she'd escaped. What would have happened if Cal hadn't come? He'd saved her life. Why was she surprised? He'd been trying to save her from the first time they'd met.

It hurt to think what he'd faced in order to do it now. To enter a burning building after . . . Why had he told her? Did it matter that he'd suffered a crisis? Even that he'd weathered it badly? He was Cal. It scared her more than the flames.

A wind chilled his face when Cal caught sight of the highway. He forced his legs to move, in spite of the raw, burned skin on the back of his calves. Every part of him hurt. Laurie was silent, and, after baring his soul, he was glad to stay quiet too. Why had he told her?

Maybe, in the midst of victory, to show her he was fallible. She'd called him a hero. But he hadn't done this alone, hadn't saved her. Someone higher, someone bigger, some real savior had intervened.

God? The Big Man? The Lord Jesus? Those moments of alone-ness haunted him. It hadn't been Laurie he needed. It was a more primal need, a spiritual need. A God need. Something no person could fill. But he couldn't talk about that, didn't understand it. So he'd told her his story.

Cal swallowed the ache in his throat, the tears just behind his eyes. Until that moment with Laurie, he hadn't cried, hadn't shed a tear for Ashley Trainor or her family. He'd raged. He'd drunk himself into a stupor. He'd numbed his mind with pain-killers. But he hadn't cried. Nor had he described, even to Rita, what he'd just told Laurie.

He'd joked, he'd argued, he'd rebelled. But now it seemed his rebellion was crumbling away. He couldn't summon the self-depre-cation, the anger, the guilt. He looked around him. Where was the smoke, the orange, the shakes? If anything should have brought it on, that burning barn . . . He wiped the sooty streak from his left eye.

Now was not the time to give in to the sobs building inside his chest. Later. He'd visit it later. With God's help? He dropped his chin, recalling Reggie's words. *"It's not what happened to the circumstances; it's what happened here."* In his heart. Cal shuddered. Maybe Reggie was right. Maybe he couldn't do it himself, his way.

He and Laurie reached the edge of the pavement and stopped

together. Cal scanned the empty expanse of blacktop, spackled now with snow. Maybe this was his road to Damascus. *"You remind me of someone, the Apostle Paul. Took a mighty wallop to get his attention."* And Reggie's story had stuck more deeply than he knew. Cal's side was shooting pain, the burns screaming a chorus while his head kept up a pulsing ache. He looked up at the sky, aswirl with white feathers.

He had told God to have His way. In the burning barn he'd said, *"change me, take me, do whatever you choose."* He'd surrendered, and somehow he couldn't take up the fight again, couldn't resist. God was bigger than his rage, bigger than his shame and horror. Cal felt the truth of it. And the dark loneliness shrank away.

He glanced at Laurie. She was pale and shaking. His shirt had soaked up her blood like a sponge. She must be in pain. He released a slow breath. "We'll rest."

She nodded, leaning into him more than she realized, he guessed.

He let her lean, though her weight made him compensate in a way that didn't help the ribs. "Are you cold?"

"I don't know."

That wasn't good. She'd lost blood on top of trauma. She could be in shock. "Maybe I ought to look at your knee." Though with no first-aid equipment what could he do beyond binding it with the shirt as he already had?

"It doesn't matter." Her head sagged against his shoulder.

He smelled nothing but smoke and gasoline in her hair. "When's the last time you slept?"

"I can't remember."

"Ate?"

She shook her head.

He needed to keep her talking. And walking. As soon as they caught their breath a little . . . Cal shifted to relieve the pain in his side and scanned the highway both directions. It was one of those country roads that leapt and bobbed through the farmland like a discarded ribbon in the wind.

He'd accept a ride from any good-ol'-boy who came by, if any came. The road was still and quiet, but he didn't worry about that. Something would happen. It had to. He didn't suppose God would work halfway. Not now, not . . .

"Cal?" Laurie's voice broke.

"Yeah?" He dipped his head to her.

"Brian's dead." So that was what occupied her thoughts, numbed her mind.

"I know."

She didn't ask how, just gave a low moan in her throat, as though she hadn't been certain until that moment. "They killed him. I thought . . . I thought I'd be the one to die. Or the children. Or you. Or all of us." She started to shake again, hysteria building in her voice. "Where are Luke and Maddie?"

"With Mildred at my grandpa's cabin." In the fire, he had told her they were safe, but maybe she didn't remember. She was running on overload, the same as he. "They're safe, Laurie. I promise you."

That calmed her at least. She must be on an internal roller coaster worse than his own. Maybe talking would help, and he sure had questions. "How did you get mixed up with cocaine?"

Her eyes came up to him, large and haunted. "Brian flew it in with his private jet. I don't know how, I don't know why." She waved a hand as the words built and spilled from her. "I found it by accident. I couldn't believe he'd be that stupid. That's why I left."

Not because she didn't love him, didn't want the marriage, the life she had as Mrs. Brian Prelane. Cal knew himself for a fool. A familiar thought.

She drew a jagged breath. "But before I did, I washed it all down the pool drain."

Cal let out a low whistle.

"I know. It was stupid. I just didn't think. I reacted. How could I know . . ."

Cal pressed her head to his chest. "You didn't go to the police?"

"And turn my own husband in?"

Her own husband. It hurt to hear it, but he could face it now. He had to. He didn't say her husband might be alive if she had turned him in. Saying it wouldn't change things now. Brian Prelane had made a stupid choice of his own. Cal swallowed the hardness in his throat. Why would any man who had Laurie risk it all for . . . for what? Money? Power? The thrill of the illegal?

"And he could take the children."

Cal glanced down. What did she mean?

"He threatened it, several times when . . . we disagreed. He said he'd take them where I couldn't find them. I know he could have."

She was not painting a picture of marital bliss now. But that wasn't his business.

"Cal?" She turned her face up. "What did you do? They said you had the cocaine. I heard them through the floor. They said you had it."

"Well," Cal grinned, "between Mildred's suitcase and Cissy's cornstarch . . ." Her look made him laugh, which he wouldn't do again.

Laurie gripped his arm. "What if they'd—"

"Well, they didn't. And I doubt they'll have time now. I sent Ray for Sergeant Danson. There's probably an APB on those two already." Cal could only pray Ray had accomplished that much at least. After all he knew where to find Danson—in the shed, cuffed with his own cuffs and gagged with the bandanna from his back pocket. This wasn't over yet. Not by a long shot. Even if Ray did convince him to look for two punks in a Mustang.

Laurie sagged, and he staggered with the pain that shot through his ribs, then jerked his head up, listening. A car. A hint of an engine through the cold air, but a car engine nonetheless. "Do you believe in God?"

Again her eyes searched his face. "I used to."

"Now might be a good time to try again." Cal steeled himself to wave the car down, then saw Danson's cruiser top a rise and plunge down again, lights flashing in the growing dusk. Oh boy. At least he wouldn't have to wave.

He relaxed his shoulders and drew a careful breath. "Laurie, I might not have much chance to talk here."

She pulled back a little. "What do you mean? What's wrong?"

The car was nearly to them. Cal released his hold of her. "Will you make sure Annie gets fed and—"

Laurie gripped his arm again. "What are you talking about?"

"Cissy knows where to find the kids if Mildred hasn't brought them down." Cal turned as Danson slid to a stop and climbed out of the cruiser. He'd brought backup in the form of Pete Rawlings, but didn't need it as he pulled himself up to his full six feet four, broiling with animosity.

"Calvert Morrison. You're under arrest." He slipped the cuffs from his belt and yanked Cal's arm.

"Aah!" Fire shot through Cal's side and shoulder and head, and he couldn't stop the cry.

Laurie shouted, "Wait. He's hurt. What are you doing?" She might have been a flea circling Danson's head.

"I won't list all the charges I have against you, Morrison, but I'll give you your rights. Just so there's no possibility you'll slip through."

"He hasn't done anything. He . . ."

Officer Rawlings took Laurie and led her away.

Danson yanked Cal's other arm and cuffed it behind him. "You have the right to remain silent . . ."

"Do I have the right to talk?" Cal spoke through gritted teeth, scarcely breathing through the pain. One question only. Had Danson put an APB on the punks?

Danson slapped the cuffs shut. "Get in the car, wise guy." He jerked his jaw toward Pete to climb in beside him. "Give him his rights."

Laurie moved to follow, but Danson motioned her up front. Even if he wanted to, Cal couldn't talk now with the car lurching and rising and falling. His breath came in short grunts with each bump and swerve. Rawlings read the Mirandas, then he, too, was quiet.

Cal understood Laurie's confusion. Once she glanced back, and he smiled crookedly, giving her the look she expected, a little rebellious and a lot more confident than he felt. Danson muttered something, and she turned around. The glass between them muffled her words, but Danson nodded shortly. Something she'd said must have penetrated his pigheaded rage. Not that Cal blamed him. Assault on an officer was right up there. But he'd been desperate.

They passed through Montrose and drove to the emergency room at the hospital in Melbourne. Cal hadn't been there since the incident with Ashley Trainor and was not eager to go inside again, but Danson was covering his bases, leaving no room for complaint. Laurie was taken off to one curtained area, he to another. Cal hoped they realized her emotional shock must be as bad as the gash in her knee. Maybe now Rita would talk to her. Maybe . . . He shook away the fuzzing.

A young doctor Cal hadn't seen before came in to assess his injuries. Pete Rawlings stayed close as a hovering mother, Cal guessed at

Danson's orders. Too bad he didn't have any fight left in him. He might have made things interesting. But why? Cal's head throbbed. What was the point here anyway?

Laurie was safe, her kids were safe. He didn't have anything left to fight for. "Yuh—right there." He tensed against the probing of the doctor's hand on his side.

"We'll X-ray that."

"What happened to your ribs?" Rawlings asked.

"Flashover." Or was that the last time? "Roof came down." That was it.

"What were you doing out there?"

Cal glanced up. Rawlings looked innocent as a suckling babe, but Cal had no doubt Danson had primed him. One didn't assault an officer without earning the ire of the entire force. "Out for a stroll," Cal said, though why he didn't just answer was beyond him. Habit of recalcitrance. That would have to stop. But just now his head hurt, his side hurt, and most every square inch of skin as well.

Rawlings frowned. "You can do it easy for me, or hard for Danson."

Good cop, bad cop. Unfortunately it was true. Cal jerked when a nurse applied something to the wound on the side of his head.

"Just washing it up." Her voice sounded shrill in his ear.

He recognized her but couldn't find a name. He sucked a shallow breath. "If you want the story clear, you should get it from Laurie."

"Danson's doing that."

So they would compare notes. Well, the sooner he cooperated, the sooner they'd leave him alone. "Laurie's husband was mixed up with a couple of drug punks. I had nothing to do with his death. I never even saw him unless you count the number he did on my shoulder with a baseball bat. Even then I didn't see him, since he was masked."

"Masked?" Rawlings had taken out a pad.

"Came at me in the dark wearing a ski mask."

"Then how do you know it was him?"

Cal felt awash with guilt. "He told me to stay away from Laurie."

"Where did he attack you?"

Cal thought about that. He could picture Brian's silhouette, bat raised, but he couldn't place the incident. He winced as the doctor pressed another soaked cloth to his head, scrubbing lightly. He recalled Annie on Brian's ankle. "Mildred's yard."

"He attacked you at your place?"

"Outside, yeah."

Rawlings wrote. "You filed a complaint?"

Cal shook his head, then wished he hadn't. "No complaint."

"Why not?"

"I didn't know what was going on." Or did he? What had he thought? He'd gone to Laurie's. He remembered that much. That's when he learned she was married—no, *still* married.

"A man attacks you and you wait to understand why?"

"Pete, I'm not thinking real clearly right now."

"Mild trauma to the brain." The doctor pushed aside the curtain and spoke for him.

Not mild, Cal thought. The physical trauma might be mild, but the mental? He had yet to deal with that.

"So what were you doing at the barn?"

"Getting Laurie out."

"Did you abduct her?" Rawlings poised his pencil.

"What do you think?" Cal frowned.

Rawlings tapped the pencil against his chin. "A woman's husband is dead. You just admitted he attacked you. Rita told us you have past history with the woman. Yeah, I'd say it's a good chance you flipped out, took her off to some secluded place . . ."

Cal pushed the nurse aside. "And what?"

Rawlings lowered the pencil. "Why don't you tell me?"

"Why don't you take a flying leap."

"We'll X-ray those ribs now." The doctor stepped between them. Cal glared over the doctor's shoulder as he was edged out of the room. Still steamed, he submitted to the X-ray. Stripped down to his skin, he realized the burns were superficial, though still painful. He'd had worse. The last time. He pictured himself wrapped in gauze, newly stitched chin, broken tibia, bruised heart and kidneys. It was the emotional damage that didn't heal. What would the fallout be this time?

Don't go there. He wouldn't have to invent his torment this time. Danson would provide it. Deservedly so. Cal felt the fight leak out.

Pete Rawlings was doing his job; he looked defensive when they went back in.

"Pete, I didn't kill Laurie's husband. Find the two punks who came out here with him. They've got a trunk full of cornstarch and probably the murder weapon."

"We're working on that."

Relief coursed through him. "Danson established a search?"

"What would we charge them with, possession of cornstarch?"

"Murder. Kidnapping. Attempted murder. Come on, Pete. Tell me you're doing something substantial."

"That's not your concern."

Cal's body tensed. "Not my concern? Have you seen Laurie's house? Did you notice her condition? They tried to burn her alive! What do you think they'll do if they stop and find it's cornstarch they're hauling, not cocaine?"

Pete looked honestly confused.

"They thought I had Brian Prelane's cocaine. So I brought them Baggies of cornstarch in trade for Laurie. They decided to kill us both instead, torched the barn and . . ."

Pete put his pad back into his coat pocket. "Let me do you a favor, Morrison. Tell Danson the truth. He'll get it one way or another."

Cal shook his head. "Yeah."

The pain was just bad enough to keep exhaustion at bay. If Rawlings was through asking questions, Cal would just as soon stop talking. Every word was painful. He had to figure Danson would hold Laurie for questioning. She'd be safe until they let her loose. But the children . . . Those punks couldn't have held Laurie and followed him, could they?

"Pete . . ."

"Save it, Morrison. Danson will love getting a crack at you."

And Danson's face when he came in showed exactly that. "All right, wise guy—"

"How's Laurie?"

"*Mrs*. Prelane is stitched up and fine."

Cal raised an arm for the nurse to take his blood pressure. "She's still in shock—"

"We've got it under control."

269

Danson obviously wasn't giving an inch. Cal stopped talking. He'd have to trust others to look after Laurie now. His own goose was cooked.

Danson looked at Rawlings and Pete shrugged; the old "did you get the statement"—"not exactly" routine. But Cal had told the truth, the best he could recall it. Danson must have gotten the same from Laurie. And he must believe it, or . . .

"Are you letting Laurie go?"

"We've driven her to the station and sent an officer to fetch her children."

Cal hoped Mildred didn't put a bullet through his breadbasket.

His throat tightened. "And you're looking for the dealers? In the Mustang?"

Danson pursed his lips and narrowed his eyes.

"At least keep Laurie and the kids under protection until . . ."

"Are you telling me how to do my job?" Danson's neck reddened. "You're in no position—"

Cal raised his hands, wincing. "I know. I just have to know they're safe."

Danson studied him a long moment. "The bacon you better worry about is your own, Morrison." He rubbed his jaw.

Cal didn't see much evidence of the blows he'd landed, lucky blows that brought Danson down. But he knew they would not be forgotten. The reality of a cell seeped in. No twilight walks, no woods, no Annie at his side. Not even Mildred's hi-fi, and Ray's odd-jobs. No trips to the nursing home, no sea of children's faces. He swallowed harder this time. He'd made his choice. But he dropped his chin to his chest.

The doctor came in. "X rays show three hairline fractures to the ribs. We'll wrap them up. A slight swelling on the brain. You'll probably be fuzzy. Here's something for the pain." He turned to Danson. "That'll make him fuzzier. You might wait to finish questioning."

Danson hooked his thumbs into his belt, drawing himself up. "Is he released?"

The doctor nodded. "The burns are superficial. I think the concussion's mild enough. Let me just wrap the ribs."

Wincing, Cal raised his arms and held them while the doctor

rendered his rib cage somewhat immobile, waiting for the pain-killers to take off the edge. When there was nothing left to delay his extradition, Danson slapped the cuffs back onto Cal's wrists and drove him to the Montrose police station. He didn't try to question him, probably due to the doctor's remarks, though Cal figured Danson hadn't appreciated that young man's input into his business either.

Cal was escorted directly to the one holding cell, and he lay kissing the bunk where Danson shoved him before uncuffing his hands and walking out. Any position was as bad as the next, but it was a bed, and if he didn't move one muscle he just might be able to ignore the pain. The only problem was breathing.

———

Like a wrung out rag, Laurie repeated the answers to questions asked one way and then another. She was still reeling. It was too much to take in. Too much to explain. And it was obvious Sergeant Danson didn't believe her, though her account of Dieter and Luís matched Ray's. He admitted that much. He didn't go so far as to charge her with Brian's murder, but he obviously suspected her involvement. He would tell her nothing about Cal except that they held him in a cell somewhere in the building.

At her insistence he also told her Cal's injuries were minor, fractured ribs and a slight concussion, his burns as superficial as her own, though painful, she was sure. Her cut knee had been stitched and bandaged. It was the emotional strain that exhausted her now, and Cal's wouldn't be much better. She hoped he cooperated, but he was just rebellious enough to make it worse. And Danson certainly had an ax to grind.

"If you just catch Dieter and Luís, you'll see that it's all true." She had told the story all the way from her finding the cocaine in Brian's pool house to Cal's rescue in the barn. She wasn't sure about the parts Cal had handled on his own, only going by what he'd told her.

"Every department in the state has been alerted. If they're out there, we'll pick them up."

"It's Alex Dieter. But I don't know the other man's last name. I never saw him before the other night."

"Tell us again about the other night."

Raggedly she described the scene in her kitchen once more.

"They took your father's gun."

"Yes."

"Which would have your fingerprints."

"Yes."

Danson tapped his pen. "And that's the last time you saw your husband alive?"

Tears surprised her. "Yes." She swallowed the sudden swelling in her throat. "He looked frightened, but I didn't think . . . Why would they kill him? He was in it with them. He always thought he could get away with anything."

Danson slid the lid onto the ball-point pen and laid it on the table. "I'll need you to make a positive ID on the body we believe to be your husband's."

Laurie shook. "Now?"

Danson nodded.

She drew a jagged breath. "All right." She followed him to the temporary morgue at the back of the building, quaking inside. But when the body was revealed, it was like a blow. Brian's face—her insides seized. It was his hair, his jaw, his neck with the gold chain she'd given him for one of their Christmases together. She staggered back, a hand to her face, and nodded.

A call came to Danson's cell phone, and he said, "Yes? Okay. Keep outside surveillance." He hung up and looked at her. "Are you all right?"

She couldn't answer. She'd never been all right, and never would be.

"My officer has delivered Mildred and your children to Mildred's house. She insisted it would be too traumatic for them to be taken here to the station."

Laurie nodded, blessing Mildred's insight. And now one thought burned away all others, one thought she hadn't allowed herself, hadn't dared hope for. Luke and Maddie. Cal had kept them safe . . . and saved her. As she'd known somewhere inside that he could. Without ever formulating the thought, she'd flown to him like a homing pigeon seeking a safe haven. And he'd done all he could and more.

"Your car is in the lot. We found and impounded it yesterday. I'll sign the release forms."

Laurie nodded mutely and followed him up from the cold room that was Brian's temporary tomb. She couldn't think about that now. She had to get out, had to see her children, touch them, hold them.

Danson handed her the tag for her car and her purse, which they'd found inside it with her keys. "You're free to go for now, but you're not to leave town."

She nodded again. Words had been purged by the sight of Brian's face.

"Can you drive?"

She forced an answer. "Yes." She had washed up at the hospital but still felt bedraggled as she climbed into the car. She drove to Mildred's, anticipation choking her. Heart racing, she climbed out and rushed for the house. An officer stood off to the side, but she ignored him and hurried for the front door. Cissy pulled it open, and the children ran down to her. She bent and grabbed them against her, tears streaming. "Oh, Luke. Maddie." She'd never let go. Even if she wanted to, her arms would never release them, never.

"Don't cry, Mommy." Maddie patted Laurie's cheek.

Laurie smiled and kissed the damp palm of her daughter's hand. "Oh, my baby." She hugged them hard again. Just to feel their warmth, their heartbeats, their breath. Just to touch them and hold them and—

"Where's Cal?" Luke struggled free, his eyes probing.

Laurie dropped her chin, taking Luke's hand between hers. "The police are keeping him tonight. They're trying to find out what happened to—" She'd almost said what happened to Daddy. But that was more than she could deal with just now. She would tell them, had to tell them. But . . .

"Can we go home now?" Maddie caught Laurie's face and turned it back to hers. "I want to go home now."

Laurie nodded.

"Can we get hamburgers?" Luke kept hold of her hand as Laurie straightened slowly.

"And French fries?" Maddie tugged the other.

Laurie's stomach revolted at the thought, but she rejoiced that the children were so innocent, so unaware. She looked up at Cissy standing in the doorway, thanked her with her eyes when words would be so wasted. Then she looked behind to Mildred and swallowed the lump that formed in her throat. These two women, these unlikely women, had risked themselves for her and her children.

"Thank you." It was totally inadequate.

"I hope you set Chuck Danson straight." Mildred's hands went to her hips. "Cal had him hotter than a hornet in my shed." She glanced at the children. "Well, that's neither here nor there."

Laurie nodded, a fresh wave of guilt assailing her, and she didn't know what Mildred meant by the shed. She had tried to convince Danson that Cal was not responsible. But the sergeant had implied that there was more to it than she knew. He wouldn't say what, though he'd rubbed his jaw with a look of pure fury. What had Cal done?

Seeing Brian had driven all her questions away. She wished she could force the memory from her mind. Would it ever fade? Leading the children to the car, Laurie shuddered. That image of her husband would be with her always. That, and the sight of him in her kitchen, weak with fright. And human. So human. So much more so than he'd ever seemed before. Six years she'd spent with him, six broken, disrupted years of lies and betrayal. But there had been times of tenderness. Or had she imagined those?

She buckled Maddie, then climbed in and drove like a zombie. She ordered their burgers and fries through the intercom, sounding like a machine herself. The smell of the food in the car gagged her, but she passed it to the children automatically, and they dug in. Danson had allowed her to go home, but not to leave town. She shook her head. What did it matter? What more could she tell him? Without Dieter and Luís it was her word against all the evidence to the contrary.

Danson suspected some sordid affair between her and Cal, believed Cal had murdered Brian. Cal, who refused to have anything to do with her once he learned there was no divorce? Yet he'd come. He'd played into their hands, braved the fire. She owed him for more than her life or her children's lives. She owed him . . . what?

"Look, Mommy. I got a ring." Maddie held up the cheap plastic toy that came in her kid's meal.

It reminded Laurie of the one Cal had magically pulled from Maddie's ear and of her little girl's giggles as Cal had played with her, down on her level, connected. Cal loved children. Why didn't he have a houseful by now?

"See, Mommy?" Maddie persisted.

Laurie nodded, no words coming. She drove up to the house and parked, startled by the yellow police tape and the gaping doorway. Danson had told her it was a crime scene, but it hadn't registered. Her head swam.

Maddie's dismay matched her own. "Who broke our house?"

Laurie put the car in reverse, shaking with this new invasion. "Let's go to Grandma's."

Luke shouted, "Did someone mess up my room? I want my bear."

"Luke . . ." Laurie shot a look over her shoulder at him. "We're going to Grandma's now. There are things I'll tell you, but not here. Not now." She shivered. Until Dieter and Luís were apprehended, none of them were safe. They could be watching now. Why had she gone to the house? She jerked her head both ways, but the neighborhood was still and silent as always.

She had to get out of there. Even if Dieter had driven straight away, how long would it be before they realized Cal had duped them with cornstarch? They weren't stupid. They'd taste it, or do whatever you do to check its authenticity. They'd know. And they'd come for her. She should have asked for protection. But would Danson give it?

She was forbidden to leave town, yet were they safe staying? She had to let the police handle it, if Danson would even try to find them. He had to believe they were the ones who killed Brian— She pressed a hand to her temple. He was dead and she felt nothing. Tears had come before, but they were not connected to any feeling.

Once again she realized how inadequate she was. Shouldn't she care? Shouldn't she hurt? In a way she did. For him. For the waste of his life. He was her children's father. She could hurt for them. Then she felt a real pang for Luke and Maddie.

Though Brian had scarcely found time for them, the children would hurt. What would she tell them? What could she say? For years she'd covered up, made some normalcy out of his deficiency. She wasn't even bitter. Not for herself. Because she'd known, known that if he stayed home, if he did love her, her own lack would show.

As Laurie pulled up to Mother's house, Maddie wadded her kid's-meal bag and handed it to her. With a fresh wave of nausea, Laurie brought the children inside and went straight to the bathroom. There was nothing to empty but her own bile, yet she heaved and heaved, then dropped to the floor and sobbed, gripping her head between her palms. *Why? Why? Why?*

The pain that came was real. Pain for Brian. Pain for her children. Pain for the emptiness and futility that filled her. Pain for herself and all the mistakes. Pain for Cal, lying in a cell injured and distrusted because of her.

"Do you believe in God?" Did she? Did she believe in anything? How could she when God wore Daddy's face? They were inseparable—frowning, disapproving, unsatisfied. But she had once. She'd given her life to Jesus and trusted, then turned away when it got too hard.

Why did Cal ask? She'd been safe in his apostasy, his irreverence. Had that, too, changed? A lot of good it did him now. But hadn't her own thoughts turned to heaven when she thought she would die? Had she prayed? Had Jesus heard her heart cry and sent Cal? Was it possible?

A knock came on the door. Looking up, Laurie sniffed. "It's open." She ran a hand under her nose.

Her mother stood in the doorway, lips pulled tight, face drawn. Her hands trembled at her sides, and Laurie thought for the first time she looked old. Then her mother's eyes softened, and she stooped, reached out her hands. Laurie took them.

She could hear the movie Luke and Maddie watched in the spare room as Mother led her to the kitchen and poured her a cup of tea. Surprisingly, Laurie found herself sipping it. It's warmth and bitterness soothed the shuddering of her stomach. Then Mother sat.

Laurie looked into her eyes and saw what she'd hungered for for so long. Love. Mother loved her. Now. In this . . . nightmare. How could she, when Laurie felt so utterly unlovable? "Brian's dead." There, she'd said it, summed up her failure.

Mother's eyes reflected her pain, but no condemnation followed.

"He's dead, and I never loved him." Laurie spoke the truth, letting Mother know how badly she'd failed.

Her mother's hands trembled as she raised the cup and drank her tea. The lids of her eyes had tiny ridges and the lashes overshadowed the eyes as she stared into her cup. "I buried your father thinking the same thing."

Laurie's breath leaked from her lips. Was it true? Mother, who had never said one word of disagreement, never contradicted one action of Daddy's, never uttered one single defense to all the criticism and scorn?

Mother's eyes met hers. "I grew up in a shack in the Ozarks. A hillbilly urchin with nothing but beautiful eyes. Your father offered me escape."

Escape. But not love. Laurie saw the pattern, how it had been subtly woven to form and shape her own thoughts and expectations. Brian had offered more than escape. He'd opened the world of privilege . . . but not love.

And she'd snapped it up like a greedy child, willing to sacrifice something real for something vain. Love was too dangerous, too uncertain, too painful. She had hoped that wealth would cover the lack. But it hadn't.

Laurie pressed her palms to her eyes. She felt so lost. She hadn't turned to her mother for answers in so many years, not since she was small, too small to see that she didn't trust the answers. Now she reached out in desperate hope. "What do I do?"

"I don't know."

The words were blank, empty. But she must know. Mother had lived too many years to have nothing, nothing at all to say. Did she have a thought, a single independent thought that Daddy hadn't burned from her brain?

Laurie dropped her hands and grabbed her mother's. "Cal asked me if I believed in God. Do I? Do you?"

Her mother sighed. "You know what Daddy said about that."

Laurie's face screwed up as she shook her head. "Not Daddy's God. Jesus. Grams' Jesus."

Mother shook her head. "Grams was a dreamer. She never understood."

"What? What didn't she understand?"

Mother met Laurie's eyes, and her mouth hardened again into the straight, pinched line. "That if there was a God, life wouldn't be so hard."

Laurie sat back, hope waning. She stared at the tea, unappealing now in the rose-flowered china, dull with an iridescent film. Why had she thought it possible? Why had she hoped?

She drew a slow breath and released it. "I need to talk to Luke, to tell him—tell them both—about Brian." She stood, uncertain for a moment if her legs would hold. Just as she straightened, the phone jarred her, and she gripped the chair back, tensing as her mother stood and answered it.

"Yes. One moment." Mother held out the receiver. "It's Sergeant Danson."

Laurie took the phone. "Hello?" Relief washed her like a flood at his words. Relief and vindication. They'd apprehended Dieter and Luís just outside of Kansas City, trying to steal a different car. It was her first feeling of total safety since she'd found the knife in her table. She put a hand to her heart. "And Cal?"

"Mrs. Prelane, you'd do well to leave that alone."

"But now you see—"

"Good day, Mrs. Prelane."

Laurie hung up the phone and closed her eyes. She was safe. Her children were safe. But Cal . . . She leaned her forehead to the wall. It would take time, that's all. It would come right. And then?

She drew herself up. She couldn't think of then. This moment had enough to deal with. She went into the den and looked into her children's faces.

19

THE FIRST THING CAL REALIZED when he woke was that he wished he hadn't. If he tried hard enough he might find something that didn't hurt, but it wasn't worth the effort. He rolled to his side and groaned.

"If you didn't already look half dead, I'd return the favor." Danson towered over him and rubbed his jaw.

Cal looked up, wishing Danson wasn't quite so tall. "I'm sorry. I couldn't wait until you listened."

Danson's expression was stone. "You've been bailed out."

"I have?" Cal sat up, wincing. "Who?"

"Mildred. But that doesn't mean I won't still nail your rear to the post."

"Look, Chuck—"

"Save your breath." Danson ushered him out to the office. Pete Rawlings turned and motioned him to the chair. Cal eased himself down between them.

Chuck closed the door. "Let's have your statement."

"Did you apprehend Laurie's abductors?"

"It's your turn to tell." Danson pushed the button on the tape recorder.

"Just tell me that much." Cal held a hand to his side, the ribs more sore than yesterday.

Danson loomed over Cal's chair. "You don't give it up, do you?"

"I wouldn't be here if I could."

Danson held his scowl, then straightened. "We've got two guys in custody."

Cal released a sharp breath. *Ouch.* "Then you know I didn't kill Brian Prelane."

Danson didn't answer.

Rawlings said, "You want some coffee, Chuck?"

Cal's mouth almost watered.

"Get three." Danson sat down on the edge of the desk. Cal had to tilt to look at him. Danson pointed to the phone. "You got one call. Want a lawyer?"

Cal shook his head. No, he didn't want a lawyer. He'd gotten himself into this.

"Then start talking."

Cal closed his eyes and collected his thoughts. It wasn't easy. Coffee might help, but he still felt confused and battered. That wasn't all of it, though. He'd been dreaming of Laurie, and that gave him a visceral confusion he was wholly incapable of putting into words.

Inside his head, he laughed. *You see, Sergeant, this girl showed up in my life, and nothing's been easy since.* He cleared the sleep from his voice. "Well . . ."

"From the beginning."

Cal's lips cracked. "Got a few years?"

———

Mildred and Cissy were solicitous, Dr. Klein surprisingly gentle with his follow-up check, Annie beside herself with glee. With a prescription of Vicodin in his pocket, Cal felt considerably better but foggy enough to sit back and let Ray take over. Ray must have had a squadron of guardian angels to catch only one bullet through the fleshy part of his upper arm. He wore the bandage like a badge as he sat at Mildred's table regaling their misadventures. Laid on a little thick, Cal thought, but that was fine. Ray was reveling in his part. At least Danson hadn't connected him to the shed episode.

Cissy *tsked* and Mildred *humphed*, but Cal noted the change in their demeanor. Mildred especially, though she'd deny it. They'd liked him before, in a way. But now he was one of their own. He rested a hand on Annie's head, taking comfort in the softness of her ear in his fingers. He wanted to call Laurie, but hadn't.

It was her call, not his. Did she know he was out? Did she care? Could she even think of him with all the rest she had to deal with just now? Cal drew a painful breath. Not even Vicodin could kill it all.

That thought brought Rita to mind. He was supposed to report the prescription, an unofficial checkup system she'd initiated with his release. That was one call he could make. He left Ray to his aunts, took Annie, and made his way up the stairs, a little woozy and stiff with the burned skin on his legs.

Doc Klein had said first- and second-degree. Cal had known worse. He opened the door to his place and stood a moment, just staring. The peaked and dormered ceiling, the graying windowpanes, the tired furniture. His place. After the cell it looked immense.

Annie bounded in. *Come on, Cal. Where's the spring in your step?* Her eyes said it all. He followed her in and closed the door. Annie made a quick case of the joint and returned to him, tail wagging.

"Guess we'll stay, huh?" He petted her head. Then he dialed Rita's number and waded through her receptionist and nurse. Rita's own voice was subdued. "Hello, Cal."

"Just so you know, it's Vicodin talking."

"How many?"

"Five left." He settled gingerly into the recliner. "How are things in the fun house?"

"I take it you're out of jail." Rita never was one for prevarication.

"A temporary reprieve if Danson has his way." He heard her nails tapping the receiver.

"So I heard. You certainly tipped the scales this time. Assault on an officer, false imprisonment of same officer, interference with a criminal investigation."

"I did what I had to do."

She sighed. "It's not you against the world, Cal. Societies have rules."

"I know that." He stiffly shifted his position. "The good thing is I beat it."

"Beat what?"

"My former condition."

She was silent.

"That should brighten your day. We did it, Dr. James. No shakes, no screams, no orange air—none that wasn't really there, anyway."

Still she didn't speak.

"Here's where you congratulate yourself on a job well-done."

Her voice came flatly. "I've recommended you not be returned to service until your competency is established."

"What?" Cal pushed Annie's paws down from his lap.

"Your criminal behavior and lack of judgment—"

His chest tightened with a rage all too reminiscent. "Haven't you heard a word I said? No post-traumatic stress."

"PTSD is not the full scope of your problems. I can't take the chance . . ."

"What am I, delusional?"

Her pause was just long enough.

Cal took the receiver from his ear and stared at it, then brought it back. "That's right, kids, the one and only fully deluded fire-clown . . ."

"Stop it, Cal." Her voice broke. "I didn't say that."

"You didn't have to."

"Don't you understand I put myself in jeopardy? I released you, believing you were fit. Yes, I knew you still had episodes, but I staked my reputation on your integrity. And you assaulted an officer."

Cal swallowed hard. She was against him. But she was right.

"He wouldn't listen, Rita."

"I don't care."

His grip tightened. "They had Laurie. I had to do something."

Her voice was cold. "Like the last time, when you directly disobeyed the orders of your superior?"

He shouted, "Yes, like the last time! I made a judgment call. I might have saved that child. It was worth the risk."

"And you paid the price."

"Fine."

Her words came clipped, "Chuck Danson is not the enemy. He's not a door you need to ax down. He's an officer of the law doing his duty, the same as you."

Cal had no response to that. She was right again, technically. But— He rubbed his face. "Would Danson have gone into that burning barn?"

Rita didn't answer.

Frank had stood outside the old house and balanced Ashley Trainor's life against his men's. Danson would have done the same. Laurie would be dead.

Cal hung up and dropped his head back against the recliner cushion. He'd done what he had to do. Didn't Rita understand? Just like the last time, he'd done what he had to do. Hurt welled up like a stain inside him. Hurt and betrayal. He raised the phone and dialed Frank.

"Am I in the rotation?"

Frank didn't ask who it was. He cleared his throat, and Cal could picture him working the gum to the other cheek. "I can't risk it, Cal. Wait till things have cleared up."

Cal pushed the disconnect button. There was nothing he could do. He was tired and sore and disillusioned. Only God knew what would happen next. *It's in your hands, Big Man.*

Laurie lay awake for the second night in a row. She looked around the room that had been hers through her two years in Montrose, two awful and wonderful years—her coming of age with Cal, then leaving it all for something "better." Brian Prelane. And he was dead.

They'd performed the autopsy and confirmed what everyone knew already. Death by a single gunshot to the head. Surprisingly no evidence of alcohol or cocaine in his bloodstream. Brian had been aware and lucid in his last moments. What had he been thinking? Did he regret his actions?

What of her own? She'd lived a lie for six years. Now Brian was dead. The last vestige of that lie dissolved. Yet she wasn't free of it. Maybe her whole life was a lie. Maybe everything, since praying that simple prayer with Grams, had been a lie. She'd believed that the prayer would change her life. But it hadn't.

Daddy was still Daddy, still criticizing everything she did. She had to watch every step under Mother's grim gaze and Daddy's disapproval. God hadn't changed them.

When they'd come to Montrose, she'd already begun to grow numb. Only Cal broke through with his persistence, his insistence. Not even Daddy cowed him. She remembered the time Cal had stepped between her father and her, put his body at risk as a verbally abusive man got violent.

No one had reported it. No charges of assault. Daddy had never repeated physical blows. But he'd pummeled her mind, her heart, her spirit. And Cal had hurt for her through it all. When Grams died, he'd held her so close. Maybe what followed shouldn't have. Laurie hardly remembered the act itself. But the joining of their hearts . . .

She started to shake. That's why she'd run before. She would not surrender her heart, not when it meant caring what someone thought of her, felt for her . . . and hurting when it wasn't enough. Not when it meant ripping open all the defenses she'd taken so long to develop. Laurie covered her face with her hands.

She could not give Cal her heart, but there was something she could give. Maybe that was the answer, the thing they both needed. It might lead to more trouble and heartache, but she had to do something. She owed him something. Maddie stirred. Her daughter had slept beside her both nights, as she had with Cal in the cabin. Maddie had told her he took away the scary thoughts and let her sleep with him. Laurie knew how it was to have Cal's arms around her, chasing the fear and grief from her dreams.

What had he thought, cradling Maddie like that? Helping her not to be afraid. Laurie pictured it only too well: his protective arms, his gentleness, and always the promise of strength and devotion. Cal Morrison, her knight in shining armor. A fallen knight now. Disgraced.

Because of her. Like Lancelot. Laurie had always blamed Guinevere more. As she blamed herself. She hadn't called, hadn't spoken with Cal. Sergeant Danson had told her he was out on bail, nothing more. She could find him at Mildred's. But if she did? Again the guilt assailed her. Didn't she owe him anything he asked? What if he wanted more than she could give?

───────────

Close to euphoric, Cal hung up the phone. He'd spent the last two days doubting himself, humanity, and God—and fighting the demons that threatened sobriety and sanity. If Mildred hadn't put up bail, he might have done something radical, rebellious, something . . . desperate. But he wouldn't betray her trust.

After talking to Rita and Frank, he'd refused conversation, hunkered down, and licked his wounds. Reggie had called, but Cal hadn't picked up the phone. Ray had knocked on the door to go fishing, but he'd declined. This time, though, when it was Laurie's voice on his machine . . . and she wanted to see him. Balm for the wounds. Not that Ray and Mildred and Cissy hadn't tried. Reggie, too, he supposed. But none of them mattered like Laurie.

She was coming over. He'd see her, smell her, feel her. He'd won her back from death. She was his. He'd heard it in her voice. He stood up, ignoring the pain. A few days' worth of dishes cluttered the small counter, most from before he'd taken the kids to the cabin. He wouldn't subject Laurie to the mess. He moved like an old man, cleaning up, but some of the stiffness eased as he forced the kinks out. Lastly, he saw to himself.

He'd showered already, but his hair was looking shaggy and he needed a shave. With the circles under his eyes, he could be a bum like Flip Casey. Cal sobered. He supposed he'd never know what part that poor old man had played, how he'd crossed paths with Brian Prelane and the other two. Maybe it didn't matter. Maybe Flip was better off.

As Brian was? Cal kicked himself for the thought. He didn't want to think of Brian Prelane, not with Laurie on her way. Not with all the possibilities Brian's death opened up. But there it was—the hope. He squelched it fast.

She'd lied and protected her husband. She'd only left him because of his criminal behavior. Maybe they would have reconciled. Maybe she would have gone back to her fairy-tale life, a life Cal could never give her and didn't want to. He drew the blade over his chin, revealing the half-moon scar that hung, a little drunkenly, to the right of his shallow cleft.

He wasn't sure what had scarred him, something sharp in the explosion. The memory brought no shakes, no screams. He'd told Rita the truth. He was cured. Whether by God, or by facing it, or both, he didn't know. But that was all in the past now. And Laurie would arrive soon. He cleaned up his neck and face, brushed his teeth, and put on a clean shirt. He drew as broad a breath as he could inside the rib wrapping, closed Annie into the bedroom where she was curled at the foot of his bed, then went to the window to watch for Laurie.

He pressed his hand to the pane as car lights appeared, neared, and turned in. He looked for the children, but saw only Laurie. A private meeting then, as he'd hoped. They could say all the things that needed saying. And when the words were done . . .

Laurie got out and climbed his stairs. He had the door opened by the time she reached the top. She smiled, her eyes large and inviting, her hair soft, smelling of Beautiful. He pulled her inside and closed the door.

She didn't resist, melting into him like butter on hot bread. It was all worth it—the ribs, the burns, the destruction of his reputation, and all the trouble he'd yet to face—worth it because she was there in his arms. He tipped up her face and kissed her, putting all of his love and need and desire into that kiss. She wrapped her arms around his neck and returned it.

"I love you," he breathed into her hair, stroking her shoulders with his hands.

She said nothing, only pulled his mouth back to hers and cranked his desire up another notch.

He eased back to hold her face between his hands. "I love you, Laurie."

"Just kiss me."

He did, but a sense of loss was growing inside. "I want you to know—"

"Don't talk, Cal." Her eyes brightened with tears, and her lips trembled.

"What, then?" He threaded his fingers into her hair.

"You know what."

Did he ever. He wanted her more than he'd thought possible. He could have her now. No more longing, no more needing. *Really?* The voice inside threatened to spoil it. *Just like the last time?*

He kissed her again, trying to regain the simple need, the physical need. "And after that?" his voice rasped.

She shook her head. "Just now. Just this."

He swallowed the pain that grew in his throat. "Why?"

"You saved my life, my children."

The pain went deep inside. "And you owe me?"

She rested her palms on his chest. A tear broke free and started down the side of her face. "Don't make it sound like that."

The hurt was turning to anger. "So we have a romp for old times' sake, and you don't have to feel indebted?"

Her mouth hardened and, for the first time, he saw her mother in her. Her tone, too, was defensive. "It's what you've wanted."

He dropped his forehead to the crown of her head, drew her scent into his lungs. "Not it, Laurie. You." Didn't she understand? "I want all of it this time." He spread his fingers through her hair. "Love, marriage, sex. I want you."

She pulled back. "Well, you can't have that."

"Why?"

She turned her face to the side. "I don't love you."

It was worse than the ribs, worse than the burns. It topped any pain he'd known. No, she'd never said she did. But she'd never before said she didn't. He had clung to the possibility like a drowning man to a splinter, and now she'd torn it away. Why now, after everything that had happened?

She sniffed. "I can't . . . love."

"You love Luke and Maddie."

Her face screwed up as she fought tears that came anyway. "That's different."

"No, it's not. It's laying down yourself for someone else." As he'd done for her.

She swiped the tears from under her nose with the back of her hand. "I don't have a self to lay down."

Not for him anyway. He wasn't rich enough, famous enough. He couldn't give her anything but a simple home . . . and his love. He wanted to strike something. Then he heard the utter hopelessness in her tone. *"I don't have a self to lay down."*

The anger faded. Cal's hands dropped to his sides. She was telling him the truth, not what he wanted to hear, not what he needed. But the truth. Did she have to love herself before she could love someone else? Maybe that was the hole in her he'd never been able to fill. He looked at her now, as beautiful as any woman he'd known, yet empty in a way he couldn't fix.

His voice rasped, "I'd do anything for you, Laurie, if I thought it would make any difference."

She looked away. "It won't."

He dropped his chin, cocking his head to the side and fighting the ache. He stepped back, putting space between himself and the woman he loved, space that would only grow with time. "You don't owe me anything. I'd have done what I did for anyone. It's my job." The words were a slap, he knew. But the hurt was burning out the one small piece of his own worth he had left.

She closed her eyes, stood for a moment without speaking, then turned and reached for the door. Cal felt her absence as keenly as the cold wind that blew in. He dropped to the chair at the kitchen table and rested his head on his palms. He was insane, passing up sex with the woman he loved for some reason he couldn't begin to understand.

He picked up the phone and called Reggie.

Reggie hung up the receiver and went out to Suanne in the living room. He glanced at the cross-stitched ornament she was working on. Would she mind if he . . .

She looked up with her slanting cat's eyes and knowing smile. "I know. God's called Moses to the promised land."

Reggie grinned, then bent and kissed her forehead. "Like Moses, I am ill fit to the task. But God knows best."

"Mm-hmm. He sends them as are willing."

Reggie took his coat from the closet and pulled the knit cap over his head. "I've had a burden for this man a long time now."

"Don't I know?"

He picked up his Bible, leaned down, and kissed her on the lips. "Keep supper hot for me."

"I might even keep it for three."

Reggie nodded. "I'll bring him if I can."

He drove to Cal's and climbed the stairs with no more certainty of success than Moses in Pharaoh's court. But Cal had called, and that was something. Reggie banged his fist on the door.

Cal pulled it open. Was it unshed tears, alcohol, or just stress that made his eyes so hollow and bleak?

"You clean, bro?"

Cal nodded and turned back inside. Reggie followed him in and set the Bible on the small table. The kitchen was overly warm, and Reggie stripped his coat and hung it on the chair back. Cal walked to the refrigerator, pulled out a Coke, and handed it over. Reggie popped the tab and drank.

Cal leaned on the counter. "You told me God had a time and a purpose for everything, an order to the universe. You said if I did things the right way, they'd work out." His fists clenched and unclenched.

"That's not exactly what I said." Reggie pulled off his cap and laid it on the table. "Yeah, you gotta do things the right way, but sometimes what you think should happen isn't God's plan." He slid out the chair and sat. "What's goin' on?"

Cal forked his fingers through his hair. "Laurie. She came to pay her dues."

"What dues?"

"One night of great sex in return for saving her life."

Reggie frowned. He did not want to be hearing this.

"And you know what?" Cal paced across the room, hands tight again. "I turned her down."

"Why?"

Cal slapped the wall. "You tell me."

Reggie took the risk. "You knew inside it was wrong."

Cal turned, raised his hands, and dropped them. "Why? Seven years ago it wasn't wrong."

"Sure it was. You just didn't know it then."

"I was in love with her, Reg." Cal spun the opposite chair and straddled it.

"Then you should have married her."

He spread his arms. "She wouldn't have me. She said no."

"So you took what you could get."

Cal's head dropped heavily. "It wasn't like that. Her grandmother died. Laurie was upset. She needed comfort."

"Comfort—not sex." Reggie knew he was pushing, but somehow he guessed it was time.

Cal's brow contorted. "I loved her, Reggie. I did what came naturally out of that love."

"And then what?"

Cal stood, took a step, and turned. "Then she . . . went berserk. We fought. She left . . . and married Mr. Drug Lord."

"Don't you see? You betrayed her."

"What?" Cal's look was sheer amazement.

"You took what didn't belong to you."

Cal shook his head. "I didn't take it. She was just as willing."

Reggie indicated the chair and waited until Cal sat down. "She might've been willing. But it was your responsibility to protect her, from herself even."

"Come on, Reg. What kind of prosaic thinking is that?"

"God's thinking." Reggie let that sink in.

Cal folded his arms around the chair back in front of him. "So, because I slept with her one night, God took her away forever?"

Now they were on treacherous ground. One wrong word could turn Cal away, set a root of bitterness in his spirit. "There are consequences to sin. The wages are death. You killed your possibilities by sinning with her."

Cal slammed his fist on the table. "It wasn't sin!"

Reggie didn't let go. "Sex outside the covenant is wrong. You can deny that all you like, but it won't change things. Here." He took up his Bible, thumbed a tab, and opened. He flipped some pages and handed it over. "Read the story of David and Bathsheba. There was a man after God's own heart, yet he stumbled in the same way you did."

"And God punished him?"

"The consequences of his own sin punished him. And he paid the rest of his life for those consequences."

Cal glanced down at the page and back up. "Then what's the point?"

Reggie laid a hand across the page. "God's sovereign mercy reunited David to Himself. Read it."

Cal read. Reggie waited, sipping on the Coke, and prayed. Cal read all the way through the murder of Uriah, the coming of Samuel, the death of Bathsheba's baby, and David's response. Then he looked up. "I didn't murder, Reg. I didn't take another man's wife. Not knowingly, anyway."

Reggie nodded. "But the principle is the same. In God's eyes all sin is abomination. Men label some acts worse than others, but not God. In as much as ye have lusted after your sister, ye have defiled her."

Cal crossed his arms on the chair back and rested his chin. "All right, so I've done things wrong. I've also done things right. Doesn't that count for anything?"

"Of course it does."

Cal raised his head. "Then why won't God give me the one thing I want?"

"Which is?"

"Laurie."

The man was in pain. It came through his voice, his eyes, his stance. But Cal didn't know what it was he really needed. Reggie opened one hand. " 'Cause He's got something better."

"What?" Cal's brows scrunched together.

"Life."

"Life." Cal rubbed his palm over his face. "Look around you, Reg. Look at these walls."

Reggie looked. It was Cal's place, a little tidier than he'd seen it at times. He returned his gaze to Cal.

Cal spread his arms. "This is it. I don't even have my work anymore, thanks to Dr. James."

Reggie shook his head. "She's in a battle of her own."

"Well, I never signed on to her army."

"Yes, you did, bro. When you entered her world."

Cal's face contorted. "She has the entire department believing I'm a nut. She and Chuck Danson. Now that's a pair. Lock me up and throw away the key." He stood up, stalked to the refrigerator, yanked out a Coke, and sucked it down.

Reggie stood, too, crossed the narrow space to Cal, and rested his hand on his friend's shoulder. "Rita cares more than you know."

Cal shook his head. "Then why's she in the crowd shouting 'crucify him'?"

"You're not crucified, Cal. Jesus did that for you." Reggie wrapped an arm around Cal's shoulders and led him to the couch. Then he sat down in the recliner across from him. "When I said life, I didn't mean this one. This one is temporal. What God has for you is eternal."

Cal dropped his head back. "Then why won't He just end it?"

"He has a plan for you."

Cal sat quiet, matching Reggie's gaze. He spread his hands. "What plan?"

"No one knows the whole of it. But I know the beginning. He wants you to give Him yourself."

"I did."

"When?"

"In the fire. With Laurie. I told him to do what He liked with me."

A burst of excitement began inside. "That's a start, bro. Did you tell him you were a sinner and make him your Lord?"

"I didn't really have time to go into detail."

"Then do it now."

"What's the point?"

Reggie crossed to the couch and sank in beside Cal. "The point is, until you give over control of your life to Jesus Christ, these walls are all you've got."

Cal's brow furrowed and his jaw tensed. He dropped his face into his hands. "I just want to love her."

"You gotta do first things first. I don't know where Laurie fits in. But you can't jump ahead of God's will. Right now, it's you He's concerned with."

Cal looked up. "So I surrender, and God delivers her, priority mail?"

Reggie shook his head. "No promises. God wants you whether you ever see Laurie again or not."

"Kind of a one-sided deal."

"Not when you consider you don't take a breath that isn't God's gift to you." Reggie sat back. "I won't argue, bro. You know." He pressed a hand to his chest. "You know here what's right. You decide."

Cal looked slowly around the room. "All right."

Reggie dropped to his knees. He could almost hear the angels singing as he led Cal in the sinner's prayer. "You are set free, my man. Ransomed by the blood of Jesus."

"Does it include a get-out-of-jail-free card?"

Reggie laughed. "I doubt it, but at least you know He'll be right there with you."

Smiling, Cal leaned back into the couch. "Well, misery loves company."

"You can't do this alone, Cal. You gotta find you a network, a church, a support system to uphold you when the enemy tries to steal your victory."

Cal's throat worked. "You said Wednesdays and Saturdays?"

Reggie read Cal's thought. "That's right. At Brother Lucas's house. And he's the Sunday pastor of a small fellowship, about twice those that meet for prayer."

"You and Suanne are there?"

"You know it. And speaking of which, she's holding dinner for us. Lasagna, if I smelled right."

Cal smiled. "Sounds like heaven if I know Suanne."

Reggie gripped his shoulder. "Amen, bro. Amen."

Weren't things bad enough? Did the children have to make it worse? Laurie looked from Maddie's face to Luke's, both mouths tremulous and insistent, eyes pleading. She couldn't. She couldn't give them what they wanted. "Luke, some things are complicated. You just have to trust me."

Eyes condemning, he looked away, but Maddie wasn't so compliant.

"I want to." She stomped her foot. "Fluffy has to say good-bye."

Maddie had no idea what she was asking. To face Cal after . . . Laurie pressed her fingertips to her forehead and glanced up at Mother. For once she seemed to have no opinion, at least not one she would share. What possible good would it do to see Cal? To let the children wring his heart as she knew they would?

She had to leave, had to bring Brian's body to his family, see to all the other affairs, the house, the will . . . Sergeant Danson had released her to go, released the body for burial. Everything Brian had was hers, or so she suspected. They'd laid out their wills accordingly. Death didn't activate the prenuptial agreement as divorce would have. His estate was hers and the children's, and she had to see to all of it. And she was glad. She couldn't get out of Montrose fast enough. But Luke and Maddie . . .

"Please, Mommy?" Luke touched her shoulder. "We didn't get to say good-bye to Daddy."

Laurie's heart seized. He was cruel, this child of hers, cruel and unfair. No, she was the unfair one. Luke was only earnest, only needing. He'd taken Brian's death stoically, too stoically. Maybe in some way he needed Cal in order to act out his grieving for his daddy. Cal would understand. He'd suffer his own pain to help them through theirs.

She sighed. "All right. I'll call. But he might not . . . be able to."

Maddie beamed. "I'll get Fluffy!" She ran to the den.

"He'll see us!" Luke chorused. "I know he will."

Laurie sighed. Of course he would.

No promises, no guarantees, no expectations, no disappointment. Cal left the dishes in the sink. Neither had he shaved, but the single day's growth wasn't as disreputable as it might have been. Either way it didn't matter. Laurie had told him plainly it was the children who wanted to come.

They needed closure, she'd said. Closure. He drew a breath, caught it at the point of pain, and released it slowly. The problem would be seeing her. How could he control the electric connection that had jolted his system at the sound of her voice over the phone?

Why did he open himself time after time to be electrified, burned, electrified, and burned out. It wasn't smart. It wasn't right. But what could he do? Say no to two little children who had to be hurting and confused? He rubbed his jaw, went to the closet, and pulled out the box.

He opened the flaps and dug through until he found the squirrel hand puppet and the water gun he'd used in a skit about safety around power lines. They would do. He had nothing for Laurie, but she'd accept nothing he had anyway. He pulled on his jacket, as it wasn't cold enough for his heavy coat, and stuffed the toys into the pockets.

Better to meet them on neutral ground, to make it easier for Laurie. He went down as the car pulled into the yard. Laurie climbed out and opened the back door. Maddie was first, dressed in a woolly blue jacket with pink lambs across the waist. Her legs in the pink leggings were impossibly small and shapely. Perfect legs on a perfect child.

Clutching the stuffed dog he'd given her, she ran to him, her smile piercing his control as she held up her arms. Cal caught her up, closing his eyes against the pain, both the ribs and the heartache. He remembered her snuggled next to him at the cabin, her fear melting away as he soothed her. He recalled her laugh, and the way she'd balanced on his knee and hooked her arm around his neck. He wanted to be there for her, to be something to her.

What was he trying to prove anyway? To be to one little girl the hero he couldn't be to another? Or was it because she was Laurie's, because he'd envisioned it differently? Maddie's palm against the back of his neck had a spongy warmth and softness that made tears burn behind his lids.

Cal opened his eyes and looked at Laurie. She wore an old flannel shirt over a turtleneck, and the knee of her jeans was frayed through. With no makeup and her hair in a ponytail, she looked like she had all those years ago when he'd gone to pick up his schedule and had first seen her. This was difficult for her, he could tell.

Luke hung back at her side, and Cal looked down at him. He stooped and let Maddie down, then held a hand out to Luke. Luke came slowly. Cal could only guess the boy's confusion and grief. He gripped him by the shoulder and brought him into his arms.

Luke circled his neck and squeezed. "I wish you were coming with us."

Cal's throat tightened. "I don't know what to say to that, buddy."

"Could you ask Mommy?"

Cal glanced up at Laurie, standing close enough now that he could smell her. Giorgio, not Beautiful. Cal studied her, trying not to memorize the line of her cheek, the shape of her eyes, the soft quiver of her lips. "I already did, Luke."

Laurie turned away.

Luke started to cry, an almost silent crying so wrenching Cal held him close, fighting tears of his own. "You'll be okay, Luke. You'll be okay."

Now Maddie was crying and pressing close. The tears crested in Cal's eyes. Well, what did he have to lose? He stopped fighting them and pressed his face to the children's heads. "You'll be all right," he said again, rubbing his tears into their hair and just holding them. But would *he*? He stood and led them back to the car, saw them into the seat, and produced the toys. He smiled grimly at Maddie gripping the life out of the squirrel as he closed the door.

Laurie's breath came sharply as he turned to her, and tears ran from her eyes as well. "I'm sorry. Please try to understand."

"I do. I know what you need. And it's not me."

She searched his face, questioning.

"You need to know who you are to God." Even as he said it, the truth of it settled inside him. Laurie didn't need him. She never had. And as long as he kept trying to be what he couldn't, she'd never find what she did need.

A fresh tear broke free and started down her cheek. He bent his head, and his mouth lingered on her lips, savoring one last contact, one moment of might-have-been. Then he stepped away.

20

To have that sense of one's intrinsic worth which constitutes self-respect is potentially to have everything: the ability to discriminate, to love and to remain indifferent. To lack it is to be locked within oneself, paradoxically incapable of either love or indifference.

Joan Didion

CAL ADDED HIS BARITONE to Cissy's warbling and Mildred's monotone rendition of "O Christmas Tree" as Ray reached the tin star with lighted tips to the top of the white fir. Looking at the tree, hung with antique glass and beaded ornaments, he had to agree with Mildred that it was a little thin. But considering his condition, they were lucky to have a tree at all.

After Mildred took the story to the newspaper, word had spread about Ray's part in Laurie's rescue, and the way he sent the drug dealers running with Mildred's shotgun. He was too busy these days to cut a tree for his aunts, and feeling a little self-important about non-paying jobs. He'd even had the luxury of turning down a job or two. Cal hoped it wouldn't go to his head; then again, he hoped it would. Ray needed a little confidence, a chance to realize his worth. Cal had taken him along to Reggie's group where they'd loved him up like some lost relation. Ray had beamed like the star he now shoved into place.

With the star set, Ray turned with a grin and added his tenor to the final refrain. It was strange to hear the high, clear voice coming from someone Ray's size, but maybe his vocal cords, like his brain, had stayed at a more youthful stage. Cal wouldn't have him any other way. Ray soared to a high harmony that was near angelic, and Cal felt his own chest swell with only minor discomfort.

Cissy clapped her hands. "It's a darling tree. Isn't it, Millie?"

"It's thin as a rail. Next time it'll be a twig."

Cal straightened a branch that sagged again as soon as he released it. "Next year it'll be the grandest tree you've ever seen. Once I can swing an ax again."

"Humph. If you can stay alive that long."

He couldn't miss the warmth in Mildred's eyes even though she turned away to hide it. Some switch had turned on in her, maybe stemming from her part in the goings-on, from having done something adventurous. Cal hadn't revealed much to Danson, only her care for the children in his absence. He might have given credit where credit was due, but Danson was mad enough to implicate her in obstruction as well. He'd been careful with what he said about Ray, as well. Cissy hadn't been in on enough to carry any responsibility, but for some reason, they all felt thick as thieves. Cal couldn't have done it without them.

He looked around the room. They were like family, this mismatched group. His family. Life could be worse. Probably would be when it all came down. But right now a powerful love for each person there made him content. God was filling in the gaps, and whatever happened, it was in the Big Man's hands.

The smell of the turkey in the oven was wonderful, and he gladly followed the women to the table set with Mildred's and Cissy's grandmother's china. The purple turkey pattern didn't do much for him, but he'd been informed that it was invaluable. He'd take their word for it.

Cal pulled out a chair but stopped when a knock came at the door. He glanced up at Mildred. "Expecting someone else?"

"Nope."

Cissy sidled around him to answer the door, and Cal tensed at the sound of Chuck Danson's voice in the entry. What on earth was he doing there on Christmas Day? Didn't the man ever give it a break? A moment later Danson followed Cissy in and narrowed his gaze to Cal.

Cal drew himself up. "I haven't broken bail. I don't have so much as a parking ticket." And there was no way he would miss Christmas dinner when he'd been smelling it these last four hours.

If he looked defensive, Danson looked downright uncomfortable. Of course, Mildred had him pinned in her stare. Cal would have pitied anyone else.

"Well?" Mildred asked.

Danson turned and motioned Pete Rawlings into the room. Pete dropped a large canvas sack to the floor.

Cal looked from the bag to Danson. "What's this?"

"Part of the nearly two thousand letters from the people of Montrose, some twelve hundred of them from school children handwritten on notebook paper, pleading for leniency on your behalf. The general idea being that in light of your service to the community and the extenuating circumstances of your misconduct, charges against you should be dropped."

Cal knew better than to think public opinion would sway Danson, especially when he recalled that Cal had put him down like a baby with two blows. But what was this Miracle-on–34th-Street charade?

"I don't care beans about what's in those letters, but some high-and-mighty folks don't want this business going to trial."

Cal frowned. "What high-and-mighty folks?"

"The Prelanes out in L.A. Some senator."

Ex-senator, but Cal didn't say so. Why would Laurie's in-laws care what happened to him?

"With their pressure and the local hue and cry, the mayor's leaned on the chief."

Cal was not sure he was hearing this correctly.

Danson drew himself up, hands on his hips. "Therefore, I'm here to inform you that all charges have been waived in lieu of community service. It's all in this letter from Judge Kinzer." He drew it from his shirt pocket and held it out. "And this is a letter from Frank reinstating you to the Montrose Fire Department, full seniority and benefits."

Cal stood, uncomprehending. "Charges are dropped?"

"Waived." Danson narrowed his eyes. "But not forgotten."

That part he understood. "Look, Chuck . . . I do apologize."

"Yeah? I've had that TMJ for weeks." He rubbed his jaw.

Cal fought the grin.

Danson raised a warning finger. "One crack from you, and you'll seriously regret it. And if I hear it whispered around . . ."

Cal held his hands palms forward. "Not a word, I swear."

"Well, then . . ." Danson turned to Mildred and Cissy. "Sorry to interrupt your dinner. Sure smells good."

"Won't you join us?" Mildred held the potato spoon like a baton. She included both Rawlings and Danson in her gesture.

Pete Rawlings bowed out. "I've got the wife waiting dinner."

Danson hesitated. "Well, it's sure a homey smell."

Cal wouldn't have chosen him to spend Christmas with, but looking around the table, he realized he wouldn't have chosen any of them . . . before. Now, he angled a chair in Danson's direction. "Then sit down already. I'm starved."

Lights glittered from the greenery decking everything from the curved banisters to the archways. It had all been ordered months in advance, though now there were black velvet bows along with the shimmery gold French ribbon. Laurie hadn't wanted to decorate, but Brian's mother had insisted. "You must keep up appearances. Brian would want it. He'd want his home as festive and . . ." Laurie had rested a hand on Wanda Prelane's shoulder when she broke down. More would have been too personal, too presumptuous.

Laurie looked across the room at Wanda, elegant in black chiffon. The party, too, had been arranged long before she had left town, before Brian came after her. If not, they would never have gotten the caterer.

There was some comfort in the knowledge that Dieter and Luís had confessed to the killing as part of a plea bargain, dropping felony kidnapping with intent to murder, and other charges she couldn't remember the legal terms for. Brian's murder was enough for both to get life in prison, but it could have been worse. She was certain the deal included an under-the-table agreement to keep Brian's illegal connection quiet. Stuart, Sr. had seen to that, reputation control an art for him. Wasn't that cause for celebration? Laurie sighed. It was all about putting on a face, and she was learning to do it well.

Wanda had insisted the party occur. "Darling, they'll want to come. To comfort you in your grief."

"I'd rather be alone in my grief."

"Sometimes we don't have that luxury. You'll do it for them, Laurie, for all those who loved Brian. To honor his memory."

So she stayed silent while the decorators came, then the caterers and the orchestra, and the Santa Claus for the children. She'd even smiled when Luke and Maddie showed her the extravagant trinkets he'd pulled from his bag for them. A Madame Alexander doll and a replica of a classic Corvette with real working headlights. No squirt gun and squirrel puppet.

Laurie turned away from the stoically grieving face of Brian's mother in conversation with a solicitous guest whose name Laurie scarcely remembered. All these people in her home, people of privilege. With her eyes she searched out Darla, one friend of whom Brian had never approved.

Actually, Laurie hadn't been close to her either. But she'd confided more than she should have one lonely night. And Darla had listened. Laurie was tempted again to take her aside, to pour out her confusion and . . . and what? She'd made her decision. This was her life, for Luke and Maddie to have more than she'd had, for Mother to believe she'd done right. If she left it now, she might never enter that world again. Slowly she crossed the room, smiling, though sadly, as the widow of the tragically murdered Brian Prelane.

The men's eyes were on her. She knew she looked stunning in the tea-length black velvet Dubois Couture gown. Her eye was caught by Brian's brother, Stuart, darkly handsome, taller than Brian but not as broad in the shoulders. More preppie than athlete. He waved her over. His arm came around her shoulders, and he bent to her ear. "I'm sure you're enjoying this as little as I am. Why don't we sneak out for espresso?"

Laurie looked around the room at the glittering lights, the glittering people. She nodded, and they went out the back. The hired valet brought his BMW, and Stuart let her in before walking around and taking the wheel.

"Am I allowed to leave my own party?"

He smiled. "You're grieving. Anything's forgivable."

Laurie stared out the window. Grieving? She was grieving, but was it Brian's death? They stopped at an upscale espresso bar. He let her out, set the car's security alarm, and held out his arm. Tentatively she slipped her hand into the crook.

He ordered espresso. She had an almond cappuccino. They sat at a table for two against the windows. There was no chill in the California evening, not like the cold December of Montrose.

He sipped, then set down the cup. "May I be blunt?"

Laurie raised her brows. What was this? Had she failed somehow, and he would chastise her? "Say whatever you like."

"I don't think there was much love lost between you and my brother." He raised a hand as she started to protest. "Maybe that's an overstatement. But you did leave him."

She looked down at her cup. "Under extenuating circumstances." Would she have gone otherwise, walked away from all she had, even if it was empty and false?

"Don't think I blame you. Brian was never easy to live with." Stuart's voice was sincere. His voice was always sincere, confident, connected, as though the person he was talking to was his only concern. No wonder he was so dynamic and successful. No wonder Brian had struggled to measure up. Not easy to live with? Try it from Brian's side.

"The thing is, the family's concerned."

"Concerned?"

Stuart took another sip. "You know, and I know, that this hyped-up version of Brian's unfortunate death is not exactly factual."

Laurie pressed her hands to the cup. Was he admitting what she'd already presumed? That the Prelanes had managed to spin the story, leaving Brian totally without guilt, and therefore her as well? She waited.

"They're concerned that, well, as time passes, you might . . . move on. You're a beautiful woman; you can't have missed the attention already directed at you."

Had they appointed him spokesman? Laurie could almost hear Stuart, Sr. *"Feel her out, son, see if she's with us or against us."*

"I don't understand, Stuart. What are you telling me?"

He reached across the table and took her hand. "Do you remember the night Brian brought you home to meet the family?"

She nodded. How would she forget? It was her first sight of Camelot.

"Well, I remember it too. I remember thinking, why did Brian find you and not me?"

Her pulse quickened, but it was uncomfortable. What was he saying? He'd coveted Brian's wife? Stuart, the most eligible bachelor, who was never without a dazzling partner, though if he'd felt a passion for any of them it was the best kept secret of all. "Stuart . . ."

"I'm sure you think it's horribly soon and tasteless for me to be saying this. But I want you to understand that my parents are in full agreement. They don't want to lose you or the children. They don't want to—"

"Lose control of the story?"

He cocked his head, one eye narrowed. "That was low."

"I'm sorry."

"Of course they're concerned with their son's legacy. You should be too. For the children's sake. Do you really want them knowing their father flew drugs over the border, then double-crossed the dealers and was killed for it?"

How suave of him to leave her part out. "Of course not."

"Then listen, Laurie." He closed her hand in both of his. "If we begin a quiet engagement now, we can be married in a year, and everyone will benefit."

She ought to laugh, but she didn't. It was her invitation to remain permanently Prelane. As the older and now only son, Stuart was well on his way to a quarter-billion-dollar inheritance. The crown prince of the Prelane empire. He was handsome enough for the stage and had in fact done a significant number of quality amateur productions before his father's reentry into business claimed his time.

And if Laurie was truly honest, she had wondered at times what it would be like if she'd married Stuart instead. He had the grace and confidence Brian lacked—and lacked the recklessness. He would be a solid presence, a father for Luke and Maddie. *Married in a year, and everyone would benefit.*

"I suppose there would be a prenup reverting everything to you in case of divorce."

"That is the protocol." Stuart's face softened. "But not reverting everything to me. This isn't some trick to cheat you of your assets, though it's understandable you'd be dubious. There wasn't much trust between you and my brother." His jaw twitched. "With his infidelities and . . . well, I'm surprised you stood it as long as you did."

Laurie flushed. Had everyone known?

He threaded her fingers through his. "I'm not concerned with any of that. No prenup if you're not comfortable, though for that matter it could protect you as well." He stroked his thumb over her index finger.

It started to sink in what he was offering. She thought of Brian's impetuous courting. He'd proposed on their first date. But then, wasn't Stuart doing the same? But he did it so coolly, almost detached.

"Is this a proposal or a merger?" The words were out before she considered how rude they sounded.

He quirked an eyebrow. "Are you asking if I love you?"

She shrugged. Was she? Did she want to know?

"I thought we'd do better if I refrained from . . . anything too personal." Then he smiled, Brian's smile, with amusement in his eyes. He brought her hand up and kissed the fingers.

It was remarkable, really, how little she could feel. Maybe they were better suited than she knew. Laurie raised her cup and sipped the cappuccino.

———

The fire station lot was full when Cal pulled in, overflowing onto the street. What was going on? He circled and exited, parking the jeep on the grassy rise just off the pavement. Maybe Frank had called in all the volunteers for a meeting.

He set the brake and climbed out. It was warm for two days after Christmas. Not so warm you forgot it was December, though. He walked into the garage and stopped. Rob and Perry and Frank, along with at least two-dozen volunteers were packed in around the two trucks. Cal took in the crowd, all eyes on him. Had he worn his clown nose? "What?"

Rob stepped forward, holding out a wrapped package. "A little something from all of us." He gave him a crooked grin. "Welcome back."

Cal took the package and weighed it in his hands, again scanning the group. He could tell by the feel it was a fire ax, short handle. He pulled the paper off. They had spray-painted it gold.

"It's the golden ax," Rob said, "to replace your golden tongue now that you'll be doing more than shooting off your mouth at banquets and civic events."

"Yeah." Perry squeezed to the front. "And the first thing you can use it on is that idiot puppet."

The group laughed.

Cal shook his head. "No way. Rocky and I are partners. Inseparable. I might let him handle a hose someday."

He shifted the ax to his right hand and felt its balance, like an extension of his own arm. He flipped it around and held it by the head the way he would to search for victims in low visibility conditions. As he had for Ashley Trainor. The thought brought sadness, but no shakes, no screams. "I don't know what to say, guys."

"Never thought *you'd* be at a loss for words." Perry smirked. "I still say ax the puppet."

"I think I'll put him on the engineer's panel."

"You're both wrong." Frank pushed forward and held up his hands to quiet the chatter. "It's true Cal's coming back active, but there's something else too. The city of Montrose has requested we not fold the educational project. Rather, they've funded a pilot program to be of Cal Morrison's design for use throughout the city and any neighboring cities and townships that choose to implement it."

Rob raised his brows to Cal. "That right?"

Cal shrugged. "It's the first I've heard of it."

"One thing we've learned is that safety education makes our job easier. I'd like to expand what Cal's done so far and make it a cooperative effort. So any volunteers, see Cal Morrison. Cal, see me."

Cal met his gaze. Was he hearing correctly? Had Frank and the department and the city of Montrose actually validated his work as fireclown? He stood holding the ax as one firefighter after another gripped his shoulder, patted his back, welcomed, and ribbed him on their way out.

"Upstairs, Cal." Frank directed with his head.

Cal followed, entered the office, and waited as Frank closed the door.

"I didn't intend to spring that on you like that, but I just got verification that it made it through the budget committee, and I thought all the gang should know it's now an official program."

"So what exactly is the program?"

"That's up to you. It's your baby. I know you wanted back on the line, and I'll rotate you in as necessary. But what you do with the kids and the elderly and, frankly, what you do representing the department at city functions, is of more importance than any of us imagined when we cooked up this scheme."

He and Cal and Rita. Cal felt a twinge of bitterness.

"I got more letters, I think, than Danson on the subject. Cal, you're a hero in a lot of people's eyes."

"You have a hero complex." Maybe he did. Maybe this was what he lived for. To be there when people needed him. To risk what other's wouldn't risk. Wasn't he the only one who went in after Ashley Trainor?

But what if he could do the same by teaching them, even the little ones, how to be safe? That's what he'd believed in, clung to, while he bore the smirks and sneers of the Perrys of the department. If he could develop a program that was entertaining enough to hold their interest while ingraining the safety rules, there might not be the need to go in. Not as often anyway.

Cal watched Frank work the chewing gum with his tongue, then blow a pink bubble that popped loudly. "You work up a program, Cal, and I'll see it implemented in every city from here to Kansas."

"What about the line?"

"Like I said, I'll use you. You know there are times I'll need to. But Perry's coming along. He's nowhere near as boneheaded as before. Rob's gotten used to giving orders. We'll make do." He switched the gum to his cheek. "I believe in this, and Montrose wants it."

It was good to hear. Cal had suspected that in the back of his mind Frank had dismissed the benefit of Spanner and company. That it was a make-do until Cal could come back to his real work. Cal pinched the pink stress head on Frank's desk. "And Rita?"

Frank raised his brows, looking more than ever like the Munchkin Mayor. "Don't know. I haven't heard from her lately."

Probably not since she'd recommended his suspension from duty. Cal nodded. "What's on the docket today?"

"You and Rob. Just to get you back in the swing. 'A' shift all week. Once you've worked the rust off, you can start on the puppets or whatever you decide to do with this project."

Cal grinned. "As I told Perry, Rocky stays."

"Fine. But, Cal?" Frank raised his pen like a poker. "Try not to show Perry up too bad. I do need him on the line."

Cal saluted. He went downstairs and saw that all but a few of the men had gone home. He joined Rob in the lounge. Glancing briefly across, he pulled the clipboard down from the wall and studied the schedule. "I'm 'A' shift with you all week."

"I know."

"You okay with that?"

"What do you think?" Rob went to the coffeepot.

"I'd like to hear you say it."

Rob poured a cup.

Cal kept on, not sure what he was trying to prove. "This job's as much in the head as anything. Gotta know you can trust your partner with your life."

Rob drank. "I trust you."

"How's it been with Perry?"

Rob took a seat at the table. "Perry's all right." He looked up. "You weren't an easy act to follow."

"Yeah. Especially the shakes and twitches."

"Especially that you went in when no one else dared. Not even me—speaking of trust . . . partner."

Catching Rob's meaning, Cal leaned on the wall. Had Rob's guilt over not supporting his partner been the real cause of separation? Cal hadn't even considered dragging Rob in with him. It was his own decision to disobey, to try in spite of the risk. "You might not be sitting here if you had."

Rob stared into the cup, then looked up. "Next time I'll be there."

Cal's throat tightened with emotion. He nodded, then went to the coffeepot himself. "What do you say we do a polish job on 'old Susie' there."

"Yes, sir."

"That wasn't an order."

Rob laughed. "Just responding to the voice of authority."

Cal poured a cup. "Was that ax thing your idea?"

"Sort of."

"Thanks." His chest swelled—not with pride in the honor, but pleasure in the gift. Friendship was definitely up there with food and water.

They hadn't even started to clean up the truck when Rob took the dispatch call. "Man down, fourth and Elm."

An unconscious person, no time to waste. "Let's hit it." Cal took the wheel as Rob opened the door, leapt in beside him, and hit the siren. As he pulled out of the station, the adrenaline surged his system. He was back, and this was living.

Life. God had given him life. Not just the eternal one Reggie had meant, but purpose in this one as well. As they approached the corner, Cal saw a huddled group on the frozen lawn before the bank. "There's our man down. Can you make anything out?"

Rob leaned to the window as Cal maneuvered the vehicle. The group opened as they pulled to a stop, and Rob leapt out. Cal secured the truck, allowing Rob to get the preliminaries. Within seconds he joined him.

"Cyanotic blue," Rob said, indicating the bluish discoloration of skin and lips.

Cal could see the victim's breathing was fast and abnormally deep, his limbs stiff. Even as he dropped to the man's side, the breathing stopped. "Bag him."

As Rob ran for the equipment, Cal reached into the patient's mouth and checked the airway. No obstruction, but excess saliva. Rob was back with the Ambu bag. He attached the valve mask to the man's face and squeezed rhythmically until the victim's lungs took over, then Rob removed the Ambu bag and replaced it with an oxygen mask. "He's pinking up."

"Diaphoretic." Cal felt the cold, clamminess of the skin, noted excess sweat, fast pulse. He pulled the eyelids up. "Pinpoint pupils." He looked up at the spectators. "How long has he been unconscious?"

"Twenty minutes maybe," Tom Wilson, the bank guard, answered. "He was in line at the bank, then got disoriented and disruptive. His speech was slurred. I thought he was drunk." He glanced around the group. "I told him to leave, and he came out here and sat down, kind of jerky. Just sat there. I was going to call the police if he didn't move on soon."

As the man talked Cal pulled up the patient's sleeve and found the diabetic bracelet. He nodded to Rob to continue monitoring the man's ABCs, then opened his med kit and started an IV. Besides Frank, Cal was the only one on the force with standing orders from Doctor Klein to administer IV drugs, but it was Ringer's lactate and D 50 sugar solution he delivered now. He didn't need a dextrose stick to identify a hypoglycemic diabetic coma. Especially with Tom Wilson describing the preliminary symptoms.

Tom shrugged. "I got busy, then happened to look outside. He'd fallen over and didn't respond when I shook him, so I thought I ought to get you guys."

Cal nodded to Rob. "Call the ambulance." Cal had a good flow from the IV bag going into the patient's arm. It should be only minutes before he responded, even though things had progressed to a dangerous point. Much longer and they'd be looking at brain damage.

Rob climbed into the cab to radio Melbourne and give the details to the paramedics en route. By the time he climbed down, the patient was stirring. His eyes flickered open, but Cal could see his disorientation. "Welcome back, buddy. Lie calm now. Transportation's on the way." Rob covered him with a blanket as Cal asked, "Have you eaten today?"

Lots of things could contribute to high insulin in a diabetic, a skipped meal, an infection, a drug interaction. Cal was more interested in getting the man to talk than in his answer, since he was already administering the solution.

The man looked from him to Rob, then at the crowd standing around. "What happened?"

"Blood sugar got low. Very low. Do you have trouble monitoring it?"

Definite confusion. Cal hoped the patient's brain was only temporarily dysfunctional, though the hippocampus, the part responsible for memory, was especially susceptible to damage from lack of blood sugar and oxygen.

"Can you give me your name?"

"David." The speech was still thick, sluggish but the answer cognizant. The bracelet had said David Miller.

"David, we're going to make you comfortable until the ambulance gets here." While he talked, he took out a dextrose test kit and checked the man's blood sugar level. Though he hadn't done a preliminary test since the symptoms indicated immediate treatment, he could assume the reading had risen dramatically.

As Rob slipped a folded blanket under David's head, Cal tucked the cover blanket under his sides between the man's body and the frozen ground. In a minute they'd let him sit, but he wanted to get more oxygen to the brain first.

Cal smiled up at Tom Wilson. "A lot of conditions resemble drunkenness. It's usually wise to go ahead and give us a call. Anything strange could be a medical impairment."

Tom nodded. "Yes, I can see that."

The crowd started drifting away. Cal loved that. The urgency of catastrophe drew them like flies, but the resolution was not exciting enough to hold them. They'd go off and say they'd seen a man fall into a coma, but Cal would recall bringing him out.

When the ambulance arrived from Melbourne, Cal handed off the information he'd gathered and the treatment he'd already given. As he repacked his med kit, he mentally disengaged. David was in their care now. Stepping back, he watched for a moment, then nodded to Rob. They climbed into the truck and fired up the engine. Cal drove back to the station while Rob filled in the report.

As the truck eased into the garage, Rob tucked the clipboard under his arm and eyed Cal. "Feel good?"

Cal set the brake and turned off the key. "Feels great."

"Nothing like saving a life to start off your day."

No, there wasn't. Cal rested his wrists on the wheel and basked in it. Maybe God knew what He was doing after all. Maybe there wasn't room in his life for anything but this. He offered up a silent thanks.

"And by the way, Cal, you took charge back there."

Cal stopped with the truck door half open. "Guess I did. Old habits . . ."

Rob swung down. "Well, if the shoe fits . . ."

"I think I'll be wearing a few shoes now."

Rob leaned against the locker. "I'd never admit this in front of the others, but I think you did a great job of education. I even thought Rocky was funny."

Cal grinned. "Rocky is funny. And there's a place for Spanner too. Education is a good thing. There's no replacement for it."

"You certainly convinced someone. Funding? From the budget committee? You've got clout."

Cal shrugged. What Rob didn't know was that Cal had nothing at all to do with it.

21

WE PARDON TO THE EXTENT

THAT WE LOVE.

François, Duc de La Rochefoucauld

"T HE BIG SURPRISE WAS PERRY volunteering to help build
the sets." Cal sprawled on Reggie's olive green couch. In just
two month's time he'd developed four safety education shows and
was scheduled in three cities to demonstrate the pilot program to the
fire departments there.

Reggie nodded, his lower lip protruding thoughtfully. "It's amazing how funding a program legitimizes it."

"You can say that again. I've gone from laughingstock to idol."
Cal scratched the side of his leg where the skin was still dry from the
burns.

"Don't let it go to your head."

Cal reached down and picked up the football he and Reggie had
tossed outside earlier. He fingered the laces. "I know how I got there,
Reg. Even though I don't get the shakes or hear the screams, I still
remember. Sometimes I dream."

"So God left you enough to keep you humble."

"You could say that." Cal tossed him the ball. "What's the word
on Smilin' Sal?"

Reggie's big hands covered the ball like a net. He lined the fingers of his left hand along the laces and tossed it. "She went home."

"Yeah?" Cal hadn't realized Reggie was a southpaw until he'd thrown, though he must have seen him write and eat a hundred times. "That's great." He rolled the ball off his fingers in a smooth lateral.

Reggie caught it and lowered the ball to his lap. "You seen Rita?"

"No." Cal closed in, shutting down at just the thought of her. She'd stabbed him in the back, turned on him when he needed her most. Though he didn't actively despise her, he certainly hadn't sought her out.

"She asked about you. Wednesday, I guess it was."

Cal didn't answer.

"You could talk to her."

"She knows where to find me." Cal touched his ribs, healed but tender still, like the wound Rita had given him.

"You could forgive her."

"There's nothing to forgive." Cal met Reggie's eyes. "She did what she felt professionally obligated to do. It's not her fault the rest of the town thought otherwise."

"A little thing can lodge inside, like a splinter, harmless in itself until it starts to fester."

"I don't bear her a grudge." Cal got up and walked to the window. "We all do what we have to."

"Then talk to her. Let her know that."

Cal looked out at the crumbling walk, the brown February landscape, the tiny houses across the street. He always felt like an oversized doll in a block village when he came there. Especially after knocking around at Mildred's. Alice shrinking and growing in the oddest way.

"It's better to leave it alone." Rita had been a lifeboat in a rough sea. Cal would give her that. But he didn't need to prolong it for either of them.

"Better for whom?"

Cal turned.

Reggie's eyes were earnest—not pleading, but convicting. "She has no rudder but herself. If she makes a mistake, there's no one to fall back on. She's alone."

Cal considered that. Part of him wanted her to regret her actions.

Maybe the splinter Reggie mentioned. Rita had been wrong to turn on him, to lose her faith in him. But then, he wasn't the one she needed faith in. He scratched his neck. "I don't know, Reg."

"Then take it from the Big Man. If He urges you—"

"I don't have quite the pipeline you've got."

Reggie tossed him the ball. "That's where you're wrong. You've got the same access I do. Just exercise it."

"In other words, pray about it." Cal spun the ball by its points.

"That's right."

"Then I may as well call her."

Reggie held out his hands and caught the ball Cal tossed. "Don't call. Go."

Cal laughed. "What is it with you and face-to-face."

"It's better that way. You can't hug over the phone."

Cal went back to the couch and sat down. "I'm not leaving before Suanne's burgers."

"You got that right, honey," she called from the kitchen.

"I suppose you've heard the whole thing," Cal called back.

"Mm–hmm. It's about time you got up the gumption."

Cal shoved his fingers into his hair. "Why do I always feel out-numbered here?" But he knew why. Reggie and Suanne were a matched pair. And he? A lone pin waiting to topple.

After lunch, he drove to the center. It had been long enough, now, that the place felt foreign. That was a good thing. He no longer entertained notions of climbing back inside. In fact, the last thing he wanted was to climb those stairs.

He parked the jeep, got out, and took the stairs with purpose, pushing through the front doors. Maybe Reggie was right. Give her the chance to come clean, get this over with, and move on. He checked in with the receptionist, but asked her not to call Rita. It took a little male manipulation, but she succumbed.

He followed the hall to Rita's office and tapped the door. Before Rita could answer, he opened it himself. "Got a minute for your pet nightmare?"

Rita pressed both palms to her desk with a look that told him he should have let the receptionist announce him. But she composed herself by the time he reached the chair across from her desk. He slouched into it, reminiscent of his once-rebellious form.

"Cal." Her voice held more than he'd hoped to hear. Reggie was right. He'd left her too long to pay for what she'd done.

"What are you doing Friday?"

Her mouth came together in silence. Her wedge of hair had more gray than he remembered, but it was exactly the same length, her makeup flawless, her nails immaculate. Did she ever let herself go? Spend a day in her pajamas?

"Poker night. I've been on a roll. No Rita James to call my bluff. Reggie's all right, but Rob's no competition, and Perry's just pathetic."

She folded her hands purposefully. "It was a mistake to mix personal and professional."

"Well, we all know you don't make mistakes, Dr. James." He saw her stiffen. "Or is it possible, just possible, you're human like the rest of us?"

"What do you want, Cal?"

"I want you to know there're no hard feelings. You trusted your professional judgment and acted on it."

She sat back in her chair, and her features softened. What load had she been carrying? He saw her throat work and thought she'd answer, but then she stood and walked to the window behind the desk. "It wasn't my professional judgment I acted on. It was personal."

Cal hadn't expected that. He shifted in the seat.

"I was so . . . angry that you could overcome what I couldn't get you past. That on your own, you'd faced the fear and didn't need me. I felt so . . . useless."

That was an admission he'd never expected. Rita angry that he'd healed? Without her? He stood and walked to her, turned her from the window, and held her. She was thin and hard like a bird with no feathers, too short for his height. Her hair smelled of shampoo. She started to cry.

"It's all right, Rita."

She looked up at him, mascara making streaks down her cheekbones. "Sometimes I'm so alone. What am I doing? Do I really make a difference? Or is it all out of my hands, just some random accident when someone recovers. Do I have any purpose at all?"

"Of course you do. You've helped too many to deny that. You helped me."

"Did I?" She looked up accusingly.

"It was all part of the process. I was definitely taking the wrong track. You steered me back."

She shook her head. "I don't know why I'm here. Don't you ever feel alone?"

Cal's stomach clenched. More than he wanted to consider. "Yeah. But maybe it's supposed to be that way." God hadn't gift wrapped Laurie. She'd walked away, gone back to her fairy-tale life. "Maybe it's so we can serve a greater number in a bigger way. You here, me with the department."

She dropped her forehead to his chest. "I'm sorry, Cal. I'm so sorry."

"It's all right. Things worked out in spite of you." He raised her chin and smiled into her wretched features.

She sniffed. "Not totally in spite."

He quirked a brow.

"I did have a part in funding your program."

He cupped her face in his hands. "*You* did? You're the one who got it through committee?"

She pinched her nose with a tissue from her pocket. "I had to do something." She dabbed the tears beneath her eyes. "At least if you never spoke to me again, I'd know I'd done something to make it right."

Cal shook his head. "Poor Rita. Trying to carry it all. You and I are two nuts, you know it?"

She tossed the tissue into the trash. "Well, I . . ."

"There's an easier way. It's just that overachievers like us need to be knocked up side of the head to see it."

She searched his face as though knowing where he was going but not sure she was hearing it from him.

"There's a function Reggie introduced me to. It's a little off the wall, but if you want to know how I really recovered, you might find it enlightening."

"I don't . . ."

"Why don't you let me pick you up, six-thirtyish. Dress casual." Which meant Rita's attire would match the others' Sunday best.

She sniffed. "Well, I suppose it wouldn't hurt."

He bent and kissed her forehead. "Not too much."

Driving home, he felt ten pounds lighter. He should have gone to her sooner, should have listened to the other nudges Reggie had given him. He was right as usual. Rita needed a friend.

Laurie applauded with the crowd around her. She glanced at Stuart and smiled. The show had been amazing, a truly original performance as only L.A. or New York could provide. Though the reviews had been scathing, Stuart insisted they'd missed the point. And he was right, of course.

She stood up beside him as the applause swelled and the ovation continued. Diamonds dangled from her ears, his latest gift. They matched the solitaire diamond in the thick gold chain on her throat. There was no one in the crowd more elegantly attired, no couple more eye-catching. Especially Stuart. Laurie saw the envious stares.

Yet as she stood there, loneliness tore a hole inside her. It was happening more frequently, the hollow, futile feeling. Maybe she needed to spend more time with Luke and Maddie. There just didn't seem to be enough hours in the day. Between Stuart and his mother, she was on more committees, involved in more events and entertainments, than she'd thought possible. The hours she'd put in at Maple's seemed a vacation. But she didn't want to think about that dreadful time. How shocked would Wanda Prelane have been to see her there! And Stuart . . . would he have come and sat in a booth and ordered coffee— She stopped that thought in its tracks.

Stuart caught her elbow. "Ready?"

"Yes." She gave him a falsely bright smile.

They sidled out between the seats. Keenly aware of the eyes on Stuart, Laurie followed him to the lobby, then out the doors. He gave his receipt to the valet, and she watched the people watching him. He commanded the space around him. No one could look at Stuart Prelane and not think "man of substance," even if they didn't know who he was. Unlike Brian, he had always known the ascendancy of the firstborn son. He needed nothing more.

Something shrank inside her. Did he need her? He was solicitous and attentive. He never said he loved her and never asked her in return. Wasn't that exactly what she wanted? No expectations of a romantic attachment they both knew was impossible. Did he think she would come to love him? Would she? He was everything Brian had been and more. He was too responsible to cheat on her. She would never deal with embarrassment from Stuart Prelane. He could do no wrong. He was perfect.

She shuddered. Maybe through Stuart, she'd attain perfection herself. Or maybe all that she lacked would show that much more. That was her real fear, wasn't it? Stuart never criticized, never corrected her. But it wasn't the same acceptance she'd found in only one other place. It was as though he didn't look deeply enough to notice her flaws. He was satisfied with the surface.

The car arrived and she climbed in. Luke and Maddie would be asleep when they returned, but she needed to see them, even if it was only to look at their sleeping faces all tucked into designer sheets and comforters.

"You're quiet tonight." Stuart took his hand from the wheel and rested it on hers.

"Still taking it in, I guess."

He smiled. "The sign of a true theatre aficionado."

She smiled back. It was true. She loved the theater, the performances that stirred memories of her own meager attempts in that area, attempts Cal had convinced her to make. Cal. When would the pain lessen? When would she think of him without her chest seizing up and her stomach knotting?

"What is it?"

She startled and turned. "What?"

"You had a pained look."

She sighed and dropped her gaze to her hands. "Just a memory." It would be enough. Stuart would think it was Brian she recalled, and he was very careful not to probe there.

He petted her fingers. "You still haven't given me an answer."

She looked at his hand, noted its smooth texture on her skin, the long, well-formed fingers. She remembered another hand, soot-stained and bleeding. Cal's hand leading her out of the inferno. "It's too soon."

"To make it public, or to know?"

She looked out the window at the city lights flashing by. When she didn't answer, Stuart let it go, tact embodied. He kissed her at the door and strolled back to the car, his suit coat parting slightly in back as he took the keys from his pocket. He glanced up and waved, then climbed in and drove away.

· Laurie closed her eyes and leaned against the doorjamb, then went inside and shut the door behind her. She locked it and set the alarm, then went up the swirling staircase to the bedroom suites that housed her children—their own rooms in the house she and Brian had bought with the down payment that was their wedding gift from the Prelanes.

Luke had thrown his covers to one side. She pulled the sheet free and placed it softly over his form. He stirred and rolled, then settled back in without opening his eyes. Maddie was nestled in a cloud of lavender and cream. One hand cradled her cheek, the other was tucked inside the gray squirrel puppet. Fluffy was lodged between her soft belly and the sheet.

Laurie looked up at the wall shelf filled with stuffed animals. Why those two? Why would she only sleep with those two? She bent and kissed Maddie's cheek. Maddie's eyes fluttered, and she reached an arm around Laurie's neck. "Sleep with me, Mommy."

Laurie knelt and laid her head on Maddie's chest.

"All the way." Maddie shifted over.

Laurie climbed into the bed beside her, as Maddie snuggled close. She lifted the squirrel that had come loose from Maddie's hand and brought it to her face. It smelled like Cal. She couldn't say how, just knew that it did. She buried her face in its plush.

"Don't cry, Mommy," Maddie murmured, then drifted into soft breathing.

There was nothing like the smell of spring, not in the woods after a rain. The last few months had been wetter than usual, and the blooms would be profuse once they started. Cal squelched the wet leaves under his boots and watched Annie bound off after a squirrel. The critter led her on a merry chase, staying close enough to tantalize, then blithely going its own way. Annie returned frustrated and panting.

Cal laughed and reassured her with his hands. "Maybe next time, girl." He breathed the March air deeply into his lungs. There was still a twinge sometimes when he fully expanded his diaphragm, but it was good to breathe without having to guard himself. Cal bent and picked up a long, straight branch, stabbing it into the earth as he walked.

The new buds gave the woods a hazy green hue that the evening light played on through the shadows. It was the kind of beauty that choked you up if you weren't ready for it. It still got to him sometimes.

Annie bounded off again. She obviously hadn't taken her defeat too badly. There were more squirrels, more opportunities. More roads not taken. Cal caught that thought and held it, though it brought an all-too-familiar pang.

Pastor Lucas had spoken on the aftereffects of forgiven sin. Forgiveness didn't negate the effects of wrong actions. There was still a price to pay. Cal had made love to Laurie when she wasn't his by covenant. He hadn't known it was wrong when it felt so right. But his ignorance hadn't changed God's immutable law. He'd taken what didn't belong to him, ruined her virtue, and hurt her in a way he only now understood.

Maybe that was why he'd never have her again. He had stood at the fork and taken the wrong road. What if he'd taken the other?

Cal stopped and eyed the gnarled feet of a granddaddy oak, then perched on one woody knee. He leaned his head back against the trunk and watched the night steal into the woods. The sun had departed, but the aura of it still remained, leaving streaks of fire across the sky, fading from gold to gray. Twilight.

One star winked at him overhead. Not a star really; it was Venus. Annie came back and lay panting at his feet, turning her head occasionally to follow a sound, then licking her chops and settling in again. He reached down and stroked her ears. If this was all he ever had, he'd be grateful.

Annie whined softly and licked his hand.

"I know. You want your supper." He stood and headed back with Annie making circles around him.

For some reason, he pictured Laurie, stooping down and fondling the dog's head. *"So this is Annie. Why would anyone dump such a nice dog?"* And his smart-mouth reply: *"I don't know, but she keeps my bed warm at night."* "That's right, Annie." He stooped and fondled her head. "Guess dog is man's best friend."

She bounded ahead and returned, faithful in every part of her nature. They reached the house, and he scooped the daily paper from the stoop where it had lain all day, then climbed the stairs. He could smell the new coat of beige paint he and Ray had given the place. That had been an adventure he wouldn't repeat soon. Ray meant well, but don't ask him to hold your ladder.

He went inside and tossed the paper on the table, filled Annie's bowl, and changed her water. Then he sat. He should eat something, too, but some nights it just wasn't worth the trouble. He opened the paper and perused the pages.

He was on his forty-eight hours off after two twenty-four hour shifts on the line. He made sure his other job description didn't keep him from active duty as often as Frank allowed. To accommodate the community service hours ordered by the court, he volunteered for small "rescue missions" with the Christian Fellowship Church Brother Lucas pastored. Through the winter, he'd delivered meals or groceries to shut-ins, mainly elderly folk who couldn't go out in the cold on bad roads. He'd done whatever odd-jobs they had for him.

Now with spring on the way, he still made the rounds. They needed conversation and attention as much as any errand he might run. Missie Jones always had something. She'd been crankier than Mildred the first time he brought her a meal, even accused him of conniving to get inside her home and steal her china. Now she had tea or lemonade waiting in the pitcher and a dozen little things she couldn't quite manage on her own.

Cal looked up from the paper and smiled. Missie was a little wasp of a woman with a terrier temper, but he'd won her heart somehow. Then there was Douglas Walberg, a stately gent who hated the fact that his arthritic body would not allow him to care for himself entirely. Cal was careful never to overstep what Douglas actually could do.

That went for Donny too. Highly functional Down's syndrome meant Donny just needed checking on. Cal had quietly taken care of a few potentially dangerous situations in Donny's trailer, but mostly just befriended him. Donny smiled more than anyone, and wouldn't you know, his grin was as contagious as Reggie's. Cal was a sap.

Annie finished her meal and lay down at his feet. He kicked off his shoe and stroked her with his foot as he flipped a page of the paper. Maybe he'd write a new skit. Maybe not. These days he gave himself permission to do nothing. He turned to the classifieds, saw Ray's ad for odd-jobs right there, top billing. Good for Ray.

He turned the page again, and there she was. Laurie's face, radiant and lovely, heartbreakingly so. He felt it deep inside, just looking at her in ink on newsprint. Reluctantly, he took his eyes from the photo and read the caption. *Announcing the engagement of Laurie Sutton Prelane, daughter of Marjorie Welks Sutton and Leonard Sutton, deceased . . .*

Engagement. Cal's throat tightened as he scanned the words. Engaged to Stuart Frederick Prelane, Jr; son of Wanda Prelane and former-California senator and business mogul Stuart Prelane, Sr. Nuptials are set for . . .

He expelled his breath with a sharp laugh that actually hurt. Brian's brother. Did it never end? He dropped his face into his hand, fighting to find the gratefulness he'd known in the woods, the acceptance of God's will. He looked again at Laurie's picture. At least he knew now that road would never be taken. He snatched up his jacket and headed back out to the woods.

———

Laurie hadn't expected Stuart. She had the table set with paper wrappers from the McDonald's burgers and plastic packages of ketchup beside the fries. Luke was sucking noisily on his soda when she went to open the door.

"Hi." Stuart handed her a single rose.

"Stuart, I . . . did we have something I forgot?"

"No. Thought I'd surprise you." Something spontaneous from Stuart Prelane?

She touched the rose to her nose, breathing lightly, and forcing a quick image of peach roses and baby's breath from her mind. "We were just having dinner."

He glanced past her to the dining room, partly visible from the entry.

"We're in the kitchen, the kids and me—having McDonald's. If I'd known you were coming," she sent him an impish smile, "I'd have ordered you a Big Mac."

His smile was passive and indulgent. "No thanks." He took her into his arms. "I thought I'd steal you away to the Douglas party." As in Michael Douglas. Malibu Colony.

"Oh." She'd known Stuart's theater work and political contacts had opened doors to Hollywood's activists and that he'd developed relationships with actors, writers, and producers. But she hadn't realized . . . Brian had mingled with the big names in sports, but to walk into a room filled with faces she'd seen larger than life on the screen . . . And here he was asking her along.

But she had two eager children waiting for her at the table, and a burger—no ketchup, extra pickles—on her own paper wrapper. They hadn't had dinner together in too long, thus the splurge to McDonald's. "Well, come in."

He cocked his head. "Am I interrupting?"

"Of course not."

"Then . . ." He lowered his eyes to her lips.

She reached up and kissed him. People Magazine had done an article on the men women most wanted to kiss. Stuart had been among them.

"What about my offer?"

She settled back and looked toward the kitchen. "The children . . ."

"Isn't Gail here?"

"Yes, but . . ."

He pulled her back to his chest, caressed her hair. "Is it too much to take my fiancée to a great party unexpectedly?"

She smiled. "No. I had just planned on an evening with the kids. I've been so busy. Why don't we . . . I could make you a sandwich?"

"Now that's exciting."

She couldn't tell by his smile if he were irked or not, but he motioned her on. As she led him into the kitchen, she hoped the children would behave. Lately Luke had been acting out in small but annoying ways. And Maddie was not her best in the evening, even with McDonald's.

"Hi, Uncle Stuart." Luke's greeting was at least congenial.

"Hi, Luke." Stuart patted his head.

Maddie drenched a fry in ketchup and held it up. "Want a French fry?"

"No thanks." Stuart removed his suit coat and started to hang it on a stool back, then folded it onto a far counter instead. Smart man. Meticulous.

Laurie walked to the refrigerator. "Turkey, ham, or beef?"

"Why don't you just have your burger while it's semi-palatable."

She glanced at him. "I can cut it in half."

Maddie held up her own half-eaten burger. "Want mine?"

Stuart held up his hands. "No thanks, Maddie."

Now Laurie did detect annoyance. Her appetite died. The levity they'd shared moments ago when Luke walked his French fries like stilts had evaporated. It wasn't Stuart's fault. He just changed the dynamic.

Maddie dipped a French fry in her Coke and tried to feed it to Luke. Luke pushed her away.

Maddie wiggled it under his hand. "Eat it. It's good."

Luke pushed again.

Giggling, Maddie slipped out of her stool and ran over to climb the legs of Stuart's stool. "Eat it, Uncle Stuart." Her exuberance carried the fry into his cheek.

"Stop it, Maddie." He pushed it away and wiped the salty moisture from his face, then caught her hand when she lunged once more with the French fry.

"Maddie." Laurie went around and caught her. "He doesn't want it." She took the fry from Maddie's hand, then scooped her up and replaced her in her stool.

"Cal would eat it." Luke opened his bun and pulled out a pickle.

Laurie tensed.

Stuart dabbed his fingers on an extra napkin. "No one would eat a soggy French fry soaked in Coke."

"Cal would." Luke rolled the pickle into a worm. "He ate a grasshopper once."

"Yucky." Maddie scrunched up her nose.

"I think your friend is telling you tales, Luke." Stuart rested his elbow on the chair back.

Luke shot him a glance that sent Laurie's warning flags to full mast. "Cal doesn't lie. I asked him why the fish liked eating bugs, and he said they were good."

"Sometimes kids say things."

"He's not a kid."

"Luke." Laurie handed him a fresh napkin for his messy fingers. "Don't play with your food."

"He did it on a dare."

Laurie could hardly doubt it. Knowing Cal, it wasn't the worst thing he'd done on a dare. But she did not want that discussed now. "Finish your hamburger, Luke." The meal had lost all magic. It was now a marathon.

"He ate a grasshopper and an ant, but the ant was covered in chocolate."

"Uh-huh." Stuart flashed a quick smile, then looked at Laurie and tapped his watch. "Do you think . . ."

"You wouldn't eat a grasshopper." Luke poked his finger at Stuart.

Stuart turned back to Luke. "No, I wouldn't. Neither would you."

"I would too. I'd do anything Cal did."

Laurie noted the flush creeping into Luke's cheeks. *Please let him stop now.* "Honey . . ."

Stuart cocked his head. "So if your friend jumped off a bridge, you would too?"

"He wouldn't jump off a bridge. It's dangerous. He teaches *safety*."

"Is that right." Stuart stood and reached for his suit coat.

"He's a clown." Maddie soared her French fry into the ketchup and sank it up to her first knuckles.

"Maddie." Laurie lifted her hand and rubbed the fingers with a napkin.

Stuart raised his eyebrows. "They're nearly finished. I think we should go."

"Mommy's reading stories." Maddie stood up on her stool and wrapped her arms around Laurie.

Laurie looked from her daughter's upturned face to Stuart. "I did promise."

"You could tell me a story." Luke's tone was almost belligerent. "Cal's a fireman. He fought a wildfire. They have these little tents they carry, and if the fire turns back they zip themselves into the tents and the fire burns right over them."

Laurie had sudden images of smoke and flame and Cal's grip on her arm, pushing her to safety when the roof crashed down around him. They'd had no little fireproof tents then. When had Luke gotten all this from Cal? What time had they spent . . .

"I bet *you* never fought a fire." Luke jabbed a finger toward Stuart.

"No, you're right. But I fly a jet. Want to hear about that?"

Caught off guard, Luke cocked his head. "Okay."

Laurie turned to Stuart. He raised his brows, and she quickly hid her surprise.

Luke slid out of his stool. "Did you ever crash one?"

"No." Stuart leaned on the bar.

"Did you see one crash? If you saw one crash would you rescue the people?"

Laurie scooped Maddie up. Maybe the child would be content with one story, or two short ones. Then she could go to the party and satisfy Stuart as well. As she started for the library she heard Stuart's voice, "Let me tell you about the cockpit."

Laurie rushed through the stories with hardly any voice inflection, except when Maddie insisted, "He doesn't sound like that. You have to make it growly." Laurie's tension mounted. What else was Luke telling Stuart? She turned the last page, hardly realizing she'd finished the story. As she surrendered her daughter to Gail, Maddie threw a tantrum. Laurie tried to reason, then left her screaming and went to change clothes for a party she now had no interest in attending.

If she had snuggled into the couch in the library, Luke on one side, Maddie on the other, lit the candles and immersed them all in stories . . . But Stuart was there. Soon he'd always be there. Yes, he traveled sometimes, but not like Brian's job had required. Or was it his job? She spread on lip conditioner, then added color. Stuart liked a more dramatic look, especially when they went out at night. But she didn't feel dramatic. She felt . . . empty.

As they drove to the party, she expected his questions. Luke had rubbed his face in Cal, but Stuart had missed it. Or he didn't care. He expostulated aloud that this person or that would be there tonight. And he wanted to pick a few brains. "I just hope Barbra Streisand doesn't corner me. She sinks in her fangs like a snake and injects her causes into your bloodstream."

Laurie stayed on his elbow most of the night, like a decorative ornament. In the pauses she walked on eggshells and planned her responses, but Stuart never asked about Cal. Luke's jabs had only hurt *her*. Why did he have to keep bringing up Cal? They'd only met a half dozen times, not enough to create the hero worship in her son's voice.

When they left the party, Stuart turned with a new intensity in his eyes and said, "Why don't we go to my place?"

It took moments for his intentions to sink in. She caught a half breath when they did. "I think . . . I really think we should wait."

He let her into the car. "Does it really matter now? We are engaged." He tucked a finger under her chin and held her eyes.

Swinging her legs inside, Laurie felt like a dope, out of step, out of sync. Her reluctance had her worried; her worry made her cross. "Brian waited."

"There's a surprise." Stuart shut her door, circled, and climbed in. "Of course your engagement was only six weeks before that lovely beach ceremony."

Sarcasm an inch thick. "I'm sorry, Stuart." Most of what she'd done since agreeing to marry him was apologize. The pattern was too familiar. "I'm tired, and I have an appointment with your mother in the morning for . . ."

"Fine, fine." He lifted his hand from the wheel.

They drove in silence. As they passed the entrance to her neighborhood, he slowed. "Is there something I should know?"

Her stomach seized. "What do you mean?" She'd thought she was ready, had all her denials in place. But if he asked now about Cal . . .

He turned. "I blamed Brian for his infidelity, even addressed it with him twice. But . . ." He brought the car to a stop and looked at her. "Did he have a reason?"

Laurie started to shake. "You mean . . . am I frigid?"

After a long moment, Stuart nodded.

Laurie expelled a half laugh. "Because I want to wait until we're married, I must be frigid? Because my husband, your brother, had no self-control, it must be my fault?"

"That's not what—"

"What would you do if I were? If you found yourself in the same predicament? You'd be discreet, that's certain. You wouldn't flaunt it for every tabloid."

"Laurie, don't make this more than—"

"Oh, certainly not. We wouldn't want a scene—you might actually react." She pictured Cal on the couch, intense in every pore of his being.

Stuart looked straight out the windshield. "Listen, if you don't want to sleep together tonight that's fine. We'll have it soon enough." He turned the wheel and pulled out from the curb. "I'm sorry I upset you."

She stared at him. Did he even have nerves? He circled her driveway and pulled to a stop. When he let her out, he drew her up against him and kissed her head. "Let's forget it, okay?"

Forget what? She was angry at his insinuations, but did she really care?

He turned her face up and kissed her lips. "It's better to wait. The best things are worth it."

Cal hadn't. He'd used her distress to take what he wanted. No! They'd been kids, confused, hurting, and in love—but it had ruined her. She started to shake again.

Stuart must have felt it; he pulled her tighter into his arms. "I shouldn't have brought up something painful. I guess my ego got stung."

That was the first personal admission she'd heard from him. "It's not you." How many times would she say that to him?

"I know this is complicated, with Brian's death and the children . . ."

What did the children have to do with it? That they were Brian's? That hadn't mattered to Cal. That they were there at all? Would Stuart be a father to them?

She pushed back to look at him. "What about the children?"

"Just the way you're trying to balance it all. I shouldn't have interfered. Tonight was a mistake. No—I'm thinking out loud. What I meant is I should have seen you were tired, had other plans." He cupped her shoulders. "I wanted to show you off." His smile was boyish and sincere and achingly close to Brian's.

"Stuart . . ."

"Laurie, don't say anything. We've both had enough wine to color things. I shouldn't have put you on the spot. I'm sure if this were a normal engagement it would be different." He cupped her cheek. "But it's all right."

How understanding. But what exactly did he think he understood? And how could he possibly understand what she couldn't herself? She looked into his face. "Why are we doing this?"

"Doing . . ." He tipped his head. "Are we getting deep?"

She swallowed.

He slid his fingers into her hair. "Because we're right for each other."

She felt a terrible sinking. It was true. "You could have anyone. All those gorgeous women who wanted a part of you tonight."

"They expect too much."

She looked into his face. "What do you mean?"

He shrugged. "I don't like demands on me. I have enough of that in the rest of my life." He looked into her face. "You're the only woman I've known who doesn't cling like Saran Wrap."

Because she didn't love him. "Then why marry at all?"

A smile flickered on his lips. "We talked about some of it before. You saw the rest tonight. As long as I'm an eligible bachelor . . ." He squeezed her shoulders. "It's like swimming with sharks."

"You think that'll change when you marry?"

He flexed his hands and rested them beside her neck. "I'm not Brian. I won't embarrass you; not because I'll be discreet, but because it won't happen." His face dropped, and he looked more real than she'd ever seen him. "I'm tired of trying to please women who want more than I can give."

If he had reached in and plucked out her heart it could scarcely have felt different. He was her. He knew there was no love between them, and he wanted it that way. He'd asked her to sleep with him, but not because he loved and needed her. They might have that, but only to ease physical needs. She should rejoice; she'd found someone as empty as herself.

"Good night, Stuart."

He kissed her lightly. "Good night."

———

It was strange to see Smilin' Sal outside the psych center. When Cal bent beside her chair in the small garden, she gave him the smile he remembered, but then her lips parted and she said, "Hello, Cal."

He'd never heard her voice. "Hi, Sally."

"It's nice of you to visit." Gray streaked her hair, but she was younger than she looked.

"Reggie wanted to stop by as well, but he got called in. How're you doing?"

She dropped her head to the wooden chair back and looked around her garden, still mostly fallow, but with green shoots in the beds all along the fence. "There'll be roses this year."

Cal looked at the climbing vines, just starting to green, tangling their way over the slats. "What color are they?"

"Red and apricot. Gil planted them when we first moved in. My anniversary present."

The car accident that took her husband had sent her to the center, unable to speak for almost two years. Reggie had soaked her in prayer and finally melted away the hard shell that had kept her trapped. Did she know it? "They'll be beautiful."

"Only I'll see them."

Cal sat back on his haunches. "I like to think the ones in heaven can too." He imagined Flip Casey looking down, his whiskey-soaked clothes replaced by robes as white and light as down. He had no way of knowing Flip's place with the Lord. Maybe he'd arrived bewildered and broken. But that was God's business, and Cal gave him the benefit of the doubt.

Sally looked up at the sky. "Gil loved the Lord."

Cal nodded. "You'll be together again some day."

"That was it, you know. I just couldn't let go." Her lips trembled. "I put on the smile that believers expected me to wear. Wasn't it glorious that God had called him home, they said? It didn't feel glorious. But I smiled. And soon I couldn't do anything but smile. The pain went deep, then deeper."

"It's all right, Sally. We all cope the best we can."

She turned. "*You* know that, don't you?"

He cocked his head. "What do you know about me?"

"All of it."

"Reggie told you?"

She shook her head. "You did. All those times you ranted and joked and swore and hollered."

Cal pictured the group therapy room, and Sally in her chair smiling away, never making a sound, never moving. "You heard me?"

She laughed. "I cheered. You said all the things I wanted to say but hadn't the courage."

"Huh." Cal rested his forearms on his knees and studied her.

"Between Reggie's prayers and your raving, you punched a hole in my wall big enough for me to walk out."

A warmth stole over him, seeping into his pores and flowing through his veins. More good than he'd known had come from his trouble. "I'm glad for that, Sally. But now that you're out . . ."

She waved a hand. "I know. I still need to live."

He nodded. "It's like starting over."

"I get up, I get dressed, I eat. I come out to my garden."

That's how he felt about the woods. But if Sally didn't get a job soon and show she could be self-sufficient, her caseworker would order her back into psychiatric care.

"Is there something you'd like to do? Some way you can support yourself?"

She tapped the back of her head against the chair. "It's time, isn't it?"

Cal nodded.

"Know of any openings?"

He handed her the classifieds. With the information he'd been given about her, he'd circled several possibilities.

She glanced at the paper then back to him. "You doing social work now?"

Cal dropped his chin. "In a way. Actually, I'm working off community service hours in lieu of jail time."

She raised her eyebrows. "You got in trouble again?"

He nodded.

She laughed. "So that's why you're here?"

"No." He straightened from his crouch. "I'm here because I want to see you make it."

"What did you do?"

"Assaulted an officer."

"Sergeant Danson?"

He jammed his hands into his pockets. "How'd you know?"

She shrugged. "From what you'd shared before . . ."

"Well . . ." He shook his head. "No excuse, really, except I had no other choice."

She watched him a moment, then tapped the newspaper. "Which of these jobs do you think I should take?"

"I don't think it matters. It's just about that next step, you know?"

She nodded. "You're a good man, Cal."

He met her gaze. "Do you have a community? Sounds like you struggled with the believers you knew before."

She turned away. "That bunch has no room for pain."

"You might try Pastor Lucas's church. They've been praying for you."

"They have?" She looked up.

He nodded. "Here." He took the card from his pocket that had the mission statement and service schedule.

She took it and laid it in her lap. "Are you still . . . do you still have the dreams, the shock episodes?" Without the smile, her face was painfully real.

"I haven't climbed under any tables lately. But I dream." He drew a quick breath. "Maybe that'll stop someday, in God's time. Until then . . ." He spread his hands.

"I dream too."

Cal nodded.

"Thank you for coming." She smiled.

He made a note to go again on his own time.

———

Wanda Prelane's Bel Air mansion had scarcely looked so festive before. She had outdone herself for this night's event. Laurie took it in with a sense of awe. Even after all the years with Brian she could never quite be sure the Prelane mansion wouldn't vanish in the mist.

"Come in, come in." Stuart's mother waved them brusquely through the massive marble entry. "Honey, don't touch that."

Luke removed his fingers from the gilded florals in a Chinese vase, which was shaped something like a dog with dragon's feet that stood beside the door.

"Darren, take their coats. Laurie, I can't decide whether to have the orchestra in the garden as usual or in the hall. They're calling for rain, and it looks dreadful." She sighed. "I wanted everything to be perfect for your engagement party."

She must have forgotten to notify God. Laurie was surprised by the cynical thought, but then, her view of many things had grown increasingly darker these last weeks. She waved her recently manicured hand, which now displayed the two-carat diamond with baguette accents Stuart had presented her. "The hall would be better. There was a light drizzle as we drove up."

Laurie looked across the great room, through the twelve-foot floor-to-ceiling windows to the panoramic view from the house perched above the domains of mere humanity. A storm was coming, but to her it *was* the perfect ambiance.

Maddie tugged her hand. "Look at the pretty egg tree."

"Don't touch it, honey. Those ornaments are Tiffany glass." Wanda made a motion to stroke Maddie's head, but Maddie ducked it. "Now, what do you think of the meat trays, Laurie? The roast beef is positively stringy, but it's too late to change that now. I've put it to the back of the buffet behind the prosciutto and smoked salmon."

Laurie followed her to the long tables arranged with plastic-wrapped trays of food from fresh sushi California rolls to melba rounds with caviar. "I think the trays are fine."

"Well, they'll certainly hear about it before they get final payment."

Laurie looked up as Stuart entered from the mezzanine off the great room. "Ah." He met her with a kiss, then looked her over appreciatively. "I'll be the envy of every man."

"You're that with or without me."

"I'll choose with." He kissed her again, then turned. "Mother have you seen my onyx tie tack? It must have fallen off somewhere around here."

"Did you check your overcoat?"

"No. That's a good thought. Darren . . ." Laurie watched him go in search of his pin. Exit stage left. She wanted to laugh. Only it wasn't funny.

"You'll have to excuse me, dear. I haven't finished dressing." Wanda, too, left the spotlight. Dressing. Now that could mean makeup, perfume, jewelry, or simply that she needed the ladies' room. She'd never be so gauche as to admit to normal human functions.

Luke and Maddie took off for the porch. Laurie let them go in spite of the light drizzle. Once the rain started they'd have to stay in with the untouchables. She wandered the house, waiting for the guests who would offer such plentiful congratulations and good wishes and even solicitudes over her recent loss and how precious it was that Brian's own brother . . .

But that was biblical, wasn't it? That the brother should marry the widow? It kept it all in the family, Brian's portion reabsorbed. All according to God and the Prelanes. God. What had Cal said? She needed to know who she was to God.

Why would she think of that now? What could it possibly matter? She had what she wanted. Who she was, who she might have been, who she had intended to be—it was all a farce anyway.

She sighed, fighting the gloom that matched the lowering skies. A door banged, and she heard the trampling of little feet and Maddie's shrill giggle. Turning, Laurie hurried to catch them before they were scolded. She rushed for the candlelit mezzanine where trays of champagne flutes and iced bottles stood waiting in silver ewers.

Stuart, too, had hurried in, just finishing with his tie tack. Laurie entered from the opposite side and caught sight of Luke chasing his sister with claw hands and growls. She opened her mouth to call out, but Luke leaped and Maddie spun into the table.

"Maddie, watch out!" Stuart jumped back, whisking his coat free of the tumbling candelabra. It was a natural motion, instinctive. But Laurie couldn't stop staring. He had jumped away from the danger, away from her child, who cringed now against the table as the candles kindled the thick Turkish carpet.

Stuart stomped at the smoldering rug but still made no move for Maddie. Where Cal had lunged for the child, Stuart had protected his suit. Catching sight of her mother, Maddie burst into tears and ran, arms outstretched.

Laurie snatched her up. "It's all right, honey. It's all right."

"Hardly." Stuart picked up the candles and laid them on the table. "Mother will be livid over this rug."

"Better the rug than Maddie's hair or dress."

Stuart looked up from brushing the blackened fibers. "Well, that goes without saying. But if she hadn't . . ."

"Maybe there shouldn't be burning candelabras where a child could get hurt."

"Maybe there shouldn't be a child where there are burning candelabras."

They stared at each other, Stuart too well-mannered to raise his voice; Laurie too shaken to raise hers.

She swallowed. "I should take them home."

He stood and came to her. "I'll drive. That way we'll both be late returning."

She looked up into his chiseled face, but all she could see was Cal collapsed and shaking, hands pressed to his ears against the screams of a child he couldn't forget. Her breath came, tight and sharp as she stood. "You don't need to. I won't be returning."

He grasped her arm. "Laurie, for heaven's sake, don't overreact. This is nothing. We'll have the rug replaced."

"It's not the rug, Stuart." She pressed Maddie's head to her thigh, stroking the curls. "It's . . ." She looked around the room, the glittering crystal, the monogrammed silver, Luke's solemn, large-eyed face, Stuart's equally solemn and now distressed countenance. "I don't belong here."

"Of course you do."

She shook her head slowly. "I tried to. I thought I needed to." Luke came to her, and she tucked him to her side.

Stuart smoothed his hair. "You're upset. I understand that. We'll take the children home and . . ."

Laurie smiled grimly. "I know why you're so effective in the boardroom. But it's no use, Stuart. I don't want this." *I don't want you.* And she suddenly realized she wasn't empty. Something inside was crying out to be recognized.

He turned his face to the side. "Bit of awkward timing, wouldn't you say?"

"I'm sorry." She really was. But not half so sorry as she'd be if they went through with this fraud. "Luke, Maddie, go get your coats from Darren." They walked out with dragging feet as she turned back to Stuart.

"Laurie, can't we work this out? My parents will be so . . . disappointed."

She took the ring from her finger and held it out. "Good-bye, Stuart."

He took the ring, his face showing distress for the first time. Was it for his image he grieved, or his failure? Either way he'd put a spin on it to save both his ego and the Prelane reputation.

Laurie fought the tears as she drove the children home, though she was certain they weren't tears of loss. It was ugly what she'd done. The Prelanes would never forgive her. The door to their world would be irrevocably closed. No more Malibu Colony parties, no women's functions with Wanda, no society pages with her name beside Stuart's.

Luke leaned forward in his seat. "Aren't you marrying Uncle Stuart, Mommy?"

She looked at him through the rearview mirror. "No, Luke." She watched for his reaction, but he showed so little. He would have done well in that world where nothing real was said, nothing real was shown. He had too much of his father in him. She would do everything she could to change that. "Does that make you sad, honey?"

He shook his head.

"Maddie?"

She shook her head like Luke. "I don't want him for my daddy."

Laurie drew a long breath. Well, that made it unanimous.

Three hours later it hit her, as she huddled in the huge teakwood bed she'd shared with Brian in the room overlooking the pool. It hit her that all this was dust. And she cried for what she'd rejected in the lust for it.

22

THEY THAT HOPE IN THE LORD WILL

RENEW THEIR STRENGTH, THEY WILL SOAR

AS WITH EAGLES' WINGS.

Isaiah 40:31 NAS

C al watched some two hundred children scour the field, bright plastic baskets swinging from their hands, searching for the multicolored plastic eggs filled with enough sugar and caffeine to guarantee stomachaches all around. The sound of their squeals and laughter rose and fell on the breeze.

He stretched his mouth down to let some air in under the red plastic nose. Spanner was doing Easter magic with live chicks today. At least he hadn't been asked to be the Easter Rabbit. That job had gone to a most appropriate individual.

He watched Ray lumber from one clump of children to the next, shaking hands with his white fluffy paws and giving hugs. He'd been hired by the city, paid an actual wage.

"Hey, bro." Reggie's grip on his shoulder brought Cal around.

"Hey, Reg. Careful with the clown suit. It's dry-clean only." Cal primped the collar.

"What's this I hear? You're getting a smoke trailer?"

Cal grinned. It always amazed him how news reached Reggie's ears. "It's on loan only, from K.C. Kind of a trade out. Our program for theirs."

"That's great. You've been drooling for that a long time."

"I haven't drooled in over a year, Reg." Cal stooped and re-adjusted the elastic ankle of the baggy pants, then flopped the big-toed shoe to ease the itch on the side of his foot.

"Speaking of which, did you hear about Smilin' Sal?"

Cal straightened. "My grapevine only works your direction."

Reggie grinned. Cal grinned back. He'd stopped fighting it. If Reggie grinned over his coffin, he'd crack the undertaker's makeup grinning back.

"Well." Reggie reached into the cage and brought out a peep with one gargantuan hand, a little like King Kong with Jessica Lange. "She's got a job at an insurance office. Doing fine."

Cal released a long sigh. "Good for her."

"She called about our fellowship last night. Thought she might come tomorrow for Easter Sunday service."

"That's great." Cal watched the peep cuddle down in Reggie's cupped hands.

"Reggie, what are you doing to that poor chick?" Rita rounded the tent in her cream tapered slacks and mint blouse.

Reggie turned. "It's happy as punch."

"Hi . . . Cal." She stopped and assessed him with a wry smile.

Cal scooped up Rocky and worked the lever. "That's right, Dr. James. Spanner's in rare lady-killer form today." He spread his arms. "As you see."

"Quite." She sauntered past.

Cal reached out and flipped her perfect wedge of hair. "Congratulations on Smilin' Sal."

She turned. "I can't take credit for it, now can I?"

"You can take some."

She caught his hand in hers. "Come on. Buy me a snow cone."

Cal sat with her at the picnic table under the elm, licking the sugary dyed ice. The breeze lifted wisps of Rita's dark hair as she bit into the mounded snow cone and tipped her head back to catch the drips from running down her chin.

She melted the ice in her mouth, swallowed, and turned to him. "I've had an offer for a position in a hospital in St. Louis."

"A good offer?" Cal leaned his elbow on the table.

"Yes. I've accepted it."

Cal digested that. "What about Montrose?"

"They have a replacement in mind. Once I give the final word, they'll make him an offer. He's from Independence."

"I don't like him."

She smiled. "You don't need to."

Cal looked out across the field, unsure what he felt. "You could really leave all this for some prestigious, high-paying position in a big hospital?"

She laughed. "Well, since you put it that way . . . yes."

He tossed his cone into the barrel chained to the tree, then took her hand. "The department will not be happy. You've held our hands through too many incidents to let you go easily."

"I'll miss you too, Cal."

The ache began. Rita knew him better than his own family. She'd seen him at his worst and not judged him. She'd made him grow in ways he hadn't wanted to. And he was better for it. "You'll do a fine job wherever you go, Rita."

She raised an eyebrow. "You think so?"

He nodded. "I know so." He slipped the plastic nose down below his chin and kissed her cheek. "Just don't take life too seriously."

Her eyes went down his face to the nose strapped beneath his chin. She covered her mouth with her hand and laughed softly.

"What?" He sat back, hands spread.

She pushed his chest playfully. "I'll call you when I need a laugh."

"Call me if you need a cry too."

She nodded, her eyes tearing up on cue. "I'll miss Friday nights."

"I'll be raking it in."

"You're all bluff." She sniffed.

"Not all." With a squeeze to her hand, he left her in the dappled tree shade and walked back to the fire-safety tent feeling empty.

Reggie still sat on the edge of the table with the chick cradled in his hands. "I guess she told you."

Cal nodded. "Who's the imposter taking her place?"

"Robert Beam."

"As in beam me up, Scotty?"

Reggie grinned. "That's right. Dr. Beam."

Cal toyed with the rubbery nose he'd removed. "Why?"

"Just time for her to move on, Cal. Life goes on."

Life goes on. Cal looked out across the field. One day those kids would be standing on the edges watching kids of their own. Would he still be here wearing the clown suit and pulling chicks from his sleeves?

As weary as the children napping in the backseat, Laurie pulled into Montrose and drove to Mother's house. It was only two weeks past Easter, but it amazed her how quickly real estate could turn in Orange County, how quickly everything that had been hers and Brian's could now belong to strangers, except the children's things and the few items she'd put into storage until she was settled. It was a cash deal, quietly and swiftly completed. She was a wealthy woman, with money enough to . . . to what?

She carried Maddie as Luke stumbled sleepily beside her to Mother's door, the afternoon light hazy on the walk. She reached up and rang the bell, then smoothed Luke's hair and gave him an encouraging smile. They'd find another place at the earliest opportunity. A nice place, no junky rental this time. Maybe she wouldn't stay in Montrose. But she had so many unresolved issues—she had to start somewhere.

Mother opened the door, eyes pained and mouth tight. She had not taken the news of the broken engagement well.

Laurie hadn't expected her to. She raised her chin. "May we come in?"

"Of course." Her mother turned aside. "Lay her down in the guest room."

Guest room. But they were family. Did Mother know it? Did she know there was something missing that they could have had all these years?

The room smelled of lemon oil and rose potpourri. Laurie laid Maddie on the bedspread and pulled the blue crocheted afghan over her. Luke had already wandered to the TV. Laurie went out and found her mother still in the entry as though she'd forgotten where else to go. She waited for some further explanation, Laurie knew, but she wasn't ready yet. "May I leave them a little while? I . . . want to see Grams."

At Mother's silent nod, Laurie went out, stifled to the brink of suffocation. Was there any person alive she hadn't disappointed or infuriated? Laurie fumbled with her keys. She hadn't actually planned to go to the graveyard. But there, in Mother's house, she'd felt the full impact of this final failure.

She had to get out, go somewhere. Even dead, Grams was her port, her dock, her guywire. She knelt at the grave, the grass a thick blanket beneath her knees, the dampness seeping through her jeans. There was no mound, of course, only the stone, the new kind that didn't even stand up but lay flush with the grass. *Grace Emaline Welks. Beloved wife and mother.* And grandmother. It ought to read grandmother.

"Oh, Grams . . ." Laurie covered her face. She had loved Grams so much. Just as she loved her children. She wasn't incapable of love; she was only afraid. Afraid to let anyone hurt her, judge her, reject her. Grams wouldn't. Her children wouldn't. But a man could. Would God?

God. Cal's words, spoken through his tears when they last parted, had been planted deeply in her thoughts. "Grams, what do I do? How do I learn who I am to God?" The question had persisted through all her preparations, the sale of her property, furnishings— nearly everything but their clothing and toys for the children. It had persisted through the long hours on the road. Through the nights in the hotels. Through her dreams, through her musings.

She touched the smooth stone, warm from the hazy sun. "Who am I, Grams? What am I?"

"You are fearfully and wonderfully made." The memory was vivid. *"Say it, Laurie. Fearfully and wonderfully made. Before the dawn of time God knew you. There's nothing wrong with you. You are just as God made you."*

"Then why is everything I do wrong?"

"It's not wrong in God's eyes. He hates sin, yes, but not our mistakes. Does a mother hate her child for stumbling when she takes her first steps?"

"My mother does. Daddy does."

"*But not Jesus, Laurie. In His eyes you are precious. He's bought you with his blood.*"

Laurie pressed her palm to the stone. Precious. To God she was precious. She had worth. "*Jesus gave His life for you.*" God had made her, had known her before the dawn of time. And Jesus had died for her. Her heart swelled. No matter how she failed, He loved her. Enough to die for her.

Love so incomprehensible filled and surrounded her. As she had been willing to die for her children, so much more had Jesus done for her. She had quailed and fought against it, yet He had submitted, denying His power, giving himself over to wicked men. Like a sheep He had been slaughtered, for her.

She grasped at the faith of her youth, found it there inside. Her heart broke at the rebellion that had kept her from seeing. Yet even as it broke, her heart was filled with comfort, deep and sustaining. Her breath eased out of her lungs. Then she was seized with an almost violent need, a need to throw off her past and become what God had intended for her to be.

She stroked the gravestone. She'd had it all, all she needed, before Brian. His wealth, his prestige, his power; it was all an illusion. Nothing compared to the knowledge that God loved her, that she was precious in His sight.

"*Red and yellow, black and white, they are precious in his sight; Jesus loves the little children of the world. . . .*" She could almost hear Gram's scratchy voice singing. She'd had the truth but ignored it. Jesus loved her through everything.

And Cal. Hadn't he mirrored that love and acceptance? Even risked his life for her? In a very real sense, he had been Christ to her. But she was too afraid to accept it, to return it. So she'd lost him.

But she hadn't lost her Lord. "*He will never leave you, Laurie. Nothing can separate you from the love of God.*" Not even herself. On her knees, she begged God's forgiveness. "I've been so blind. But you've made me see. I'll never turn away again."

She stood up and looked down at the grave. "Thank you, Grams. Thank you, Jesus!"

She drove back to Mother's with a joy she could hardly comprehend. Nothing had changed. She was still adrift, uncertain what to do next, where to go. Her children were hurting and confused. Too many changes, things beyond their understanding. They'd lost their father, and she'd been a stranger to them these last months. But now hope kindled. The Lord would see her through.

That hope staggered, though, when she reached the house. The very air was oppressive, as if something was trying to suck the life from her. When she entered the kitchen, Mother was waiting, two cups set out to be filled with tea. Laurie wanted to tell her the epiphany she'd had, the truth she'd found.

But Mother's face was so grim as she took the kettle from the stove. "Are they keeping the site up?"

"The site?"

Her mother poured water over the tea bags already draped into the cups. "The grave."

Laurie took the cup Mother handed her. "Yes." She supposed they were. She hadn't noticed anything amiss, though she hadn't gone there to scrutinize the landscaping. She'd gone there to be near the one person who had given her unconditional love. No, not the only one.

"So your engagement is broken for good."

A rope of tension started down the back of Laurie's neck, as she struggled to retain the peace. It had always been that way, sensing God's love with Grams, then losing it the moment she walked into her own home. Not this time! This time God's love was real, potent, viable. "Yes. I've sold everything."

Stuart had made only one attempt, one phone call asking to work things out. She had told him calmly that her mind was made up. He hadn't argued.

Mother drifted into her chair, a dry leaf without the will to oppose the forces that carried her down. "I suppose you'll be seeing Cal Morrison."

Laurie looked up from her cup. "Why do you suppose that, Mother?"

"Because you love him."

Laurie's fingers tightened on the handle. She raised the cup and drank. How strange for the truth to come from Mother's lips after all the years of telling her why Cal was wrong. If only those simple words could change it all. She set the cup on the table, watched a drip slide down its side. "I doubt that's enough anymore."

Mother's tone had a bitter, despairing tone. "It better be. You've given up everything else for it."

Laurie understood the condemnation, but it didn't hurt as it once had. God knew. She had given up the things that didn't matter. Now she needed to find what did. Luke came and stood beside her, one hand on her shoulder. Laurie's heart jumped. God's acceptance embodied in her small son. No wonder Jesus said, "Let the children come to me." He knew. He saw their precious spirits. And she realized again that what she felt for Luke was no more than God felt for her. *Thank you, Lord! Thank you.*

If there was heaven on earth it was the woods at twilight. Cal had found the grandfather oak and hunkered onto its knee. Annie was off for the moment proving her prowess, and he felt the silence deepen. There was just enough chill to accent the dampness, the afternoon haze becoming an evening mist.

Cal's wool jacket pearled the droplets as he sat, eyes upward toward the leafed branches above. The sky held that indeterminate hue between steel and charcoal. The stars would be milky smears of light when they came. Annie padded softly back and licked his hand.

Cal reached for her ears without changing his view. He wanted to see the first one, the first star. No, he didn't believe in wishes, but there was still something magical, something that stirred inside when that first prick of light showed the heavens beyond earth's domain.

Under his hand, Annie's ears perked, and Cal looked in the direction she'd turned. A wood muse with Laurie's face pressed aside a damp branch and stepped over the brush. Maybe just searching for the first star could make dreams come true.

Cal kept his head against the trunk and watched. As a hallucination it was better than any the drugs had induced. Not that he'd had any of those lately. He was so squeaky clean the guys were calling him the Reverend. But he'd accept this trick of the light, this wood magic, this twilight gift.

The swelling in his throat made him swallow hard when the

apparition caught sight of him and adjusted her path. She stopped beneath the silver maple, with its leaves curled like chrysalis buds just opening into jagged fingers. Her eyes were dark and solemn. Her hair hung loose. His imagination had conjured her exactly as he liked her best, jeans and an oversized shirt.

She took a step and another, coming closer than any dream he'd had before. He stayed where he was, lounged against the oak, its solid mass a witness to the depth of its roots. It was real and he was real. But what he saw . . .

She wrapped her elbows with her hands. "Hello, Cal."

Her voice put that tremor in his chest, made him aware of each breath. If he spoke would she vanish? Had he fallen asleep in the woods?

She ran her fingers along a slender twig of redbud full of pink petals. "Do you want me to leave?"

He rested his forearm over his knee. "No."

Annie padded over and Laurie stroked her head. Surely Annie could tell an apparition. But then she might be part of the dream as well.

Cal brushed a tiny gray moth away from his cheek. "What are you doing here?"

"I came back."

"What about your engagement?"

She shook her head. "It shouldn't have happened."

The oak bark was rough against his back, the mist chilling his neck at the collar.

She let go the branch. "I hope you don't mind that I came without calling."

That's how she always came, when he drifted off to sleep or sat mesmerized in a daydream. Why should this one be different? Although she didn't always talk. He shouldn't waste the opportunity.

"Why did you?"

"I wanted to see you."

"Why?"

She folded her hands, looking up into the darkening sky. He'd pushed and she might vanish, fade into the night sky with one last sad look. She didn't, but he could see her struggle.

He caught his tongue between his side teeth, not wanting to antagonize her, yet unwilling to play the same old game. "Say it, Laurie."

"Does it matter so much?" Her voice was rough and breathy.

"That from a lover of words? 'Two roads diverged in a wood, and I—I took the one less traveled by, And that has made all the difference . . .' "

Her eyes widened. "You read it?"

"It was kind of sleep inducing at first, but after a while I caught on. I even got to where I could almost smell the woods the old guy described."

Laurie folded her hands together, smiling slightly. "You would."

Cal raised an eyebrow, waiting.

She drew a deep breath, then released it. "I'm afraid that if I do . . ."

He pushed himself up from the tree root. If she vanished, so be it. He crossed the distance, reached for her. She had substance. He ran his hands from her shoulders down her arms, smelling the wet cotton and . . . Beautiful.

He tucked one finger under her chin and raised her face. A tear broke free from her eye and ran down her skin. "Say it, Laurie."

Her lips parted, and she breathed, "I love you."

He pulled her into his arms and kissed her mouth, sinking his fingers into her hair. "You can't take it back."

"I don't want to." She pressed in close and more tears fell, landing between his finger and thumb as he cupped her cheek. "I don't know if I can do it right."

"That's okay." He'd learned not to expect too much. He was no longer in control of things. But then, he'd never been in control anyway. *Your will, Lord.*

"You were right. I had to remember who I was to God, but even more, who God was to me." She swiped a tear aside. "And more importantly who He wants me to be."

Cal nodded. That was certainly the right direction.

"I could have made it so much easier. I already had everything I needed . . . and even what I wanted." She reached up and touched his lips. "I was just too stubborn to accept it."

No more stubborn than he'd been, trying to move ahead of God's plan.

Her fingertips trailed across his cheek. "Can you forgive me?"

"It was my fault. I messed things up for us." He pressed her palm to his face. "But we can make it right."

She sucked in a tiny sob. "What did I do to deserve you?"

"That's not how it works. Love's a gift, Laurie, not earned, just given." He'd had to learn that himself. *Lord?* He caught her neck between his palms, felt her pulse under his thumbs. "Will you marry me?"

"Yes."

His chest swelled. He hadn't imagined the word; she'd actually said it. He wrapped her in his arms and kissed her again. "Think you can stand it here in Montrose for the rest of your life?"

"Wherever you are."

He kissed her eyelids. "There's a place off Route D for sale. A few acres, a big stone farmhouse. I could do it up nicely. You'd never know it was old."

"Does it have a woods?"

"And a creek."

She smiled. "Luke and Maddie would like that."

"There's even a carriage house. You could set up your wheel, make a studio."

She looked up then, her mouth quivering.

He drank in the coffee of her eyes, pictured her with the potter's wheel spinning between her knees, the clay coating her hands. "Anything you want, Laurie."

"I want you, Cal."

How many years had he waited to hear that? How many times had he given up? But never completely. God had given him this one love, this one chance. "You've always had that."

She drew a jagged breath. "I know."

He hooked an arm over her shoulders. "Where are the kids?"

"With Cissy and Mildred. They're beside themselves wanting to see you."

That thought reached down inside him to a place left empty just for them. A place that could expand with a baby of his own, maybe two, maybe six. Anything was possible with Laurie as his bride. He looked up again at the milky stars, the seat of heaven. *Thank you, God.*

He curled Laurie into his arm and headed for the house. But not too quickly. He wanted to savor the moment. On the other hand, he could hardly wait to see Mildred's face.

Acknowledgments

This book would not have come to be without our friend Steve Schopper of the Colorado Springs Fire Department. Thank you, Steve, for all the technical fire fighting and medical information, for taking the time to answer questions, and for all the work you do educating children in fire safety.

Thanks also to Sergeant Rick Tudor of the Monument Police Department for, likewise, answering questions and imparting information and experience.

Thanks to Sarah Long, Barb Lilland, and the others who read and improved my work. Special thanks to Jim and Jessica for multiple readings and great feedback. I love you both. And to Charlotte and Melodie for input and encouragement, many thanks.

Thank you, Lord, for this calling, and your abundant grace to fulfill it.